THE CRESCENT DUNES

THE CRESCENT DUNES

STEVEN BARCLAY

Refractory Books
New York

Published by Refractory Books

ISBN: 978-0-9845741-0-0

Set in 10.5/13 pt Sabon

Manufactured in the United States of America

First Edition

1

The leather sandals were dilapidated, the soles worn almost to the point of depletion. The patched and stained *galabiya*, the ubiquitous garb of the rustic Egyptian, with its loose arms and hanging lower skirt, was noticeably ragged at the edges. The listing head was wrapped in a considerable length of remarkably clean white fabric, making up a turban of no small stature. Below the substantial headgear the features were visibly weathered, the expression curious and pensive.

Framing this solitary figure, an entry recess of vaulted stonework merged with an austere wall of chiseled limestone rising block upon block to an intricate and crenellated cornice. High above this ornate edge an unembellished and windowless dome capped the underlying structure, its crown radiant in the morning sky. The sun was just emerging from behind the cliff-like Muqattam hills, flooding the streets in a golden incandescence, the raking light exaggerating the roughness and details of the plastered walls and stone faces of the adjacent buildings.

Martin Colbrook observed all this from where he stood in a dusty and debris-filled roadway on the very fringe of the City of the Dead. In his khaki pants, blue oxford shirt, and gray blazer, with a small canvas bag slung over his shoulder, Colbrook looked like a tourist who had taken a wrong turn.

The City of the Dead, a vast Islamic necropolis of medieval origin, blended so completely into its surroundings that when seen from the window of a speeding tour bus few gave it more than a passing glance. Its mixture of domed and square tombs arranged in a predictable grid-like pattern across the eastern edge of Cairo appeared to be nothing more than an extension of the city—albeit a ramshackle one. Its fame was related not only to the highly prized funerary architecture still dotting the district, but also to the fact that certain inhabitants of Cairo had seen fit to take up permanent residence inside the tombs.

While many of these sepulchral buildings were constructed on a modest scale—simple box-like structures with small iron-barred windows and an access door—others were almost villas for the dead, containing multiple rooms, courtyards, and second floors. The most impressive were built of stone, their surfaces decorated with elaborate masonry. Beneath the structures were the crypts themselves—small caverns scooped out of the earth.

It was customary for Egyptians to visit the cemetery on Fridays, and Colbrook was pleased to find the roadway almost empty on such a morning. Walking toward the narrow unpaved alleys formed by the vast network of tombs, he cast a sideways glance over his shoulder. The turbaned man was already following him, a walking stick now visible in his right hand, swinging rhythmically alongside his smock-like garment and jabbing at the dusty ground.

Shortening his stride, Colbrook allowed him to catch up.

The man's smile widened considerably when he realized that he had been tentatively accepted as a guide, and soon he arrived at Colbrook's side with a slight wheezing sound. He fumbled in the pocket of his *galabiya* for something, and Colbrook paused to let him retrieve it.

Producing a flat metal case that fit in the palm of his hand, he opened its tarnished cover and extracted a partially squashed cigarette, placing the end loosely into his mouth. Recovering a faded plastic lighter from the folds of his garment and igniting it, he held the fluttering flame to his cigarette, drawing in a deep breath.

"Mameluke?" Colbrook asked, pointing towards a nearby dome-topped building.

He did not expect a satisfactory reply, and he did not get one. The Cairene shrugged, puffing a cloud of acrid white smoke from his mouth.

Colbrook was looking for a famous landmark—a mausoleum. More than likely this Egyptian man could lead him to that location, but first he had to determine whether he understood any English.

"Tomb of al-Ashraf?" questioned Colbrook, motioning towards the intersection of two distant streets.

"Al-Ashraf," muttered the Egyptian. He seemed to be thinking hard, but Colbrook could sense it was all a ruse to stall for *baksheesh*. He was in Egypt after all. Nothing could get done without a little money changing hands. The man looked completely lost until Colbrook handed him ten pounds.

His listless demeanor then evaporated quite suddenly. Resting his walking stick on his right shoulder, he began to lead Colbrook steadily toward one of the overgrown footpaths on the side of the road. Plunging into the weed-choked path, Colbrook followed his guide, who now sported about with a much reduced limp.

They passed many tumbledown brick and plaster structures, and soon came out onto a wider street. Several old cars lined its edge, wheels and other critical parts missing. A few ragged children ran in the street kicking a soccer ball. They seemed curious, but did not approach either of the two men.

The Egyptian dexterously weaved around piles of rubbish and debris that frequently clogged the street. Some of the brick structures here had almost completely collapsed, leaving just the outlines of the original walls on the ground. Most of these open spaces were filled with heaps of dusty trash.

They were moving west now, their shadows cast ahead of them. Colbrook slowed briefly to swing the small canvas bag over his other shoulder. Stepping among the weeds and rubble, he watched his guide carefully, continuing to follow him towards what he assumed was the famed mausoleum.

Emerging from a crumbled gateway of stone blocks that arched over the roadway, they were soon standing in front of a large building. It rose several stories high, the exterior covered in moldering brown stucco. Crowned by a dome of considerable proportions, its surface flaking away and revealing the brickwork beneath it, the decaying roof rested upon an octagonal-shaped support drum pierced by small circular apertures. Imposing double doors of carved wood sealed its entrance.

The Egyptian was leaning on his walking stick now. He pointed at the structure and bobbed his turbaned head, spitting the already spent cigarette from his mouth. Colbrook did not pay much attention to the building. He started to walk towards a smaller, reddish-colored tomb across the street. The Egyptian guide seemed to be tired now. He moved off and sat down on the wide stone steps leading to the entrance of the large mausoleum.

Pausing briefly at the front of the reddish tomb, Colbrook soon resumed his walk, turning left into the first narrow alleyway which ran perpendicular to the front of the building. Vines and weeds hung down from a crumbling stone wall on his right, making the passage almost a tunnel. Behind the stone wall was a tall fence made of rusted metal bars. He turned to see if his guide was following him; he was still resting on the steps. Colbrook moved quickly down the alley.

Following the uneven pathway littered with countless shattered bricks, he was approaching a squat one-story tomb constructed of yellowish stone. It appeared quite old from the wear and damage on the steps and facade, but the doorway, a slab of dark wood with oversized metal strap hinges, seemed relatively new compared to the rest.

Arriving at the front of the structure, Colbrook examined the stone facing. It was smooth and rippled like limestone, but crumbling at the corners where the blocks were fitted in an alternating pattern.

Kneeling down, he examined the lower half of the door. Near the bottom a small V-shaped notch was carved deep into the wood. It was meticulously done, and looked very similar to the Roman numeral five. He stood upright again, peering around to see if anyone was watching him.

He was in a fairly confined area. The alleyway he had come down was the only apparent approach to the building he stood before. The structures on either side had collapsed entirely, leaving a wall of rubble that could not be easily surmounted. The long vine-covered wall that ran the length of the pathway faded into a heap of rocks to his right, and his immediate view to the left was blocked by the remains of a stone mausoleum.

After checking for the Egyptian again—he was nowhere to be seen—Colbrook pushed at the wood door.

Much to his surprise it swung in soundlessly.

He felt a rush of cooler air flowing out of the opening and briefly swirling around him. It was dark in the interior, but as his eyes adjusted to the dimness he could vaguely sense that someone was inside.

Stepping through the entryway, he swung the door closed. It latched an instant before making an ominous thud.

The interior was quite large and airy, the floor paved in a smooth, dark stone. The ceiling appeared to be slightly vaulted, reaching at least fifteen feet into the air. The only light entering the building came through narrow horizontal openings located above the wide entablature dividing the walls from the ceiling.

Two rectangular stone monuments of substantial bulk filled the center of the tomb. These, Colbrook recognized, were the ceremonial sarcophagi, marking the locations of the underground burial chambers. Composed of marble, with ornate brass fittings along their tops and sides, they blocked his view into the back of the tomb. Arabesque designs covered many of the interior surfaces, executed with an intricacy and scale that was astonishing.

A sudden creaking sound drew his attention. Moving soundlessly but steadily towards the back of the tomb, he made his way past the imposing monuments.

A man was sitting on a wooden stool, facing away from him. Dressed in a blue *galabiya,* he was hunched over a small crate. White tennis sneakers were poking out from underneath the garment's folded edge. The faint sound of bubbling water emanated from somewhere close to this figure.

Colbrook continued forward, his canvas bag clutched suitcase-style in his left hand.

The man leaned his head back, as if listening intently. His right arm was extended forward, tracing a narrow and somewhat circular movement. The sound of bubbling water was louder now. Soon Colbrook heard a new sound—the sound of tearing paper. The bubbling sound stopped abruptly.

Uncertain as to what was happening, Colbrook froze. He smelled the distinct odor of cinnamon. Stepping closer, he was alert for any unexpected movements from the hunched man.

Colbrook could now see over the man's shoulder.

He was tending a medium-sized aluminum pot resting on a small butane-powered camp stove. He did not turn to look up at Colbrook, who now stood by his side, but held out his hand, palm-side up. It contained several packages of oatmeal.

"Which flavor do you prefer?"

The suddenness of the question briefly astonished Colbrook. He continued to stare at the outstretched hand.

"Have a seat," said the man in the blue *galabiya*. He pointed to a very small wooden chair on the opposite side of the crate. It appeared to have been taken from an elementary school classroom. He continued to tend to his breakfast, adding several more packages to the pot.

Colbrook stepped around the crate and carefully lowered himself down onto the offered chair. He was now facing the blue-robed man, his knees much higher than they normally would be when sitting in a chair. Pushing his canvas bag off to the side, he looked more closely at the man preparing the oatmeal. He had a small beard and mustache, carefully trimmed and combed. His dark brown hair was slightly on the disheveled side, but of average length. He was middle-aged and heavily tanned, as if he spent a lot of time outdoors. He spoke with an accent originating somewhere in the Midwest.

"I'm Harry Mercer," stated the man, sensing Colbrook's inquisitive stare. He scooped out a lump of oatmeal with a large serving spoon, placed the contents in a plastic bowl, and then handed it to Colbrook. "Here, let me get you a spoon." He reached under the crate and produced a cardboard box filled with plastic spoons.

Taking one, Colbrook lowered the disposable utensil into his oatmeal, stirring the steaming, increasingly thickening contents. Mercer began vigorously eating his, so Colbrook tried a spoonful. The oatmeal tasted better than he thought it would. His most recent meal had been served to him on a plane many hours before. Glancing around, he noted some things that he had missed on the way in.

A small aluminum cot was against the opposite wall, two wool blankets draped across the top. Not far from the cot was another wooden crate, this one much larger than the one they were using as a table. On the top of this crate were several disassembled cell phones, a collection of small cables, and a thin laptop computer. Adjacent to this larger crate, sitting on the floor, was an oversized and partly open duffel bag made of brown nylon. It appeared to be filled with more laptops of varying sizes and colors, more cell phones, a handful of flat plastic batteries, flashlights, and various cardboard boxes and clear plastic bags with numbers written on them in bold red marker ink.

"The command center," stated Mercer, aware that Colbrook was staring intently at the pile of equipment. "I would be more productive if I always had power, but I don't."

Looking at the ground near the crate, Colbrook could see a single orange extension cord twisted into a loop on the floor. He was going to ask where it was plugged in, but Mercer sensed what he was thinking.

"The government put up some streetlights around one of the better-preserved tombs down the road a piece, to try to hinder squatters. I rigged up a rudimentary connection to the pole, and buried the cable when I was done. It works fine—that is, when the main power is switched on. Apparently lights are not a high priority in this part of town. I've sometimes gone for days without electricity."

Colbrook finished his oatmeal and put the empty bowl down on the crate. The whole tomb setup seemed almost comfortable, and he suspected it had been here for a while.

"I have something for you," Mercer suddenly declared, reaching for the empty bowls. He tossed the used plastic spoons into a nearby garbage bag and sealed the bowls inside of a much smaller but thicker bag.

"I'll clean those out later. The place has rats. Big ones."

He started rummaging around under the crate. Pulling out a roll of paper towels, he tore off a few sheets and began wiping his hands, staring intently at the canvas bag lying on the floor next to Colbrook.

Mercer pointed to the canvas bag. "Did you bring any cell phones or computers?"

"No."

"You're sure."

"Positive. I packed everything myself."

Mercer seemed satisfied and dropped the subject. He pushed his stool back and stood up. It was obvious he was wearing regular clothes underneath his *galabiya*. Stepping towards the larger crate, he reached down and grabbed the nearest intact cell phone. He turned towards Colbrook, displaying the small phone in his hand. "Here, you'll need this."

Colbrook leaned forward, and Mercer walked closer before carefully tossing the phone. It landed safely in Colbrook's outstretched hands.

"Before you leave the country, destroy it," declared Mercer. "Don't just drop it in the Nile."

Colbrook examined the cell phone. It looked like a cheap one. "Is it traceable?"

"Of course not," said Mercer. "And you'll never need to buy any additional minutes. Its a bit heavier than when it came out of the convenience store, but the battery should last for several weeks without charging."

Colbrook slipped the cell phone into his pocket.

Mercer stood with his hands drawn behind his back, looking down at the larger crate with a thoughtful expression on his face. He started slowly pacing back and forth. Colbrook thought the white sneakers looked a little ridiculous, but the rest of the getup was fairly convincing.

Suddenly Mercer stopped, veering off towards the brown duffel bag. He stooped down, pulling at packages and boxes until he found what he was looking for. He carried two marked cardboard boxes over to the smaller crate. One had a large handwritten G on it, the other had H for G marked on it.

"I think this is a good choice," Mercer said.

Colbrook turned the first box around, pushed his thumb through the circular tab on the front, and lifted the cover. Inside was a black nylon shoulder holster wrapped in clear plastic.

Pushing the first box aside, Colbrook pulled the other one over. It was much heavier. He opened the top, revealing a dull black handgun. It seemed rather small.

"That's a Glock 36. It's what the manufacturer calls a subcompact slim-line. Uses a single-stack six-round magazine. It's .45-caliber. It may be smaller than usual, but it's certainly no compromise. Lightweight and virtually indestructible," said Mercer. He then added, "A considerable portion of that gun is made from a synthetic polymer. Perfect for concealment. It's a popular choice."

"For who?" asked Colbrook.

"People in your line of work."

Mercer reached across the crate and pulled the gun from the box. Then he pulled the plastic-wrapped shoulder holster from the other box and began unpacking it. Colbrook watched as he made the necessary adjustments, customizing the holster so that it securely held the unusually flat pistol. Mercer placed the holstered gun down on the crate when he was done.

Shrugging off his blazer while still sitting in the ridiculously small chair, Colbrook lifted the holstered gun over his shoulder, latched the plastic snaps, fiddled with the various fasteners, and eventually secured everything comfortably.

"It's double-action only," warned Mercer. "And it doesn't have a conventional safety."

"I'm familiar with the Glock trigger system," replied Colbrook, staring down at the holstered weapon.

"A perfect fit," Mercer declared.

Colbrook reached across himself with his right hand, undid the end of the strap that secured the handgrip, and pulled the gun from the holster. He made some further adjustments to the height at which the holster sat under his arm. He put the gun back into the holster and repeated his last draw. Comfort was not the only consideration.

"I have a Heckler & Koch Mark 23 in 9mm," said Mercer. "It's kind of clunky though, if you ask me. It'll be harder to conceal."

Colbrook was still too absorbed by the changes he was making to the shoulder holster to make any reply.

"Then there's the SIG Sauer p229. I don't have it in 9mm, but I have it in .40-caliber Smith & Wesson. It's your choice."

The gun was now back in its holster again. Colbrook patted his side and said, "It's fine." He reached for his blazer, slipping his arms through the sleeves.

Mercer at first seemed unsure of Colbrook's sincerity, but he finally lifted the empty boxes off the crate and put them back into the brown duffel bag. He returned with two spare magazines, handing them to Colbrook. Both were filled to capacity.

Reaching down for his canvas bag, Colbrook unzipped it and dropped the magazines inside.

Mercer stood staring sideways at the duffel bag. Then he turned towards Colbrook. He seemed lost in thought as he spoke. "You don't seem like someone who works for the government."

"I don't," said Colbrook.

"So you're an independent contractor."

"Something like that."

Mercer seemed satisfied. He started pacing around again. "I'm just a logistics man. They don't really brief me on anything." He abruptly stopped pacing. A sound had come from outside.

A few tense seconds passed, during which Colbrook watched Mercer's anxious face.

After a pause, Mercer walked closer to the back of one of the large rectangular stone monuments, his hands in the narrow pockets of his *galabiya*.

Colbrook tried to stretch his legs without making a sound, but his body was hunched forward at an awkward and uncomfortable angle. The tiny chair was not suited for extended use.

"Do you hear anything?" Mercer's voice was low, but not quite a whisper.

Colbrook concluded his struggle with the chair by managing to extend one of his legs.

"I did a few seconds ago."

"So did I." Mercer moved away from the small crate, disappearing around the stone monument.

After distinctly hearing the door open and then close, Colbrook heard two voices. Mercer reappeared with an Egyptian man in tow.

Colbrook immediately recognized his guide of the dilapidated sandals. He rose from his chair saying, "I made sure he wasn't following me."

"He wasn't following you," replied Mercer. "He knew where you went."

Colbrook was puzzled. Mercer soon clarified the matter.

"He works for me. His name is Abdullah."

Abdullah nodded, smiling.

"He always stops by for morning tea," explained Mercer. He settled down onto his stool and looked up at Colbrook. "I assume you know where you're going next."

"Luxor."

"I mean specifically." Mercer was looking under the crate. He seemed to be searching for something. "I made all the arrangements for your stay in Luxor."

Colbrook waited.

Mercer soon found what he was looking for. It was a tall aluminum teapot.

Colbrook glanced over at Abdullah, who seemed to be drowsing on his feet. "Was there much to arrange?"

"A few details." Mercer lifted the pot onto the crate, sniffed the inside, and seemed satisfied.

Abdullah's gaze was now focused on the teapot.

Mercer put the teapot down on the floor. "You have the top unit for the month."

Crouching down next to the crate, Abdullah started examining a shoebox filled with tea bags. He seemed captivated by the vast selection. Eventually he pulled a few out and handed them to Mercer. Reaching behind his stool, Mercer retrieved a one-gallon plastic jug of bottled water and quickly filled the teapot while Abdullah held its dented top open. Mercer placed the bags of tea into the pot, told Abdullah to close the lid, and then put the pot on the camp stove.

Retrieving the faded lighter from his pocket, Abdullah leaned forward on one knee and ignited the butane burner. He then turned to see what Colbrook was doing. When he was satisfied that he was not returning to the small wooden chair, he scrambled for it himself, settling down after much squatting and twisting. It was tea as usual.

Colbrook, who was now standing over Abdullah, noticed something odd on the top of his turban. It was a small white card stuck into the many folds and twists of his head covering. He was staring at it when Mercer noticed his gaze.

"Abdullah," said Mercer, tapping the top of his own head.

Abdullah began searching for the card with his long brown fingers. Before he could find it, Mercer had reached forward and plucked it from his turban.

Mercer examined the card for a moment. He reached down and picked up a pen from the crate, rapidly scribbling a few lines on the back of the card. Flipping it over, he circled something at the very bottom. "You'll need to contact Salah for transport to Luxor. He's got his own plane out past the pyramids. Does mostly sightseeing tours, but he'll be more than happy to do some longer jaunts if the price is right." Mercer handed the card to Colbrook. "I wrote the address for the apartment on the back."

Colbrook glanced at the business card. It was printed in both Arabic and English. Mercer's handwriting was cursive but acceptably legible.

Mercer reached into the left pocket of his *galabiya* and pulled out a tiny yellow envelope. He leaned forward, stretching his arm towards Colbrook.

Colbrook reached over Abdullah and took the small envelope. Something was sliding around inside it, small but heavy. He opened the folded end and dumped the contents into his hand. It was a brass key, completely ordinary in appearance.

"The key to the apartment. I had the locks changed," said Mercer.

Colbrook slipped the key back into the envelope and dropped it into his pocket.

"The key opens both locks. There's a padlock on the outside gate and a regular deadbolt on the door. Most of the villas in Luxor have a padlocked gate for extra security. There's also a main gate on the street, but that's never locked."

Abdullah muttered something to Mercer in Arabic which Colbrook did not understand. It sounded like a mild complaint. In response Mercer carefully adjusted the position of the teapot on the burner. Steam started to rise from around its trembling lid, the smell of brewed tea filling the tomb.

Colbrook picked up his bag and zipped it closed. He looked down at the two crouched figures, tending their teapot as if engaged in some archaic ritual. Neither looked up at him as he started walking towards the tomb's entrance.

He had almost reached the door when Mercer called out in an oddly echoing voice: "Tell me, Colbrook, does this operation have anything to do with that helicopter that went down in the Sudan?"

Colbrook turned to look back into the tomb. It was obvious the tea-brewers did not expect an answer.

They did not get one.

2

The Nile's course was a bright green ribbon against the monochromatic brown landscape. Cruising at an altitude of eight thousand feet, Colbrook viewed the expansive scenery from the co-pilot's seat of a Beechcraft Musketeer. The cabin was larger than he would have expected for a single-engine low-wing aircraft of its size, and when he commented on its spaciousness, Salah told him with great pride that it was a Super III model.

Salah had sensed Colbrook's uneasiness upon seeing the aircraft for the first time, and had tried to reassure him of its airworthiness by declaring that he did all of his own repairs. Having far from allayed Colbrook's growing concern with that statement, the pilot made matters even worse when he cheerfully admitted the plane had been in service since 1969. Despite the initially rough ignition and smoky engine, the Musketeer, orange with a wide yellow stripe down the side, had safely climbed away from the airstrip located on the large plateau outside of Giza.

Now twenty minutes into the flight, they were approaching the Fayum Oasis, a vast basin of greenery in the otherwise parched terrain. Soon the northward-flowing Nile would start curving gradually westwards.

Gazing through the thick, yellowed windscreen, his eyes still following the river up ahead, Colbrook could tell they were already steadily angling away from the Nile, heading out over the inhospitable Eastern Desert, flying a more direct course to their destination. He watched the river fade from sight on the starboard side, eventually disappearing altogether.

He hoped Salah's mechanical skill would see them through the flight.

A few hours later—after consuming a bottle of warm lemonade and a slightly flattened sandwich—Colbrook began to see the river again, curving back into view.

They landed in Luxor without incident. The long walk across the blistering tarmac was something of a relief after three hundred miles of constant engine noise and vibration. Salah, who gave the impression he was impervious to fatigue, planned on making the return trip to Cairo later that afternoon. Colbrook was not sure how well the pilot knew Mercer or Abdullah, but he was very helpful in finding a taxi driver to take him into town.

The taxi, an old Peugeot sedan, rattled violently, the suspension bottoming out every time it hit a bump or a pothole. On both sides of the road vast tracts of flourishing crops covered virtually every inch of arable land. Scattered throughout the fields were mud-brick houses, many of them set in small groves of palm trees. In the distance several large canals guiding water from the Nile ran roughly perpendicular to the road, with smaller feeder canals leading to the cultivated areas.

They soon passed over two concrete bridges spanning these larger canals, reaching the outskirts of a small village only minutes later. The driver began muttering to himself as he negotiated its narrow and crowded thoroughfare. Groups of people and livestock walked both in and along the sides of the dusty road. Many undersized wooden carts pulled by donkeys temporarily blocked the way. Guiding these animals were the *fellahin*, the farmers of Egypt, their long *galabiyas* stained with dirt and toil.

As they were leaving the village they passed a large potter's shop. Clay vessels of all shapes and sizes were lined up alongside the dusty road. The driver swerved at a crossing junction, heading southwest, barely missing a fruit stand and its shouting proprietor. After another turn, this time to the northwest, taller buildings loomed on the horizon. They continued to barrel towards what could only be Luxor.

Soon the car was lurching down paved streets and swerving around curbed corners, the driver struggling against the traffic which surged from all sides. Slowing the taxi at a tangled intersection he blared the horn a few times and then veered through the oncoming traffic, forcing his way onto a smaller side street, narrowly avoiding several collisions.

Blasting through a series of narrow alleyways, the driver haphazardly merged with other cars onto a wider roadway. Colbrook recognized it as the Sharia al-Karnak, one of the main thoroughfares in Luxor. Tourists were now highly visible. They walked in packs along the sidewalks, congregating near the ancient sites. The driver made another violent maneuver—a right turn—passing onto the Corniche, the roadway that paralleled the Nile along the waterfront of Luxor.

The avenue of sphinxes and the imposing structure of the first pylon of the Luxor temple were now visible through the grimy windshield. A considerable obelisk stood just outside the temple's entrance. The rest of the temple stretched away to the southwest, a mass of colonnades, courts, and chapels.

The car was slowing rapidly now, and soon it stopped on the edge of the road. The driver turned and pointed out the passenger window. "Follow steps down to river. Ferry will take you across."

Colbrook nodded his thanks and leaned his canvas bag against the edge of the seat. He pushed open the creaky back door of the Peugeot, stepped out to stretch his legs, and then reached in for his bag. After paying the driver, who shook his hand vigorously at the generous tip, he stepped away from the side of the road to get a better look at the ferry docking area. The heat and dust of Luxor swirled around him, mixing with the cloud of dissipating exhaust from the taxi.

Making his way down to the docking area, Colbrook watched the many locals standing patiently in line to board a relatively small boat. It did not seem possible that so many people could fit onto the aging vessel, but they all eventually filed on. It left for the opposite shore only minutes later.

Hanging back from the crowd, Colbrook waited to see if another ferry returning from across the river was going to stop at this particular dock. When he was certain one was, he headed down the last flight of steps to the edge of the river to meet it. This ferry carried only a few people coming from the western side of the Nile, so he could board quickly.

After paying a few pounds for the ride—apparently a much higher fee than the locals paid to cross by the smaller vessel—he sat down on a worn bench near the stern of the ship. A canopy covered most of the deck, blocking the searing sun but not the sweltering heat. A few other passengers boarded—mostly tourists, easily identifiable by their colorful knapsacks and large water bottles. The total barely equaled a dozen when the ferry departed ten minutes later.

Whether it was the Valley of the Kings, the tombs of the nobles, or the temple of Hatshepsut at the foot of the Theban hills that his fellow passengers sought, Colbrook knew they would all be given the same choice of transportation: various domesticated beasts—with saddle or without—or for the less adventurous, a rusty old taxi. Colbrook had more practical reasons for his visit to the western side of the Nile: he had to find the Amenti House. The town near the river where this residence was located was very small on the map he carried in his pocket, and he was certain he could find the address without local assistance.

The ferry soon docked on the west bank, several grubby-looking Egyptians onshore seizing the lines as they spiraled off the bow of the ship. The captain kept the diesel engine idling, waiting for the passengers to go ashore. The tourists were immediately thronged by prospective guides who pointed out their various decrepit means of transportation.

Colbrook slipped from the crowd and quickly made his way along the waterfront, heading towards a group of low buildings. Several Egyptians asked him if he needed a ride, but when he told them he was going to Ramla, which was within easy walking distance, most of them wandered away, though some persisted in following him for a hundred yards or so. Then even these gradually drifted away in disappointment.

Strolling along a dirt road bordered by a swath of low-growing vegetation separating it from the river's edge, he watched the many feluccas sailing close by. He was soon greeted by a spotted dog with curling triangular ears and a narrow snout, who emerged from another street and arrived at his side with a friendly stare. The dog trotted alongside as he made his way down the roadway.

After exploring several different dirt streets, consulting his map a few times, and turning back once, Colbrook arrived at a small store. It was made of rough bricks coated with cement. A low doorway was flanked by two giant soft-drink signs. A small window looked out onto the street, covered by an elaborate metal grill. The rooftop was arrayed with a variety of loose building materials and tarps, along with many ancient-looking television antennas. Not a single one was truly upright. Behind the rusty aerials was a large satellite dish.

Colbrook wiped perspiration from his brow. The sun was very strong, and he had not anticipated such a long walk. His clothes were already coated with a fine film of sand and dust. Stepping under the low overhang that stretched across the front of the store, he consulted his map again. The piebald dog lazily dropped into a patch of shade nearby.

After a few minutes he refolded the map and stepped back into the bright sunlight. The dog appeared to be fast asleep, so he gave him a wide berth, walking a bit faster as he headed back the way he had come. Before he had gone very far, a small boy dexterously intercepted his path and offered to give him a ride on a gray donkey.

The good-natured beast seemed almost too small to ride, but at the sight of the doleful expression on the boy's face, Colbrook told him he was trying to reach the Amenti House. The boy nodded happily, indicating he knew where it was by pointing with his finger in its apparent direction.

Waiting patiently for his passenger to mount the animal, the boy held a frayed rope tied to the rudimentary bridle. Colbrook soon realized the donkey was so short that he could simply sit down on its back and then swing his leg over to the other side. He found the large padded blanket to be a suitable substitute for a proper saddle, and when he was at last settled, the animal began plodding its way down the road.

Though Colbrook worked the reins, the animal resisted his control. Resigning himself to the donkey's erratic path, his only consolation was that he was heading in the right direction.

Sightseeing from the surprising comfort of the donkey's back, he was immediately aware of the dense vegetation that surrounded the town and the stark contrast of the higher desert not far beyond it. The age-old comment about the Nile being the lifeblood of Egypt was certainly not an exaggeration.

Several minutes later, the boy—who had been wandering along the side of the road staring down at the wide variety of industrial rubbish that littered the ground, as if souvenir hunting—came running up behind the donkey and grabbed its tail with an expression of glee. It was an effective brake, and the donkey stopped almost immediately.

Colbrook looked away from the river's edge which had held his interest the whole ride. They had halted in front of a high stone wall with a metal gate. A three-story structure made of concrete, its footprint about the size of a large house, stood not far beyond it. It was very basic and block-like in design. There were matching rows of windows on each level, and two wide balconies across the front of the first two floors. The top sported a parapet of sorts. The building appeared to be fairly new, or at least well maintained. In comparison to the mostly dilapidated dwellings nearby it seemed almost palatial.

Colbrook swung his right leg over the donkey and stepped with both feet onto the roadway. The donkey immediately wandered to the side of the road to nibble on some tall grass. The boy accepted payment for the ride, and then began begging for some *baksheesh*. Slipping him a few more pounds, Colbrook waved goodbye to the boy, who now turned the donkey with its simple lead and made off in the opposite direction.

Standing for a moment in the road, his canvas bag now hanging from his shoulder by its leather strap, Colbrook stared up at the Amenti House. It was certainly a quiet and secluded location, away from the crowds of tourists.

Walking to the metal gate, he pushed it inwards, passing into a small but well-tended ornamental garden. Various shrubs and flowers grew in abundance, and several clusters of tall palm trees flanked the property. A gravel path led up to the front of the building, surrounded by an expanse of closely cropped grass.

Following the path, his shoes crunching on the loose surface, he spotted an exterior set of concrete stairs attached to the left side of the structure. They appeared to lead all the way up to the rooftop. Turning onto a narrower pathway, he walked along the front of the building until he reached the exterior stairway. Confronted with a metal security gate at the bottom of the steps—this one set into an arch made of concrete—he stopped to unlock a gleaming brass padlock using the key Mercer had given him.

Pulling the padlock out of the retaining ring and swinging the gate aside, he stepped through. After closing the gate he looped the lock through the ring again, but did not snap it closed.

He started up the wavy concrete stairs. The risers were not all of equal height, and he found himself stumbling a few times as he tried to anticipate the next step. He soon reached the top, moving beneath a wooden trelliswork which covered about a third of the rooftop.

With a network of vines thickly interwoven across it, the trellis provided a vast canopy of shading foliage. At either end of the short side of the framework two long wooden planters were filled with moist dirt—the water supplied by a drip irrigation system—and from these grew the vigorous climbing plants. Staring out onto the sunny patio, Colbrook took a welcome respite from the hot sun.

The rooftop was covered with large limestone tiles. The low wall that encircled it on all sides was made of concrete blocks plastered over with cement. A set of cushioned chairs surrounded a round metal table in the middle of the roof, its center-mounted umbrella folded loosely on a wooden pole. A barbecue and a few small benches were against the opposite wall. Under the trellis were several wicker chairs with wide wooden arms, a wooden table, a wicker sofa, and an ornate plant stand. Large potted plants and a few hanging ones were scattered around the rooftop.

To his right, not far from where he stood under the trellis, a partially enclosed stairway went down through the roof into the apartment below. There was a small landing at the bottom of the steps. A set of very narrow French doors provided entry into the interior.

Walking out onto the exposed rooftop, shading his eyes from the sun's glare with his hand, Colbrook looked westward. The Theban hills rose steeply in the distance. A thick haze seemed to hang in the air behind these craggy prominences, where the real desert began. Higher up the sky was cloudless and a deep azure blue. Turning in the opposite direction—to the east—he could see the Nile slowly winding its way through the greenery below. Several large cruisers were moored on the opposite side of the river, serving as floating hotels for those who preferred to see Egypt from the deck of a ship, and beyond these a few of Luxor's taller structures were conspicuous on the skyline. To the south were the modest buildings of the local farmers, which also dotted the ground some distance to the north and west.

Moving towards the covered stairway, Colbrook made his way down the steps to the French doors. He unlocked them, entering into the apartment.

Though the air conditioners were not running, it was still much cooler indoors than up on the roof. The kitchen was small, but appeared to have all the modern amenities. Dropping his canvas bag onto a nearby chair, Colbrook stood thinking for a few moments. He realized he was quite hungry.

Apparently Mercer's arrangements included stocking provisions, because the array of food neatly stacked within the surprisingly large refrigerator was simply an embarrassment of culinary riches.

When his lunching was complete, Colbrook picked up his canvas bag and walked out of the kitchen and into the bedroom. He took off his dusty blazer and then carefully removed his shoulder holster. The wrinkled button-down shirt he wore underneath was replaced with a casual short-sleeved shirt. He concealed the pistol in the bottom of his canvas bag, wrapped in a pair of pants.

He made his way back up the staircase to the patio. Briefly stopping to clean off his sunglasses on his shirt, he studied the shimmering Nile. Moving out from under the shade of the trellis he slipped his sunglasses on and walked towards the front of the building. This side of the rooftop was clear of furniture and plants, and he could walk right up to the wall and look down into the garden. The scene below was quiet and tranquil, the afternoon sun creating bright splashes of light across the flower beds and lawn, contrasting vividly with the inky shade cast by the taller shrubs and trees.

Colbrook's eye caught the movement of a man walking below in the garden. He was holding a large camera in his hand, and appeared to be sneaking around, snapping photos of the flowers and trees. Colbrook suspected it was Dr. Trevor Beckwith, an Egyptologist of some note. He was one of the reasons this building had been selected.

Beckwith had retired from teaching at a university in England some years before, and his knowledge of ancient Egypt was con-

sidered by many in the field to be unparalleled. He was also a pro-
lific writer on the subject, something he apparently spent most of
his time now doing. Colbrook was not all that interested in the
specifics of Beckwith's Egyptological qualifications, but he was interested in making his acquaintance.

He immediately headed for the exterior stairs.

When he pushed his way through the arched gateway at the bottom, planning on intercepting Beckwith in the garden, he practically
bumped into him passing by on the gravel path.

Breathing heavily, as if from excessive exertion, Beckwith was
wearing a pair of dusty brown khakis and a blue short-sleeved shirt.
A pair of sunglasses were tucked into his shirt pocket, a narrow-
brimmed sun hat perched on his head. His swarthy complexion
indicated that he spent a considerable amount of time at these
latitudes. He was carefully fitting a plastic cover onto his expensive SLR digital camera's lens. Beads of perspiration were running
down his face.

Colbrook tried to act as casual as possible, as if he was just going
for a stroll in the garden.

"Did you see it?" Beckwith asked, his accent decidedly English.
"A good chase he made for me, but I think I got him anyway." He
started pushing buttons on his camera, looking carefully at the small
LCD screen on the back. "There he is. Look."

Colbrook leaned over and peered down at the camera back. He
could see the image of a small black and white bird sitting on the
top of a shrub.

"Those are very rare." Beckwith's breathing was less labored
now. He was rubbing his forehead with his hand, his hat pushed
back on his head. "Say, did that boy stick you for more *baksheesh*?
You've got to be stronger! Some of those boys can play their act so
well they could step onto the London stage and have the audience
swimming in tears."

Colbrook gave Beckwith a careful look. "I'll learn with time I
suppose."

The Egyptologist suddenly looked up from his camera and said,
"I haven't properly introduced myself. I'm Trevor Beckwith." He
turned a switch on the top of the camera, and then swung the long
padded strap onto his shoulder.

"Martin Colbrook." He held out his hand and shook Beckwith's.

Greetings now aside, the two men began to walk down the pathway, gravel crunching under their shoes. As they reached the front of the building, Beckwith stopped and reached across his shoulder, pulling at the heavy camera which kept sliding around. Soon both men stood staring up at the building.

Colbrook, realizing that Beckwith was about to depart for his apartment, quickly said, "You could probably get some good shots from the rooftop."

Beckwith tilted his head back and looked up at the roof. "Is the view that good from up there?"

"You can see just about everything," replied Colbrook.

Beckwith paused. "I suppose you're right. I've never been up there."

"Be careful on the steps. They're a little uneven." Colbrook turned and walked back the way they had come, heading for the exterior staircase, not giving Beckwith a chance to refuse.

"I see you've just arrived," said Beckwith, trailing along.

Colbrook paused at the cement arch at the bottom of the steps to pull open the metal gate. "I landed in Cairo early this morning."

"Nothing to see in Cairo, eh?"

Colbrook could barely suppress a smile when he thought about that innocent question. He was glad his back was turned. The image of Mercer and Abdullah hunched over their morning tea reappeared vividly in his mind.

Beckwith now followed Colbrook carefully up the wavy stairs. "Didn't you at least stop at the pyramids?"

"I've seen those before," said Colbrook. "They always look better in photographs anyway."

"That's true."

Halting halfway up the stairs, Colbrook peered over his shoulder. Beckwith had now taken off his hat and was using it as a fan to cool his face as he continued climbing. Colbrook waited until he was a little closer before moving once more up the stairway.

"Can you see across the river?" asked Beckwith as he continued to make his way up the steps.

Colbrook had now reached the top of the stairs, and in answer he moved aside to let Beckwith ascend the last few steps. They both moved under the trellis, gazing out over the tops of the palm trees.

"You weren't kidding," said Beckwith. He pulled the lens cover off his camera and peered through the viewfinder. A few seconds later he was snapping a series of photos looking towards the Nile. Then he turned to look the other way, to the west. Stepping out into the sunlight he took some pictures in the direction of the Valley of the Kings, and then retreated back under the trellis.

"How about a cold drink?" asked Colbrook. "Some iced tea, maybe?"

Beckwith hesitated. "If it's no bother."

"Wait here, I'll be right back." Colbrook went down into the kitchen and returned a few minutes later with two glass bottles of iced tea.

Colbrook handed one of the beverages to Beckwith and then walked to the wicker chairs and the small wooden table in the dappled shade of the trellis. Beckwith followed, and soon both men were sitting comfortably. Lifting the camera strap over his head, Beckwith carefully placed the camera on the table.

"I got a shot of you riding up on that donkey," said Beckwith. "You don't mind, do you?" He twisted the top off his iced tea, waiting for Colbrook's response.

Colbrook leaned back in his chair. "Not at all."

He thought he had arrived unobserved. Beckwith must have come out onto his balcony after he rode up.

"I bought it just a few weeks ago." Beckwith pointed at the camera. "I haven't figured out what half the buttons do yet."

"Those instruction manuals aren't very well thought out," said Colbrook.

"They usually aren't," agreed Beckwith. "This one is no exception. Hopefully I can figure the menus out by trial and error." He drank some iced tea. "When I'm giving lectures on Nile cruise tours I often see people struggling with their digital cameras."

"Cruise tours?" asked Colbrook, sipping his beverage.

"I give them. Not tours, lectures during the tour." Beckwith took another swig. "It's a good way to sell books."

"Oh," said Colbrook.

"I'm an Egyptologist," declared Beckwith. "Retired."

"Your name sounds vaguely familiar," said Colbrook. "I read

quite a few books on the subject in preparation for this trip. Didn't you write *Along the Ancient Nile?*"

Beckwith looked briefly astonished. "You know my work?"

"Your material is readable, which is more than I can say for some authors on the subject." Colbrook studied the contents of his bottle. "I'm just a travel writer. Strictly a layman when it comes to Egyptology."

Beckwith was pleased with the compliment.

"In all the years and innumerable lectures, not a single tourist has ever once told me that they have read my books. I'm not even so sure they know I'm actually an Egyptologist. They all seem to have the same blank expression on their faces during my lectures, and the only time they appear to get active is when the lunch service starts."

"It's a shame."

"It is, isn't it. Why do they come to Egypt if they have no interest in its ancient history?"

"So they can say they've been to Egypt."

Beckwith nodded in agreement. "Yes, I suppose that's it." He continued drinking his iced tea.

A period of silence followed, both men resting comfortably in the shade. During this interval they finished their beverages, and Beckwith, following Colbrook's example, placed his empty bottle on the wide arm of his own wicker chair.

"I guess you're not involved in digs anymore," said Colbrook.

"Not officially. I don't have an affiliation. You need one to apply for an excavation permit." Beckwith lifted his hat to cool his head. "You can't just show up with a shovel. It's all handled by the Supreme Council of Antiquities."

Colbrook allowed himself a modest grin.

"I kid you not," insisted Beckwith. "That's what it's called. Most people just refer to it as the SCA."

"I imagine it's very difficult to get permission even when all the requirements are met."

"Submission to the SCA with the appropriate credentials is hardly a guarantee," replied Beckwith. "The project must be approved by the permanent committee of that organization. Even if it's accepted one must still provide evidence that adequate financing is available for the duration of the dig."

"Sounds complicated."

"Official endorsement brings another set of headaches," explained Beckwith. "Stacks of paperwork must be filed before starting. The committee also expects full reports at the end of the season, and that includes a required translation into Arabic. Compliance with these rules is taken very seriously. If you don't follow the regulations chances are your concession will not be renewed for the following season."

Colbrook leaned back in his chair.

"And when you find something newsworthy," Beckwith went on, "you can't go public with it. The SCA must be notified first, and then they decide whether to grant you press clearance. You're essentially signing a contract to that effect."

"What about funding?"

Beckwith shrugged his shoulders. "That depends on the organization conducting the dig." He looked over at Colbrook. "If it's a museum the funds naturally come from contributions. Large universities typically finance their own projects, but they also actively seek wealthy individuals to enhance their funding, just like the museums."

"What about corporate sponsors?" asked Colbrook.

"It does exist in a roundabout way," said Beckwith, now staring out into the bright sunlit portion of the patio. "It's more of a mutually beneficial system, though." He looked at Colbrook across the table. "The 1970 UNESCO treaty prohibits the export and transfer of ownership of any ancient artifacts without official permission. Clearly one cannot expect to legally profit from archeological finds anymore. Even if you managed to smuggle artifacts out, no museum would buy them without proof of prior ownership."

Colbrook was not sure where this topic was leading and let Beckwith continue.

"All is not lost though, because there's still the entertainment value of the dig." Beckwith removed his hat, placing it on his lap.

Colbrook waited for an explanation.

"It's interesting material for a documentary or special," said Beckwith. "If the budget is sufficient, the production company will allocate funds for the whole project. Naturally this can cause some contention between the producer and the Egyptologist, because the former is looking for maximum entertainment value, while the latter is trying to conduct legitimate field research. It's not a good combination. I've been involved in a few of those myself."

Colbrook was about to express his interest in Egyptologists who actively worked in the field—those who ended each day with dirt under their nails—when Beckwith suddenly interrupted his line of thought.

"Are you writing about digging in Egypt?" Beckwith was staring at Colbrook with earnestness.

"That's what I had in mind," replied Colbrook. "I'd like to find something unique and unusual. Away from all the tourists. Not just your typical dig. Maybe something out in the Western Desert."

Beckwith furrowed his brow in contemplation. "There's an ongoing excavation in the Kharga Oasis. That's a very remote area in the Western Desert. It's completely away from tourists and the usual haunts of Egyptologists. About four hours from here by car."

"Sounds promising."

Beckwith swatted at a fly. "It's Gus Lowell's dig. I haven't been out there, but I've met him a few times in town. I'm not sure it's going all that well, but he seems to have found enough funding to keep it active, which is an accomplishment in itself."

"Do you think he would allow me to visit the site?"

"I don't see why not, but you can ask him yourself," said Beckwith with a faint smile. "Lowell spends every Friday night at the Karnak Club."

"Where's that?" asked Colbrook.

"Luxor," said Beckwith. "It's the local spot for Egyptologists, so to speak. It's where we discuss our latest finds and argue our theories. Don't expect any entertainment, though. It's more of a research center than a club."

"Is it hard to find?" inquired Colbrook.

Beckwith put his hat on and leaned back in his chair. "Not really, but it's such a dump from the outside that you wouldn't believe you were at the right place. The inside is actually quite comfortable if you like old libraries."

Colbrook got up from his chair and lazily stretched. Beckwith rose soon after. As they turned and gazed towards the glittering Nile, Beckwith described how to find the Karnak Club and

Colbrook pretended to listen carefully. He already knew exactly where the club was situated.

"I guess you probably want to get back to your photography," said Colbrook. He sensed Beckwith wished to excuse himself, but could not find a polite way to do so.

"Oh, yes. I almost forgot." Beckwith had started to reach down for his camera, but suddenly stopped. He turned back towards Colbrook. "Before I go, here's my card."

The Egyptologist handed him a crumpled business card. "It has my phone number on it in case you want to reach me. Of course you can just yell down off the roof if you want. I spend most of my time writing out on the balcony." He paused and then added, "I have a tour group coming off a river cruise tomorrow morning at dawn, otherwise I'd go along with you. Crossing the river at night is always interesting."

"How so?"

"There are no regular passenger ferries. You'll have to use whatever happens to be around."

Colbrook retrieved the two empty bottles from the arms of the wicker chairs while Beckwith picked up his camera and excused himself. He left in no great hurry.

Colbrook stood listening to the sound of Beckwith's footsteps fading down the concrete stairs. He consulted his watch. If he wanted to get to the police station on time he would have to leave now. Tucking one of the bottles under his arm, he headed for the kitchen below.

Blotched and faded, the facade was consistent with the building's bunker-like design. The only windows visible from the street were on the second floor, and these were narrow and tall. The structure was purely utilitarian in design. It was connected by an overhead walkway to a much smaller concrete building constructed along more classic lines.

Colbrook began to walk up the cracked cement stairs, aware that he was being watched carefully by an Egyptian police officer who stood just inside the entrance of the building. Reaching the door, he pushed it inward, nodding to the uniformed man. "I'm Mr. Colbrook. I have an appointment with the chief of police."

"Follow me, sir." The uniformed man motioned for Colbrook to accompany him.

Colbrook found himself walking through the empty lobby towards a flight of metal stairs ascending to the second story. He trailed along silently, making his way up the staircase on his tired legs; he had walked from the passenger ferry. When they reached the top he could see rows of wooden doors on either side of a linoleum-tiled hallway that stretched away to the back of the building. A doorway was partly open on the left side of the hall, and it was towards this that his guide walked.

Colbrook followed the policeman into the room. It was a small working office. A wooden table and several old swivel chairs covered in a garish fabric made up the extent of the furniture. The table was clear of any of the usual materials one might expect to find in an office, such as loose papers and books, though it did have an old laptop computer on it, along with an ancient-looking rotary telephone. A faded Egyptian-flag sticker was peeling off the back of the phone, revealing another even older sticker beneath it.

A metal fan rattled away on a battered filing cabinet. Several maps of the Nile Valley drawn in bold and multi-colored lines fluttered on the wall in the artificial breeze. The room was considerably cooler than the outside air temperature, but it was not air-conditioned.

Behind the wooden table was a utilitarian metal door. It was closed. As Colbrook studied it he sensed that the man who had directed him into the room was no longer standing beside him. When he turned, this proved to be the case.

He heard a faint clicking sound and turned towards the table again. The doorknob was swiveling on the metal door, and when the door swung inwards a gray-mustached and relatively tall man entered. He was wearing ordinary casual clothing: a pair of jeans, a maroon short-sleeved button-down shirt, and a brown baseball cap. Plucking the hat off with an exaggerated flourish, he dropped into the chair on his side of the table. He leaned his close-cropped head forward.

"Mr. Colbrook?"

Colbrook nodded in reply.

"I'm the chief of police. My name is Ali Hassan."

Hassan's English was remarkably well spoken for a man who undoubtedly used his native Arabic in most of his daily discourse.

"Please, take a seat. Do you have your passport?"

Colbrook placed his passport down on the table. Hassan had no reaction beyond a quick, friendly nod. Colbrook then put two more documents down, one after the other. Pulling a chair around, he sat down facing the chief of police.

Hassan ignored the documents for a moment, leaning back in his squeaky chair to begin the conversation. "There seems to be some confusion about the reason for your visit. I'm sure you can clear it up." He leaned forward to give a cursory glance at the additional documents. "You are with the United Nations Office on Drugs and Crime, correct?"

"I'm doing some work for the United States Drug Enforcement Agency. Consulting and research. The DEA sometimes cooperates with the UN."

"And you are actively engaged in something specifically involving Egypt right now?"

"That's why I'm here."

"Are you trying to obtain a specific permission from the Egyptian government?"

"Just a mutual understanding," stated Colbrook.

"That's good, because I can't really help you if you're seeking a diplomatic-level clearance." Hassan grinned. "I'm just the local police chief." He then continued in a more serious tone. "Is this an investigation of some kind?"

"You could say that."

Hassan leaned back in his chair. "Do you need local cooperation? Or help of some other kind?"

"For now I just need you to know what I'm involved in. I don't want someone snapping a set of handcuffs on me."

Hassan was amused. "Why would anyone do that?"

"My research sometimes results in incidents. People frequently sustain injuries in these incidents."

"This is under whose authority? The United Nations?" Hassan was leaning forward and staring at the documents on the table again.

"I operate under U.S. government authority. The UN has nothing to do with it. They're a security risk," said Colbrook. "They can't be trusted with information."

"They can't be trusted with much of anything," said Hassan, folding his arms. "This strikes me as being a bit more than consulting and researching. Sounds like field work to me."

"Regulations and technical suggestions don't accomplish much unless strictly enforced."

Hassan reached across the table and slid the documents towards himself. He frowned as he thumbed through them. Glancing up he said, "I can't authorize you to arrest anyone. You're not an officer of the law."

"I don't plan on making any arrests," replied Colbrook. "That's your job."

Hassan leaned back in his chair and folded his arms again. "What are you investigating?"

"A large shipment of cocaine," answered Colbrook. "The point of departure was Venezuela. It left aboard a Cessna Conquest II from a remote airstrip in the jungle. The flight was obviously never scheduled with any aviation authorities."

"Where did they fly to?"

"Western Africa—Guinea-Bissau to be exact. It's just north of Senegal."

"That's a considerable flight, isn't it?"

"Thirty-five hundred miles at least," replied Colbrook. "This certainly confused some people at first, because the Conquest II only has a standard range of thirteen hundred miles. The cruising speed is around two hundred and fifty knots. That means at least a twelve-hour flight, not including the time needed for the initial climb and then the descent."

"If it had the fuel to get there in the first place," stated Hassan with a piercing look.

"Additional fuel tanks were installed. The plane's empty weight is around fifty-five hundred pounds, but it can easily carry another four thousand pounds. It's a turboprop, seats eight passengers, and can attain a cruising altitude of close to thirty thousand feet."

"That must be a very expensive modification."

"I'm sure it is, but the value of the cargo is estimated to be at least forty million dollars."

"Now it doesn't seem so absurd," replied Hassan. "How do you know so much about the plane, anyway?"

"The aircraft was seized in Guinea-Bissau."

"Not the drugs, though."

"No. The cargo had already been unloaded," explained Colbrook. "Aircraft are not their only means of transport. They also regularly use large private boats and sometimes even standard commercial freighters. The freighters are considered risky because they have to dock at ordinary ports, which means they're exposed to search and seizure operations. The larger ships typically stay offshore, unloading the goods into smaller boats for local landings."

"Who controls the drugs once they get into Africa? How do they stop the locals from just taking everything?"

"The cartels have their own men in the region who run the whole show. They handle the logistics. Nothing is left to chance. In return for cooperation from the locals, the cartels pay them in cocaine. Most of this trickles its way into Europe by way of individual Africans who get onto commercial flights. Nigerians seem to be the largest group involved in this practice. A large percentage are caught. They're the amateurs."

"And the main flow?"

"The majority of the material is managed by the cartel itself all the way to Europe. They use local people to physically haul it around. The Africans are hired hands in this part of the business."

"Why aren't the West African authorities doing something about it?" Hassan asked.

"They have little or no law-enforcement infrastructure to stop shipments after they arrive," answered Colbrook. "I won't even begin discussing the fact that probably a considerable number of the officers who are authorized to seize such goods are on the payroll of the drug cartels."

"They must be seizing some of it, or how would we know about it?" declared Hassan.

"It's frequently reported that forty-six tons of cocaine have been seized in the past three years. That may seem like a large amount, but no one knows what percentage of the total that makes up. Probably only a very small part. Some say twenty-eight percent of Europe's cocaine goes through West Africa at some point."

Hassan put his hands behind his head and leaned back as far as his chair would tilt.

Colbrook continued. "Guinea-Bissau and Ghana are the hubs where most of the cocaine arrives before further transport. Obviously once it's on land it's almost impossible to track. Most, if not all, is destined for Europe. Spain and the UK are the largest markets."

"How do the large shipments get into Europe?"

"Now that's an interesting question. A considerable quantity—if not the majority—of the drugs are shipped into the Sahara desert on camels or in trucks. Outposts and temporary airstrips are set up to facilitate flying the cocaine into Europe via private planes. Most of these land in Spain, in very remote desert regions."

Hassan looked thoughtful.

"We have received reports," Colbrook went on, "from some locals under our sponsorship, that this specific shipment passed into Algeria from Guinea-Bissau via Mauritania, ultimately destined for trans-Saharan shipment. They have Tuaregs in pay, who load their trucks with the drugs and then drive across the desert. These convoys typically consist of four or more vehicles, the front and rear cars carrying enough guns and ammunition to provide ample protection for the rest of the group, and sometimes enough to start a small war."

"Where were they heading?" questioned Hassan.

"East."

Hassan looked directly at Colbrook.

"If my sources are correct," concluded Colbrook, "this particular shipment is destined to arrive in Aswan."

"And then?"

"Down the Nile."

"In what?" asked Hassan. "A ship would be impossible. The river is silted up north of here. You might be able to pull it off in August or September, but not now."

"Felucca," stated Colbrook. "Small boats. Whatever can make it."

Hassan did not respond, and as Colbrook looked at the police chief, he felt a tinge of remorse.

He almost believed the whole story himself.

3

The sound of buzzing insects and chirping frogs echoed along the river's edge. The lights of distant Luxor sparkled across the flat expanse of dark, flowing water. A faint odor of decaying vegetation drifted with the fitful wind. In the limited illumination of a kerosene lantern a group of men were playing cards at a small plastic table on the shoreline. Two of them were yelling something while the others laughed and pointed at the table. Another man, sitting on a concrete wall a short distance away, discreetly smoked a cigarette. A couched camel being coaxed to rise nearby made a growling noise that soon changed to a loud bellowing. It was night in Upper Egypt.

Colbrook stood on the western edge of the Nile, waiting for a small wooden felucca to maneuver into position so he could climb aboard. As Beckwith had told him, the regular passenger ferries did not operate this late at night—the sites on the west bank were closed to visitors after sundown—but the local Egyptians were always eager to provide transport across the river for an appropriate fee.

The felucca's owner stood in the bow, pointing and shouting in Arabic to a teenage boy who struggled with a coil of heavy hemp rope on the shoreline. The boy pulled the line taut, trying to get the nose of the boat to turn parallel with the shore and into the river's current. He eventually succeeded, motioning for Colbrook to wait.

The owner reached down into the hull and lifted a long plank over the side, gradually sliding the free end into the water. The boy waded into the river, grabbed the end of the board, and positioned it on the shore. With this makeshift and very unstable gangway now in place, the owner waved for Colbrook to come aboard.

Steadying himself as best he could, Colbrook clambered up the plank and into the aging vessel. Making his way to the center of the craft, he lowered himself down onto the worn seat as the boat rocked gently from side to side. The felucca was quite small compared to the others he had seen floating on the Nile. The owner swept past him, gathering his robes together as he steadily moved towards the tiller. He soon seated himself on a bench at the stern.

The wind was light, but still sufficient for crossing the river. It was only a third of a mile in distance from one side to the other. The sail ruffled lazily from beneath the yard, the mast a long curving timber rising far above into the darkness. The sailcloth was threadbare in more than a few places, and appeared to have been patched many times.

The boy, now shouting what sounded like a warning from the shore, cast the heavy rope back into the boat with considerable effort. Colbrook ducked instinctively. The coil of rope landed far forward of him.

Soon the boy was running up the crude bridge, his footing far more certain than Colbrook's had been on the warped and pitted board. The felucca started to rapidly drift away from the muddy shore, leaving the boy scrambling to haul the plank over the gunwale. He dexterously wrestled it into the boat and then staggered towards Colbrook, dropping down next to him. With a satisfied grunt of relief, he propped his muddied feet up on a disintegrating milk crate.

Colbrook was beginning to wonder when they planned on getting underway when he heard the unmistakable sound of lines sliding through pulleys. He turned to see the owner struggling with the rigging, his arms flailing about as he tugged violently at the lanyards. The sail was tighter now, slowly filling with air. The felucca made a gradual turn and began angling across the Nile towards the opposite shore.

Watching the tranquil river ahead, Colbrook listened to the sound of water slapping the hull. A stronger breeze suddenly filled the sail, the sound of stretching ropes carrying down from above. He zipped his gray windbreaker up higher. It got cold in the desert after sundown, which was one reason he had worn the coat. The other reason had little to do with personal comfort—he was wearing his holstered gun. He didn't think he would be needing it at the Karnak Club, but one could never be too careful.

The owner shouted something in Arabic from the back of the boat. The boy turned and nodded his head in agreement, now rising from the center seat. He made his way to the bow, and when he arrived there he turned on a small but powerful electric light. The water ahead of the vessel was flooded with illumination of vast spread but limited distance. The boy remained kneeling, staring out across the river's surface.

A few motorboats cruised slowly across their direction of travel, churning up frothy wakes visible in the pale glow of the Christmas-style lights that ringed their overhead metal frames. During the daytime hours these supports were covered with canvas awnings. Much longer than a typical motorboat, with narrow benches on either side providing seating for fifteen or twenty people, they were crowded with Egyptian youths.

Listening to the incessant creaking and rubbing of old wood, Colbrook peered up at the approaching shoreline. He could see a few large Nile cruisers stationary along the docks, their many lit cabin windows showing in neat rows. A modest fleet of small feluccas, their sails folded, was nearby. Higher up, the whole town of Luxor was bathed in the golden glow of artificial lighting. The sprawling stone mass of the Luxor temple showed up vividly against the night sky, illuminated by numerous ground-based floodlights.

Several minutes later the felucca was steering towards an empty berth, the owner skillfully using the tiller to maneuver into position. The dock was illuminated by only a single light mounted on a tall post, but the captain did not appear concerned in the least. He was already working the rigging, letting the sail out.

The boy kneeling in the bow stood up to seize the forward lines. Crouching in anticipation as they came alongside the dock, he vaulted out onto the wooden gangway, the ropes trailing in his hands. A minute later the felucca was secured both fore and aft.

The walk along the dock was not long, and soon Colbrook was climbing up a short flight of steps that led to the top of the river wall. He crossed the Corniche, walking rapidly northeast, away from the Luxor temple and the areas frequented by tourists. Checking his bearings from time to time by looking up at the occasional signpost, he turned onto a narrow side street with cracked and uneven sidewalks. The buildings were much smaller here, and in generally poor condition.

As he continued his rapid stroll down the road, a small gray cat darted in front of him before turning and disappearing into the darkness of an alley. A few lone Egyptians passed him on the sidewalk. Unlike Cairo, Luxor was a quiet town at night.

Colbrook looked at his watch. It was almost a quarter to nine.

Turning once again, this time to the east, he emerged onto a dirt road that curved through a section of deteriorating buildings. On the right side of the road a modest but certainly more modern building, with large windows facing the street, sat oddly among the older structures around it. Colbrook slowed as he passed it.

The interior was fully visible from the street, almost stage-like in its display. It contained an array of old pinball machines and small two-chair tables scattered about the floor space. Many local men of all ages sat talking, playing pinball, or smoking intricate and large floor-standing hookahs.

When he reached the corner of the street he stopped. It was very quiet now. Two men in dusty overalls were climbing into an idling car parked alongside the curb. It soon departed with a whining sound. A window closed somewhere with a thump. An old man trundled a handcart full of slippers and shoes towards him, the wheels squeaking as it passed.

On the opposite side of the road there was a one-story building made of brown brick, its roof a plain cement-plastered dome. The doorway was badly warped, and the wood sign proclaiming its name, hanging above the entrance from two rusted chains, was peeling and faded to the point of near illegibility. A bare electric bulb attached to a bent metal fixture provided the only light for the establishment's street front.

He had found the Karnak Club.

Colbrook made his way across the road to the entrance of the building. The door required a solid push to get it moving, and not being knowledgeable in its idiosyncrasies, he struggled to provide the proper leverage and angle necessary to force it open. It swung inwards unexpectedly, catching him by surprise. He stumbled over the threshold and into the dimly lit interior.

In terms of solitude and lack of noise, the atmosphere was not unlike a Coptic monastery. Dark woodwork stretched from floor to ceiling, and intricately carved oak bookcases lined the walls, the shelves overflowing with volumes of assorted thicknesses and heights. A dusty oriental rug covered most of the aging hardwood floor, its muted maroon color and geometric design reminiscent of the Bokhara style. Above the shelving, boldly painted in black on yellow, was a wide band of hieroglyphs that ran all the way around the top edge of the wall.

On the curved ceiling overhead, someone in the distant past had painted all the constellations of the night sky in great detail across the whole swath of plaster. The work was faded now, and several wide cracks obliterated some stars, but it was otherwise in good condition.

In the center of the room sat several heavy-looking wooden tables and chairs. Gleaming brass lamps, their shades made of thick green glass, illuminated the leather-inlaid tabletops. Despite the vast collection of undoubtedly rare books, there were no patrons.

On the right side of the room were two ancient-looking reading stands, each with a very worn volume resting on top, stitched into matching covers of heavy Moroccan leather. A gap in the shelving was visible in the far left corner of the room, forming a narrow doorway. There was a small sign above it indicating that it was the *Map Room*.

A man was sitting behind a small desk a short distance from the entrance. He wore a tweed jacket and gray slacks that fit in well with the setting. A register book sat open on the desktop, an expensive-looking pen lying by its side. The man was certainly of Egyptian descent, but when he spoke it was with an accent that suggested a British education.

"Please sign the register, sir."

His voice was barely above a whisper.

Colbrook glanced around the room again, and then moved to the desk. He stooped as he signed his name.

"Are you a member?" asked the man, still barely audible.

"No. I'm looking for Gus Lowell." He tried to speak suitably low.

"Dr. Lowell is in the map room." The man gestured towards the open door, and then studied the latest entry in the register.

"A friend of Dr. Beckwith," explained Colbrook.

After a brief pause, the man nodded with a faint smile.

Walking as quietly as he could across the room, his footfalls masked by the woolen rug under his feet, Colbrook passed through the doorway and into the map room.

The lack of bookcases was made up for with deep, box-like shelving lining the walls. Inside of each hand-lettered cubbyhole sat two or three tightly rolled maps. Most were yellowed and clearly very old, though some were still almost white in color, indicating that their printing was not so distant in the past.

A long desk-height counter ran the entire length of the back of the room. On it sat stacks of bound map volumes in thick plastic covers. A variety of smaller books, apparently referencing catalogs of some sort, were ordered in a neat and accessible row.

A long wooden table without chairs filled the entire center of the room, a variety of heavy paperweights resting on its surface in a haphazard fashion. Some of these were in use, holding down two maps rolled out at the far end of the table. A man stood staring down at them with seemingly riveted attention. He held an over-sized rectangular magnifying glass in his hand, moving it slowly over one of the maps lying on the table.

Colbrook waited.

When the man realized that someone was watching him and not searching the many shelves in the room, he looked up expectantly. When he could see Colbrook was about to speak, he moved quickly towards the six-panel wood door. He pushed it gently closed and then turned to face Colbrook.

Lowell seemed to be about ten years younger than Beckwith, with a head of reddish hair, all straggly and windblown. His face and arms were brownish-red, his hands callused and scratched. His attire, a brown safari shirt and khaki pants, while reasonably clean, were badly wrinkled and appeared to have been brushed off with a coarse broom, giving the impression that he had just surfaced from an excavation pit. The pair of worn leather boots on his feet looked to be of ancient origin themselves.

"You must be Gus Lowell," said Colbrook.

"Yes," replied Lowell. He seemed vaguely uneasy.

"I'm Martin Colbrook."

Lowell nodded. Clearly the name meant nothing to him.

"I spoke with Dr. Beckwith. He suggested I contact you regarding your Kharga dig."

"What about it?" asked Lowell, his accent unmistakably Australian. He was walking back to the maps on the table. If he had been uneasy before, he was trying to hide it now.

"I'm looking for an interesting story," said Colbrook, following a few steps behind the Egyptologist. "I'm a travel writer."

Lowell stopped at the table. He was looking down at the maps with a contemplative expression.

"I thought you might be able to provide some insight into what goes on during a dig," said Colbrook.

"To tell you the truth, we don't get many visitors out there. The Egyptian authorities are reluctant to provide security clearance for anyone not directly involved in the excavation. It's pretty far off the tourist track." He was still studying the maps. "We haven't found much anyway. Why, what did Beckwith tell you?"

"He just told me you had a dig in Kharga," replied Colbrook.

Lowell was obviously not enthusiastic about his interest in the site.

"It is in the Kharga Oasis, but it's much closer to Baris than the actual town of Kharga," replied Lowell. "More than ninety miles south of it actually."

"What sort of dig is it?" asked Colbrook.

"A temple—or more accurately the remains of a temple." Lowell pointed down at one of the maps and said, "It's right here. Take a look."

Colbrook glanced down at the map spread on the table. Lowell had placed his index finger on it, and Colbrook stooped lower to examine the spot he was pointing at. He could see three triangular red marks and a line of small print indicating it was classified as *unknown ruins*.

"The map is outdated," said Lowell. "It's from the 1950s. What's marked as unknown ruins is actually a well-documented mud-brick structure dating to the Roman Period. The site I'm working on is adjacent to that. At this scale, though, they almost overlap."

"Looks like the middle of nowhere," said Colbrook. He picked up the magnifying glass and studied the area more closely. An uneven brown stripe ran vertically on the map, just slightly west of where the ruins were marked.

"Those are the crescent dunes," declared Lowell. "That's been our biggest problem. Drifting sand. We've been trying some lightweight fencing around the pits."

"Does it work?"

"It's better than nothing."

"What have you found?" asked Colbrook.

"We located a foundation deposit," replied Lowell. "A mud-brick pit underneath the front cornerstone on the east side of the temple."

Colbrook gave Lowell an encouraging look. He wanted him to discuss the site in detail.

"Foundation deposits were put in place before construction began on any important building. They're associated with both ritual and symbolic purposes," said Lowell. He lifted a paperweight off the corner of one of the maps. "The more practical purpose they serve today is that they're basically self-contained time capsules. They're frequently used to definitively date structures."

"What do you find in a foundation deposit?"

"It's rare that anything very valuable is included in a deposit," replied Lowell. "We've found clay cups, a few small baskets, unused chisels, the head of a wooden goose, model bricks—things like that."

"No scarabs or amulets?"

"No." Lowell had a humorous expression on his face.

"Anything inscribed?"

"Nothing in the deposit was," said Lowell. "We did find a loose stone block, some distance away on the north side, with what appears to be Nakhtnebef's cartouche inscribed on it. The hieroglyphs are very faint."

"A pharaoh?" When Lowell nodded in agreement, Colbrook asked, "Which period?"

"Late Period." Lowell removed the rest of the paperweights, letting the maps roll up by themselves. He reached down and began tightly rolling one. "I'm fairly certain the temple is Thirtieth Dynasty, based on the cartouche. But I'm looking for more solid evidence. If I were digging in Luxor I wouldn't put much faith in a random stone block."

"Why is that?" asked Colbrook.

"Because so much of the stone came from older structures. Finding a loose block with an inscription will only prove when the stone was inscribed. It can't reliably date the building it's found in, unless, for example, it's located within a wall or floor that's still intact," replied Lowell. He had finished rolling the map. "The problem is that the Egyptians were practical when it came to construction matters. If old blocks were available when they were erecting a new temple, they did not hesitate to use them. You would be surprised how often older blocks were used as fill, or turned backwards to hide the previously worked side."

Colbrook held out one of the soft Velcro fasteners that had been lying on the table. He was beginning to understand the complications that arose from trying to date the jumbled remains of ancient buildings. For someone actually writing a travel article or book it would have been an interesting topic.

Taking the loop of nylon, Lowell carefully fitted it around the map and secured it without applying too much pressure. He started rolling the second map.

"The ruins are much more limited in the area I'm working in. The likelihood that the block came from another temple, or more specifically an older temple, is far more remote," said Lowell. "There is that mud-brick structure nearby, but as I mentioned earlier, it's Roman."

"How much of the temple still exists?"

"Not much. Just a few footings, most of the flooring, and a few scattered limestone plinth blocks. We hope to uncover a lot more." Sensing that Colbrook was disappointed, Lowell added, "It doesn't sound like much, I know, but you must understand that the majority of the temples built in the Late Period were constructed in the Delta—that is, Lower Egypt. These structures did not fare as well as those in the drier south. And after the Muslim invasions, many of them were quarried away for building material. As you might imagine, remains are virtually non-existent in the north."

Colbrook wondered if Mercer's tomb in the City of the Dead contained stone spoils of ancient Egypt, and did not doubt that Lowell could probably answer this question.

"Given that the site is in the desert, anything buried will probably still be intact," said Lowell. "The rot factor of the Delta is not an issue in the Western Desert. Mind you, that's not a scientific term, so don't quote me on it."

Colbrook suppressed a smile. He had no intention of quoting Lowell on anything. "What do you hope to find?"

There was a loud knock at the door.

Lowell moved to open it, but it swung in before he could reach for the brass knob. A man with prematurely graying hair and a narrow, carefully trimmed goatee and mustache stepped in. He stood looking at the two men with a mildly surprised expression on his face.

"A meeting without me?" he said sarcastically, eyeing Colbrook with a friendliness that could have been easily taken as disguised suspicion.

"We're discussing Egyptology," declared Lowell.

The gray-haired man glanced at Lowell, but soon directed his attention back to Colbrook. He appeared to be studying him as he walked closer, trying not to stare. This was not possible, and so reaching out his right hand he suddenly said, "I'm Carl Graf."

"Martin Colbrook." Shaking Graf's hand, Colbrook glanced briefly at his face. It was heavily tanned, with deep creases. He was certainly not someone who had spent his life in an office cubicle. His speech was infused with a very faint Germanic accent—possibly Swiss.

"You don't look like an Egyptologist," said Graf.

Colbrook, wondering what he did look like, replied, "I'm not."

"He's a writer," said Lowell.

"Journalist?" Graf's eyes narrowed.

"No. Travel writer," answered Colbrook.

"Oh." Graf seemed oddly relieved.

There was a moment of awkward silence.

"Carl runs an aid agency for those unfortunates in the sub-Saharan region," Lowell abruptly declared. "Commendable work, I suppose, if you don't mind being shot at."

"He exaggerates," replied Graf nonchalantly. "I've only been shot at once."

Colbrook looked at Graf.

"I started it about five years ago," explained Graf. "It's called the Displaced Fund. I do a lot of work in Sudan. It's a small dent in a big problem, but I hope to make a difference in the long run."

Colbrook refrained from commenting on the practical results of such activity and who profited from these enterprises. When he realized Graf was expecting him to say something sympathetic, he inquired, "Doing work in Egypt?"

"No—not here," said Graf. He seemed startled by the directness of the question. "But this is where our supplies are based, and I have other business to attend to in Luxor."

"What he means," explained Lowell, "is that he's hobnobbing with diplomats. You see, Mr. Colbrook, he has connections in high places."

Graf gave Lowell a withering look before saying to Colbrook, "An overstatement, believe me."

"He knows everyone at the American Research Center in Egypt and most of the members of the Supreme Council of Antiquities," said Lowell. "He also used to work for the UN—need I say more?"

"I'm impressed," said Colbrook. He was actually thinking quite the opposite.

Graf seemed pleased at the last remark. He turned to Lowell with a fading smile and said in a serious tone, "The reason I stopped by is because I got a call earlier today."

"From who?" Lowell had a worried look on his face.

"The director of the documentary team," declared Graf.

"They left the site yesterday afternoon with a lot of their gear," said Lowell. "No one told me anything. Why, where are they now?"

"In Luxor," replied Graf.

"What for?" asked Lowell.

"Establishing shots or something," Graf replied. "They told me they're doing some work at the temple of Seti tomorrow. The director was having trouble getting a filming permit, though he did finally obtain one after I pointed him in the right direction."

Lowell was rubbing a scrape on his arm. He nodded, but didn't appear concerned about the latest news. "How long are they going to be in Luxor?"

"I'm not exactly sure. I think they told me a day or two."

"Why do they keep calling you?" asked Lowell.

"Apparently they think I'm the official liaison for the mission director."

"I'm the mission director," declared Lowell.

"I know. But I didn't want them to annoy you with endless requests," said Graf defensively. "You'll have to deal with it soon enough anyway. I'm flying to Sudan tomorrow. I won't be back until early Monday."

"I'll deal with it," said Lowell.

Standing silently by the table, Colbrook gave Lowell an intentionally curious glance.

"I was low on funding," explained Lowell. "I needed to keep the dig open for as long as possible. Once we shut down, that's it for the season."

"It's not like he had much choice," Graf interjected.

"I used most of the initial funds building the magazine over the winter. The SCA wouldn't let us keep digging without a permanent storage house," added Lowell hastily. He was now looking directly at Colbrook.

Graf said to Colbrook, "I made the arrangements with the documentary people in order to provide additional funding."

"It's not an ideal solution, but they haven't been much of a bother. I thought it would be worse," said Lowell. "They've tangled a bit with the SCA inspector, but he's more interested in making tea than keeping an eye on correct dig procedures."

"All's well that ends well," declared Graf with a smile.

Lowell looked at Graf. "The director is a bit pompous, but I can hardly understand what he's talking about half the time anyway."

"That's not surprising," stated Graf. "They're all from Serbia."

Lowell murmured *sotto voce*, "Well, wherever they're from, without them the dig would be finished until next season. As it is I only have a little more than two weeks left, unless I'm granted an extension."

After some further conversation relating to the future success of Lowell's dig, and a parting comment on Graf's honorable work, Colbrook politely excused himself. He made his way out of the main room of the Karnak Club, stopping only momentarily to acknowledge the tweed-jacketed man at the front desk, and managed to open the entrance door with a minimum of fuss. Getting out seemed to be a lot easier than getting in.

The outside air temperature had dropped a few more degrees since he had entered the club. A pervasive stillness seemed to hang in the air, along with the lingering odor of sun-baked garbage. Except for the occasional bark of a dog or the brief swoosh of a car passing down some nearby street, there was little in the way of activity. A full-sized Toyota pickup truck, its blue paint gleaming under a nearby streetlight, was the only vehicle parked along the black and white striped curb. Colbrook detected the faint glow of a cigarette through the driver's side window as he turned to walk in the opposite direction.

Slipping his hands into the pockets of his windbreaker, he began strolling down the sidewalk. He mulled over his conversation with Lowell, thinking back to Graf's sudden intrusion. He had a nagging mistrust of Graf, but could not decide what it was he found so odd about the man. Perhaps it was his smugness and demeanor, though the same could be said of most of the politicians, diplomats, and aid agency executives he had met over the years.

As he crossed the road to retrace the same path he had taken earlier, Colbrook began to sense that he was not walking alone. He distinctly heard footsteps behind him, but every time he turned to look back he could see nothing but an empty street. When he stopped, the footsteps suddenly ceased. When he moved, they started up again. He did not require heightened powers of perception to realize that someone was following him.

After moving into an area with better overhead street lighting, he was able to catch a brief glimpse of a man keeping pace with him. Trying to stay in the shadowed part of the sidewalk—the side against the storefronts—the man pursued him with dogged earnestness. He was too far away to be seen clearly, but Colbrook could have heard his scuffling shoes from a mile away. Suspecting the man was unaware that he had been noticed, Colbrook pretended he was ignorant of his presence.

Despite the seemingly amateur nature of his stalker, Colbrook found the whole development mildly disconcerting. It suggested the possibility that the chief of police, against all indications to the contrary, had assigned someone to keep track of his whereabouts.

When Colbrook reached the shop with the large window framing the hookah-smoking patrons, he abruptly stopped. He stood facing the glass, pretending to look into the shop. Out of the corner of his eye he could see that the man had halted further down the street, leaning against a darkened storefront with his hands in his pockets. His acting abilities were as poor as his shadowing skills.

Colbrook resumed walking, moving briskly towards the street corner, heading in the direction of a wider crossing thoroughfare. As he reached the intersection of the two roadways he started to walk even faster. The scuffling sounds grew louder as the man following him struggled to keep him in sight. Apparently soft-soled shoes were not in his personal inventory.

Abruptly ducking into the inset entryway of a closed and shuttered tobacco shop, Colbrook peered back the way he had just come. The man who was following him was now walking very fast, his head darting around in a hawk-like fashion as he searched the roadway for a sign of his vanished quarry.

Colbrook pressed himself against the side of the entryway. He turned his head and watched the approaching figure, careful not to shift his feet on the crumbling cement.

The man continued to walk toward the shop's doorway, frequently halting to look around with considerable hesitation. He was wearing what appeared to be predominantly black clothing. In fact he almost resembled a priest in his dark garb, but his sacerdotal likeness ended there. His physical size was well beyond the average in both height and girth; his head was bullet-shaped and covered with short bristly hair. He was walking with a purposeful stride that indicated his intentions were anything but friendly. He did not seem so amateur anymore.

Watching the man stop only twenty yards away at the edge of the curb, facing away from the tobacco shop, Colbrook determined it was time to vacate his observation post. If he let the man get any closer he would risk being cornered. Quickly stepping from the entryway he moved at almost a jog, heading for a side street dimly illuminated by only a few scattered streetlamps.

As he rapidly distanced himself from the black-clad man, the glow of the Luxor temple lights came into view on the skyline. The temple was a popular spot to visit at night, and despite the fact that it was getting quite late—nine thirty according to his luminous watch dial—he suspected a few stragglers might still be wandering about. Once there, he would have the advantage of being able to blend in with the tourists.

He patted the gun under his windbreaker. It was strictly out of habit—he had no intention of using it. More than likely the bullet-headed man did not plan on dispatching him unceremoniously in the streets of Luxor. He had given his pursuer plenty of opportunities to close the distance.

Rounding another corner, Colbrook caught sight of the avenue of sphinxes, each crouching human-headed lion lit with an individual ground-based floodlight. At their far end, the first pylon of the temple looked even more staggering in size when illuminated from below, the giant seated statues of Rameses II casting eerie shadows against the towering wall.

There were no pedestrians about.

Heading straight for the sphinx-lined processional way, Colbrook walked down the middle of the double row of stone statues. At least he could use the bright lights to his advantage. At the end of the pathway two guards were seated on stone blocks, having already closed and locked the large metal gate at the entrance to the temple. They only briefly looked up as he veered off the wide path and began making his way down to the Corniche. Looking back, Colbrook could see that the man with the bullet-shaped head had stopped indecisively at the beginning of the long avenue, staying just outside the throw of the brilliant lights.

Nearing the riverfront, Colbrook glanced over his shoulder again. The black-clad man was now jogging, trying to close the distance which had opened up when Colbrook had entered the temple grounds. Lengthening his strides, Colbrook decided to put an end to this game.

The area he led the man into was a vast open-air butcher shop. The shops themselves were locked and covered, but the courtyard where the livestock and poultry were processed was accessible from the street by way of narrow alleys. It was lined on all sides with long tables and high wooden stands for hanging carcasses. The smell was appalling, and Colbrook covered his mouth and nose with his hand as he darted across the courtyard's uneven paving stones.

Crouching behind a plywood table, he watched as his pursuer walked past without even a glance in his direction. A minute later Colbrook quietly made his way back to the sidewalk, looking after the retreating figure.

The man hurried briskly along, still peering from side to side. As he got further down the street he seemed less interested in his surroundings, and simply walked along the sidewalk with his head down.

Colbrook followed him carefully, keeping a close watch on his movements. He need not have bothered—the large black-clad figure never once turned to look back. Several minutes passed as Colbrook trailed him through the unevenly lit streets. As they approached a more upscale area, he soon began to suspect where his former pursuer was heading.

A short distance down the street stood a building that was much taller than the others in the immediate vicinity. It was a high-rise hotel, built for the tourists who each day took in the sights of Luxor and visited the tombs and temples across the river. Colbrook slowed, anticipating the man's next move. With only a brief sideways glance, the shadowy figure slipped through the entrance of the large hotel.

Colbrook headed in the direction of the Nile.

He had determined one thing for certain—bullet-head wasn't one of police chief Hassan's men.

4

The view from the comfortable wooden chair was unquestionably interesting. Seated in the shadow of the first pylon of the temple of Seti, Colbrook observed the entire layout of the complex—or what was left of it. The morning was still early, and not a single tourist walked the grounds. Though it was only a short drive from the Valley of the Kings, the site attracted few visitors at any time of the day.

Colbrook's attention was drawn to a stone portico some distance away, constructed with a row of columns made to resemble bundled papyrus plants. Beyond these lay the remains of the hypostyle hall, the only structurally intact portion of the temple that still contained a serviceable roof. The portico, much like the hypostyle hall, was never intended to be seen by anyone but the pharaoh and the priests—being, in fact, the rear wall of the second court—but the ravages of time had reduced the front superstructure to a mere outline in the dry desert floor, exposing the inner sanctum to all who cared to look.

Walls abounded on the rest of the site, some just mere strips of stones in the ground, others whole for a few feet before the tops went missing. To Colbrook's far right, a maze of stunted mud-brick walls gave more than a clue as to the whereabouts of the temple's vast magazines, where the priests had stored their goods. To his immediate left, the remains of the ritual royal palace consisted of only confusing patterns of thick footings. An enclosure wall of considerable size surrounded the entire temple, largely the result of modern reconstruction work.

With such a limited portion of the site still whole, Colbrook assumed that the documentary crew would be primarily focused on the standing structures near the western end. To determine if he was suitably positioned to watch their production work and remain unobserved would require them to arrive, something they had not yet done. Colbrook certainly hoped Graf had been correctly informed when he had told Lowell about the documentary crew's plans.

The sound of crinkling cellophane interrupted his thoughts. He turned to glance down at the temple guard squatting in his shapeless *galabiya*. He was carefully unwrapping a new package of cigarettes. Colbrook did not feel guilty that the guard had so readily relinquished his seat for such a trifling gift. He knew that most Egyptians liked to smoke, and the guard was clearly no exception.

Colbrook had arrived early that morning by taxi. Tickets could not be purchased at Seti's temple, so he had been forced to stop on the way at the antiquities inspectorate office. For a modest fee he had purchased the necessary entrance pass. After a drive lasting not more than a few minutes, he had staggered out of the back of a taxi that smelled strongly of gasoline, soon to be greeted by several Egyptians who professed to be official guides. Colbrook had dismissed them with a few well-chosen Arabic words, and had entered the temple through the entrance in the northern wall. It was here that he had made the guard's acquaintance.

So far his plan was working.

Ten minutes later he was not so sure. Surrendering the chair to the guard, he made his way towards the columned portico. Entering into the darkened hypostyle hall, only giving a passing glance at the famous reliefs of Seti I worshipping the gods, he continued through to the sanctuary. Behind these mostly ruinous areas was a set of stairs providing access to the top of the enclosure wall. A portion of the mud-brick wall was parapeted, and visitors could walk on it.

Colbrook climbed the stairs, followed the flat paving stones along the top of the wall to the corner where the north and west walls met, and then turned east. The wall traveled the entire distance of the north side of the temple complex, and the parking lot was on this side of the site. By following the wall for most of its length he was able to position himself near the entrance but remain largely hidden from below.

The rudimentary parking area of the temple was little more than an unpaved gravel-strewn expanse along the side of the road. Not surprisingly, it was empty.

Colbrook assumed the documentary crew would arrive from the direction of the Valley of the Kings. He removed his sunglasses and wiped the dusty lenses on his shirt, squinting at the sudden glare from the ground below. Beads of perspiration were beginning to drip down his face. It was very warm up on the wall. There were no trees nearby.

Several large palms were located just outside the south wall, beyond which a patchwork of sugarcane fields rolled towards the southwest, and others loomed to the east, where a small village lay adjacent to the temple's walls. As he put his sunglasses back on he heard the unmistakable sound of a slowing vehicle.

In the distance a red minivan was gradually drifting off the pavement, a plume of dust trailing and then swirling up behind it. Soon the sound of tires crunching on sand and gravel reached him. The battered and dirty minivan crossed the parking lot and came to a stop a short distance from the entrance, facing the wall.

As the cloud of dust dissipated, the front doors of the minivan opened and two men stepped out. One was the driver, an Egyptian man of advanced age, the other a taller man with black hair and a sallow complexion. His garb consisted of jeans and a white shirt with numerous pockets. A pair of very small sunglasses hung from a flexible cord around his neck. He peered at the landscape as one might examine insects in a jar. Colbrook had more than a hunch it was the Serbian director that Lowell had mentioned at the Karnak Club. He waited for the rest of the passengers to emerge from the vehicle.

The sliding door of the minivan opened—it was on the right side, allowing him only a partial view—and two men clambered out, one after the other. The first was a younger man with unkempt and uncut hair, his T-shirt a garish yellow and green affair. He sported a beard that looked like the fur of a hibernating grizzly bear. More than likely he was an assistant cameraman, soundman, or possibly both.

The second man had a light meter hanging around his neck and several other gadgets on the front of his belt in little square cases. Shorter than the director, with a receding hairline which was soon hidden beneath a mesh baseball cap, his clothes were badly wrinkled, as if he had slept in them. There was little doubt he was the cameraman. It was a small crew by any standard, but not surprisingly small given that they were documentarians.

Colbrook waited to see what their plans were. The director had already walked some distance away from the minivan, in the direction of the entrance, the cameraman following just a few steps behind. The Egyptian driver had moved around to the front of the vehicle, pushing at one of the headlights with the palm of his hand. The assistant, now leaning against the passenger door with his arms crossed and his head turned towards the open sliding door, appeared to be talking to someone inside the minivan. The side windows were tinted and the windshield had too much glare on it to determine who else might still be inside.

A large camera case dropped into view outside the sliding door; smaller cases soon followed. They continued to flow from the side door. The shaggy assistant was not lending a hand, standing with his arms crossed during the whole procedure.

The last member of the crew finally stepped out of the side door carrying a handcart. Colbrook waited for him to turn in his direction. When he did, there was no doubt that it was the man with the bullet-shaped head who had trailed him from the Karnak Club.

The long-haired assistant suddenly recovered from his bout of lethargy and began lifting cases onto the handcart. The director shouted something from the entrance. The assistant looked up from the cart. A few seconds later Colbrook heard the director and the cameraman laughing together as they passed into the temple grounds. He could only assume the remark was related to the assistant's earlier idleness.

Turning from the scene outside the wall to the one just getting underway inside, Colbrook watched the director and the cameraman walk into the middle of the outer court. They stopped to look down the stone-paved approach to the temple proper. Clearly they were interested in the columned portico. The two men talked in an animated fashion, the director turning to point at various landmarks within the complex from time to time, the cameraman nodding.

The temple guard emerged shortly after from the remains of the first pylon, a stump of a cigarette smoldering between his fingers.

Walking purposely towards the director and cameraman, he said a few words as he approached them. The director pulled a folded sheet of paper from his pocket and handed it to the guard. The cameraman, seemingly uninterested in the proceedings, was now walking in the direction of the portico. He lifted the light meter from around his neck and held it in his hand.

Colbrook turned to watch the progress the other two men were making with the equipment. Most of the cases were now either neatly stacked on the smaller handcart or resting on a larger cart with four wheels. As the shaggy assistant prepared to roll the handcart towards the entrance, Colbrook directed his attention back to the inside of the enclosure wall.

The guard stood languidly at the director's side, scrutinizing the unfolded sheet of paper with exaggerated care. Apparently satisfied, he carefully refolded the piece of paper and placed it in the pocket of his *galabiya*. The director smiled and walked away, heading towards the cameraman.

The sound of squeaking wheels attracted Colbrook's attention, and he just caught sight of the assistant and the bullet-headed man passing through the entranceway, pushing the equipment carts. Emerging into the outer court, both men stopped to stare around the temple complex. The director was now strolling in their direction, while the cameraman stood looking up at one of the large papyriform columns.

Feeling a bit exposed standing on the wall, Colbrook knelt down and edged closer to the inside parapet. The temple guard was closing on the two men pushing the equipment carts, while they, in turn, continued to move towards the processional pathway that bisected the temple—the same means that the director was using to intercept them. The guard was walking much faster, and he was not encumbered with carts. He stopped the men before they ever reached the center path. The director had to walk a considerable distance to reach the three men, who now stood only fifteen yards or so from where Colbrook knelt looking down at them.

The director was pointing at the two other men as he drew closer, trying to communicate to the temple guard that they were with him. The guard seemed to understand what he was trying to say, and reached into his pocket to retrieve the sheet of paper. The director strode up to the guard and started jabbing at the open paper with his finger, pointing to the two men across from him. Colbrook could hear him talking, and though he was sure the director was now speaking English, he could not make out the words.

After making a cursory examination of the two carts full of plastic and metal cases, the guard wandered away towards the first pylon and his comfortable chair.

The director wasted no time in ordering the shaggy assistant and the bullet-headed man to start pushing the carts again. The cameraman, returning from his architectural tour, walked towards the others. They had now reached the intersection of the entrance pathway and the processional pathway. It was here, at the central axis of the temple, that Colbrook suspected they would set up their camera. The unloading and unlatching of cases soon proved him to be correct.

While the documentary crew worked to assemble their equipment, Colbrook stood and walked a little further down the wall. A loose stone block was the perfect size for a seat, and he settled down on it, rubbing his sore knees. The documentarians were making some progress in their work, but it was a slow business.

The cameraman was soon cradling a large video camera while waiting for the shaggy-haired assistant to set up a shiny black tripod. After the tripod was placed down and the legs adjusted to level, the bullet-headed man handed the assistant the camera head. Quickly fastening the head to the tripod, the assistant reached over to help the cameraman attach the camera to the baseplate. Several minutes passed, during which a matte box and rods were fitted to the camera. The director stood by impatiently, waiting for his crew to finish.

When all was ready the director looked through the camera's viewfinder, adjusting the drag on the pan and tilt controls while performing a few mock shots. After several minutes he stepped away from the camera and motioned for the cameraman to take over.

Colbrook was getting bored with the whole operation. Having experience in this sort of work, he knew nothing out of the ordinary was going on. He still had no explanation as to why the bullet-headed man had followed him the previous night. There had to be a reason, but so far he could find none hidden within this activity.

The assistant and the bullet-headed man finished stacking the various cases in a neat pile. Both men then walked purposefully toward the entrance, apparently heading back to the minivan to get additional equipment. Moving over to the other side of the wall, Colbrook watched as they emerged into the parking area. When they reached the van the assistant climbed into the passenger seat. Bullet-head opened the sliding side door and ducked inside, pulling it closed. The Egyptian driver was already behind the wheel. Seconds later both front doors slammed shut and the engine started with a growl. The vehicle turned sharply and proceeded onto the paved roadway, making a left, heading back in the direction it had arrived from earlier.

The whole event caught Colbrook by surprise. He looked back towards the inside of the enclosure. The director and cameraman were trying out various camera angles. Apparently half of the crew leaving in the middle of a shoot was not unusual. He quickly turned to see where the minivan was going.

The red vehicle traveled for a short distance in the direction of the Valley of the Kings and then turned right onto a much smaller road that crossed through a Muslim cemetery. It entered the town of tangled streets located behind it that some maps called Tarif. Though at times disappearing from view, the van's progress soon became easy to follow—it had made another right, and was roughly paralleling the main road.

The van stopped at a small house. Only the parking lot, the road, and the cemetery lay between Colbrook's position and the vehicle. The distance was not more than a few hundred feet, and he was able to observe the goings-on with ease.

The passenger door and sliding door both opened. The assistant and bullet-head stepped out. After a quick look around the deserted street, both men ducked through the sliding door of the vehicle.

They soon reappeared outside the minivan, each carrying an equipment case roughly the size of a piece of large luggage, but wider. Based on the speed with which the assistant slid the door closed and retrieved his case from the ground, it was obviously empty. Bullet-head was already heading towards the side entrance of the house, his case likewise not hampering his movement in the slightest. There was no hesitation in their course of action, and

Colbrook suspected they had done this before. The Egyptian driver was certainly familiar with the maze of streets leading to this particular house.

Colbrook walked rapidly towards the stairs which would bring him to a spot close to the temple's entrance, keeping a careful watch on the director and cameraman once he began to descend. Reaching the bottom of the steps, he made a rapid exit from the temple.

Crossing the parking area with long strides, he stepped up onto the edge of the paved road and surveyed the wall of the cemetery. It was too high to climb, but a narrow opening was located a short distance to the north.

No vehicles were approaching from either direction, and he jogged across the road.

Reaching the wall, he walked along it until he arrived at the opening. He then began following a footpath that appeared to lead through the center of the necropolis. Soon this path split into many smaller courses, and when the rear wall of the cemetery blocked his view of the town's streets, he maintained his direction by glancing up every so often at the skyline and locating the roof of the house.

The wall separating the town from the cemetery was constructed of giant orange-colored bricks with alternating spaces between them. Arriving at it, he knelt in the hot sand and stared through one of the wide rectangular gaps.

The van was less than thirty feet away.

Colbrook heard a door slam and the two men came into view, now struggling to carry their cases—or more accurately, the assistant struggled and the bullet-headed man moved as one would with a slightly heavy suitcase. Bullet-head kept his case off the ground until he reached the sliding door of the minivan, whereas the shaggy assistant was forced to frequently place his down, take a breather, and then resume his effort. Though the bullet-headed man did his best to look unfazed by the weight of his own case, he rubbed the back of his hand as he waited for the assistant to arrive at the vehicle.

When both cases were inside the minivan, the assistant dropped into the passenger seat while the bullet-headed man disappeared into the back. Doors slammed, the engine coughed to life, and the vehicle soon disappeared into the maze of streets.

Rising slowly from his kneeling position behind the brick wall, Colbrook surveyed the immediate area for any further signs of activity. Satisfied nothing unusual was going on, he made his way along the wall until he reached a gate. Pushing through it, he stood on the edge of the dirt and gravel street, opposite the small house. He now regretted not having brought his handgun.

He glanced around one last time and then crossed the street, heading for the entrance of the house the two men had recently entered and then exited.

The door was windowless and metal, with peeling paint and a rusty knob. The stucco surface on the outside of the house was falling off in small pieces, littering the ground. Hesitating for only a moment, Colbrook thumped his hand on the door.

He heard a dog barking somewhere deep inside the house, and then the sudden jangling of many locks being unlatched. The door swung open, revealing a disheveled and rotund man squinting in the doorway. He stood staring out with an expression of surprise mixed with suspicion. Wearing the conventional garb of the rural Egyptian, the loose-fitting robe poorly concealed his protruding stomach and stocky build. His head seemed almost perfectly spherical, crowned with a ring of black hair receding from its summit; his jowls sagged. On his upper lip was a wide mustache resembling a variety commonly observed in some parts of the Middle East.

He looked more like a Turkish bey than an Egyptian peasant.

Colbrook waited. He did not want to speak first.

The fat man shuffled forward, looking into the narrow alleyway on either side. "Can I help you?" His English was serviceable.

"You might just be able to," replied Colbrook enigmatically.

"How's that?" questioned the fat man, his eyelids half closed.

"Maybe you can tell me."

The fat man was at first confounded by Colbrook's ambiguous statements. Then, with a faint smile creeping onto his face, he declared, "Are you buying?"

"That depends," replied Colbrook.

"On what?" demanded the fat man.

Colbrook gave him an arrogant look. "What you have to offer."

"I have much to offer," spluttered the fat man, his jowls shaking with anger. "You won't find anything like it anywhere else."

"I must see before I buy," stated Colbrook.

"Of course—of course," replied the fat man. He suddenly moved aside, waving Colbrook into a narrow hall.

Stepping through the doorway, Colbrook eased past the overweight man.

Ignoring his visitor for a moment, the man now turned his attention to securing the door again. When he was done he held out a pudgy hand and said, "I'm Hamed."

Colbrook shook his hand briefly and replied, "Martin."

Hamed's face now seemed to have a perpetual smile on it. His earlier reserved demeanor gave way to genuine friendliness. He ushered Colbrook into a small living room, offering him some tea. Colbrook politely refused.

"Follow me then," said Hamed. "You will soon see wonderful things."

Trailing a few paces behind the bulky form of his Howard Carter-quoting conductor, Colbrook followed him into another room that resembled a kitchen. After a brief stop to get a set of keys, Hamed moved into a narrow hall that ended at a wood door. Unlocking it with a quick turn of his wrist, the stout Egyptian motioned for Colbrook to follow him down a steep flight of stairs. These led into a dark basement.

Hamed turned the lights on. They were bare bulbs hanging from the underside of the warped, wooden floor rafters. The basement was small, and more noticeably, empty.

"Nothing in here," Hamed declared. "It's all in there." He pointed to the wall across from the stairs.

The only thing Colbrook could see was a large piece of furniture, the kind typically used to display and store china. It was tall and wide, taking up most of the wall space. It was also empty.

Hamed stepped up to the side of the cabinet with his hands raised. He leaned forward and pushed against its side. It moved across the floor with surprising ease, accompanied by the sound of metal wheels rolling over concrete. A door was revealed, and this one had two locks.

Hamed was either overly cautious or involved in something of a highly illegal nature. Colbrook suspected the latter.

With a jingle of keys, Hamed pushed through the door. He

beckoned for Colbrook to enter through the darkened doorway, as if saying, "Now we can get down to business."

Stooping slightly to pass under the low doorframe, Colbrook found himself in a chamber that was hewn from stone. The walls and ceiling were undecorated. A series of gleaming metal shelves bordered the outer periphery. Hamed was still reaching for light switches, and as each bare bulb lit up, Colbrook became increasingly certain he was standing in a storage room. A narrow corridor was situated across from the doorway they had just entered through, dark beyond its first few feet.

Colbrook stepped closer to the shelving on his right, peering through a clear plastic bag tied at the top. Inside was the unmistakable shape of a cat mummy. A little to the right of that was a perfectly preserved Osiris statue in dull bronze. On the shelf below, row after row of shabtis stood quietly in repose. Colbrook had read about these little mummiform statues. They were put into tombs for the purpose of performing agricultural work for the tomb owner in the afterlife. Most of these examples were simple, but a few were unusual enough to warrant closer inspection. The whole shelf was devoted to a congregation of the small statues. Against the wall between two more crowded shelves of cat mummies were several limestone stele, the incised reliefs of superb quality. Canopic jars and broken pieces of pottery filled another shelf. Colbrook walked along the outer edge of the room, staring at the unique and possibly priceless historical treasures.

He had just stepped into the den of a tomb robber.

"Like I say before," said Hamed, inching forward. "All wonderful things."

Colbrook turned to eye Hamed.

"You've got quite a collection."

Bowing with exaggerated delight, Hamed shuffled to the center of the room. Placing his flipper-like hands on his bulging stomach, he said with a flourish, "Do you have a particular piece in mind?"

Colbrook hesitated. He knew that shabtis were common to the point of abundance—the museum in Cairo had over forty thousand of them. One of these mummy-shaped statuettes could not be all that expensive.

He turned to the artifact dealer and said, "A shabti."

Hamed frowned. "I've plenty of those. How about something more interesting?" He was smiling again.

"No—I think a shabti will do just fine. Preferably a simple one," said Colbrook.

Stepping over to the shelf of shabtis, Hamed studied several before he carefully removed one with his pudgy hand. It had a distinctive bluish glaze and a narrow back-pillar with painted hieroglyphics. Most of these glyphs were faded and worn away. It was roughly four inches tall, the base heavily chipped on the bottom.

"A faience shabti," declared Hamed.

Colbrook did not want to linger here much longer, but he also did not want to appear too anxious. "How much?"

"Don't you want to know when it is from?" questioned Hamed.

Colbrook nodded. He really didn't care.

"Saite Period, Twenty-sixth Dynasty or thereabouts," stated Hamed. "The owner's name is missing on this one—a pity—but the inscription of spell six of the Book of the Dead is still partially legible. Three thousand pounds and it is yours."

"You'd better mean Egyptian," said Colbrook. He was already calculating the exchange rate in his head. It was a little more than five hundred dollars.

"Of course," replied Hamed.

Colbrook pulled out a roll of bills. Separating out the required amount, he handed the money to Hamed. The sooner he finished the transaction, the sooner he could get back to the temple across the road.

"It is a pleasure doing business with someone who does not waste time." Hamed quickly counted the bills, and then slipped them into a shirt pocket under his *galabiya*. "Let me get a box for it."

Waiting for Hamed to carefully wrap his purchase in paper and stow it in a sturdy cardboard box, Colbrook scanned the shelves again. It was not difficult to find legitimate antiquities in Egypt, and he knew from his travel writer's research that every so often a few surprising objects would surface, usually by means of the less law-abiding hawkers of the Khan el-Khalili, a sprawling medieval-aged bazaar in Cairo, but the quantity and variety in this Tarif residence was remarkable.

Hamed handed Colbrook his purchase. Then he turned and pointed across the room to the entrance of the narrow corridor on the opposite wall. "It is best if you leave that way."

Colbrook sensed that Hamed was not going with him. "Where does it go?"

"A friend's house," replied Hamed. "You see, this is part of an underground passage we are standing in. The passage goes a short distance northwards. You'll find another door at the other end. Just knock twice, hard—like this." Hamed turned sideways and rapped his knuckles on the door.

Colbrook nodded in agreement, though he was suspicious about these arrangements for departure. The bullet-headed man and the shaggy assistant had not exited this way, but then again their purchases had been considerably more unwieldy than his own.

Bidding Hamed farewell, Colbrook walked into the passage. It got darker the further he moved from the lit storage room. Soon enough, as Hamed had indicated, he was confronted with a small metal door at the end of the passage. He knocked twice and waited.

The door opened after a few tense seconds. An Egyptian man of considerably advanced years smiled a toothless grin as a greeting, guiding him inside with a frail arm. Colbrook realized that this too was no ordinary basement. It was cluttered with what appeared to be the detritus of a stone yard.

After closer inspection he realized that the stacks of what he had initially assumed were modern building materials were actually ancient carved blocks of stone, pieces of columns, chunks of capitals, portions of flooring slabs, and broken and scattered plinth blocks. Some of the pieces were quite large, and it was difficult to imagine how they had been moved down here in the first place. Other than the narrow passage connecting to Hamed's cellar and a set of rickety wooden stairs that resembled a ladder with unusually deep rungs, there did not appear to be any other means of entrance or exit.

The octogenarian began showing his wares, stooping occasionally to lift the corner of a tarp to point out a particularly well-preserved piece of stonework. Colbrook was not interested in purchasing anything, though he was tempted to ask the man how he planned on delivering the goods. It was now very obvious why Hamed had requested he leave by the narrow passageway. Colbrook was growing impatient with wily Egyptians always looking to make a sale or commission.

While the old man was poking in one of the dusty corners of his basement, Colbrook quietly ascended the ladder-like steps and reached the living area of the man's house. He hunted around for the exterior door, finding it before the withered man had time to haul himself from the nether regions of his house.

Retracing his path through the necropolis, it was not long before he stood alongside the opening in the cemetery wall, checking to see if the red minivan was again parked across the road in front of Seti's temple.

It was. The doors were closed, and no one was near it.

Jogging across the scorching roadway, Colbrook made his way cautiously towards the entrance to Seti's compound, not wanting to meet bullet-head unexpectedly. The temple guard was resting on a canvas camp chair outside the wall. He smiled as Colbrook drew closer, an unlit cigarette clamped between his teeth.

Edging past the wall behind the guard's chair, Colbrook stood in the entrance. Moving forward a few paces, he cleared the thick enclosure wall and peered around the corner.

All four crew members were under the columned portico. The camera was low on the ground, aimed at the top of one of the pillars. Both the director and the cameraman were kneeling, the former peering through the eyepiece while the latter appeared to be adjusting focus. Stepping back from the entryway, Colbrook stood before the guard, the small cardboard shabti box held in one hand.

"Good cigarettes," the guard said. Removing the cigarette from his mouth, he drew it under his nose, smelling the paper wrapper. He was eyeing the cardboard box.

"That's all I had," replied Colbrook. He watched the man put the cigarette back into his mouth. "How much for the paper in your pocket?"

"Paper?" intoned the guard. It was obvious he knew exactly what Colbrook was talking about.

Patting his own left side, Colbrook illustrated what he was referring to.

The guard reached into his *galabiya* and pulled out the folded sheet of paper Colbrook had seen earlier.

"How about ten pounds," said Colbrook. The fact that he had suggested a price indicated he was an amateur.

"Twenty," said the guard.

"Fifteen," Colbrook countered, knowing the guard would probably have sold the permit for three or four pounds.

The guard shrugged, handing him the folded paper. Colbrook gave him the fifteen pounds and walked a few paces away. Leaning against the outside of the mud-brick wall, he unfolded the sheet.

It was the typical product of a bureaucracy: signed, stamped, and entirely too ornate for the purpose it served. Ignoring the Arabic, which he had limited ability to transliterate anyway, Colbrook scanned down the page for the English equivalents. He found a block of text towards the bottom dealing with the listed permit holders. In neat hand-printed lettering, the names of the documentary crew were registered. The director was listed as Aleksandar Coslovich, the cameraman as Vladimir Cavoski, the assistant cameraman as Nerman Gvero, and the name at the bottom of the list—Radovan Nedic—had a word that looked like *security* written beside it.

Colbrook folded the paper carefully and slipped it into his pocket. Walking back towards the guard, he stopped once more at the entrance to the temple complex. The documentarians were still shooting under the portico. The bullet-headed man—undoubtedly Nedic—was holding a large reflector board, aimed at the ceiling of the portico. Colbrook stepped away from the entrance.

He knew the Serbians could potentially be at the temple for hours, but based on their recent behavior they might pack up in the next ten minutes. If they did, he would have no way of following them.

The guard was still smiling when Colbrook wandered to his side.

"I'm looking to hire a taxi," he said.

The Egyptian man held his prized cigarette between his fingers. He shifted his eyes to the east and struggled out of the low canvas chair, rising to his sandaled feet. "See building?" He was pointing at a ramshackle abode. Only a narrow alleyway separated it from the temple's looming enclosure wall.

Colbrook nodded. It was a two-story mud-brick house. The first floor on the street side was almost entirely taken up by a wooden garage door.

"My friend have good car. Fair price. He take you anywhere you want," the guard said. He held out his hand, still smiling.

Colbrook almost reached out to shake it, but then realized the man expected more *baksheesh*. Slipping him a five-pound note, he turned to take one last look into the temple compound.

The Serbians were still at work.

Walking along the dusty shoulder of the road, Colbrook approached the house. The garage door was missing some panels, and the faded green paint looked as if it had been applied only a short time after Seti's temple had been built. A splintered plank was jammed between the handles on the barn-style doors.

Colbrook peered into the darkened garage through one of the openings. A rusty Peugeot station wagon sat inside. There was the sound of movement on the opposite side of the door and a man's face came into view. Colbrook stepped back. An arm reached out, removing the plank with practiced dexterity. The doors swung open on squealing hinges seconds later.

An Egyptian of indeterminate age stepped out into the sunlight, squinting at Colbrook. "You need taxi?"

"Yes," replied Colbrook. He would have said more, but he was distracted by the vehicle in the garage. The Peugeot was without a right rear wheel, a rusty hand jack in its place.

Sensing Colbrook's dismay, the man hurried back into the garage. He soon emerged from its dusty and dim recesses rolling a wheel.

"New tire," he said. "Good tire."

"There's no rush. I'm waiting for some friends," said Colbrook.

He watched as the man fitted the wheel onto the car, pushing it over the bolts. Threading on the nuts, he tightened each with the wrench end of a tire iron. Working the rusty jack, the man lowered the station wagon to the ground. Sliding his tools and jack to the side, he quickly made his way to the driver's door and got behind the wheel. Stepping aside from the belching exhaust, Colbrook waited as the man backed the car into the street. When it stopped outside he opened the back door and climbed in. The driver got out and pushed the garage doors closed, dropping the plank back in place. He returned to the car and settled down in the driver's seat, peering expectantly into the rearview mirror.

Angling his legs across the wide bench seat for maximum comfort,

Colbrook told the driver to maneuver into the shade of a nearby palm tree that was overhanging the shoulder of the road. The back of the car was only yards from the garage when the driver shut the engine off. Colbrook carefully tucked the shabti box into a safe place on the back seat. The driver popped open a plastic container of nut pastries. He offered one to his passenger, and when Colbrook declined, proceeded to noisily eat them all. When he was finished he pulled a moderately clean rag from the glove compartment and wiped his crumb-covered mouth.

Fifteen minutes passed, and then half an hour. The driver was getting restless. He began wiping the dashboard and the instrument panel with a powerful bottled cleaning agent that he produced from under the passenger seat. Feeling light-headed from the fumes, Colbrook pushed open the back door.

A few minutes later the director, Coslovich, appeared in the entrance to the temple complex. He was wiping his forehead with his hand, staring at the minivan. The cameraman, Cavoski, soon joined him. They both stood talking in the shade of the enclosure wall. A few minutes later their Egyptian driver appeared, wandering down the side of the road from the direction of Jebanah, a small town a stone's throw to the east of the taxi driver's house. He opened the front door of the van and seated himself behind the wheel.

Nedic emerged from the opening in the wall, trundling the four-wheel cart stacked with cases across the parking lot. He slid the large door open on the side of the minivan and began loading the equipment inside. The shaggy assistant, Gvero, made his appearance soon after. He was pushing the handcart filled with smaller cases. The minivan was loaded with an efficiency that was mildly astonishing. After Coslovich and Cavoski returned to the vehicle, doors opened and closed, last minute checks were made to be sure nothing had been left behind, and soon the minivan was crunching its way across the dirt parking lot, heading for the paved road.

Colbrook pulled the car door closed and told the taxi driver to follow the red van.

"Are they your friends?" asked the driver. He peered into the rearview mirror.

"Yes—friends," replied Colbrook. "The van is too small for all of us. I'm tired of sitting on equipment cases." He anxiously watched the minivan. It was gaining distance on the roadway, heading west, back toward the Valley of the Kings.

The driver started the station wagon and immediately put his foot down on the accelerator. The Peugeot fishtailed in the loose sand, only aligning itself properly after it had reached the asphalt roadway. The transmission threatened imminent failure, but somehow made it into the next gear.

The taillights of the red minivan briefly flashed as it turned left at the Valley of the Kings road. The taxi driver quickly closed the distance, swerving across the intersection with little regard for possible oncoming traffic. An approaching tour bus blared its horn, and Colbrook began to consider the possibility that his driver's recklessness might draw attention to their vehicle. Then he remembered where he was. It was unlikely anyone would notice—everyone drove like maniacs in Egypt.

Following the minivan at a leisurely distance, they made their way southwest along the long line of mortuary temples. A few turns later the Colossi of Memnon were flashing by, a throng of tourists gawking at the giant statues. The minivan appeared to be heading back to the ferry landing area.

Several minutes later Colbrook told the driver to pull off the road under a clump of shady palms. He watched as the minivan sat idling near the ferry docks. The sliding door eventually opened and shaggy Gvero stepped out. He carried a case made of black plastic. Roughly the size of a large briefcase, it was much smaller than the containers he and Nedic had carried into and out of Hamed's. Without looking back, Gvero walked down to the docks. The red minivan pulled away and made a sharp turn onto a narrow side street, disappearing around a corner.

Colbrook tapped the driver on the shoulder and said, "I need to get out here." Then he remembered the shabti entombed in the cardboard box, resting on the seat. "I was wondering if you could do me a favor."

"Certainly," said the driver—meaning certainly, for the right price. He had turned in his seat at the prospect of further profit.

Colbrook handed him one hundred pounds in Egyptian currency. "Do you know where the Amenti House is? It's on this side of the river."

"What does it look like?" The taxi driver stared at the cash in his hand.

Colbrook described the building, and where it was located.

"Take this box to my friend who lives there." The driver was more than happy to make some additional cash for such an insignificant and certainly very convenient trip. "I need to get on the ferry."

The driver took the box from Colbrook's hand. "What is your friend's name?"

"Beckwith," replied Colbrook. "Just ring the bell at the front door. Give him the box. Tell him it's from Martin Colbrook. If no one answers, push open the mail slot and place it on the floor inside. Be careful with it, though."

The driver nodded, slipping the cash into his shirt pocket.

Colbrook pulled out some more currency and paid his fare. Getting out of the taxi, he repeated the name and the address one last time, and then walked down to the ferry docks. He started looking for Gvero.

One of the local ferries was approaching from the east, a frothy wake of churning water trailing out from its stern as it neared. Colbrook mingled with a crowd of tourists that had just climbed off a bus, trying to appear as if he had arrived with them. He spotted Gvero standing at the end of the dock with the plastic case held in one hand, facing away from the local Egyptians and the tourists. Weaving his way through the crowd waiting for the worker's ferry, Colbrook stepped onto the concrete dock, moving towards the shaggy Serbian. He stopped well short of him, loitering like any other passenger waiting for the ferry.

When the ship finally arrived at the pier, Gvero hurried up the gangplank onto the lower deck. He soon appeared on the top level, making his way to the stern of the vessel.

Colbrook waited until he was sure the Serbian had taken a seat, and then boarded the ferry. He climbed to the topmost deck and maneuvered cautiously through the line of benches, sitting down a few rows forward of the Serbian, screened by a considerable number of intervening passengers. The trip across the river was uneventful, though it was certainly crowded and very hot. Soon they were disembarking on the east bank, near the Luxor temple. Colbrook followed Gvero discreetly, shadowing his every move.

The bearded Serbian made his way northwards on the Corniche. Colbrook kept his distance on the crowded sidewalk. Gvero never turned his head or stopped to look back. Soon he was approaching the gate of an impressive five-star hotel overlooking the Nile. He turned into its drive.

Colbrook waited for a short interval before entering the grounds himself, doing so only after Gvero had entered the hotel. Strolling to the entrance, he pushed his way through the glass doors and stepped into the air-conditioned lobby.

At its center was a circular kiosk. Gvero was standing on the right side of the counter, talking in a low voice to one of several gray-suited Egyptian men who were assisting guests. Colbrook made his way towards the kiosk, stopping when he was only ten feet from Gvero. The disheveled Serbian gave him a quick but disinterested glance. Colbrook pulled some brochures from a nearby display.

Gvero was talking quietly, and the only distinct words Colbrook caught were *tour* and *overnight*. Money was exchanged, and Gvero wandered away into the hotel restaurant, still clutching the plastic briefcase.

Colbrook sauntered up to the counter.

"Can I help you?" asked the man who had just assisted Gvero.

"I'd like to go on the same tour."

The man stared at Colbrook for a few seconds.

"You mean the Dendera tour?"

Colbrook nodded.

"It's a boat ride to Qena. Then a tour bus to the temple." The man was looking at the brochures Colbrook was holding.

Colbrook suspected none were for the Dendera tour.

"When does it leave?" asked Colbrook.

"One hour," replied the man. "It's an overnight trip. You'll see the temple first thing tomorrow morning. You should be back by late tomorrow afternoon."

"And the cost?" inquired Colbrook.

"Six hundred pounds," answered the man.

Colbrook peeled some bills from his dwindling roll of cash, handing them across the counter. He picked up the ticket and the additional brochure the man had placed on the counter, and then turned to look into the dimly lit restaurant.

Gvero was sitting alone at a table in the corner, drinking lemonade out of a bottle. The plastic case was standing on the carpeted floor between his feet.

Whatever his reasons for heading north on the Nile, he was taking no chances with his luggage.

5

The *Papyrus* was a river cruiser of moderate proportions. It consisted of two full decks of cabin space and a truncated top deck over the forward section of the vessel, making up the bridge. The teak-covered expanse behind the bridge was a sundeck running very nearly from bow to stern. A similarly styled and elevated platform continued over the roof of the bridge, accessible by narrow side stairs. Almost dead center on the main sundeck was an oval swimming pool, providing a rapid means of cooling off when temperatures soared during the afternoon. Passengers who were seated on this upper level had a choice of exposing themselves to the fury of Helios, or resting under the protection of a white sailcloth awning.

Colbrook reclined lazily in a chair on the sundeck, staring at the receding shoreline as the vessel was maneuvered into the center of the river. The ship had left the dock only ten minutes before, during which time many of the passengers had stowed their knapsacks and bags in their cabins below. Most had now made their way up to the open deck to view the passing scenery while the vessel made its way north towards Qena.

As he gazed across the teakwood planking at the distant fields in the fertile valley, Colbrook had to admit there was a certain practicality to river cruising. It allowed one to appreciate the scenery at a distance, without the frequent and undesirable contact with nefarious touts likely to occur on land. One could slip through the landscape in relative silence on the river, without the blaring of car horns, the stench of animal droppings, and the endless flow of boys clamoring for *baksheesh*. Except for the low rumble of the diesel engines and the soft murmur of voices on the deck, it was serenely quiet. Colbrook sat idly thinking about the earlier confusion of the embarking process and the limited opportunities of surveillance it had afforded.

Boarding the vessel just after the case-toting camera assistant, he had watched for any signs of familiarity the shaggy one might show towards fellow passengers. Gvero had been entirely unsociable, carrying his plastic briefcase with the utmost attention to its safe passage. He appeared to be alone, traveling to Qena for a purpose which Colbrook could only speculate upon, though it was no doubt connected with the vigilantly guarded case.

After having positioned himself in the ship's central passageway to observe Gvero entering his assigned cabin, and noting the number when he walked by the Serbian's door, Colbrook had then continued down the passage aftward to where his own cabin was located.

The accommodations consisted of a small bed, a nightstand, a sink and toilet in a closet-like room, and one small rectangular window which looked out over the murky Nile. He had exited his cabin as fast as he had entered it, heading for the sundeck above.

Now, fifteen minutes had passed, and still Gvero had not made an appearance with the rest of the passengers. Only two obvious possibilities existed—he was either still in his cabin, or had gone to the small cafeteria-style restaurant in the rear of the vessel. It appeared to have limited fare during the day, but promised to serve a lavish four-course meal for dinner—or so the brochure claimed. Colbrook had read the brochure several times while waiting to board the ship.

With Gvero not topside, Colbrook could only continue to observe the layout of the ship and the sightseers on the sundeck. He assumed the shaggy assistant would leave the case in his cabin, since carrying it around the ship would likely attract unwanted attention from fellow travelers.

Most of the passengers sat reading guidebooks or quietly watching the scenery. The majority were seated at the medley of tables and chairs under the awning, trying to stay out of the strong sunlight. It was an innocuous lot altogether, except for one questionable passenger of Serbian nationality.

Rising from his deck chair, Colbrook walked to the starboard side of the ship. He stood by the low rail, looking down into the brown water below. It was placid, except for a thin line of churning froth flowing past the hull, the resulting surface ripples widening as they advanced towards the shoreline. The ship continued downriver, heading north, its rate of speed steady, following a course more or less centered between the banks of the Nile.

Colbrook turned his attention to the countryside.

Thickly planted crops covered the dark soil of the floodplains on either side of the river. Between these vast agricultural fields, primitive houses constructed of mud brick dotted the landscape. Most were in a state of advanced decomposition, the roofs being merely thatched reeds. The dry climate allowed one to live without undue fear of the elements.

Private docks were scattered along the shore, many with ancient-looking wooden feluccas tied to them. The *fellahin* used these vessels for transport, the river in many cases being more convenient for travel than a road, and a boat capable of carrying more cargo than a truck. Small villages drifted into view from time to time, nothing more than collections of mud-brick buildings.

Colbrook returned to his chair. A few minutes later Gvero appeared on deck. He was walking away from the top of the rear companionway that provided access to the sundeck from below. He soon passed between the tables and chairs under the sailcloth awning, and stepped out onto the exposed teak decking near the pool. His hands were empty. A few passengers, their legs dangling in the water as they sat on the raised edge of the splash pool, glanced up at him as he stood uncertainly on the deck. Sensing their momentary interest, Gvero quickly retreated under the awning. He sat down in a chair just inside the edge of the line of shade, his face expressionless.

Colbrook settled into his chair, adjusting his sunglasses. He eyed Gvero, still looking for any sign that he might be meeting someone on board. A few minutes passed. The shaggy assistant slouched further down in his plastic chair, scratching his straggly beard intermittently. His head was turned slightly, his eyes partly closed. He looked very tired.

After another minute or two had elapsed, Colbrook rose from his chair. He walked to the front of the ship, passing the splash pool on the way. Climbing a short flight of steps, he now stood on the roof of the bridge, one level higher than the main sundeck.

He looked out over the brass rail towards the bow. A few other passengers milled about, staring at the passing scenery. One of these cruise-goers wandered to his side.

The man's gray hair was combed straight back and kept in place by the use of some chemical product designed for the purpose. A garishly printed Hawaiian-style shirt was his primary covering, and a pair of baggy brown shorts that went practically down to his knees his nether garment. He held a bright blue baseball cap in his hands, and soon set it atop his thinning crown. There was nothing remarkable about the man, except that he was the perfect representation of a typical Western traveler in a warm climate.

"Nice view from up here," declared the man in the baseball cap, revealing himself to be an American. He turned to Colbrook, waiting for a response.

"It's quiet," replied Colbrook. "Nice and quiet."

The man nodded. "I'll say. I couldn't wait to get out of Cairo last week. It's so noisy, and it never stops." He grabbed the brass rail with both hands, pulling himself closer to the wall at the front of the deck. "What have you seen so far?"

"Just Luxor," said Colbrook. "I've only been here a few days."

"Vacationing alone?" inquired the blue-capped man.

With some trepidation, since the reaction was sometimes alarming, Colbrook replied, "I'm a travel writer."

The man swiveled his hands on the brass rail, a smile spreading on his face. His loose Hawaiian shirt fluttered in the breeze. "Ha! A travel writer in the flesh. I've always wondered what you guys looked like."

Colbrook hoped the man would soon relent. He didn't.

"I retired a few years ago," began blue cap. "I started writing a novel last year. I used to write when I was younger." He looked expectantly at Colbrook.

Colbrook glanced in the direction of Gvero. He began to suspect he was about to be told a plot for a bestseller, chapter by chapter.

"I never write fiction," stated Colbrook. He made a show of looking at his forearms. "I can already feel myself burning. I'd better apply some sunscreen. It's in my cabin. Good luck with the book." He turned to face the stern as he said this, checking to see if Gvero was still resting comfortably in his chair.

The Serbian had not moved.

Colbrook walked away from the man in the blue hat with a departing nod. The man touched the bill of his cap. Colbrook drifted along the rail toward where several unsuspecting passengers had taken up station.

Retracing his steps, he descended to the main sundeck. Taking one last gander at Gvero, he quickly crossed the deck in a few rapid strides. He was now standing above a gleaming chrome ladder. Below was the small teakwood-covered section of exposed deck between the bows. Somewhere on that level, against the forward superstructure, was another door. Colbrook hoped it wasn't locked, because if it was, he would be coming back up the same way he had gone down.

Swinging his leg over the rail, he dropped down onto the top rung of the ladder with one foot. A brief glance around told him no one had taken notice of his unusual activity, and he was soon descending. After reaching the narrow deck below he could not at first locate the access door. It turned out to be concealed under a wide storm ledge, its handle recessed in a steel frame. Releasing the handle and using his shoulder to force the door inwards, he swung it open on its well-oiled hinges.

Stepping over the sill, he turned and pushed the door shut.

He was standing in a narrow L-shaped space at the end of the deck's center passageway. Cautiously walking into the deserted corridor, he made his way briskly to Gvero's cabin door. He stood in front of it and listened. Satisfied no one was inside, he tried the door handle. It was locked.

He removed a small sliver of flexible metal from his pocket and slipped it into the keyhole. A few quick turns of his wrist and the lock popped open with a satisfying click. Pulling the piece of metal from the keyhole, he put it back into his pocket. Seconds later he was inside the room, closing the door without a sound.

The cabin was a duplicate of his own, the space identical in both size and shape. He surveyed the room's contents for several seconds, and then walked rapidly to the side of the small bed, examining the compact nightstand. The drawer seemed too small to fit the case, but he checked it anyway. It was empty, with the exception of a few yellowed scraps of paper which proved to be old receipts for shore excursions. He slid the drawer closed and knelt down to look under the bed.

The plastic briefcase was lying on the floor, pushed against the wall. He pulled it out by the handle and placed it down on top of the bed. There were two plastic snap closures, hinged and latched with metal bands. There was no lock. He undid both of the plastic tabs and opened the case.

The interior was fully lined with foam, and gave off a pungent plastic odor. Nestled on the cushioned bottom were two flat objects encased in bubble wrap, each roughly two-thirds the length and width of the case. The end of one was slightly exposed, showing a card-edge connector. They were circuit boards. Colbrook unwrapped one and lifted it out of the case, studying the green-colored surface. There were hundreds of tiny letters and numbers printed along one edge.

Turning the board around, he peered at the opposite side. Etched in small silver letters on the lower left corner he could distinctly read *Hamilton Sundstrand*. Setting the board aside, he lifted the other one from the case. Removing the bubble wrap, he noticed that this board was damaged in one section. The plastic was deformed and melted, as if it had been scorched in a fire. He placed it carefully down on the bed, turning his attention to the case again.

He tugged at the foam padding on the bottom of the case. It was loose. He lifted it out, sliding his hand along the smooth plastic it had covered. He turned the foam piece over to look at the back. Inspecting it thoroughly, and turning it over again to the other side, he squeezed it with his fingers. Disappointed, he placed it back in the bottom of the case.

Pulling at the thin piece of foam that covered the inside of the lid, he worked his fingers around the seam between the foam and the lid. The corners were slightly free, but the rest was solidly glued down. He pushed at the foam across its entire surface, and then paused for a moment, listening.

Quickly rewrapping the boards and placing them back into the case exactly as they had been, he lowered the lid and pushed the two metal bands over the notched tabs, pressing down hard with his thumbs on the plastic closures. They snapped shut with a loud popping noise. He positioned the briefcase back under the bed as he had found it.

Colbrook continued his search. He checked the curtains over the window, the cabinet in the bathroom, the small wastepaper basket in the corner, the pillow, and the bedcovers. When he was done, he stared up at the ceiling. It was blank, with the exception of four recessed lights. He stepped over to the wall and flipped the light switch on. All four halogen bulbs glowed. He turned the switch off.

He moved to the cabin doorway and eased it open. The hallway was empty in both directions. He stepped out into the passage and pulled the door closed, reaching for the piece of flexible metal in his pocket. Seconds later the lock was secured.

Having made his way back to the sundeck using the conventional method, Colbrook sat down under the awning. Gvero still rested in his chair, entirely oblivious of the recent intrusion into his quarters. Glancing around at the other passengers, Colbrook leaned back in his chair, slipping his sunglasses back on. No one paid any attention to him.

More than two hours passed, and except for obtaining a light snack from the ship's cafeteria, Colbrook remained in his chair. Gvero, on the other hand, disappeared for at least half an hour at one point, heeding the call of his stomach, as many of the other passengers did with predictable frequency.

The sun slowly sank towards the western horizon, a fiery aura soon lighting up the sky. Long shadows stretched and lingered like spectral fingers playing across the teakwood deck. The air was noticeably cooler, and many passengers began snapping photos of the picturesque sunset.

Colbrook rose from his chair. He strolled past the splash pool, heading in the direction of the bridge, but still keeping an eye on the Serbian. Gvero took no notice of his movement. Approaching the narrow side stairs that he had climbed earlier, he walked by them and moved out onto the breezeway, a narrow deck encircling the bridge. He continued forward until he reached a low rail overlooking the bow of the ship.

In the near distance a long causeway spanned the Nile, its concrete piers reaching high above the water. As the ship drew closer, the sound of the engines dropped a note, the rumbling now deeper in pitch. They were slowing noticeably. A small police launch closed on their course, moving alongside to escort the ship into the Qena docks.

A few minutes later the *Papyrus* passed under the bridge, the engine noise reverberating off the steel girders on the structure's underside. The vessel slowly made its way towards the docking area on the east shoreline. Crew members now appeared at the bow and stern, waiting to secure the ship.

Colbrook turned and retraced his path, heading for the aft companionway.

Gvero was no longer on the sundeck.

Looking over the side rail, Colbrook could see rows of vendors and their wares set up alongside the dock, waiting for the passengers to go ashore. Considerable security forces patrolled the area. On more than one occasion he spotted a policeman carrying an automatic weapon slung over his shoulder, walking the length of the dock.

A narrow gangway was being fitted and lowered. When it was secured, several Egyptian policemen boarded before anyone was allowed off.

Leaving the ship would be a slow process.

Entering into the passageway below, Colbrook walked to his cabin door. There was now considerable activity below decks. Doors were opening and closing, and passengers rushed about, moving in both directions. The shaggy camera assistant stepped out of his cabin a few minutes later, carrying a large yellow shopping bag. The flexible plastic handles were pulled tight in his hand. The bag was not empty, and whatever was inside clearly had some weight to it.

Colbrook pretended to lock his own door, dropping the key into his pocket afterwards. Stepping into the middle of the passageway and behind three elderly tourists discussing what there might be to buy onshore, he pulled a crumpled brochure from his pocket. The bearded Serbian approached, turning sideways to pass the group, the yellow bag held stiffly at his side. Glancing down into it as Gvero moved by, Colbrook could see the black plastic briefcase resting inside.

Remaining for a moment in the passageway, still staring at the brochure in his hand, Colbrook turned to follow the Serbian at a vigilant distance. They were soon on the narrow side deck, Gvero moving rapidly towards the forward section of the ship, his intent, evidently, to disembark. His progress was soon checked by a crowd of passengers bottled up at the head of the gangway. A member of the crew was handing out small paper tickets, telling the passengers they would need to show them when they re-boarded.

Shuffling forward, Colbrook took a ticket and moved to the top of the gangway. It swayed under his feet, the angle steeper than he had expected. He gripped the handrail and began descending the non-skid metal ramp. Gvero was already at the bottom of the platform, turning left into the mélange of vendor stalls. Stepping from the gangway to the pavement, Colbrook extended his stride, keeping his eyes on the distinctive yellow shopping bag.

Weaving his way in and out of the stalls, he followed the Serbian as best he could under the circumstances. The dock was crowded with both locals and travelers. With alarming frequency, vendors plucked at his shirt and shouted at him as he walked by, vying for his business. Colbrook ignored them all, moving at a steady gait to keep Gvero in sight. A young Egyptian man suddenly stepped into his path, waving a Tutankhamen T-shirt in his face. The article of clothing blocked his view for several seconds.

Pushing the man aside, Colbrook scanned the dock ahead.

Gvero had disappeared.

Moving faster now, his eyes skimming across the crowd, Colbrook approached a group of food stands. Smoking grills, bubbling pots of water, and condensation-covered cans of soda were in haphazard profusion as he stepped up to a nearby stall. The proprietor, an older Egyptian man in a glaring white *galabiya*, waved a bowl of unidentifiable food under his nose. It looked vaguely like porridge, but smelled like beef stew. Colbrook craned his neck to see around a stack of flatbreads, thinking he had spotted the yellow shopping bag somewhere up ahead.

Threading his way further into the maelstrom of humanity, Colbrook was finally able to locate Gvero. He was at a not too distant stall. Edging closer, Colbrook observed the proceedings closely.

The Serbian was talking to a ragged-looking Egyptian man

wearing a white *kufi* skullcap over a head of dark curly hair. Colbrook watched as Gvero lifted the yellow bag onto the stall's counter. The Egyptian removed the bag from the counter and put it down somewhere inside of the temporary hut which formed the rear of the stall. Moments later a similar bag appeared back on the counter. Gvero took the bag, walking briskly away with it at his side.

Colbrook moved towards the stall, ignoring Gvero for the moment. It was more than likely that he would be getting back on the ship, since Qena was considered off-limits for tourists. The police turned back anyone who tried to enter the town on foot.

It did not take long for the *kufi*-wearing Egyptian to step out of his stall, now carrying the original yellow shopping bag with the briefcase inside. He was heading towards the water's edge. Colbrook found a clearing in the crowd and made his way hurriedly across the concrete dock, on a rough intercept course with the skullcapped Egyptian. They both reached the edge of the dock at the same time, Colbrook only ten yards away from the man. In this area, a short distance north of where the *Papyrus* was moored, most of the vessels tied up were small motorboats and wooden feluccas in varying degrees of disrepair. The *kufi*-topped Egyptian was heading towards a motorboat with a metal roof. It was painted in bright primary colors.

Colbrook watched the *kufi*-wearing Egyptian climb into the boat. Another man of similar but more disreputable appearance helped him aboard. Less than a minute later the man in the skullcap clambered back out of the boat, his hands empty. He stooped to untie the fore and aft lines which were looped around a metal pipe running the length of the dock. Casting the lines into the vessel, the man turned and walked back to his stall. The motorboat's engine started with a belch of thick blue smoke, the man at the controls steering the craft out into the glittering orange glow of the Nile. The sun was just slipping below the horizon, the sky a vast dome of purplish cirrus clouds stretching from east to west.

Dusk was settling over the dockyard as Colbrook worked his way back to the *Papyrus*.

When he reached a position from where his view of the ship was unobstructed, he noticed a second gangway had been installed, this one leading down from the aft section of the ship. At the top of the ramp was a low rectangular doorway, inset into the hull, facilitating the movement of larger items into and out of the ship. The ramp was considerably wider than the one in the forward section of the ship, and set at a lesser angle. Passengers who tried to board by this means were turned away, directed to use the original gangway instead.

Colbrook slowed his pace. A rusty six-wheel truck was maneuvering in reverse, backing up to the aft ramp. When it stopped two men got out of the cab and a third man climbed down from the open bed. A policeman wandered by, his automatic weapon slung diagonally across his back. At the top of the gangway two men in the garb of lesser crew appeared, descending towards the truck. Another Egyptian made his appearance soon after, following the two men down the ramp. He was wearing the uniform of a chef, his crumpled hat stuffed under his arm.

With growing interest, Colbrook sat down on a nearby bench to watch the activity. The chef had reached the truck, pointing and gesturing with his hands, giving instructions to the other men now staring into the back of the truck. One of the men pulled the tailgate down with a clatter, and two others hauled themselves up into the uncovered back. Boxes and cartons were neatly stacked in the bed of the truck.

With two men on the ground and two in the truck, a slow but methodical process of unloading began. Colbrook watched as the cartons and boxes were carefully transferred to the ground. The driver magically produced a handcart from somewhere, and began stacking boxes on it. He trundled up the gangway a few minutes later, holding the top carton with his free hand. The boxes contained fruits and vegetables. Leafy foliage was sticking out of several of them.

After a few minutes of continuous observation, Colbrook was beginning to lose interest. The whole scene was making him hungry. Coming aboard were nothing more than the ingredients for the upcoming four-course meal.

His whole perspective on the matter soon changed.

At the side rail of the ship, very close to the aft ramp, Gvero appeared. He stood in the failing light, his unkempt hair blowing in the wind. Moments later he disappeared into the deepening shadows, and the better part of a minute passed before he could be seen coming down the larger gangway with a determined look on his face. The men at the bottom were still unloading boxes of foodstuffs.

Colbrook rose from the bench and slipped into a knot of people, trying to maintain his anonymity while still preserving his view of the truck. Gvero reached the bottom of the ramp, and instead of being given the same treatment his fellow passengers had been when they had tried to embark on this gangway, he was greeted with familiarity by the working men.

Most of the cartons and boxes had by now been removed from the truck, and four men climbed up into its open back. They appeared to be struggling to move something heavy.

Colbrook watched with riveted attention as a large wooden crate neared the edge of the tailgate. It was roughly six feet long and maybe a little more than three feet high. The width was more difficult to determine, but he guessed it was at least as wide as it was tall. With two men in the back pushing, and three on the ground at the rear of the truck guiding it out—the chef had already gone back aboard the *Papyrus*—the five men managed to unload the crate by sliding it down a makeshift ramp of timbers.

Once the crate reached the ground, two men began pushing it from the short side. It moved easily—it had wheels on the bottom. The shaggy camera assistant suddenly held out his hand, motioning for the men to stop. When they did, he reached down and pulled off a sheet of paper that was attached to the lid. He folded it carefully, slipping it into his pocket. He then retreated as the two Egyptian men resumed their effort, gaining speed as they approached the gangway. Significant momentum was needed to ascend the metal ramp.

The other three men walked back to the truck, two of them getting into the cab, the last closing the tailgate and then climbing up and over it. The truck started with a roar, belching black diesel exhaust, and began crawling its way through the crowd. Gvero walked briskly up the ramp, following the crate.

Colbrook headed for the smaller gangway, removing from his pocket the ticket he had been given earlier. When he reached the top of the ramp no one was waiting to receive it. He stepped onto the narrow walkway that circled the outer edge of the ship, moving steadily towards the rear of the vessel. Below the aft companionway sliding double doors of painted steel provided access to the hold. He stopped and listened. A muffled bang reverberated through the floor plates, followed by the echoing shouts of workers. He began climbing the stairs.

The ship's exterior lights blinked on just as he was reaching the restaurant. Dusk was turning to night. He passed a lone policeman walking the perimeter of the deck. With the ease with which he had just boarded, Colbrook was not surprised such precautions were being taken. Pushing open the tinted glass door, he stepped into the ship's mess.

After a satisfying meal of chicken cutlets and eggplant, both laced with a shockingly sweet but appetizing sauce, Colbrook engaged in some desultory conversation with the passengers at his table. He had other things on his mind beside the latest travel warning or tomb closure, the merits of the alabaster factories on the west bank, or the current exchange rate. Eventually he politely excused himself, and after a brief visit to the small gift shop, went to his cabin. He had not seen Gvero at the dinner service.

Colbrook's luminous watch dial indicated it was one o'clock when he rolled from his bed. Walking off a slight cramp in his left leg, he reviewed the plan he had hatched many hours previously. His opinion of the situation had not changed.

Exiting the cabin, he softly closed the door and locked it. The hallway was deserted. Moving with great care, he soundlessly walked the length of the passage, heading for the rear companionway which would take him, after one flight of steps down, to the steel doors of the hold below.

While the lights were dimmed in the interior passages, the exterior walkways were still brightly lit—something Colbrook had not anticipated. He was well aware that security forces protected the dock at night, and while it was unlikely anyone would be paying much attention to the moored ship, they would certainly be patrolling the wide roadway between the docking area and Qena. The risk of being spotted and confronted was very real for someone walking along the ship's rails at this hour of night.

Staying on the shadowed side of the companionway, Colbrook

descended rapidly to the main deck. The lights were brighter down here, several almost blindingly so. He sprinted across the metal decking to the doors of the hold. It took him a moment to unlatch them. When he started to slide one of the doors open it creaked noisily. He paused for a few seconds before continuing to apply steady pressure. When there was enough room to pass inside, he slipped through.

He found himself standing in an enclosed area with a level floor made of non-skid steel plate. The only illumination was the faint glow of a low-wattage overhead light. He slowly pulled the door shut.

He had expected to find a staircase behind these doors, but instead found what appeared to be a freight elevator. There was a small control box on the nearest wall. It had two recessed green arrows—one pointing up, one down—with a single raised red circle between them. The elevator's operation appeared to be manifestly self-explanatory, but he was far more concerned with the loud noise it would probably generate when activated.

He turned away from the elevator, moving towards the opposite corner of the space. Here he found a narrow steel ladder affixed to the wall. In the dim light he could faintly see the floor of the hold at its bottom. Stepping onto the ladder, he began to descend. The rungs were narrow and slippery, and when he reached the decking below he breathed a sigh of relief.

The darkened hold stretched for some distance into the central portion of the vessel's lower hull. Walking past the freight elevator's shuttered gate, Colbrook removed a small flashlight from his pocket—his only purchase in the gift shop after dinner. He aimed the very narrow beam of light into the gloom.

Moving cautiously forward, he made his way deeper into the hold. He could smell more than he could see. The odor of garbage was strong, and further ahead he found the source: a pile of trash-filled plastic bags sitting in a heap on the floor. Working his way around them he moved into a wider section of the hold. Boxes and cartons containing every variety of material needed on board a passenger ship abounded. Paper products, cleaning chemicals, canned goods, and other assorted supplies were placed in a somewhat orderly fashion on deep metal shelves.

Colbrook ignored these, directing his small flashlight towards the bow section of the hold. Here he could see larger and bulkier items, many in wooden boxes or crates. As he walked closer he could tell that most were spare parts for the ship—some had stenciled words on them—but one in particular stood out. It was the large wooden crate he had watched being loaded onto the ship only hours before.

He slowly approached it, the beam of his flashlight aimed at its side. The wood looked new, as if the crate had been constructed very recently. There was nothing painted on it, and there were no labels stuck to the rough boards. He looked down. Something was lying on the lid.

It was a green-handled screwdriver.

Alongside the tool were at least a dozen long black screws. Moving closer, he could see the holes that the screws had been removed from. They were evenly spaced around the edge of the lid, little splinters of wood sticking from the perforations.

A scuffling sound came from somewhere to his right. Switching off the flashlight, Colbrook crouched down next to the crate, his eyes searching the shadowy hold.

From the darkness came a faint clicking sound. It continued intermittently, sometimes with long pauses between the clicks. It sounded almost like someone repeatedly turning a deadbolt—a sliding of metal on metal and then a *click*.

Something small and metallic struck the floor. Colbrook switched on the flashlight, aiming it at the noise. A single brass handgun cartridge rolled into view, glinting brightly as it passed through the beam of light. Now he knew what the sound was—someone was loading a magazine.

The clicking sound stopped.

A figure barely more than an outline shifted against the nearby bulkhead, a sense of hesitation in its slow movement. Colbrook raised the flashlight, aiming it across the hold.

Gvero blinked back at him, his shoulders pressed against the wall, a mixture of surprise and disdain showing beneath his shaggy beard. He squinted his eyes closed as the beam of light settled on them. In one hand was a pistol magazine, in the other a brass cartridge. On a box nearby was the pistol itself.

Gvero lunged for the firearm.

Colbrook charged across the ship's hold.

The bearded Serbian tried to turn away, but Colbrook felt his shoulder make contact. They both tumbled into a row of empty cardboard boxes.

Flinging the crushed boxes aside, Colbrook struggled to his feet. He picked up the fallen flashlight, directing it at the floor of the hold.

Gvero was on his back, attempting to jam the magazine into the handgun. He had a dazed expression on his face. When he rolled to a sitting position, Colbrook slammed his foot into his chest, knocking him flat again. The magazine went spinning to the floor, striking a collection of loose cartridges lying alongside an open ammunition carton.

The pistol clattered away into the darkness.

"Someone is going to get hurt if we don't stop," declared Colbrook. He held the flashlight steady, aiming it down at Gvero.

"All right, all right," muttered Gvero, struggling to regain his breath. His passable English was slurred by his labored breathing.

"Don't go for the gun." Colbrook was breathing heavily himself.

Gvero rolled over sideways, sliding to his knees.

"Get up," ordered Colbrook.

Rising slowly to his feet, Gvero tested his shoulder to see if it still worked. His face was covered with grime and perspiration, his shirt twisted and pulled sideways. He staggered for a moment, peering uncertainly in Colbrook's direction. It was obvious he could not see behind the glare of the flashlight.

Gvero suddenly lashed out with his right hand, grabbing for the light.

Colbrook stepped sideways, seizing the Serbian's arm. Twisting it behind his back, he drove him forward, propelling him violently into the bulkhead. Gvero's head contacted the steel plate with a solid *thunk!* His body went limp, dropping to the floor in a heap.

Grabbing Gvero under the shoulders, Colbrook dragged him away from the wall and towards the center of the hold. The rubber soles of the Serbian's sneakers squeaked as they slid across the painted metal floor. Pausing to adjust his grip, Colbrook continued dragging the unconscious man through the hold.

When he reached the freight elevator he lowered Gvero to the floor. Breathing hard from the exertion, Colbrook rested for a moment, and then stepped around the shaggy Serbian, making his way to the port hull door. There was a large metal wheel affixed to its center. Turning it with considerable effort, he unlatched the door, slowly pulling it inward. When the door was more than halfway open he moved to its edge, looking down into the dark waters of the Nile. A weak moon illuminated the rising and falling surface. He breathed in some satisfyingly fresh air, and stood listening for a moment to the chirping insects and frogs.

Retreating back into the hold, he stopped to examine a metal container hanging from a bracket on the left side of the doorframe. It was tall, running almost from floor to ceiling, and at least four feet wide. At the bottom of the metal box the words *LIFE RAFT* were printed in bold black lettering. Running his hand down the side of the container, he located the primary latching mechanism, releasing it with a loud snap. The container's front panel dropped away. He barely had time to stop it from striking the deck.

Wrestling the flimsy metal cover out of the way, he turned to the container and tugged at the orange raft inside. It was deflated and made of thick nylon, a series of plasticized ropes running around its outer edge. It fell out onto the floor with a faint swoosh. It was hexagonal in shape. A long red tag hung from the left side, attached to a metal ring. Connected to the ring was a thin braided cable. It ended at a narrow stainless-steel cylinder. Colbrook pulled the ring. A short burst of carbon dioxide exploded from the cylinder, and with a hissing sound the raft began to inflate.

He waited until the raft was fully inflated before dragging it towards the open hull door. When he reached the door, he unthreaded a length of rope from the top of the raft, passed a double loop over one of the rubber cleats on the side of it, and then slid the raft over the sill. Dropping without a sound, it thumped lightly into the river and started to drift northward. Quickly pulling the raft back and tying off the rope on the door jamb, Colbrook headed for Gvero's prostrate form.

He checked the Serbian's pockets and found the crumpled shipping paper that had been removed from the crate. Most of what was written on it was in Arabic, but he could make out that the destination was Baris. This was not surprising. Baris was the closest town to Lowell's dig site, where the documentary crew had apparently been working for several weeks. Slipping the paper into one of his own pockets, he resumed searching Gvero. The only other item he turned up was a Serbian passport. He briefly glanced at it before returning it to Gvero's possession.

Pulling him by the arms, Colbrook wrestled the still senseless Serbian to the edge of the hull door. He turned him around, so that his legs dangled from the opening, and then let him slip out feet-first into the raft below. He had his doubts that this maneuver would be wholly successful, but the unconscious Serbian dropped right into the middle of the orange raft, flat on his back. Untying the rope that held the raft to the door jamb, Colbrook cast it out into the river. The raft drifted steadily northwards. It disappeared altogether a few minutes later, swallowed up in the murky night.

Colbrook leaned forcefully against the wide hull door, pushing it slowly closed with his shoulder. He latched it tightly with its substantial locking wheel. The hold was again pitch dark. He switched on his small flashlight and walked back to the spot where Gvero had been loading the magazine. Searching the floor, sweeping his flashlight back and forth over the riveted steel plate, he located the handgun. It was a Beretta. The magazine was lying not far from the gun. It contained only eleven rounds. He walked back to the pile of cartridges on the floor, chose two .380s, and filled the magazine to capacity. Checking to make sure the safety was engaged, he jammed the pistol into his belt. He walked back to the crate, perspiration now trickling down his forehead.

Shining the light onto the lid, he looked for any markings he might have missed earlier. He found none. Sweeping the screws into his hand, he placed them on the floor. The screwdriver he put in his pocket. The flashlight he set carefully down on a nearby box, aimed towards the crate. He lifted the short side of the lid with both hands.

Inside were rows of plastic bottles in shrink-wrapped cardboard trays. It was bottled water, a very common brand.

Colbrook gently lowered the top back down.

When he lifted the lid again he did so from the long side, pulling it towards himself. Gradually tilting the lid down until its edge rested solidly against the steel floor, he maneuvered it to a more upright position, leaning it against the crate.

Picking up the flashlight, he swept the narrow beam over the rows of shiny plastic bottles. He then placed the small light on the near corner of the crate, freeing his hands to search the contents.

He removed an entire cardboard tray of bottles, placing it down on the floor. Brown canvas showed in the vacated space. As he pushed the heavy cloth aside, the sharp odor of metal and fresh oil filled his nostrils.

He was looking at a row of rifle barrels.

Removing more trays of bottled water and pulling the rest of the canvas away, the whole crate was soon filled with the sinister gleam of recently manufactured firearms.

The documentary team was certainly full of surprises.

6

The trip to Dendera was as uneventful as it was informative. The guide from the ship was knowledgeable but painstakingly didactic. He seemed intent on pointing out every last detail of the Greco-Roman temple dedicated to Hathor, from the outer hypostyle hall constructed by Tiberius to the recently cleaned zodiac ceiling supported by eighteen massive Hathor-faced columns. The latter had been disfigured by the Coptic Christians, who had chiseled away with much success the facial features of the four-sided and four-faced capitals. The ancient church lay just outside the temple court.

As Colbrook and the other passengers worked their way deeper into the darkened temple, they were told that a special hidden crypt once held a gold statue of Hathor, only retrieved during the New Year festival. The statue was considered to be lifeless until it was carried up to the exposed roof and revived by the sun's rays, at which point it would be regarded as awake. This led to an impromptu discussion of the opening of the mouth ceremony performed on mummies, something that was assumed to have similar implications.

Despite the vaguely unsettling aspects of the lecture, the group cheerfully followed the guide up the western staircase and onto the rooftop. Here Colbrook, with many others, entered the chapel of Osiris on the eastern side, examining the plaster replica of the famous Dendera zodiac, the original having been removed from the temple in 1820 by French stonemasons and carted off to the Louvre. While on this rooftop, with its vast panoramic views, Colbrook wondered if he might soon see Gvero stumbling along the river bank, a deflated emergency raft trailing behind him from a thick rope tied around his waist.

Leaving the interior of the temple, the tour group circled the exterior walls. The guide pointed out with much gusto the wall relief on the southern side of the structure. It depicted Cleopatra VII and Caesarian, the son of Julius Caesar, offering to the goddess Hathor. Telling the group to turn around, the guide then told them they were looking at the temple of Isis, constructed by none other than the emperor Augustus. While leaving the complex they were ushered into the *mammisi*, or birth house of Horus, built by Trajan in AD 90, decorated with the disturbing images of the god Bes, a dwarf of unflattering and unquestionably hideous proportions.

The man with the blue baseball cap acted as if he assumed Colbrook had additional information about the temple that the tour guide was not revealing, or that he had access to areas that regular visitors did not. Colbrook assured him that as a travel writer he was far from being an expert on anything, particularly Egyptology. The blue-capped man eventually wandered off and took up a position close to the guide, his lofty view of travel writers apparently tarnished forever.

The bus trip back to Qena was thankfully a short one. By the looks of the security forces at the roadway intersections and the armed guard who rode shotgun in the seat behind the bus driver, Colbrook was constantly reminded that this was considered by the authorities to be a high-risk area. One of the earliest tourist-related attacks was perpetrated by a man from a nearby village. The Egyptian government had destroyed the man's house, not stopping until the entire village was razed, Carthage-style. Of course, they had the added benefit and speed of bulldozers as opposed to the laboring foot soldiers of Scipio.

After the passengers ate a hearty and much anticipated lunch, the *Papyrus* left the Qena docks. Gvero was still nowhere in sight. Apparently the current had actually carried him some considerable distance down the Nile during the night. He might still be on the river, or he might have made it to shore. Colbrook didn't care either way. Given Gvero's dubious dealings, he would avoid the authorities wherever he made landfall.

The cruise back up the Nile was relaxing, and without the Serbian on board, far less stressful for Colbrook. Though he kept an eye out for the man in the blue cap, he did not see him again.

The only matter of immediate concern was how he was going to safely get the handgun off the vessel. Having no luggage, he would need to purchase a camera bag. He had seen a few on display in the gift shop the previous night. Fortunately there were no metal detectors at the docks, and none aboard the *Papyrus*. Most of the large hotels in Cairo now had them.

Hours later, standing on the small sundeck over the bridge, Colbrook watched as the ship nosed into the dock at Luxor. The shipping paper for the crate was secure in his pocket, and he carried his new camera bag over his shoulder, slung from its padded strap. He glanced down at his watch. It was almost three o'clock. The air was stiflingly hot.

He descended the short stairs leading down to the main sundeck and pool. A few passengers lingered here, but most had gone below to collect their luggage. Moving down the length of the teakwood deck, he soon found himself standing near the aft companionway. Directly below this stairway the hold could be accessed via the freight elevator. He had no intention of going below into the hold, but he was very interested in keeping an eye on the crate once it left the ship, and there was little doubt the crate would leave the ship. The cruiser plied only the waters between Luxor and Qena at this time of the year.

The *Papyrus* was now stationary, the huge diesel engines idling. Hawsers were cast and retrieved, the mooring process beginning with the same methodical approach used at every dock on the Nile. The Egyptians had been doing this in some form or another for thousands of years.

The forward gangway was put in place, the railings carefully assembled and fitted. Colbrook watched with little interest, and then descended the aft companionway. Passing the hold elevator doors, he walked to the rail. He was now directly over the port hold door, waiting for the aft ramp to be secured below.

The hull door opened. Only minutes later a group of overall-clad men emerged onto the wider gangway. The slow process of unloading containers, crates, and boxes began. Colbrook leaned on the rail, looking down the ramp. Ten minutes passed before he saw the large wooden crate being trundled off. Three men were needed to apply braking pressure as it rolled its way noisily down the metal gangway, and when it reached the bottom it bounced heavily onto the concrete dock. Colbrook was reminded of the half hour he had spent in the hold putting the screws back into the top.

With the crate now on land, he made his way quickly to the narrow passenger ramp and disembarked. The crate sat unattended at the dockside, other materials now piling up alongside it.

A variety of taxis and buses waited for the passengers, parked in a narrow drive that looped down to the dock and merged back into the parking lot higher up the hill. Above the parking lot the multi-storied hotel overlooked the Nile.

Colbrook looked for a place that would allow him a degree of careful observation without being too conspicuous. He had no idea who was going to arrive to transport the crate, but he was almost certain Gvero had been arming himself from its contents in preparation for going along on the trip.

A metal shipping container, rusted but serviceable, sat not fifteen yards from the crate. Colbrook headed for it, holding the camera bag containing the unusually practical souvenir he had acquired on the cruise. From a position alongside the shipping container he could remain hidden from the view of anyone driving down to the dock, but could still watch for someone arriving near the crate.

A wider bypass road allowed commercial vehicles to drive directly alongside the dock for loading and unloading, and it was on this road that Colbrook first spotted a cab-over truck of Japanese make. The back was enclosed by a frame covered with canvas. Moving slowly down the steep grade, it maneuvered very near to where the wood crate was sitting.

When the truck began backing up to the mound of boxes and containers alongside the dock, Colbrook caught a glimpse of the passenger door.

It was white, like the rest of the vehicle, and on it was a large circle painted in light blue. Inside the circle, in bold green lettering, were two words: *Displaced Fund*. Below, in a smaller and more flowing typeface, was *Help the World—Help the Future*. From the sound of its engine the truck appeared to be in excellent condition, and as it neared, Colbrook concluded that it could not have been in use for more than a few months.

The truck stopped, and Colbrook stepped from behind the corner of the metal container to get a better look at the driver. He was a relatively youthful Egyptian. The door swung open and he lowered himself out of the cab onto the short running board. He stood there for a few seconds stretching, and then stepped to the ground, walking towards the wooden crate. He was wearing a loose-fitting brown shirt with a pair of ordinary faded jeans. Bright white sneakers covered his feet. Shading his eyes were a pair of mirror-like sunglasses with gold frames.

Walking with a slight swagger, the Egyptian driver slowly circled the crate. He was chewing gum, his hands in his pockets as he sized up the cargo.

A minute passed, and still the driver lingered by the wooden crate with his hands in his pockets. He kept staring up at the ship, as if waiting for someone. Colbrook stayed where he was, wondering if another vehicle might arrive with men to help load the crate. No such vehicle arrived, and after a few more minutes had elapsed, Colbrook walked from behind the metal container, angling towards the driver's half-turned back. The Egyptian did not take notice of him until he was almost at his side.

"Let's get the crate in the truck," declared Colbrook. "I'm supposed to be in Baris with it by the end of the day."

The driver turned, staring down through his sunglasses at the shipping paper now displayed in Colbrook's hand. After a few seconds he nodded, telling Colbrook his name was Samir and that he had only driven for the Displaced Fund once before. He worked as an independent driver for hire.

"The forklift by the ship," said Colbrook, motioning with his hand. "See if you can get it over here."

Samir nodded, heading for an orange forklift that sat idling not far from the aft gangway, the operator smoking a cigarette while sitting motionless at the wheel.

While Samir headed across the concrete dock, Colbrook stepped over to the passenger door of the truck. He pulled on the large chrome handle and swung the door open. In one fluid motion he positioned the camera bag alongside the seat and shut the door.

The shipping paper he folded and slid back into his pocket as he returned to the wooden crate.

Samir was now halfway across the dock, waving his arms over his head, trying to get the forklift operator's attention.

Colbrook strode across the dock. He arrived alongside Samir just as the forklift engine sputtered and died. The operator swung himself down from the padded seat. His grease-stained overalls were too long, the bottoms of the legs rolled up into makeshift cuffs. He wore headgear that resembled that of a desert Arab—a folded triangle of white cloth with a snug-fitting black headband. His skin was leathery and wrinkled, and a scruffy beard completed his unkempt look.

Samir said a few words to him in Arabic, turning to point to the truck. The forklift operator nodded, but remained standing alongside his machine.

Reaching into his pocket, Colbrook said, "How much does he want?"

Samir said a few more words in Arabic, and the man gave a short response.

"He says one hundred pounds," said Samir.

Colbrook pulled out a bill. "He'll get fifty—no more." He handed the money to the man, who in return flashed a brief gap-toothed smile. Colbrook knew twenty would have been sufficient.

The forklift started seconds later, Samir directing the operator to the wooden crate at a slow jog. Colbrook leisurely strolled across the dock, swatting at some annoying flies that buzzed around his head. Returning to the truck, Samir undid the chains and pins holding the truck's tailgate closed. The metal door swung down with an earsplitting shriek.

Climbing up into the truck bed, Samir motioned for the forklift operator to approach. The truck already contained a sizeable quantity of what Colbrook recognized even from a distance as boxed medical supplies. These cartons were pushed all the way to the front of the bed, against the back of the cab.

The hydraulic machine made short work of the loading process. The operator was obviously skilled, and with minimal difficulty maneuvered the crate into the back of the truck. He lowered it with only the slightest bump, and then backed away. When the forklift was gone, the tailgate secured, the crate tied down, and the canvas cover pulled all the way over the back, Colbrook climbed into the cab. Samir settled in behind the wheel.

The driver guided the truck back up the bypass road, heading towards the hotel parking lot. Within minutes they were stuck in Luxor's afternoon traffic. Horns blared and arms waved out of windows as drivers jockeyed for position on the baking roadway. Colbrook was grateful the truck had air conditioning.

Samir was not in a talkative mood as he weaved slowly in and out of the traffic, heading southwest for the nearest bridge that would take them across the Nile and over to the west bank. Once the immediate environs of Luxor were behind them, the traffic rapidly dissipated. They drove along the main road paralleling the river, and soon approached a lengthy four-lane bridge. Two large concrete statues of the hawk form of Horus, both topped with the distinctive cone-shaped white crown of Upper Egypt, sat on either side of the entrance. Samir, who had probably driven this route hundreds of times, never even turned his head to admire the modern replicas. They continued on towards the dusty town of Dabiya on the other side of the river.

There was little to see in Dabiya—just the usual mud-brick buildings and sandy streets of a small town in Upper Egypt. Most of it was on their right. They passed it and made a sharp left onto another road, continuing south along the western bank of the Nile. A large town soon appeared through the sugarcane fields. It was Armant, a more prosperous locale.

After driving through it on the main thoroughfare that was nothing more than an endless row of vegetable stands and shouting street vendors, Samir slowed the truck. He turned the vehicle onto a rutted dirt road, heading for what looked like a large farmstead. Colbrook was surprised at the detour. He had assumed they were driving straight for the Kharga Oasis and Baris. As the truck rumbled closer to the group of mud-brick buildings that made up the secluded farm, Colbrook noticed wooden cages stacked up neatly alongside the drive. There looked to be at least twenty-five or more of these wood boxes with wire-covered fronts. The truck stopped, and when the cloud of dust that billowed out from beneath it cleared, Colbrook could see that the cages were filled with chickens.

Pushing the driver's door open with his foot, Samir scrambled out of the comfortable cab, admitting a blast of dry, scorching heat. He disappeared behind the back of the truck, and a few seconds later Colbrook heard the chains and pins rattling on the tailgate. Now well aware of the probable reason for the detour, Colbrook pushed his door open and stepped out into the oven-like heat.

With a look of annoyance, Samir began carrying the chicken cages to the rear of the truck. After assembling six or seven of them into a small pyramid, he climbed into the bed and reached down for the wood and wire boxes. The chickens made little sound and even less movement. Huddled in pairs in the cages, they were no doubt stunned by the intense heat and scorching sun.

Colbrook lifted a few cages so Samir could reach them easier. After several more trips back and forth, all of the cages were loaded. Samir unrolled the canvas cover again, secured it, and then refastened the tailgate. The chickens, now under the shade of the tarp, gave them a baleful look. These birds, thought Colbrook, would be half baked by the time they reached the Kharga Oasis. Maybe that was the whole idea anyway.

Samir followed the rutted road back to the main one. After they had driven for some distance southwestward, the blacktop road no longer paralleled the Nile. Leaving the river's edge behind, they soon approached a railroad crossing. Samir barely slowed down, the truck bouncing across the gravel-filled grade. They were now traveling towards a vast limestone escarpment.

It was here, at the very edge of the Western Desert, that a naturally occurring *wadi* provided passage through the rocky cliffs, and precisely for this reason the road engineers had built the Kharga highway at its issuance. From the far end of this valley, the sun, already beginning to change from yellow to ochre as the late afternoon haze intensified, bathed the limestone outcroppings bordering the passageway in a blinding light.

As they drove towards the mouth of the *wadi*, where the blacktop road began to snake its way through the low hills, Colbrook watched the green vegetation of the fertile valley give way to an endless expanse of gravel and silt. Windblown sand crept to the very edge of the road in snow-like drifts, in some places actually covering it in thin tendrils of creeping obliteration.

Passing through the gap in the escarpment, the truck steadily climbed the gently sloping roadway. They emerged onto a low limestone plateau with rolling hills to their left. On the right was a limitless stretch of gravel and sand. More steep limestone cliffs loomed ahead, where the road faded into a thin wispy line in the thick haze of the southwestern horizon.

Colbrook knew this journey was only slightly less lethal than it had once been. While following a faint desert track on camelback was certainly more difficult than driving down a paved road of modern construction, getting lost in the desert was only the beginning of the end. Even in a modern vehicle, if the engine broke down and the water supply was insufficient, one could perish in as little as two days without help. It was more ironic to die in the shade afforded by an air-conditioned truck than alongside a camel, but the result was just as permanent.

Rising again, the road passed through a second stretch of limestone cliffs. The higher plateau here provided better visibility, but the haze still limited the distance one could see across the open desert. They were now passing an amphitheater of low hills. Stretches of yellow sand filled the voids under these prominences. Driving through the desolate landscape, Colbrook realized he was becoming mesmerized by the view. He had nothing to focus on but the roadway ahead of the truck.

Samir put a disc into the dashboard player. The music sounded like someone howling into a microphone. After about an hour of this noise, Samir hit the stop button on the player with his thumb. Relative silence filled the cab.

More widely spaced hills lay ahead, and after making their way through these, they were greeted by the site of a shingle plain resembling the surface of the moon. Bits of black volcanic rock lay scattered about, as if blasted from a giant cannon.

"Nothing to see here," said Samir quite suddenly. "Just this—for miles and miles."

"How far?" asked Colbrook.

"Close to a hundred miles," replied Samir, pointing out the window at the desolation.

An hour later, long shadows filled the shallow canyons. The sun was a fiery orange ball hovering above the horizon. The road soon lost its luster, the heat waves emerging from the hot asphalt dissipating into the cooling atmosphere.

Thirty minutes later the truck reached an area of broken ridges about fifty feet high. Following the road through a series of gradual turns that went for miles on end, they started climbing again. At the top of the incline was a high, flat area of dark brown shell limestone. Samir told Colbrook that the region had much quicksand, and that whole bands of camel traders had been swallowed up by it in the not too distant past.

The sun sank below the horizon, until just a sliver of flame was showing above the earth's curvature. The sky ahead glowed with the last rays of direct sunlight, turning from orange to pink to purple, while the cloudless heavens overhead darkened to a deep blue. Soon only the headlights were illuminating the road in advance of the truck's passage.

Not long after sunset they approached a police checkpoint. It consisted of a concrete hut without windows and only a single narrow doorway. Two four-wheel drive vehicles were parked near the building. A single officer stood on the side of the road, flashing a battery-powered lantern.

Samir shifted down through the gears, and the truck gradually slowed to a crawl. The brakes were applied with a slight squeal of hot metal. The headlights stabbing into the darkness ahead created an eerie cone of light that dropped off abruptly into the bleak desert.

The lantern-toting police officer walked to the driver's side of the truck, his shadow stretched monster-like on the blacktop road. He glanced at the door before he stepped up onto the short running board, and then peered through the window before he tapped on the glass with his fingers. Samir opened the powered window, turning his head to speak.

The officer asked a question in Arabic.

Samir replied as if listing a series of items. At the end of this list Colbrook heard him say, "Baris."

The officer was holding onto the tall chrome side mirror now, peering down at the driver's door.

"Displaced Fund," declared Samir. He dropped his arm out the window and hit the side of the door with the palm of his hand, smacking it like a kettle drum.

The policeman jumped lightly to the ground and walked around to the back of the truck. He returned a few seconds later. This time he was on the passenger side.

Colbrook lowered the window. When the glass was down, he was looking at the stubble-covered face of the Egyptian officer. More words were exchanged between Samir, who was now leaning forward in his seat, and the disheveled man of the law. Colbrook waited, hoping the policeman was not overly zealous in his duties and decided to search the truck's cab. His camera case might escape notice, but if it was searched, the firearm inside certainly would not.

Samir was now answering in short guttural phrases. The officer poked Colbrook in the arm with his finger and said a few words of his own in Arabic.

"He's telling you to be more careful," translated Samir. "You shouldn't be riding with strangers. It's dangerous on the desert roads. You might be killed by a fanatic."

"Tell him I'm fine," said Colbrook.

"I already did," spoke Samir, just visible in the dim glow of the dashboard lights.

The officer was now stepping from the running board, his back turned as he hopped to the ground. He waved the truck forward.

Samir slowly accelerated. In the side mirror Colbrook could see the policeman removing a pack of cigarettes from his shirt pocket as he walked back to his post. Framed in the doorway of the illuminated concrete hut, his partner sat reading a magazine in a sagging canvas chair.

Rolling hills with chalky white tops loomed in the headlights after another quarter of an hour. The shelf of limestone soon gave way to crescent dunes of the finest sand—endlessly shifting in the slightest breeze, Samir told him—and it was from beyond these rolling dunes that Colbrook first saw the glimmer of artificial light. As they descended from the escarpment, passing through vast fields of rippled dunes, the lights grew more distinct, casting a glow of yellow illumination into the night sky. Soon the small town of Jaja lay before them.

Limestone outcroppings loomed high along the sides of the road, the roadway itself built on a gravelly bed between the swallowing dunes. Swerving to avoid the mounds of sand that almost blocked the road in places, Samir guided the truck down the sloping grade. When they reached the bottom, a swath of crushed gravel flowed on both sides of the road all the way to the edge of the sleepy town.

Reaching the main intersection in Jaja, Samir steered the truck left, heading due south. He turned to Colbrook.

"This is the Darb al-Arba'een."

Colbrook glanced over at Samir.

"The Forty Days Road," declared Samir. "It ran from Darfur to Asyut in the old days."

"Caravan trail?" asked Colbrook.

Samir nodded. "Ivory, gold, and slaves. Everything of value from Sudan, but especially slaves."

Colbrook imagined the route as a faint cart track in the desert back then. Today it was a gleaming strip of asphalt lined with the glow of yellow and white paint.

The monotony of the desert was broken only by the occasional cluster of date palms or an empty, rubble-filled foundation near the roadside. After a little more than five minutes, a blue sign appeared on the side of the road with the word *Paris* printed on it in both English and Arabic. Samir pointed at the sign and grinned, waiting for Colbrook's reaction. Colbrook said nothing, but turning to Samir he responded with a faint smile. They continued for a few more miles until the town itself was approaching.

Samir slowed the truck as they entered Baris. With the exception of a few scattered streetlamps casting an orange light, the town was almost dark. Though it was only a little after seven, both the main road and the byways appeared to be entirely devoid of life. The few shops that existed were closed, and the street vendors—every town in Egypt had them, Samir assured him—had already packed up their carts and trundled home.

Negotiating the short and narrow streets of Baris, Samir guided the truck to the edge of town. Creeping up to a chain-link gate, he stopped the truck and set the parking brake. They were outside what appeared to be a parking lot surrounded by a wire fence of considerable height. A single metal hut was within the enclosure. It was windowless and had steeply sloping sides. Hanging from the gate was a painted sign that matched the one on the truck's door, indicating the lot was the property of—or at least currently in use by—the Displaced Fund. A series of ordinary halogen spotlights mounted on telephone poles illuminated the area from several different directions.

Colbrook waited as Samir exited the cab and unlocked the gate. It was a double gate, and both sides had to be pulled inward to allow passage of the truck. Samir climbed back into the driver's seat and maneuvered the vehicle into the small lot. He parked it near the back fence, alongside a row of trucks similar to their own. Near the metal hut that resembled a miniature aircraft hangar was parked a white Isuzu Trooper with a wide blue and green stripe painted down its side.

Samir rested in his seat with the door half open, grumbling about unloading the chickens. They had to be put into the metal hut and given some water that was stored in a large tank alongside it. Apparently the rest of the contents of the truck would remain in the back. Colbrook pushed his door all the way open and stepped out. Poised on the running board, he bent down to retrieve his camera bag from beside the seat. Samir yawned, not paying any attention to his quick movements. Bag in hand, Colbrook stepped down from the truck. The ground was covered with packed gravel. It was still radiating heat, but the air was beginning to feel cool.

Samir slipped out of his side of the truck, walking around the front of the parked vehicle towards Colbrook.

"Any hotels around here?" Colbrook asked.

Samir pointed across the road. "Turn left outside the gate. When you reach the corner, go right. Keep going and you'll see a sign for the Lotus Hotel. I've never stayed there myself. I wouldn't expect much. No tourists around here."

Colbrook began making his way to the rear of the truck, the camera bag slung from his shoulder. Samir followed him, his shoes crunching on the gravel. When they reached the tailgate, Samir started banging on it with the palm of his hand, trying to rouse the chickens. Colbrook looked into the back of the truck. The cages were only dimly visible, but he could detect some movement and what sounded like scuffling noises.

Apparently the birds had survived the journey.

"They're alive," remarked Samir. He seemed mildly surprised.

"Are you staying in town?" asked Colbrook.

He knew it was possible Samir might cross paths with Graf at some point and comment on their ride across the desert.

"No. I'm going to Kharga tonight with my cousin," said Samir, pulling a cell phone from his pocket. "Tomorrow I have a long drive to Cairo in a trailer truck." He paused, glancing at Colbrook. "Why? Are you looking for a driver?"

Colbrook shook his head. He began walking towards the open gate.

Following Samir's directions, he soon found himself standing under a sign that read *Lotus Hotel*. It was attached to a three-story brick building in a moderately dangerous state of disrepair: a dreary, uninviting structure that appeared to have been designed by an architect from eastern Europe, circa 1960. Describing it as utilitarian was a compliment.

Pulling the heavy steel door open, Colbrook stepped into the lobby. A single overhead ceiling lamp provided the only illumination. It barely allowed one to see the interior properly, and it seemed likely this was intentional. If the exterior was a disappointment, the interior was downright discouraging. Plastic plants and threadbare furniture filled the small lobby. The carpet was worn to the backing and sprinkled with a generous helping of sand. If the hotel had a cleaning staff, vacuums were not in their repertoire.

The rumpled man at the reception desk looked up from his portable television, giving Colbrook a displeased and somnolent look. Ignoring the man's obvious displeasure, Colbrook told him he needed a room for the night.

"Only one night?" questioned the man, a look of hilarious incredulity on his face.

"Yes—only one," replied Colbrook emphatically. He was beginning to think he might have been better off just stretching a hammock between two palm trees and calling it a night.

After some unnecessary delays and much stamping of papers, the man grumblingly handed a room key to Colbrook, but before he would allow him to leave for his quarters, he demanded his passport. Willing to oblige for no other reason than prevaricating would generate unwanted interest, Colbrook handed over his passport. The man scanned the pages as if searching for some hidden symbol or stamp in the booklet, and finally handed it back with a look of genuine disappointment. Colbrook slipped it into his pocket. He had several others like it back at his apartment, some with vastly different contents.

Indicating that Colbrook should follow him, the man walked to the narrow set of stairs that ascended from one corner of the lobby. Colbrook trailed behind, sliding the camera bag around to his back as he mounted the steps. Soon they were walking down a narrow hallway on the second floor. The rumpled manager led him to a room two doors down on the right. The lock required some rattling of the key before it unlatched, and once this had been accomplished, the man left him alone, departing with a half-hearted handshake and a slight nod.

As far as hotel rooms went, Colbrook had seen worse. There was little question that the contents were original from when the hotel had been built—the early Soviet-inspired period.

Closing the door, he locked the deadbolt.

Leaving his shoes on, he ignored the bed and instead moved towards a comfortable-looking chair in the corner. He put the camera bag down on a small card table near the chair, undid the plastic fasteners, and lifted out the Beretta. Sitting down in the upholstered chair, he positioned the pistol between the seat cushion and the armrest. He closed his eyes and tried to sleep, still seeing the desert road and the endless expanse of drifting sand that threatened to obliterate it.

7

Standing outside the hotel the next morning, Colbrook was greeted with the sight of a town that was primarily built of mud. Many of the windows had no glass in them, and the roofs were a mixture of plastic and metal panels, or in some cases, just woven reeds plastered over with mud. The air was relatively cool, the sun still low over the jagged limestone escarpment to the east.

Looking down the mostly deserted street in both directions, he started to walk south. Several goats crossed his path, searching for discarded vegetable matter on the parched ground. Just beyond the wandering livestock a local farmer was approaching the dusty town, pushing a two-wheeled cart piled with watermelons.

The morning breeze carried with it the smell of frying food, and after detecting a faint cloud of smoke further down the street, Colbrook began walking towards what he could now see was a small eatery. It was a shed-like building, open to the street on its first floor, with colorful scenes of the Hajj painted across its windowless second floor. The extent of its sidewalk frontage was spanned by a low counter into which were set a series of battered cooktops, manned by even more shopworn cooks.

He slowed to watch their preparations.

Not being fluent in Arabic, particularly the Egyptian dialect, he only managed to acquire his breakfast after much gesturing and nodding. A bowl of steaming scrambled eggs in one hand and a large piece of bread in the other—the bread serving as a means to extract the eggs from the bowl—Colbrook stood and ate his meal.

Finishing the eggs, he placed the empty bowl back onto the

counter and turned to look across the street. Something had caught his attention.

There was a white Isuzu Trooper parked on the opposite curb, a wide and distinctive blue and green stripe running along its side. It appeared to be the same truck he had seen parked in the fenced lot. He walked across the street and stood next to it, examining the vehicle more closely. The rearmost side window exhibited a row of small adhesive stickers, displaying everything from *Save Every Whale* to *The Rain Forest Must Live*. The last sticker in the series was a *Displaced Fund* logo.

Hearing some unusual sounds coming from the street behind him, Colbrook looked over his shoulder. A man was leading a temperamental camel down the road. When Colbrook turned back to the Isuzu he saw Graf stepping out of a narrow food stall that was little more than a cubbyhole filled with steam, holding a paper coffee cup. He acknowledged Colbrook's presence with a quick wave of his hand.

"You made it out here after all," Graf declared loudly, walking towards the parked truck.

Colbrook greeted him with deference. He watched Graf very closely, searching for any sign that he might be aware of his method of transportation to Baris. Graf's expression did not hint at the slightest suspicion.

"Decided to see the dig firsthand?" asked Graf.

"That was my plan, although Lowell didn't exactly extend an invitation."

"Don't worry about Lowell. He's always a bit standoffish with strangers." Graf sipped some coffee. "He's just under a lot of pressure lately. The dig it set to close in two weeks. He wants to find something important that will garner the public's interest for next year's fund-raising. You know the drill—as soon as the digging stops the fund-raising begins."

Colbrook nodded in reply. He began to stroll in the direction of the camel, trying to look as if he were taking in the sights of the remote Egyptian town. He walked very slowly, as if he had no particular destination in mind.

Graf sauntered alongside, but took little interest in the camel or the town. "I'm going out to the dig. Why don't you come along?

It'll take you some time to arrange transport in a town like this. Not many tourists come here. Kharga is as far as most of them get."

Colbrook studied Graf's smiling face. It would be suspicious if he turned down the ride. He suspected travel writers never refused such offers—at least not the kind who fancied themselves as something more than guidebook scribblers.

Graf was persistent. "If you go yourself, you'll probably be required to take along a few government security men. I'm surprised you haven't had dealings with them already. How did you arrive—by private taxi?"

"Yes," replied Colbrook. "Late last night."

"Oh, well that explains it," said Graf. In a more serious tone he added, "If you're a tourist you normally can't get more than ten feet down the road once outside of a major city without the Egyptian police escorting you. The last thing they want is a traveler getting shot up. Puts a damper on the tourist trade, and that's half the economy in this country."

Colbrook nodded knowingly.

"Well, come along then. No haggling with Egyptian drivers and no security detail." Graf started walking back to his vehicle, not waiting for Colbrook's response.

When they reached the Isuzu, Graf moved to the other side of the truck, speaking in a loud voice that could be heard over the roof. "The dig is only a few miles southeast of here." He opened the driver's door and slipped inside, checking to be sure the plastic lid on his coffee was secure. He pulled the door closed and put the coffee cup into the cup holder.

Colbrook pulled the passenger door open and climbed in, settling into the soft cloth seat. He placed his camera bag on the floor between his feet. Like the truck Samir had been driving, this vehicle was in excellent condition, though unlike the larger cargo-hauling vehicle, it had clearly been in service for many years.

Graf started the Isuzu and put it into gear.

As they drove down the main road, Graf asked what aspects of travel in Egypt he was writing about.

Colbrook replied that he thought a working dig would be an interesting topic.

The conversation then went from practical matters relating to dealing with assorted Third World governments to desultory comments about the weather. When Graf began to show an interest in discussing publishing, Colbrook steered the conversation onto geology. It proved a successful diversionary topic.

Graf pointed out the driver's window. "Those limestone cliffs form the edge of the depression that marks the boundaries of the Kharga Oasis. Most people think it's below sea level, but I tell you it's not. Almost all of it is at least a hundred or more feet above sea level. The oasis is quite narrow, maybe only twenty miles wide on average, but very long—at least one hundred and twenty miles. The wind prevails out of the east, forming those crescent dunes on the right." He was motioning towards the passenger window. "The whole oasis owes its existence to the plentiful supply of water stored in the porous sandstone which underlies much of the desert around here. Some of the wells are thousands of years old, and they still provide a reliable source of water. The Egyptian government is very interested in trying to expand the arable land and reclaim the desert for agriculture."

Colbrook scanned the scenery through the windshield. They were in a large bowl-shaped valley, with a vast field of dunes to the west. When the road started angling towards the precipitous limestone cliffs, Graf turned onto a much smaller roadway, the truck bouncing jarringly on the wavy blacktop.

"We could stay on the main road a little longer, but it's faster this way," said Graf, talking louder over the strained suspension. He gunned the engine as they went off-road and onto the sandy expanse that stretched to the east of the poorly blacktopped road. With the engine roaring, they started weaving their way through a field of large boulders scattered in the desert. Pointing out the windshield, Graf shouted, "Dush—the Roman fortress."

Colbrook leaned forward to look under the heavily tinted glass along the top edge of the windshield. He could see the crumbled remains of a modest structure perched atop a tall ridge to the south. It was several hundred feet higher than the ground they were now driving on. It did not seem very impressive from where he sat.

Watching Colbrook's gaze, Graf shook his head negatively. He turned to yell over the engine noise, "That's the basilica—an ancient Christian church. The fortress is on the left."

Moving his line of sight in the direction Graf was indicating, Colbrook could now see a giant ruin starkly silhouetted against the bright southeastern sky. It looked like a vast crumbling sand castle. It was below the ridge where the basilica sat, but was higher than the flat desert floor behind it. The distant limestone ridge running the whole length of the oasis showed as a dark outline on the horizon.

When they emerged from the field of boulders, they began following a set of well-worn tire tracks heading east. It was a rudimentary desert road, but appeared to carry frequent traffic. Due to his somewhat excessive speed, Graf could not at first keep the Isuzu entirely on the packed surface, but after running over a large rock he slowed down and remained within the confines of the narrow track.

The gravel-strewn sand soon gave way to swaths of pure yellow sand, and as Graf guided the truck around a low dune forming a hillock, a group of white tents came into view in a shallow depression. Near the tents several four-wheel drive trucks were parked. Not far from these vehicles was a permanent-looking structure made of concrete blocks, covered over with an unusual barrel-vaulted roof of corrugated metal panels. Graf explained that it was designed to keep sand from building up on its surface.

About two hundred feet to the right of the building, on the flat expanse of desert floor that stretched to the very edge of the depression, were the remnants of the temple. The outline of the foundation was clearly visible, but little in the way of vertical structure remained. The last intact wall was merely a low section of mostly jumbled blocks. A single column, the only element of the stone portico still in existence, lay shattered on the ground. Lowell had not been exaggerating when he had said the temple was limited in its remaining features. In centuries past, someone must have quarried most of it away.

As they drove closer Colbrook could see a number of turbaned workmen concentrated at one of the many excavation pits visible around the perimeter of the temple ruins. Various pieces of equipment, clearly fabricated at the site, lay scattered about. A patient white donkey stood staring out into the bleak desert, loaded down with dripping water jugs.

Approaching the concrete-block building at a slow rate of speed,

Graf parked the Isuzu next to the other trucks. He shut off the engine and pulled his paper cup from the center holder, removing the plastic top which had kept the liquid inside. Sipping some coffee, he made a face. "Already cold."

Colbrook pushed the door open, stepping out into the yellow glow of the morning sun. Reaching into the front seat he lifted out his camera bag. Graf soon joined him outside the vehicle, dumping the remains of his beverage into the sand while surreptitiously peering at the right front wheel and fender of the Isuzu. Finding no damage, he turned away from the truck. Colbrook kept pace alongside him as they walked towards the concrete structure. The sand was very soft, similar to that which one would find at any seaside beach, though in certain places patches of hard underlying stone showed through.

"The magazine." Graf was gesturing at the bunker-like building with the curved roof. "It's where they store the finds." He tossed his cup into an empty fifty-gallon drum nearby. "Let's see if we can find Lowell somewhere."

Turning away from the metal drum, Graf moved towards the tents. Colbrook stopped to examine the giant steel garage door on the storage house. It was padlocked at the bottom, and by the looks of the keyed metal box mounted outside the wooden frame, the building probably contained an alarm system. The whole structure was of considerable size. It seemed almost too big for the limited scale of the archeological site.

Quickly catching up to Graf, who was marching inexorably towards the row of white canvas tents, Colbrook watched the robed workers hauling basketfuls of sand from the nearest pit. These baskets were being dumped onto long wooden trestles covered in wire mesh. As the sand sifted through the metal screening into a series of wheelbarrows below, clouds of dust rolled away to the west.

Graf oriented his direction towards the largest of the tents, which sat in the exact center of the group. They were expedition-style shelters, some with metal stovepipes poking through their canvas roofs.

As they continued forward a group of four Egyptian laborers approached them carrying a makeshift wooden ladder, their *galabiyas* caked with sand and streaked with perspiration. They nodded their cloth-wrapped heads as they walked silently by. Colbrook stopped and turned to watch them march away, their bare feet kicking up puffs of dust. They were heading for one of the deeper pits nearby.

Graf had reached the door of the largest tent and was waiting for Colbrook to join him. Colbrook followed him through the covered entrance.

The interior of the tent was filled with boxes and equipment of every shape and size, forming a ring around the inside walls. Within this circle a single metal cot was situated. Next to the bed was a writing stand of flimsy bamboo. Tucked under it was a folding chair that looked as if it might have come from a cache of ancient artifacts itself. The floor was made up of plywood panels.

Within arm's reach of the cot was a low bookshelf filled with a collection of Egyptology books. Two notebook computers sat on a wooden crate being used as an improvised bench near the bookshelf. On the right was a table made of old lumber scraps, the top nothing more than a rough piece of plywood cut in half. It was caked with dirt and dust and bits of stone. A small horsehair brush lay on its surface, along with an assortment of stainless-steel dental tools.

On the opposite side of the tent was a portable generator, a pile of power cords, plastic fencing, giant spools of string, and several large black plastic tool cases. There were many other shiny metal and plastic boxes stacked in neat piles. Some were labeled, but many were not.

Graf turned from where he was standing by the cot. "I guess he's not here." He started to move towards the door.

Colbrook heard a man's voice behind him suddenly exclaim, "Watch it! I've got some delicate pieces." Turning and stepping aside, he allowed the man to enter. It was Gus Lowell.

Looking rather surprised to see both Graf and Colbrook standing in his tent, he swiftly set down the handful of broken pottery he was carrying on the dusty plywood table. Brushing his sand-caked hands off, he stared at Graf for a few seconds.

Graf responded. "We met in Baris. I gave him a ride out. Apparently he's decided your dig would make an interesting travel piece."

Lowell turned to Colbrook. He had a friendly smile on his dusty face. "Here for the tour?"

"If you have the time."

Lowell undid the buttoned flap on his shirt pocket. "It's no trouble. I'd be happy to show you around. Let me just log these items first."

Stepping to his writing table he retrieved a thick spiral notebook. He pulled a pen from his shirt pocket, and began flipping through the pages until he found the one he was looking for. A minute passed as he scribbled in the book. When he was done he turned to Colbrook and said, "You're probably wondering why I don't just use one of those laptop computers. Well I do, at night, when I log everything into the database, but when I initially find something, I prefer to write it out by hand first. Electronics aren't very reliable in the desert. The heat and sand do strange things to computers, especially laptops."

"I can imagine," replied Colbrook. He had already noticed that everything in the tent appeared to be covered in a thin film of sand, and it was not ordinary sand—it was the finest sand he had ever seen. It was really nothing more than silica dust.

Lowell put his spiral notebook away, returning to the plywood table. He was poking at the clay shards, shifting them this way and that. He looked up suddenly from his work, realizing that both men were watching him.

Graf said, "I'll figure out the puzzle while you give the tour."

Lowell quietly laughed, stepping away from the table and walking towards Colbrook. "All joking aside, he does actually seem to have a knack for it."

Both men exited the tent, leaving Graf at the worktable.

Lowell walked along the edge of the row of tents, stepping over the occasional support rope and ground peg, heading towards the remains of the temple some sixty yards away. Colbrook followed a few steps behind the Egyptologist, and soon found himself walking very near the rim of an open pit that was at least eight feet deep. Two wooden ladders built from ordinary lumber leaned against the inside. The pit was empty, but down at the bottom Colbrook could see small red tags stuck in the hard-packed sand. The walls were shored up with pieces of thick plywood and makeshift railroad-tie buttresses. Along its eastern side a length of lightweight plastic fencing blocked the encroaching sands.

"Watch your step," warned Lowell. "The ground is quite loose around the edges."

Passing the hole, Lowell marched on. Off to their right a much larger excavation pit, with sloping sides for easier access, contained four squatting laborers. They were clearing sand from a large stone block buried in the ground. Lowell did not seem too interested. He continued moving towards the temple.

Stepping up onto the wide stone slabs that had once made up the interior flooring of the temple, Lowell made his way to the center of the ruined structure. Colbrook stared down at the stones as he crossed over them, stopping a few feet from Lowell. They stood looking east, towards the shattered column. On their right was the only remaining wall. It ran the full width of the temple, providing a measurable dimension to the mostly vanished structure, but its height was not more than four feet in most places. A few plinth blocks remained at the entrance, but these were so badly worn with age that they almost looked like natural rock formations. Colbrook was surprised by the many different sizes of stones used to make up the temple's floor. A few of the larger slabs had scrape marks on their edges, giving the appearance of having been lifted out and then lowered back in place.

Lowell swept his outstretched hand from left to right. "This is what twenty-four hundred years can do to a limestone structure."

"What dynasty is it again?" asked Colbrook. He was staring down at little circular pieces of shiny metal tape stuck on one of the flooring stones.

"Thirtieth," replied Lowell. "Late Period. Nakhtnebef was pharaoh. I originally assumed it was dedicated to Amen-Re, Mut, and Khonsu, based on some preliminary findings, but now I'm leaning towards Osiris."

"The god of the dead."

Lowell nodded. "I've been finding a considerable quantity of demotic ostraca. Those are pottery shards with written texts on them. I sent a few pieces to a friend in Switzerland who specializes in that difficult script. He told me they were almost all votive offerings to Osiris."

"What about Serapis?" inquired Colbrook.

"Serapis? No. Strictly Ptolemaic. But you're right, temples of that god are quite common throughout Egypt, particularly in the Delta, and even in some of the more remote outlying oases. They were built after the Greeks arrived."

"Did you find anything under the floor?" asked Colbrook, gesturing at the slabs near his feet.

"A bronze statuette," Lowell answered. "It's quite small and badly damaged, but it looks like it could be an Osiris figure with the *atef* crown. Hard to say for certain until we piece it back together. I'm surprised we didn't find more of them. They were commonly used for temple offerings, and they're usually in abundant caches." He paused before continuing. "Our real hope was to find hidden chambers under this floor—they've been referred to in previous studies as priest holes. Some say they were used for oracles, where the priest could hide from view and speak to the visitor in a disembodied voice, while others think they were just used to hide treasure. Personally, I think both theories are correct."

Colbrook pointed his shoe at one of the silver circles. "What are these?"

"Those are for the total station," Lowell said. When Colbrook gave him a blank look, Lowell continued. "Do you know what a transit is? Well, it's an electronic version of a transit and an EDM. That's an infrared electronic distance measuring system. The total station combines these two features with a data recorder. Here, I'll show you the instrument." Lowell began walking towards the northeast corner of the temple floor.

After they had stepped from the stone slabs and down onto the sandy ground, they began climbing a low mound of sand that was situated on the east side of the temple. At the top of the mound was a large fiberglass tripod with a reflective silver bag covering something square mounted on the top. Colbrook worked his way up the sandy rise beside Lowell. When they reached the top, they were about ten to fifteen feet higher than the temple remains. Colbrook noticed that the tripod legs were bolted securely to metal pipes pounded deep into the ground.

Lowell pulled the silver bag from the top of the tripod, revealing a bright orange instrument about the size of a large toaster. "This is a total station." He pointed back to the temple floor. "Those bits of tape are used to take measurements. We also use a peanut prism

and a standard prism on a pole." He reached into a nylon sack lying under the tripod and lifted out a pole about five feet long with
a square card mounted on the top.

"You're surveying the temple," stated Colbrook, staring at the
expensive-looking instrument.

"Exactly," responded Lowell. He lowered the pole and put the
cover back over the total station. "Once we have all the data points,
we can transfer the information into a CAD system and produce
a very accurate two-dimensional map. The more data points you
provide, the more accurate the survey. We could do three dimen-
sions with a bit more labor, but as you can see"—he waved his hand
down the slope—"it's not that important for a site like this one."

Colbrook nodded in agreement. He could feel the hot sun on
the back of his neck. Now he really was thinking about sunscreen.

"We also use the total station to pinpoint any finds. The information is then used to produce a detailed Harris matrix." Lowell
stopped speaking, sensing that Colbrook was not following his
improvised lecture, but he soon picked up where he had left off.
"That's a stratigraphic program designed to improve interpretation
of the deposits. All digging is done with the basic assumption that
the deeper one gets the older the material one will find."

"Is that true?" questioned Colbrook.

"Yes. But only if the site has not been disturbed in the past."

Colbrook studied the ground. "Looks like you don't want this
tripod going anywhere."

Lowell nodded. "One must have a definite point from which to
start the survey. It's all trigonometry. The data recorder stores the
angle, elevation, distance, and the position of the instrument. I take
this down every night and remount it in the morning. With this soft
ground here I'd never get it exactly in the right place again. That's
where the pipes come in. If you put them deep enough, they won't
move. Come—I'll show you the main excavations. That's really
what you're interested in, isn't it?"

Leading the way, Lowell plunged down the slope. Colbrook already had sand in his shoes, and this sudden descent added even
more. Now he knew why Lowell wore tall work boots. The Egyptian laborers solved this problem by not wearing any shoes at all.

When they reached level ground, Lowell advanced along the

north side of the temple, where most of the larger pits were situated. Making a line for the most crowded pit, Lowell stepped around a group of Egyptian workers hunched at its rim and smacked his hand against a standing triangle of very thick wood beams. Hanging from the center was a large metal pulley with a stout rope looped through it. It was positioned over the corner of the pit, the rope snaking its way into the void below. Colbrook could hear the sound of digging mixed with guttural Arabic. Cigarette smoke drifted out of the hole.

"This is our primary pit right now," said Lowell. He pointed across the ground to a series of smaller pits staggered along the edge of the temple foundation. "The others are just preliminary excavations. We dig those first to see if we find anything of interest. If we do, we expand them outwards."

The pits were marked with strings attached to plastic stakes. Little tags fluttered from the strings in places, presumably noting some important spot. In some areas the pits had been merged into a whole series, forming what amounted to a long trench. Some of the larger pits had canvas stretched across sections of them.

"The tarps are for the sun," noted Lowell, watching Colbrook's gaze. "It makes it easier on the workers. By noon we'd be broiling out here."

"Looks like you start early," observed Colbrook.

"Seven in the morning," replied Lowell. "But we stop at one in the afternoon." He made this last remark in a disappointed tone.

Colbrook heard a whirring sound and looked towards the primitive hoisting system. A basketful of sand and gravel worked its way to the top of the pit. It hovered at the edge, swaying slightly.

"That's a *zambil*," declared Lowell. He reached out to steady the basket. "They're made from old car tires." He motioned to the group of hunched workers.

One of the men, wearing a bright green turban and an exceptionally sand-encrusted *galabiya*, dashed over to remove the *zambil* from the metal hook it was hanging from. Carrying it, he staggered to one of the long wooden trestle tables covered in wire mesh. He dumped the contents onto the table and walked back to the pit with the empty basket, refastening it to the winch. Then he rejoined his companions.

"Let's take a look, shall we?" Lowell led the way to the table.

Colbrook watched Lowell push the sand around with his hands. Most of the material sifted readily through the wire mesh, but a few small chunks remained on the surface. Lowell examined each very carefully. One by one he flung them into the wheelbarrow below. The last piece in the sieve, which looked almost like a broken seashell, he kept.

"Anything?" inquired Colbrook.

"Pottery," replied Lowell. He held the shard up. It was covered in very faint brown characters. "Probably a votive offering to Osiris written by a priest at the request of a common man." He dusted it off and slipped it into his shirt pocket.

"Do you dump every basketful through the screen?"

"The workers dig with trowels first, and always sift by hand. But when they have enough material removed that they can fill a *zambil*, they transfer it into the basket and winch it up top. Then the accumulated debris is dumped through the screening tables to do one last check. It's a two-stage process. I have an excellent pit supervisor—Daud." Lowell pointed at a bearded Egyptian man in a light blue *galabiya* kneeling at the edge of a nearby pit. "He keeps an eye on the men when they work."

"Where are the workers from? Around here?"

"No. They're from Kharga. Some of them were working on the temple of Hibis. The SCA has been doing ongoing restoration work on it for years. I pay a little better. One might say I borrowed the best of them that I could find." As an afterthought he added, "They stay here all week, and only leave on the weekends."

"I see you don't use students."

Lowell chuckled. "It's always been common practice in Egypt to use local labor. I have nothing against students, especially since they work for free, but the circumstances of this dig do not allow it."

Colbrook pondered Lowell's last statement, watching an Egyptian man approaching from the direction of the tents. He was short and squat, wearing a pair of jeans, a white shirt, and a sun-bleached straw hat. Lowell turned to receive him.

"Problems?"

"Just seeing who your visitor is," said the man.

"This is Mr. Colbrook. He's a travel writer." Then Lowell added sarcastically, "Don't worry, he didn't bring a shovel."

The man smiled and laughed. "Okay, okay. Just checking. It's my job." He walked away towards one of the excavation pits.

"That's Rashad," said Lowell. "He's the SCA inspector for the dig."

Colbrook remembered Lowell casting aspersions on the man at the Karnak Club.

"He's not all that bad. I've seen a lot worse," declared Lowell, now looking towards the row of tents.

"So how does a typical day start?" asked Colbrook.

Lowell stared at the ground, his expression thoughtful. "Well, let's see. I usually get up around six fifteen, get dressed, and eat a quick breakfast of tea and toast. Sometimes I have eggs if time permits."

"You have a camp cook?" asked Colbrook, ignoring Lowell's lack of seriousness.

"Sure, but he prepares breakfast at ten o'clock. That's too late for me. I prefer eating early."

"Then what?"

"I set up the total station and look over my map, a hand drawing that I use for sketching the site and marking the locations of any finds. The later CAD work is for absolute precision." Lowell folded his arms, his eyes roaming over the site. "Roll call is at seven. The pit supervisor checks with the SCA inspector, and both verify that the site is undisturbed—meaning nothing was taken or dug during the night—and only then are the laborers allowed to resume their previous day's digging."

"Some of the work looks pretty dangerous," Colbrook noted.

"It can be," admitted Lowell. "Most of the injuries seem to occur towards the end of the work day."

"What kind of injuries? Anything serious?"

"No. Mostly just scrapes and bumps. At worst a broken bone. Usually fingers. We've been lucky so far on this dig. But we're not moving big blocks around." Lowell was looking at Colbrook again. "A local doctor attends to things. He's on our payroll."

"Do you take your own photos?"

"Yes. I don't have a photographer on site. I do it myself. I've got a Nikon SLR—digital. Sure beats film any day," replied Lowell. He looked down at Colbrook's camera bag and asked, "What do you have? A point and shoot?"

"It's a little more complicated than that." Colbrook surveyed the dig site. "What happens when someone finds something?"

"The pit supervisor or his assistant marks the location with a tag and a number. They'll notify me and I'll bring my camera to photograph the item before it's removed. After documenting the object in place, I'll assist with its removal. Once the artifact is dislodged, I'll clean it using a brush, take more photographs, and then carry it back to my tent for registering."

As Lowell finished, a battered Land Cruiser pulled into the line of parked trucks. Two Egyptian men got out and wandered over to the temple. One of them was carrying a bolt-action rifle that looked like a relic from the First World War. Their clothes were vaguely military in style, but nothing properly matched.

"Guards," said Lowell. "Another requirement of the SCA."

Lowell led Colbrook toward the tents. When they reached the canvas lodgings, Colbrook noticed a dust trail forming on the track connecting the dig site to the paved road. A red minivan was the cause. Lowell soon spotted the vehicle.

"The documentary crew," he muttered. "I see they're back again." He turned to Colbrook. "I'll introduce you."

The minivan soon arrived and stopped beside the other parked vehicles. The front doors opened and the director and cameraman—Coslovich and Cavoski—stepped out into the blazing sun. Nedic wasn't with them.

Lowell waited as both men approached, and when they were closer said, "Should we expect any shooting today?"

Coslovich paused mid-step. He looked irritated and haggard. His eyes were rimmed with dark circles, and his black hair was sweat-plastered to his head. He seemed only vaguely aware of his surroundings, the focus of his attention somewhere else. Cavoski was not as tired looking, but he had a troubled expression that he tried to mask with a half-hearted smile.

Coslovich spoke first.

"No shooting today."

"No, not today," agreed Cavoski. He looked like he was about to add something else, but before he could, Lowell gestured toward Colbrook.

"This is Martin Colbrook," he told them. "He's a travel writer. I met him in Luxor at the Karnak Club. He's writing an article about what goes on at a real dig."

Cavoski nodded. Coslovich barely registered a response.

"Maybe I can interview you later," suggested Colbrook.

"Yes," said Coslovich in a monotone voice. "Maybe we can do that." He resumed walking.

Cavoski silently kept pace at the director's side, his smile fading as he passed by.

Colbrook turned to watch them. The two Serbians disappeared into the last tent in the row. Lowell led Colbrook to his own tent, a thoughtful look on his face. They stepped inside.

Graf looked up as they entered. He was still standing behind the plywood table, pieces of clay pottery in his hand.

"Any luck?" Lowell asked. He walked over to the table, staring down at the scattered pieces. "Anything fit?"

"No," replied Graf. "Just random bits."

Lowell nodded. He walked to a large plastic box on the floor near his cot. Opening the top he pulled out a sealable plastic bag. He handed it to Graf.

Placing the pieces into the clear bag, Graf handed it back to Lowell, who then used a black marker to scribble something on the imprinted white label. Colbrook watched as he put the bag on a nearby shelf with a jumble of others.

"The Serbians are back," said Lowell, turning from the shelf. "Not all of them, just the director and the cameraman."

Graf made a face, as if he disapproved. Lowell began searching for something. It proved to be his hand broom. He found it lodged between two plastic binders on the bookshelf. Lowell moved past Graf and started brushing off the plywood table with the long-bristled broom. Graf coughed at the cloud of fine dust, backing away from the table.

"Going down to Sudan again?" inquired Lowell. He did not seem to mind the dust. When he was done, he stooped to put the broom under the table.

"I've got a convoy set up for tomorrow afternoon," declared Graf. "I'll probably go with it. The situation is getting much worse. No food. No water. The recent refugee problem is depleting my supplies. The advance depot across the border has also been experiencing raids. One of the security guards was killed the other day." He glanced across the table at Colbrook.

"You can't help everyone," said Colbrook in a serious tone.

"Helping the right people is what matters," stated Graf.

A low rumbling noise came from outside. It sounded like an approaching truck.

Graf stepped to the entrance, thrust his head out of the tent, paused for a moment in careful observation, and then moved back from the swaying canvas flaps. He stepped alongside Colbrook, placing his hand on his shoulder. "How was the tour? Did you get everything you need for your travel piece?"

"Plenty. I'm not writing a dissertation."

Graf laughed, steering Colbrook out of the tent. Lowell followed after them.

A small box truck was parked outside the magazine, the door emblazoned with the readily identifiable *Displaced Fund* logo. Colbrook had not noticed this truck at the lot in Baris.

"Well," announced Graf, "I must see to my work." He turned and walked quickly away, heading for the truck.

Lowell turned to Colbrook. "I have to register some more things, and I'm falling behind on my drawings. If you want to get back to Baris right away, before it gets really hot, someone could probably give you a ride. You could ask Rashad. He's usually sending someone on a useless errand into town."

"I think maybe I'll walk around and take some photos," replied Colbrook. He patted his camera bag. "I was also thinking of walking over to the Roman fort."

Lowell nodded. "I usually take a break around noon. If you want, come by my tent. If you're going to Qasr Dush you might want to start now, before the sun gets too high. It's going to be brutal in the afternoon. There's usually a guard on the road to the fort, and someone in the rest house nearby. You could probably get a ride back to town that way, if you ask. But don't count on any air conditioning." Lowell marched across the sandy ground in his work boots, retreating into his tent.

Colbrook spent the next hour walking around the site. He kept a close watch on the tents to see if the Serbians ever showed themselves. They did not. Graf eventually departed in the Isuzu, following the box truck back down the desert road. Lowell eventually emerged from his tent, blinking in the bright sunlight. He soon descended into one of the shaded excavation pits nearby.

At eleven o'clock Colbrook crossed paths with Rashad. The SCA inspector guided him to the small but well-equipped field kitchen. The cook, an older Egyptian man who obviously had many years of experience working in remote locations, offered him a substantial choice of foodstuffs. By the time Colbrook left the mess tent he had a small but complete picnic lunch carefully wrapped in sheets of newspaper. He stowed the food in his camera bag and made his way towards Qasr Dush.

He followed the desert track away from the dig site, heading roughly west and then south. A hundred yards down the dusty track he veered off toward a distant set of buildings. He suspected these were the rest houses used by the guards. Pushing his sunglasses as close to his eyes as he could get them—the ground glare was extreme—he trudged on with his shirt collar turned up over the back of his neck. Soon the only thing he cared about was finding some shade.

Ten minutes later he was standing under the overhanging roof of one of the small desert buildings. It was locked and dark inside. He walked the short distance to the other building. It was in the same state. So much for hitching a ride back to Baris with the guards. Apparently they had not arrived, or maybe it was their day off.

Colbrook removed the bottle of water the cook had given him from his camera bag. Drinking only a mouthful, he placed it back into the bag and began ascending the hillside that led up to the Roman fort, following a narrow and rocky footpath. Broken potsherds littered the ground, and he stopped to pick up a few. They were unmarked and very brittle. He tossed them away before resuming his hike.

It did not take long to reach the Roman fort, and Colbrook found that it provided an excellent view of the valley below. The fort looked much further away from the dig site than the dig site looked from the fort. He could see almost every part of the archeological excavation, and he had not even climbed the fortress ramparts, which were at least another thirty feet higher.

Walking to the eastern side of the ruins, Colbrook admired the sandstone temple which merged with the rest of the structure. He spotted a small black and white sign stuck in the ground, written in English, which indicated that it was a temple of Serapis built during Domitian's reign. Continuing forward, he walked around to the northern side and entered the temple through a pylon. Passing beneath the stone gateway, he stepped into an enclosed pillared hall. Two adjacent side rooms were covered with a barrel-vaulted ceiling of interesting design. A set of crumbling stone stairs ascended to the flat roof above. Carefully climbing these steps, he soon reached the rooftop, cautious of the weakened state of the high platform.

Finding a shady spot in the corner of a tall mud-brick wall, he sat down facing the dig site. He pulled open his camera bag and began unpacking his ad hoc lunch. It was not that uncomfortable in the shady nook, and he quickly consumed his *shawarma*, a sandwich filled with shredded chicken, tomato, and sesame paste. Tossing the pita bread remnants to some friendly birds roosting nearby on the temple's cornice, he began eating a large chunk of semolina cake. He drank the bottle of water down to about half, and then packed it away. His watch indicated it was a little past twelve.

Settling in for the afternoon, Colbrook watched the dig site. He might have been better served with a pair of binoculars, but his view was superb all the same. Not only could he see the whole site from where he sat, but it was even possible to determine individual identities. On more than one occasion he spotted Lowell walking around the trestle tables, sifting through the sandy debris by hand.

The afternoon soon gave way to late afternoon. When sunset neared, Colbrook finally rose from his secluded spot and stretched. He was tired, but growing more alert with the cooling atmosphere. Reaching down into his camera bag, he removed the pistol and secured it under his belt.

Dusk arrived, the last skylight fading gradually.

In time the dig site was almost dark, its presence revealed only by a few spotlights around the magazine and the gold-colored lantern light spilling from the tents. When the wind began to blow down off the eastern escarpment, swirling particles of dust across the landscape, the tents took on the appearance of giant glowing candles stuck in the sand below. Overhead the moonless sky provided a magnificent display of twinkling stars.

Colbrook descended the stairs and emerged from the temple's facade.

Ten minutes later he was crouched behind a large boulder, not fifty yards from the outer perimeter of the dig site. He searched for the guards he had seen earlier, but could not find them anywhere. Other than the sound of his own labored breathing—the result of his quick descent—and the wind sweeping through the rocks, the camp was silent. He remained where he was for an uncomfortably long period of time. Then, without a sound, someone pushed open the flap of Lowell's tent.

Lowell stepped out, followed by two *galabiya*-wearing men. In the dim lighting afforded by the tents, both of Lowell's companions looked like laborers, but as the three men walked closer to the magazine's halogen spotlights it became readily apparent that one of them was the pit supervisor, Daud. The other Colbrook did not recognize.

Gesturing with his hand, Lowell guided the two men to the red minivan, still parked where it had been left earlier by Coslovich and Cavoski. Daud slid open the side door of the van and clambered inside. Lowell and the other man stood waiting. Soon Daud reappeared at the edge of the door, pushing a large plastic case. It looked heavy and unwieldy.

Colbrook pressed closer to the boulder. The case was one of the two he had seen carried by Nedic and Gvero into Hamed's with relative ease and then removed with much difficulty.

Lifting the case at one end, Daud tilted it out the door. Lowell and the other man grabbed the sides and pulled it from the vehicle. They placed it carefully on the ground. Daud disappeared into the back of the van, and soon reappeared with the second case. This one was placed down alongside the first. Slipping from the side door, Daud pulled it slowly closed, trying to minimize the noise of the latching mechanism.

Lowell stood by the two cases while the two men walked briskly away, heading toward the tents. They entered the nearest one, emerging from its dimly lit interior a minute later with a piece of heavy canvas mounted between two long wooden poles. It looked very much like a stretcher. Their bare feet making no sound as they walked, the two men carried it silently back to the minivan.

Daud and the other man crouched down, placing the poles and the attached piece of canvas on the ground near the cases. Lowell reached for the nearest container impatiently, waiting for someone to give him a hand lifting it. All three men then worked in unison to get both cases centered on the canvas framework, one behind the other. Lowell and the other man each grabbed a pole, while Daud, kneeling at the front, prepared to lift his end. With coordinated effort they raised the cases and immediately began trudging towards the dark excavation pits. They stopped a few times to change direction, maneuvering expertly around obstacles. Soon they were approaching one of the smaller, deeper pits.

Colbrook moved to the opposite end of the boulder.

The procession had already ended.

With both cases now resting on the ground at the rim of the pit, Lowell descended the wooden ladder that was already in place, disappearing from view. Not long after a length of thick rope flew up from the bottom of the hole. Daud took hold of it. The other man began tying a loop around the first case, passing the rope through the handle several times before pulling it tight. Lowell reappeared at the top of the ladder. He remained perched there as his assistants lifted the case and carried it over. Lowell guided the case down the ladder's uprights, the two men slowly letting out rope as Egyptologist and case descended haltingly from view.

The tension on the rope soon relaxed. A minute or so passed before Lowell resurfaced, carrying the bulky case with little difficulty. He handed it to Daud, releasing his grip before the pit supervisor had secured his own. The plastic container dropped to the ground. Lowell flinched at the hollow thump, muttering under his breath.

The second case was lowered and retrieved in the same fashion, though both Lowell and Daud exercised more caution when maneuvering it from the top of the ladder. Both cases were then placed back on the stretcher, and Daud and the other man made haste with the empty containers, retracing their path, padding along in almost complete silence. They disappeared into the tent they had emerged from earlier.

Lowell climbed back down the ladder.

Colbrook turned to observe the rest of the camp. Nothing moved. The wind was not as strong as it had been earlier, but it was steady.

He scrambled closer to the pit Lowell was within, until he was not more than sixty feet from it. Easing to the ground behind a screening station, he lay still. The sound of shoveling was faint but distinct. Soon he could hear the sounds of tamping.

Lowell was salting the dig.

8

When Lowell emerged from the pit he was carrying a short folding shovel. Standing for a moment and inspecting his handiwork, he began brushing the sand off his pants. A gust of wind blew from the east, and the Egyptologist straightened, looking across the shadowy landscape, his shirt sleeves flapping in the sudden breeze. The horizon behind him showed as a silhouette of serrated rock.

Turning toward the camp, Lowell cautiously made his way back in the direction of his tent, weaving around shallow depressions, exploratory holes, and deeper pits, stepping over strings with a familiarity which could only have been acquired through experience. The flaps closed on his tent, and he disappeared from sight.

Colbrook relaxed, rising to his feet from behind the mound of sifted debris. He waited a few minutes before moving closer to the recently vacated excavation, stepping warily between the piles of sand. Nearing the pit, he was almost tempted to climb down the ladder; after a moment of contemplation he dismissed the idea. Whatever had been buried at the bottom would no doubt be miraculously found tomorrow.

Moving away from the pit, Colbrook focused his attention on the Serbians' tent. Staring at the glow of yellowish lantern light showing through the canvas fabric, his thoughts were suddenly interrupted by the sound of a distant engine.

Two bright spots of light were rapidly approaching across the desert from the direction of the main road, their veering and bouncing movement indicating a high degree of recklessness on the part of the driver. Graf immediately came to mind.

126

Scrambling forward, Colbrook began searching for a suitable hiding place. The nearest rock, a low and sloping projection of sandstone, was his only immediate option. Flattening himself down on the ground behind it, he lay on his left side, keeping the pistol out of the sand. The engine noise grew louder, and soon a band of light swept across the ground, for an instant illuminating the dig site. As the vehicle passed and gradually moved away, Colbrook raised himself to his knees.

It was Graf's white Isuzu.

Dropping back down, he waited until he heard the truck crunch to a halt and the engine shut off, and then slowly raised his head to look over the top of the rocky outcrop. The vehicle was parked in front of the magazine, its glass and metal gleaming beneath the halogen spotlights.

Graf already had the driver's door open, and appeared to be rummaging around for something in the front seat. Pushing the door open all the way with his foot, he stepped out onto the packed sand and gravel surface. He turned to close the door, shutting it with a thump. Apparently Graf did not have the same level of concern that Lowell did when it came to making noise.

Walking at a determined pace, Graf headed for the row of white tents. Passing almost all of them, including Lowell's, he strode to the very last one in the line: the tent the Serbians were occupying. A triangle of light was cast briefly from its entrance, and then Graf vanished, swallowed up in the canvas flaps.

Colbrook shifted his attention to Lowell's tent, watching for any sign of the Egyptologist. Lowell's abode remained quiet, and there were no indications of movement anywhere else in the camp. Colbrook looked again towards the Serbians' quarters. Occasionally a dark shadow stirred and passed across the wall of the tent, but no one made use of its entrance. The only sound he heard was the faint whisper of sand shifting across the surface of the dig site. He would have to get closer to find out what was going on inside.

Taking one last quick look around the rest of the darkened camp, Colbrook moved rapidly in the direction of the ruined temple.

Reaching the thick slabs of flooring stone that made up the temple's base, he skirted their rightmost edge until he was on the southern side of the dig, away from the tents which lay to the north. Walking east, in the general direction of the high escarpment, he soon arrived at the entrance side of the temple. Turning left to avoid the remains of the smashed pillar, and then passing the mound of sand he had climbed earlier with Lowell, he made a dash for the largest debris pile. He reached it seconds later, dropping down behind it.

Directly ahead and less than sixty yards away, the tents sat like a row of giant paper lanterns.

Colbrook rested for a moment. There was no cover between his position and the Serbians' quarters. If someone stepped out of any of the tents while he was crossing the open ground he would almost certainly be discovered. Despite the lack of any moon, the starlight provided surprisingly good illumination, the desert sky being absolutely clear. Raising one knee up from the ground, he paused at the top of the sandy, rock-filled pile.

The flaps on the Serbians' tent were suddenly pulled back.

Someone stepped out.

Slowly lowering himself to the ground behind the pile of debris, Colbrook studied this solitary figure.

It was definitely not Graf. It was Coslovich.

Looking up into the star-filled sky, his back now half turned, the Serbian director puffed away on a cigarette, the tip glowing brighter as he inhaled.

The light inside the tent suddenly dimmed, the canvas taking on a distinctly orange hue. Then the tent went dark. Seconds later a glow of much whiter but more confined light told Colbrook that a battery-powered lantern had been substituted for the original gas one.

The flaps parted again, Cavoski and Graf now emerging into the night. Coslovich turned as Graf said something to him, blowing out a cloud of smoke in response. Cavoski was carrying a large duffel bag, and appeared to be struggling to hold it with both hands. Graf became more animated, almost as if he were arguing with Coslovich, but Colbrook could not make out what he was saying.

Coslovich dropped his cigarette into the sand and stood looking at Graf, nodding his head. Moments later the three men began walking along the row of tents, heading towards the magazine. Colbrook waited until they had reached Graf's Isuzu before standing up to get a better view.

Graf got behind the wheel. Cavoski opened the square door on the rear of the truck and heaved the duffel bag inside. Shutting it, the cameraman opened the side door and slipped into the back seat. Coslovich swung open the front passenger door and climbed in. Doors slammed and the Isuzu backed away from the concrete-block building. When the reverse lights went off, it turned to the west, its taillights getting smaller as it began to negotiate the desert track leading back to the paved road.

Colbrook sprinted towards the recently vacated tent. The ground he moved over was devoid of pits and strings, apparently being too far from the temple to have been yet considered for excavation. All the same he kept a wary eye out for any unexpected obstacles.

Halfway to the Serbians' tent he saw a flap opening on one of the tents further down the row. A man was stooping in its entrance, holding what appeared to be a shallow cooking pan. Colbrook slowed, dropping to the ground. He lay still, wondering if he had been spotted. The man sent the contents of the pan flying into the sand, and soon the flaps dropped back into place. Colbrook watched the tent for several minutes, the pungent odor of exotic spices drifting to him. When the man did not reappear, he stood up and dusted himself off. The desolate tract to his right was beginning to look more inviting.

Distancing himself from the row of tents and moving out into the open desert, he approached a series of wooden stakes set in the ground. He slowed his pace, turning to intercept them. When he reached one of the markers he knelt down to examine it. It was not stuck in the sandy ground as he had thought, but was slipped through a narrow hole in what looked to be a buried stone slab. A crosswise piece of wood was nailed to the marker, preventing it from falling through the hole. It seemed as if a small pit or shaft was beneath the flat stone.

After a quick glance in the direction of the tents, he cleared away the sand around the hole with his hand, revealing more of the stone. It was about three feet square, and far too heavy to move. He re-buried it. Rising from the ground, he followed what proved to be a continuous line of these markers, spaced roughly ten yards apart. On some, white numbers were painted.

Now moving at a half jog, Colbrook followed the stakes as they marched to the northwest. After sixty or seventy yards the markers disappeared altogether. He stopped and listened. The dig site remained quiet. Ahead and to his left was the Serbians' tent.

He approached it cautiously, watching the glow of the battery-powered lantern inside. Nothing moved in front of the light and he saw no shadows on the canvas walls. He stopped to listen for any sounds coming from inside the tent, but heard only the wind rushing over the ground. A hundred feet beyond the Serbians' quarters the markers resumed their steady march across the desert.

Being careful not to trip over any pegs or ropes as he moved alongside the tent, he stepped swiftly around to its front, pushing through the entrance flaps.

It was devoid of occupants. Hanging from the center post was a cylindrical LED lantern.

The Serbians' tent was almost as crowded with equipment and furnishings as Lowell's, and had a similar floor of coated and hinged plywood panels carefully fitted together. Most of the space on the left side of the tent was taken up by four large folding cots. The right side of the tent was filled with assorted production equipment and storage cases.

There were lighting stands, portable lights, cables of varying lengths and types, boxes of replacement lamps, rolls of tape, sheets of plastic in various colors rolled in clear tubes, and a quantity of reflector boards in assorted sizes, their plastic frames propped up against the tent's front wall. There was also a small lightweight dolly and sections of tubular aluminum track.

Against the back wall was a large makeshift desk of plywood, alongside which were two padded folding chairs. A pair of LCD monitors and a black computer tower sat on the desk, cables snaking from the computer in all directions.

Two portable generators were positioned almost adjacent to the tent's entrance. One of these was quite large, with pneumatic wheels, whereas the other was considerably smaller, lacking wheels, and appeared to be connected to a wiring harness. A yellow cable ran from the smaller generator to a power distribution box and a large block of batteries. From the batteries another cable ended at an ordinary power strip. It was here that the computer plugs were connected, drawing electricity from the storage cells.

The computer system looked ordinary enough, but on closer inspection it was readily apparent that the desk contained a whole host of additional and less common hardware—a portable audio mixing board, a large external case enclosing multiple hard drives, expensive-looking speakers, and a keyboard marked for use with specific software. Alongside the hard-drive enclosure was a plastic tray full of flat memory cards. Apparently the documentarians preferred to edit in the field. They certainly appeared to have all the necessary equipment for a full-fledged production.

Colbrook began systematically searching the desk. He slid trays and books around, looked under piles of stacked paper and plastic binders, shuffled compact flash cards, lifted loose CDs and DVDs, poked around behind the small speakers, and even briefly opened an eyewear case containing a pair of sunglasses. Putting everything back where he had found it, he stepped away from the desk.

He began rummaging around in the back right corner of the tent where some of the larger cases were stored. He opened all of them. They contained legitimate production equipment. Next he directed his attention to a metal cart with shelves. A collection of flat plastic cases lined the upper shelf. He pulled one out of the row and opened it. It held matte-box filters in sets of different colors, stacked in threes. He placed the case back, and opening another, found a set of lens filters in varying gradations. He opened all of these cases; they contained only filters. Snapping the last case shut and slipping it back where he had found it, Colbrook looked around for anything he might have missed.

His head down and his hands searching methodically, he spent the next ten minutes examining everything in the tent. He left no case or box unopened. Cables were pushed aside, carts moved, lights lifted, and stands tilted. He then looked under the four canvas cots, where he found only more dolly track, assorted clamps, and folded reflector boards.

Moving to the back left corner of the tent, he stopped to briefly reexamine an oddly shaped plastic storage case containing a carbon-fiber tripod. Turning from it, he stepped onto a section of the floor made of unfinished plywood. It was being used as a substitute for the hinged and coated plywood panels found elsewhere on the tent's floor. It was only half a sheet, and when Colbrook put his full weight onto it, the center sagged noticeably. He retreated from its creaking surface.

Dropping to one knee, he pried up a corner with his thumb and began pulling the plywood sheet towards himself. There was an opening in the ground, surrounded by ragged stonework. He pulled the dirty and frayed wood panel aside.

Stepping closer to the edge of the hole, he hovered along its crumbling rim. A narrow wooden ladder disappeared into the darkness below, the top of the uprights crudely sawn off to allow the plywood sheet to lie flat on the opening. It was pitch black below the first few rungs.

Colbrook went to get a flashlight. Several were lying in a shallow plastic box nearby. He selected one constructed of dull black metal. Turning it on for an instant to be sure it worked, he pushed it into his pocket. He cautiously stepped down onto the rickety ladder and descended several rungs. Stretching his arm out, he grabbed the sheet of heavy plywood. Sliding it partially over the hole, he descended two more rungs.

With one hand gripping the ladder and the other pulling the plywood sheet, he managed to work the panel back into place. Sand and pebbles showered his head, released by the passage of the plywood across the rough edge of the opening. A narrow sliver of light still showed from along one edge of the sheet. He shifted the plywood a small amount until this disappeared completely. Removing the flashlight from his pocket he switched it on, playing the beam over the panel above, making some final adjustments with the palm of his hand.

When he was satisfied the sheet was in its proper place, he began descending the ladder, one hand gripping the upright, the other holding the flashlight, directing it towards the vertical wall of smooth sandstone.

As he moved from rung to rung the ladder twisted from side to side. At one point he came across a wide board bolted across the uprights between two of the rungs, and on closer inspection realized it was being used to repair a damaged section of the ladder. He moved cautiously below this structural addition.

In several places he noticed Roman numerals carved into the wall. They were small but deeply incised.

He turned the flashlight towards the ground, continuing down. Far below, the bottom of the ladder rested on packed sand. He had at least another fifteen feet to go, and had descended at least that distance already.

When he reached the bottom he was standing in a sandstone tunnel. The walls and ceiling were seamless, as if cut through a continuous vein of rock. The width of the passage was at least eight feet, the height slightly less than that. Where the ceiling and the walls joined they formed a corner, but the floor was finished with shallow, sloping sides. Colbrook suspected it was an ancient aqueduct, probably built during the Roman era, designed to carry water for great distances across the desert.

The tunnel ended at the vertical shaft he had just descended, and he could only walk in one direction. Moving cautiously along the underground passage, shining his flashlight down the remarkably straight corridor, he came upon a small rectangular hole just above his head. He could feel air flowing from it. It appeared to be some sort of ventilation shaft, and he had more than a suspicion that far above was a slab-covered hole marked out in the desert.

Continuing down the passage, the only sounds he heard came from his own shoes on the stone floor. At one point he had to bend down to get through a section of the passageway filled with sand.

Fifty feet beyond this he reached a branch in the tunnel. One opening went roughly west, the other more easterly. The corners at the side branches were rounded, had wider mouths, and pitched noticeably down from where he was standing. He now accepted that his aqueduct theory was correct.

Since the western tunnel was nearly half filled with sand and rubble a short distance beyond its entrance, he chose the eastern passage. Residing in it were a substantial number of moderately large spiders that scuttled away from his sweeping beam of light. Twenty feet further down this passage he stepped into a large underground room.

It was bowl-shaped, with steeply sloping sides and a perfectly flat bottom. The curvilinear walls eventually merged to form a narrow dome overhead. Tunnels of various sizes connected at different elevations around the outside perimeter, many of them just out of reach, others fifteen feet or more above the floor. It appeared to be a giant subterranean cistern. The construction of such a gallery certainly intrigued Colbrook, but what he found most interesting was the modern usage it had been put to by the Serbians.

Stacked row upon row, a mixture of steel and wood boxes lined the floor. Many had stenciled letters and numbers on their sides. Moving across the cavernous space, stepping around some low wooden crates filled with unmarked metal canisters, he bent down to examine a large canvas tarp stretched on the floor in a rumpled heap. Something appeared to be hidden beneath its greasy folds. Pulling back the edge of the heavy cloth, he was not surprised to find piles of recently manufactured and unblemished assault rifles arranged on the canvas, though he was genuinely astonished by the variety.

What he initially assumed were standard AK-47s upon closer inspection turned out to be Zastava M70s. The handguards had three distinct cooling slots not found on the more common Russian rifle. The Zastava was of Serbian make, something he did not find surprising under the circumstances. Variants of the M70 that he identified adjacent to the primary cache included those with folding stocks and those with attached bipods.

Behind the pile of M70s he recognized a weapon of more recent origin—the Zastava Arms M21. A modern take on the Kalashnikov, but constructed of lightweight carbon fiber, it had a somewhat unusual solid folding stock. Chambered for the standard 5.56mm NATO round, it was particularly popular for export. Apparently part of that exportation had found its way to an obscure dig site in the southernmost oasis of Egypt, and then thirty feet below the surface of the desert into an ancient Roman aqueduct.

Pistols and shotguns in every imaginable caliber and gauge filled the other half of the tarp. In all, the number of weapons easily totaled several hundred.

Given the size and scope of what he had found in the cistern, his search was somewhat more perfunctory than his tent rummage, but he explored the contents all the same.

Many of the wooden cases were nailed shut. He ignored these and concentrated on the metal ones. These could be opened and closed with folding latches, and all contained exactly what he expected they would: rifle and handgun cartridges. Another long wooden box that looked promising contained only shotgun shells. He even found a box of targets—cardboard outlines of humans—in one of the cartons.

After a lingering look around the cistern, Colbrook consulted his watch. He had already spent far too much time investigating the aqueduct. He exited into the short connecting tunnel and returned to the main shaft.

Beyond the intersection the passage seemed to continue indefinitely in a straight line. He turned left and retraced his steps. As he drew closer to the vertical access shaft he directed his light towards the ground. When he was within twenty feet of the ladder he switched it off. Edging his way forward and looking upwards, he searched for any sign that the floor panel had been removed.

The darkness was complete. He stretched out his hands to locate the ladder.

His right hand brushed against the smooth wood of a worn rung. Looking up again to where the plywood sheet covered the opening in the tent floor, there was nothing but smothering blackness. He strained to detect any sounds, but heard only his own breathing and the swish of blood rushing through his ears.

Pushing the flashlight into his pocket, he lifted his foot onto the bottom rung. The ladder creaked when he put his full weight onto it. Reaching above his head he grabbed the next rung. The higher he got the more often he paused to listen. When he was within what he estimated to be about eight feet of the plywood, he heard a muffled voice and froze.

Subdued and unintelligible conversation drifted down from above.

He remained still for several seconds, and then continued climbing, reaching one hand cautiously above his head after each step to check for the presence of the plywood. The voices were getting clearer.

His hand brushed against the wood panel. He stopped climbing.

A voice came from above, much louder than before, but not quite loud enough to make out the words. He moved up two more rungs, until his head was almost touching the underside of the floor panel. The same voice spoke again.

It was Graf.

"Nonsense. I already gave you a demonstration. I'm not giving you another. That's final."

There was a pause, and then Colbrook heard Coslovich reply, "There are few buyers. Not many have that kind of money, and those that do will only buy what they can see."

"I can't satisfy everyone else's worries," said Graf. "I can only satisfy my own."

Cavoski intoned, "We've done everything you requested. You're not holding up your end of the deal."

"Ridiculous," snorted Graf. "The deal is the same. Nothing has changed."

"I'm not so sure," Coslovich declared. "We've had an unexpected setback."

"You mean your missing man?" inquired Graf.

It was silent for moment.

Colbrook shifted his weight to his other foot, trying to keep the ladder from creaking. He turned his head so that his right ear was facing the plywood sheet. Soon the conversation resumed.

"Yes. Gvero." It was Coslovich again.

"And that's my fault?" questioned Graf. "I gave you those circuit boards for almost nothing, and now because the boards and your tyro messenger have gone missing you've decided it's somehow connected to me?"

"The boards made it to their destination—Gvero did not. Nedic is out looking for him. He's gone to Qena. I should hear more from him tomorrow," Coslovich answered.

"Sounds like your man has gone into hiding," stated Graf.

"No. I don't think so." It was Cavoski speaking now. "Something must have happened. He's made innumerable trips without incident."

"Well, maybe he'll turn up somewhere with a perfectly reasonable explanation," Graf declared.

"I hope so. He's my assistant," replied Cavoski. "We need him for the documentary."

"I thought that was just a ruse," Graf said.

"It's real." Cavoski again. "We were just watching the Seti footage."

"Next your going to tell me you have distribution."

"We do, though we did have to pay for it." It was Coslovich now. "What better deception than no deception at all."

Graf was laughing now. "I can't argue with that."

Cavoski interrupted in a serious voice, "Why do you laugh? It's no different from your aid agency."

"The Displaced Fund supplies aid to those in need. I have to keep the funding and expenditures in equilibrium somehow."

"And we started out as documentary filmmakers," replied Coslovich.

"What happened?" asked Graf.

"It was unprofitable," summarized Cavoski.

For a moment no one said anything, and then suddenly Coslovich declared, "Vukasinov wants to close the deal."

"He's your boss—not mine," growled Graf.

Colbrook gripped the ladder tightly.

There was a pause before Graf continued. "It sounds like you've already got a buyer. Am I right?"

"Maybe," muttered Coslovich. "There is more than one party with an interest."

"So what's the problem?" Graf demanded. "They all want a demonstration?"

More silence, then Graf grunted, "That's what I thought."

"What about this American visitor?" Coslovich asked.

Colbrook listened intently.

"You mean the travel writer?"

"What is he doing here?" Coslovich again.

"What do you think? Writing a travel story."

"I think it's best if the dig site stays off the tourist maps," warned Cavoski.

A few seconds of silence followed.

Coslovich resumed the conversation. "Vukasinov must please the buyers in order to obtain the highest price. We must have another demonstration."

"It's not going to happen." Graf was obdurate.

"What if we provide some complimentary items?" Cavoski suggested.

"Like what?" demanded Graf.

"Whatever you need."

"I'm having trouble as it is getting everything shipped across the border in a timely fashion. The Sudanese are becoming wary of aid agencies. They're stopping convoys at the border," said Graf.

"They haven't stopped you." It was Coslovich.

"Not yet."

"What will you do if they do stop you?" Cavoski asked.

"What I always do when I'm in trouble. Bribe someone. It always works in Africa," answered Graf. "Actually, it works almost anywhere."

"You might have to start flying everything out," suggested Cavoski.

"That would attract too much attention," said Graf. "And not just from Khartoum."

Coslovich declared harshly, "It's not worth the risk—not when a deal this big is in the works."

No one argued with that statement.

"It doesn't do me any good to have goods in permanent transit. It cuts into my bottom line," stated Graf, pausing before he asked, "Why, what do you have?"

"RPGs from Romania," explained Coslovich. "Of recent manufacture. Considerably better than usual. We can also increase the number of boxes of 7.62mm ammunition. That's from our own private stock."

"Russian ammo? It's corrosive-primed you know. Ruins the bore of the M70s—they're not chrome-lined like the AKs," Graf intoned.

"Bulgarian. Non-corrosive primer. And much better quality than the usual," replied Coslovich.

Cavoski began to speak now. "We will continue to help you, but you must be willing to make a deal—and soon. We can't wait forever."

"It's up to Vukasinov to make the deal happen," said Graf. "I'm beginning to wonder if he's the right man after all."

"I wouldn't say that to Vukasinov," replied Cavoski.

"I wasn't planning on meeting him."

It was silent again.

"So will a complimentary shipment change your mind?" asked Coslovich.

"No," stated Graf.

"You must need some extra supplies, especially when it looks like you're trying to single-handedly save those miserable refugees," stated Coslovich.

"I'm trying to even things out."

"You are running a very odd aid agency, Mr. Graf," Coslovich declared.

"I'm providing a much needed service," replied Graf. "If that involves killing a few devils on horseback, so be it."

A silence followed.

"You don't care for politics anymore?" It was Cavoski. "Your UN experience has soured you?"

"I've learned that it's always better to be on the paying side of corruption. The UN is internationally recognized in that respect."

"We've supplied you with enough weapons to equip a whole army," declared Coslovich. "I think you should be more cooperative." He was trying to steer the conversation back to where it had begun.

"I'm not changing the deal to suit Vukasinov," Graf declared. "I made it clear that there would be only one demonstration. That's already happened. Apparently Vukasinov doesn't believe what you told him."

No one said anything for a full minute.

When Graf spoke again, his voice seemed more distant. "Maybe I can interest Vukasinov's buyers in some more helicopter parts."

"You're just stalling for time. You're already in a dangerous situation as it is. Why push it?" Coslovich again.

"Are you threatening me?" Graf snarled.

"No. Just an observation," said Coslovich.

"Sounded like a threat to me," responded Graf. "Do you think I'm foolish enough to carry something so valuable around with me?" Graf paused as if waiting for an answer. "I've found a very good hiding place. I'm the only one who knows where it is. Your threats are meaningless."

Coslovich intoned, "I would be more worried about Vukasinov, especially now that he's in Egypt. He arranged for us to shoot the documentary. He also supplied the funding to keep the dig going. Think of all the complex preparations that have been made on your behalf. Our purchase of illegal antiquities, for example."

"Necessities," replied Graf. "Due to unusual circumstances. Nothing more. If Lowell could manage to find a few things in the archeologically acceptable manner, the dig could run on its own."

"Lowell is beginning to worry me," said Coslovich.

"His Egyptological demands are getting excessive," added Cavoski.

"Lowell is harmless." It was Graf.

"Not if he gets caught," said Cavoski.

"As long as you remain in charge of his purchases, no one will get caught," said Graf.

"Don't think we like looking for his finds in underground shops," stated Coslovich. "His requirements are very specific."

"Why don't you just turn him in? That will simplify everything," said Graf.

"You make us out to be villains, Mr. Graf. We are quite friendly compared to Vukasinov." Cavoski was speaking.

"You do not understand Vukasinov. If you did, you would understand why we are telling you this. He is not a tolerant man." It was Coslovich.

"Without my contacts, none of this would be possible. And I'm the one who knew Lowell."

"I think you do not understand our position," Coslovich continued. "And possibly not even your own."

"If you want your money," added Cavoski, "you're going to have to eventually close the deal."

"Without me there won't be a deal," declared Graf loudly.

There was the sound of movement above. Cavoski said something Colbrook could not understand, because the plywood flooring just to the side of the sheet covering the opening squeaked. He heard a muffled thump.

Colbrook held his breath and listened.

Coslovich's voice seemed uncannily near.

"Where's the black flashlight?"

"Don't look at me," said Graf.

"I didn't take it," declared Cavoski.

"Someone did." It was Coslovich again.

Colbrook started to drop down the ladder at a dangerous rate, his feet barely resting on the rungs as he descended.

He heard the plywood panel being lifted away, and when he looked up a sliver of light showed far above. It grew wider until it became a squarish hole. Stepping from the ladder to the sandy floor of the ancient aqueduct, Colbrook moved back from the access shaft, still peering upwards. A dark shape blocked out the light from above, and then the wooden ladder trembled under a sudden weight.

9

Colbrook plunged into the enveloping blackness. When he was deeper into the aqueduct he switched on the flashlight. A narrow beam of unsteady light shot down the stone passage as he raced forward.

He was fast approaching the section of the tunnel choked with a deep layer of sand, and stooping slightly to reduce his height, he fought to keep his balance on the shifting surface. When his shoes again thumped on hard sandstone he lengthened his stride.

The two side tunnels he had found earlier were now just ahead. He ignored them both. The cistern had no accessible outlet and the opposite passage was filled with considerable rubble. The main passage remained clear as far as he could see.

A muffled shout came from behind—from the vertical access shaft. Colbrook switched off the flashlight and continued to rush headlong down the tunnel. Soon the floor was smoother and more level underfoot, but he was running blind, and even slight variations in the surface caused him to stumble. He hoped the passage remained straight and did not make any unexpected turns.

Several times he brushed up against the sides of the aqueduct, scraping and banging his elbows and shoulders on the sometimes smooth, sometimes rough, but always unyielding stone. He began to imagine yawning pits ahead, and the sense that he was approaching one caused him to suddenly slow and then stop.

He turned on the flashlight, keeping his hand over the reflector, allowing just a trickle of light to flow out between his fingers.

The tunnel ahead was empty, the floor solid and level.

His mind had been playing tricks on him in the unsettling void of blackness. He clicked the light off and listened intently.

Scuffling and creaking noises were coming from the direction of the access shaft.

He turned to look back. A small point of light was bobbing up and down. The sound of a voice carried towards him, echoing crazily in the confined space.

Colbrook ran, the soft thuds of his shoes and the rasp of his own labored breathing making it impossible to hear anything else. Soon the air felt cooler, the atmosphere less stale. The roof of the tunnel was now faintly visible. He slowed to a fast walk, staring upwards, his attention drawn to a narrow rectangular outline overhead. Far above he could see stars in the night sky. Standing for a moment under the opening, he breathed in some fresh air, wondering if there might be some means of climbing the shaft.

The approaching sounds of his pursuers propelled him forward again.

Sprinting down the passage, he did not slow until the echoes of his footsteps told him that something had changed in the structure of the shaft. Shielding the flashlight again, he switched it on.

The tunnel had ended. He was staring at a solid wall.

He began to retrace his steps, searching for a connecting passage. The walls of the main shaft were continuous, without any visible break. Aiming his light alternately at both sides, he moved at a steady pace. The flashlight would give him away if he continued to use it, but without it he was as good as blind.

Just when he was beginning to lose all hope a roughly hewn opening came into view only a few yards ahead on his left. As he was slipping into this narrow passageway he saw a flickering light at the junction of the cistern tunnel and the blocked tunnel across from it. No doubt they were checking the weapons cache first, and arming themselves.

Hurrying down the rough and narrow passage, he removed his hand from the front of the flashlight, allowing the beam to fully illuminate the tunnel. The floor was littered with rocky debris, its width little more than half that of the main tunnel.

He guided the light along the walls and floor. The passage was curving, making it impossible to determine its extent, or if there were other connecting tunnels. The view ahead was limited to about thirty feet.

Footsteps echoed closer.

Colbrook turned to look back. A blindingly bright light flooded the main tunnel. He watched his dark shadow bend across the pitted sandstone wall, dissipating as the light changed direction. He darted forward on the loose and jumbled stone debris scattered across the uneven floor. Apparently the weapons cache included some portable million-candlepower xenon spotlights.

Weaving his way down the rock-littered passageway, he tried to make as little noise as possible. The tunnel was getting smaller as he progressed further into it. He spotted a narrow opening not more than twenty feet away and veered towards it, hoping it was the beginning of another tunnel.

Almost completely filled with stone debris, it ended only a few feet from its start.

Colbrook ducked inside anyway, and crouching low, scrambled beyond the crumbling entrance. Making use of the minimal space to turn and position himself, he waited with his head down and the flashlight off, concealed behind a mound of rubble.

Distant pattering footsteps gradually became closer hurried strides, and soon the dazzling light was knifing down the narrow, curving tunnel, searching like a roving eye over the uneven walls and floor. Colbrook froze when he heard Graf's voice booming down the tunnel.

"Is this where you saw the light? Right here?"

"It looked like it," declared Cavoski.

"Where did it go? What direction?" asked Coslovich.

Cavoski answered. "I don't know. It just disappeared."

Colbrook heard the crunch of loose rock. Someone had entered the side passage.

"Let me take a quick look." It was Coslovich. "This tunnel doesn't go very far."

The beam of bright light shifted abruptly away, and then a much weaker light replaced it.

Crunching and scuffling noises approached. The sound of labored breathing was very distinct when the footsteps momentarily stopped.

Colbrook eased the Beretta from his belt. He slowly disengaged the safety with his thumb, gripping the gun tightly in his right hand. The crackling sound of sandstone being walked on resumed. He peered through a small aperture in the pile of rubble, holding the pistol a few inches off the ground. A narrow beam of light swept down the passage, hovering for a few seconds on the walls before settling onto the floor.

Coslovich stepped into view, the rubber tips of his canvas desert boots gleaming in the shifting light. In addition to the flashlight, he was carrying a large pistol.

The light swept toward the recess.

Colbrook moved his head to the side and kept it there, pressed against a rock. The light bobbed upwards to the unfinished ceiling. There was a moment of dead silence as Coslovich played it around the tunnel.

Then the sound of footfalls moved away.

Colbrook gazed through the small opening in the rubble, listening as Coslovich made his way further into the narrow tunnel.

A minute passed, then two minutes. Colbrook thought he heard Graf say something in a low voice—Graf and Cavoski seemed to still be in the main tunnel.

Soon a glow of faint light returned. It grew steadier and brighter, the footsteps falling evenly. Coslovich was not searching anymore—he was simply walking back to the main tunnel. He passed Colbrook's rubble-filled niche without even a pause in his stride, occasionally muttering an oath under his breath as he stumbled or slipped.

The glow of light and the sound of footsteps faded rapidly. Colbrook reached for the flashlight at his side, turning it to face the ground. He waited. There was a low murmur of voices, and then they gradually faded. After several minutes had passed he turned the flashlight on.

Reengaging the Beretta's safety, he put the gun back under his belt. His leg muscles were cramped from the uncomfortable position he had been kneeling in. When he had recovered enough strength in them, he climbed out of the recessed opening.

Hooding the flashlight with his hand, he began carefully retracing his steps back towards the main passageway. He moved slowly, his thumb on the rubber-coated switch, ready to turn off the light. As he approached the junction of the main tunnel he put the palm of his hand over the end of the flashlight, completely blocking the beam. Standing in near darkness, he waited, listening.

Voices drifted from afar, moving away. Forming a small circular opening over the flashlight's lens with the palm of his hand, Colbrook stepped out into the main passageway. In the distance, at the junction of the side tunnels, he could see a light resting unattended on the floor. The voices could no longer be heard. He began walking rapidly back towards the access shaft and ladder.

He had traveled about two hundred feet down the passage when the sound of echoing voices burst from behind him like a sudden flood of water. Extinguishing the flashlight, he began to run at a breakneck speed.

A blaze of light swept down the center of the shaft. When he could see his own shadow rippling across the stone floor directly ahead, Colbrook knew he was in trouble. The light was blinding to his dark-adapted eyes. He kept running.

A trumpeting shout from behind indicated that he had been spotted. A calm came over him as he sprinted down the tunnel—there was nothing he could do now but try to outdistance his pursuers.

As he drew nearer to what he could now see was a tall gas lantern positioned in the center of the passage, a shot rang out from behind. It sounded hollow and strangely muffled in the long tunnel. Stone chips and dust exploded from the wall to his left. A second shot echoed, this round burying itself in the hard-packed sand only a few feet in front of him.

He weaved from side to side as he neared the lantern marking the intersection of the tunnels. There was a high probability he would be shot if he stayed in the main passage for even a few seconds longer. He prepared to dive into the tunnel leading to the cistern. As he was about to move in that direction a light appeared at its far end, bobbing towards him. He hurled himself into the opposite tunnel—the rubble-filled passage he had chosen not to explore earlier. A third shot rang out as his shoes slipped in the soft sand that flowed from its entrance.

After an initial downward dip, the tunnel became more and more choked with sand and rocks. Running became impossible—the ceiling was too low. Colbrook was soon on his hands and knees, scrambling to squeeze over the top of a mound of loose stones. Rolling down the sandy incline on the other side and into the darkness, he came to a halt sitting on the hard floor. Switching on the flashlight, he stared down the tunnel.

It was mostly clear of debris.

Regaining his feet, he rushed forward. Up ahead the ceiling was cracked and crumbling, sections of stone having sheered away from the bedrock and shattered on the floor.

Beyond these broken monoliths was a sandy incline that rose almost to the ceiling, nearly blocking the tunnel. Scrambling up the slope, he found a gap barely a foot high at the top. Aiming his light through the narrow space he could see that the passage continued on the other side. Jamming the bottom of the flashlight into the soft sand, he began hurriedly scooping with both hands. When he had cleared a space large enough to fit through, he snatched the light up and wriggled through the small excavation, sliding head-first down the opposite slope.

He came to his feet and started to jog down the shaft. The floor glistened with moisture in the shifting light. He could smell a musty, vegetative odor. A hundred feet later his shoes were splashing in standing water. He slowed, moving the beam of light across the ceiling and walls, looking for ventilation shafts or connecting passages.

The odor of decaying vegetation was now almost overpowering.

His right foot suddenly lost purchase on the stone floor, sinking into several inches of soft muck. Water seeped through his shoe and then his sock. He yanked his foot out, stumbling back. He paused for a moment, catching his breath.

The water looked as if it would become progressively deeper as he advanced.

Despite its uncertain depth, the prospect of escape into the open desert above was enough to send him plunging in. As he moved forward he sank deeper and deeper into the muck until the water reached almost to his knees. Sloshing along, he tried to convince himself it was free of parasites, being naturally filtered by the subterranean sandstone which underlay the whole oasis.

Within a few short steps the depth increased up to his waist, bits of unidentifiable debris now floating on the surface. Some of this looked like seeds or bits of leaves, but when it covered virtually the entire surface of the water, Colbrook knew it was algae and fungus. The sharp and pungent odor of rotting vegetation assailed his nose. He pushed forward through the increasingly odious murk, thinking only of reaching the dry surface above.

The flashlight was getting dimmer and soon began to flicker. He rattled it and tried screwing the cap down tighter, suspecting it would not last much longer. It was now dented in several places.

A faint, even light seemed to be coming from up ahead. Colbrook switched off the flashlight to let his eyes adjust to the darkness. He stared down the tunnel, vaguely discerning a distant opening to the night sky above. Continuing forward at the best speed he could muster, he was soon amidst a choking swath of succulent vegetation that was sprouting from the stagnant water. He pushed his way through the leaves and stems until the ceiling above his head was replaced with a star-filled sky. He was now in nothing more than a very deep trench in the bedrock.

He turned the flashlight back on and plunged ahead, crashing through the riotous foliage, grasshoppers springing away from him in sudden surprise, large beetles scuttling under leaves to escape his sweeping beam of light. Frogs stared back at him, dropping into the black muck with soft splashes when he neared their perches.

Emerging from the tangled mass of vegetation, Colbrook found himself standing at the bottom of an ascending circular shaft filled with a thick bed of sharp reeds. It was similar to the shaft beneath the tent floor, with the exception that the circumference was significantly larger. It was constructed of cut stones stacked in alternating courses. At the top was the welcoming night sky. A narrow circular staircase wound around the wall of the shaft. The mold-covered stone steps were just deep enough to safely position a shoe. Set in the curved wall alongside the stairs were the rusted remains of iron handholds, most of them nothing more than tangled stumps of oxidized metal.

Colbrook turned off the flashlight and pushed it into his pocket. He needed both hands free.

He began climbing the dangerously small steps.

It was at least twenty-five feet to the top, and if he fell near the surface he would almost certainly be killed. Clearly it was a well shaft, allowing aboveground access to the aqueduct's waters. He hoped the ancient stonemasons had built the steps to last forever.

Occasionally stopping to steady himself against the wall, he slowly wound his way upwards. The iron handholds served more for guidance than to prevent a fall—they were too brittle to hold onto tightly. As he neared the top it became easier to see the steps, though he still had some heart-stopping moments when his foot slipped or a step was missing from the series.

Reaching the surface, exhausted from the treacherous ascent, he carefully climbed over the low circular wall forming the sill of the well. He sat down on its edge, facing away from the opening. His shoes and pants were coated in mud, and bits and pieces of vegetation were hanging from his sweat-stained shirt, but he had otherwise escaped the aqueduct virtually unscathed. Even the Beretta was still tucked safely in his belt, though the dip in the water had probably not done it much good.

He was surrounded on all sides by the dense and feathery foliage of an engulfing patch of tamarisk trees. From the Roman fort he had seen a few of these clumps of vegetation scattered about in the desert, not knowing what secrets they concealed. The ground in the immediate vicinity of the well was damp and muddy, allowing a thick bed of waist-high reeds to flourish. The tamarisk trees grew in a wider ring, completely encircling the thick-stalked grasses.

A noise came from almost directly ahead. Something was pushing through the slender tamarisk branches, moving in his direction.

Colbrook pulled the Beretta from his belt, holding it along his thigh.

The branches parted and Graf stepped from the shimmering vegetation. He was holding a shotgun. His mouth was drawn into a thin line, his eyes searching for a meaning to this evidently surprising discovery.

Colbrook released the pistol from his grip. For a few long seconds there was no sound, and then he heard a faint splash.

Graf advanced a few more steps. "You're a very eccentric travel writer." The shotgun shifted slightly.

Colbrook did not respond. Water and muck continued to trickle from his shoes and pants. He was cold and tired—well past the heroic stage.

Graf tested the ground with his boots. He lifted his left foot onto a partially buried rock, resting the shotgun across his raised knee. "It's a shame your story will never make it into print."

"There is no story," replied Colbrook.

"Who are you?" demanded Graf in a menacing voice, any pretensions towards professorial attitudes having dissipated entirely.

"I'm not a travel writer," answered Colbrook.

Graf's eyes narrowed. "Then what are you doing out here?"

"I can explain," stated Colbrook.

Graf was about to reply, but instead turned his head to look back into the dense vegetation.

The tamarisk branches began rustling again and the shadowy form of Cavoski materialized into the small clearing, his hands poised over the sharp reeds as if fending them off. He carried a compact, shiny pistol. A few seconds later Coslovich emerged from the thick foliage. Stepping closer to Colbrook, his face a mask in the half-light, he gradually lowered his much larger handgun.

"The travel writer," he muttered. He looked over at Graf, as if expecting an answer to his statement.

"What are you looking at me for?" demanded Graf.

"You said he was harmless," declared Coslovich.

"I was wrong," snapped Graf. He removed his muddy boot from the rock. The shotgun swung freely in his right hand. He turned and gave Coslovich a look of disdain. "He was just about to explain himself."

Cavoski edged forward to get a better look at Colbrook.

Coslovich waved his gun. "You better have a damn good explanation. I won't miss from this distance."

Colbrook stared at the three men. Cavoski held the smallest firearm, but his expression was just as unfriendly as the rest. Colbrook turned his attention back to Coslovich. His large pistol seemed to be the most immediate danger.

"Do you mind if I ask a question first?"

"What?" Coslovich grunted in disbelief. His sallow face, bathed in sweat, was almost hideous in the starlight.

Colbrook ignored him and looked at Graf.

"How did you know where I would come out?"

"That tunnel only has two exits. One of them is here." Graf

pointed at the ground. "I told Coslovich and Cavoski to check the other one. It's not far." He then pointed to the east. "We've explored most of the aqueducts at this end of the system. Some of them have even been mapped."

"That should make my work a lot easier," said Colbrook.

"He's talking nonsense," declared Coslovich. "I think we should just shoot him and dump his body in the well."

"Not yet," interrupted Graf in an insistent voice. "I want to know what he's talking about."

Cavoski was now staring at Colbrook. He was wearing a mesh baseball cap, his hair squashed under its dirty rim. Speaking in a low voice, he said, "What did you find down in the aqueduct?"

"Find?" questioned Colbrook, staring up at the cinematographer. "Oh—you mean the cache of guns?"

Coslovich raised his pistol.

"I don't care about the guns," responded Colbrook quickly. "I'm not exactly a law-abiding individual myself."

The three men waited expectantly. Cavoski finally said what they were all thinking. "What are you looking for then?"

"The same thing Lowell's looking for."

The Serbians glanced at each other in silence. Graf continued to stare at Colbrook.

"What do you know about the fort overlooking the dig site?" asked Colbrook. "The one known as Qasr Dush."

"It's a Roman fort," replied Coslovich. "Everyone knows that."

Cavoski nodded his head in assent.

"Rumor has it these aqueducts connect with the fort," said Colbrook, looking directly at Graf.

"I've heard that," agreed Graf with a somewhat puzzled expression. "But what of it?"

"Dush protected the confluence of several caravan routes," explained Colbrook in an authoritative tone. "The desert roads were critical for trade with the rest of Africa. The Darb al-Arba'een was just one of those roads. The Darb al-Dush was another. Some say as many as five tracks converged near the fort. Every day caravans would pass through with gold and slaves, crossing the inhospitable desert to reach their final destination in the Nile Valley. It wasn't an easy journey by any means, but it was worth it if your cargo arrived intact and you didn't perish at the hands of murderous bandits."

The three men were now all very still.

Colbrook continued with scarcely a pause. "The Romans built the fort to protect the caravans, but it also served as an outpost for the empire—a means of discouraging possible invaders, a visible warning to those who might stray into Roman-controlled territory. But protection came at a price. The Romans taxed the caravans in return for their safety. Have you been to the fort?" Colbrook did not wait for an answer. "Dush is really nothing more than a giant barracks for housing soldiers. It held a Roman garrison."

"It is quite large," agreed Graf. "I think it must go underground several stories."

"It does," replied Colbrook. "The structure began as a temple of Isis and Serapis during the reign of Domitian, mostly serving the ancient town of Kysis. The original Roman camp was more than likely one of temporary design. Remember, this was the extreme periphery of the Roman Empire."

Graf's shotgun was now aimed at the ground, his pose more relaxed. Coslovich's large pistol was still positioned in a threatening way.

"It wasn't until the beginning of the fourth century—Anno Domini—that the temple was converted—some say expanded—into a Roman fort of considerable size," said Colbrook. "Some people don't find Roman ruins in Egypt to be all that interesting, preferring Egyptian ones, but that fort is very interesting, even if it is Roman. I should know. I was there earlier today."

Graf's face remained impassive, but his eyes had a far-off look in them.

"By the fifth century the fort was abandoned completely," added Colbrook.

Stretching out his arm, Cavoski crushed a large mosquito that had landed on his shoulder. He brushed the sticky remains off his shirt with the handgrip of his shiny pistol. Coslovich stood like a statue, his much larger pistol now resting partially in the palm of his left hand. A sudden breeze gusted through the tamarisks, sending them into a fitful but short-lived dance.

Colbrook looked furtively around at the others. They were clearly waiting for him to continue, and so he did. "All forts had a treasury.

A stronghold if you will." He paused for effect. "Dush was no exception. It also more than likely had a sacellum, or military shrine, housing the regimental standards. The standards were considered sacred. To lose them in battle was to bring shame upon the head of every soldier. To be slain in battle, some say, was preferable. The treasury and the sacellum were essentially one and the same in most Roman forts, and their protection was not taken lightly."

Coslovich wiped his sweaty face. His hair looked like the fur of a recently surfaced water rat. He was now paying close attention.

"The stronghold was used for the distribution of pay. All soldiers were paid in the Roman army, and they were paid in coins—gold coins—but they were paid infrequently. Typically only three times a year," explained Colbrook. "The aureus used for this purpose were issued up to the beginning of the fourth century, when the solidus replaced it." Colbrook knew most soldiers were actually paid in denarii, a far more common coin, but suspected none of his audience were numismatists.

Graf stared at the soft muddy ground. He had the look of someone calculating something he was unsure of.

"Tax collection provided another reason to have a stronghold within the walls of the fort. I don't need to tell you that the Romans were inveterate tax collectors. One needed a secure place to store such ill-gotten gains. And then there was the raw gold from Sudan and Nubia. The spoils of Africa, painstakingly harvested from mines by slaves and convicted criminals. Hauled by men and beast alike over the scorching sands and endless wastes. Most eventually made it to Rome, being converted to coins and stamped with the emperor's own profile, only to fill the bottomless coffers of the empire. Some, though, only made it as far as Dush. Skimmed before minting one might say. Pilfered, others might argue. But all the same—it remained."

Graf shifted forward with deliberate slowness. He leaned towards Colbrook, his goatee filled with bits of tamarisk leaves. His eyes had a glassy look, and his teeth were startlingly white when he spoke. "Who says any of this is still in the fort? That was almost two thousand years ago."

"Haven't you ever wondered what Lowell is really doing here?" asked Colbrook, lifting his soggy shoes to drier ground.

Graf's face clouded over. He looked very thoughtful.

"I guess it does explain one thing," said Cavoski with amusement.

"What's that?" Graf asked, looking back at the cinematographer.

"How many Egyptologists do you know who keep a loaded pistol in a shoebox under their bed?" answered Cavoski.

Graf did not reply.

"Lowell isn't digging anywhere near the fort," noted Coslovich.

"Of course not. He doesn't have permission from the government," replied Colbrook.

Graf put his boot up on the rock again, resting his elbow on his knee. The shotgun had been transferred into his left hand. His eyes never moved from Colbrook's face.

"The treasury should be at the deepest level of the fort," said Colbrook. "By using the aqueducts to gain access and moving the debris and digging material into other tunnels, the aboveground section of the fort would never be disturbed."

"How do you know about all this?" demanded Coslovich. "Are you working for Lowell?"

"No," answered Colbrook with a locked gaze. "I'm a competitor."

"How much gold is there?" Coslovich asked.

Colbrook continued to look at the Serbian director's shadowed face.

"That's hard to say exactly. It depends on whether it's mostly coins or mined gold. Roman coins tended to be very pure, much more so than modern mints, which rarely exceed ninety percent. With raw gold it's even more difficult to tell because we don't know the purity, or whether it's dust or nuggets. I'd say at a minimum there must be at least two thousand troy pounds in total, and maybe a maximum of four thousand. I've pondered the same question myself, but I can't come up with an exact number. In my opinion it's in the tens of millions based on the current trading value."

Coslovich nodded. He seemed satisfied with the answer.

"Lowell is not working in the aqueducts," declared Graf suddenly.

"He isn't?" Colbrook questioned. "Have you explored every tunnel?"

"No—of course not. It's a veritable underground maze," said Graf.

"He doesn't have to go into them until he's found something of interest. It's a lot easier if you have the proper equipment," stated Colbrook. "Total station, ground-penetrating radar, sophisticated mapping software—"

Graf nodded. If he had been finding the theory hard to accept, these doubts appeared to have been dispelled.

"A few months back Lowell marked many of the ventilation holes on the surface with wooden stakes," said Graf. "He told me he did it so the workers wouldn't dump rubbish over them."

"Those are pretty far from the excavations, aren't they?" asked Colbrook.

"Yes, I suppose they are," answered Graf thoughtfully.

"Why should he be worried about anyone dumping anything that far away?" Colbrook let that sink in, and then added, "Did he survey the vents?"

Graf nodded again. "He told me it was done for a topographic map he was making of the immediate surroundings. Something about connecting contour lines at a known elevation. Fixed points on a level plane. I really don't remember."

"Do you believe that?" questioned Colbrook.

"I wouldn't know," answered Graf. "My knowledge of surveying is limited."

Cavoski, who had not said anything for a while, suddenly declared, "Who else is working with you?"

"I always work alone," replied Colbrook. "You live longer that way."

Graf grunted. "That's hard to believe. If you are really working alone, how were you going to physically remove the gold from the treasury, haul it through the aqueducts, and transport it out of the country?"

"I wasn't going to remove all of it at once. Just small amounts to start with. It's too risky any other way."

Graf kicked mud from the soles of his boots. "Well, that's all changed," he said. "Now that you have partners."

Colbrook shook his head. "I don't want partners."

"I don't think you have a choice," interrupted Coslovich.

"Look at it this way," said Graf, "you need a means of transporting the gold. We can help move the gold through the aqueducts without anyone's knowledge, and once we've stockpiled it some-where safe, we can load it onto one of my trucks. I have empty food and medical containers."

Colbrook did not respond.

"After it's on the truck, I can send it anywhere in Africa you like," added Graf.

Brushing the drying mud from his pants, Colbrook stood up. He looked directly at Graf. "This will all come at a price, I assume."

"Of course," answered Graf. "There is risk involved. And I am providing a critical service."

"I'm not in a position to argue," said Colbrook, "and it does make sense given the circumstances."

"We want fifty percent of the haul," stated Graf. "It may sound like a lot, but that's split between three people."

Coslovich stared hard at his pistol. Cavoski nodded, as if satis-fied with the arrangements.

"Half?" blurted Colbrook. "You expect me to take only half?"

"It's fair enough," replied Graf. "Without our services it would take you months or possibly years to clear even a fraction of that."

"This arrangement is not very satisfactory," Colbrook noted.

"Why is that?" Graf demanded.

Colbrook studied the three men standing before him.

"Because," he told them, "treasure hunting leads to jealousy, and jealousy leads to murder."

10

Counting himself fortunate that he had not been murdered during the night, Colbrook rolled from under the woolen blanket he had been sleeping beneath. The temperature dropped rapidly in the desert after sundown, and with his clothing still damp, the blanket had been a necessity, not a luxury. He was in the supply tent adjacent to the Serbians' tent, lying in a narrow corridor formed by stacked boxes and containers. It was clear he was still under suspicion, despite the fact that Graf and the two Serbians had taken such an interest in his imaginary plan to search for Roman gold.

When Colbrook emerged from the canvas tent, haggard and sore, he was greeted by the sight of laborers toiling away in the many scattered excavation pits. He watched as a steady flow of debris-filled *zambils* were dumped in succession onto the screening tables. A veil of orange-colored dust hung in the air. Standing motionless for a minute or two in the warm morning sunlight, his clothing stiff with dried mud, he turned to look towards the magazine.

Graf was crouched beside the Isuzu, checking tire pressures. Soon he opened the hood, and reaching down to lift a plastic container of blue liquid from the ground, began filling the washer-fluid reservoir. The red minivan was still parked where it had been left the day before.

Abruptly stepping back into the supply tent, Colbrook glanced at his watch. It was just before eight. The laborers had been at work for almost an hour; he had been awake since five.

A distant shout came from outside, followed by a clamor of voices drifting across the site. Colbrook returned to the doorway.

Pushing aside the canvas flaps, he watched a group of laborers assembling around an excavation pit located a good distance from the tents. Turbans bobbed and bare feet stamped as each worker vied to move closer to its edge. It was the same pit Lowell had climbed into the night before. In the midst of the commotion a single man stood out from all the rest, shouting loudly in both Arabic and English. It was Daud, the pit supervisor.

Nearby excavations were emptying rapidly. A few minutes passed before Colbrook saw the flaps on Lowell's tent part. The Egyptologist stepped from his quarters with a purposeful stride, his boots kicking through the soft sand with easy regularity. Hanging from his neck was a digital camera with a long lens. His expression was hard to read from such a distance, but Colbrook thought he detected a faint smile.

The show was about to begin.

Pushing through the crowd of laborers, Lowell came to a stop next to Daud. The pit supervisor was pointing down into the excavation, nodding his head and talking animatedly. Lowell stood at his side, listening for the most part, but on occasion interrupting him as they both peered down into the pit. Colbrook was too far away to understand what they were saying, but he could guess. It was remarkable to watch these two men pretend to be surprised at the discovery.

Lowell soon cleared the laborers away from the rim of the pit, lifting the camera from his neck to snap a few quickly focused pictures. Daud was already climbing down the wooden ladder, a small trowel clutched in his hand. He disappeared below ground level, leaving Lowell staring into the pit from above, holding his heavy Nikon. A few minutes passed. Lowell paced along the edge of the excavation, his eyes never leaving the bottom of the hole. Eventually two sand-covered diggers emerged from the pit, brushing themselves off. Lowell immediately swung himself onto the vacated ladder, climbing downward. The crowd of laborers surged forward again, surrounding the pit on all sides.

Colbrook redirected his gaze towards the magazine. Graf seemed oblivious to all the commotion. He was cleaning the truck's windshield with a rag, misting the surface with a bottle of glass cleaner. Occasionally he glanced in the direction of the ruined temple, as if awaiting someone's arrival. Most of the time his interest was focused on the windshield.

A movement in the foreground caught Colbrook's attention.

The brim of a sun-bleached straw hat poked through the canvas flaps of a nearby tent. The squat form of the SCA inspector, Rashad, emerged into the morning sun. He hurried in the direction of the pit, a foil-covered pastry clutched in his hand. Discovery or no discovery, he was intent on finishing his breakfast. Stopping to take furtive bites, by the time he reached the circle of laborers he was pushing the empty foil into his pocket, his jaw working hard to grind up the rest of the evidence. He descended the ladder and disappeared below ground, joining Lowell in the pit.

A few minutes later Colbrook realized what Graf had been anticipating.

Cavoski was trudging through the sand from the direction of the temple, a video camera resting on his shoulder. Coslovich was following only a few yards behind, carrying a lightweight tripod and a small case. They were both making a beeline for the crowd. The documentary was apparently still in production, the occasion too good to pass up.

The sound of the Isuzu's rear door slamming shut drew Colbrook's attention back to Graf; he was now moving in the direction of Lowell's tent. When Graf had disappeared from sight, Colbrook began walking slowly in the direction of the crowd. He tried to brush the remaining dried mud from his pants while he made his way across the rippled sand. He soon gave up.

As he approached the group of robed Egyptians, a few turned to watch him with obvious interest. A narrow path formed as he advanced through the crowd to the edge of the deep pit. Despite the fact that he knew the finds had been in the sand for less than twelve hours, he found himself caught up in the moment. The brown smiling faces, the friendly banter in Arabic, and the whispers of those closest to the edge of the pit—some down on all fours, their necks craning over the rim—made him realize that even the most humble digger felt the thrill of discovery.

Cavoski was pushing through the crowd from the opposite side of the pit. The cinematographer was repeating some practiced phrase in Arabic as he progressed through the group of laborers, his camera

still positioned on his shoulder, secured by his right hand. Coslovich was frowning as he followed behind him. He was clearly not
happy about his demotion to camera assistant. The two Serbians
reached the pit and looked over the edge.

Cavoski ignored the folded tripod that his partner set into the
sand. Instead he crouched on his knees at the crumbling rim of
the pit, looking through the camera's viewfinder. The lighting at
the bottom of the hole was almost non-existent at this early hour,
but Cavoski did not seem concerned. After pushing a series of small
buttons on the side of the camera and adjusting the lens, he began
shooting.

Coslovich briefly looked up, nodding discreetly at Colbrook
from across the pit, and then continued watching the activity below over Cavoski's shoulder. His expression was one of paramount
disinterest.

Looking into the pit himself, Colbrook could see Lowell kneeling
at the bottom. He was painstakingly sweeping sand away from a
buried object with a small hand brush. From where Colbrook stood
it was difficult to determine exactly what the Egyptologist was un-
covering. Daud was near Lowell's side, watching the work intently,
holding the digital camera in anticipation of further photo opportunities. Rashad viewed the proceedings from opposite Daud, leaning
against one of the wide boards shoring up the side of the deep pit.

Across from Lowell knelt two laborers, their hands carefully
scooping sand away from the opposite end of the object. Lowell
was now brushing vigorously, sweeping sand to either side. The
item in the ground was still only a vague outline, a little more than
two feet in length.

Calling for his camera, Lowell tossed the brush aside. He retrieved a ruler-like piece of wood painted with alternating black
and white stripes from his shirt pocket. Positioning the length of
wood adjacent to the find horizontally, he reached for his camera,
taking it from Daud's outstretched hands. Rising from his knees,
he stepped back until he was against the wall of the pit, alternately
composing, zooming, focusing, and firing the shutter. He handed
the camera back to Daud and reached for the brush again.

Still kneeling at the rim of the pit, Cavoski was zooming his lens
to get a closer shot of the work going on below. Soon he was back

on his feet, moving around the excavation. The laborers struggled to let him pass. Coslovich leaned on the tripod, inactive but following the activity below with a weary look.

Colbrook shifted sideways a few feet to get a better view. Several workers jostled to fill the space he left at the edge of the excavation. As the two laborers continued to clear sand from the buried object, Colbrook began to distinguish the shape of something emerging from the ground. Lowell leaned forward, waving off the two men. He ran his brush back and forth over the uncovered portion. As the brush swept across the object Colbrook caught a glimpse of a stone head with carved Egyptian braids. At the opposite end of the half-buried object he could now see a sandal-clad foot protruding from the sand.

Working faster now, Lowell instructed the two workers to start excavating the sides of the object. Colbrook watched as two slender arms were carefully cleared of debris. Soon Lowell began pushing aside the remaining sand with his loosely splayed fingers. Rashad leaned forward for a better view. The statue was now almost completely uncovered.

As Lowell rose to his feet and stepped aside, Colbrook could see that the stone figure was that of a woman, the left foot forward in the traditional Egyptian pose. Lowell knelt again, sweeping the remaining loose particles from the statue with his brush. The complex folds and creases of a long gown were modeled into the stone with intricate detail.

Lowell called for his camera again. Using the flash this time, the Egyptologist snapped a whole series of pictures from many different angles, documenting the find *in situ*. He handed the camera back to Daud and began giving the two laborers further instructions in Arabic.

Using small trowels and at times only their hands, the two excavators cleared away the rest of the sand around the perimeter of the figure, and then began digging beneath the stone object, creating a hollow under each side. Lowell soon motioned for the two men to clear the plinth block at the foot of the statue. After this had been accomplished, the Egyptologist helped them gently lift the statue, raising it from under the shoulders and rotating it to a standing position.

Colbrook was immediately struck by the very un-Egyptian features of the statue. The pose was typical of what he had seen throughout Egypt, but the details were very Greek-like. Instead of the symmetrical lines, hard angles, and rather stiff look of typical Egyptian work, this statue was rounded and softer in style—a more fluid and realistic shape. The face had far too much detail and individual identity to pass for strictly Egyptian sculpture of the Dynastic period.

Lowell turned to look briefly upwards from the bottom of the pit. As if on cue, workers scrambled to assemble a wooden box, accomplishing this with battery-powered drills at an astonishing rate. A series of ropes were carefully lowered into the hole. Rashad scrambled to reach the ladder before the pit got too crowded, deftly extricating himself from the swarm of activity.

Within minutes the statue was carefully padded with rolls of cloth and settled inside the shallow plywood box. Slings were made from ropes, and laborers on both sides of the pit hauled the heavy artifact to the surface with practiced coordination. Once on the surface, the ropes were removed and the small crate was carried to a low work table not far from the pit.

Lowell emerged from the excavation. He brushed off his knees and began walking towards the low table. Daud clambered to the surface soon after, cradling Lowell's camera. Rashad was already halfway to the work table, shaking clumps of sand from the crown of his straw hat.

Colbrook stepped back from the dispersing circle of laborers, nodding to the Egyptologist as he walked past. Lowell stopped with a look of astonishment, staring at Colbrook's mud-stained clothing.

"I got a little carried away in my exploration of Qasr Dush," explained Colbrook.

The excited crowd of laborers drew Lowell's attention back to the find. He pointed towards the table, now surrounded by workers. "Well, you wanted something interesting to write about. We've found a statue. Come along, I'll show it to you."

The figure lay in the plywood box. Lowell turned to Colbrook and said, "It's a granite statue of the goddess Isis. Certainly Greco-Roman Period. Hard to pin it down any further than that."

Colbrook nodded.

Lowell pointed at the stone figure. "There's Greek influence in the stylistic execution. Look at the details in the folds of the garment and the diaphanous nature of the sleeves. It's a remarkably skilled piece. In limestone it would be impressive enough, but in granite—it's just amazing."

Staring at the brown and gray speckled stone, Colbrook admitted it was masterfully done. He would have been even more impressed had he not known it had come from Hamed's storeroom.

The Serbian filmmakers soon stepped through the throng. Cavoski was carrying his video camera at his side by the handle as he moved closer to the low table, looking at the camera's small fold-out display. Coslovich stopped short of the table, holding the tripod and the small case. Both men were staring at the granite statue.

Lowell turned to Cavoski. "This should get the patrons excited. I hope you got some good footage."

"Documented the whole thing," replied Cavoski. "It'll be great material."

"Get a few close-ups," directed Coslovich.

Cavoski swung the camera onto his shoulder and crouched down on his knees.

Colbrook knew the shot could not be very good, but he suspected the Serbians had, with all the recent developments, lost interest in the technical aspects of their documentary.

Lowell turned away from Cavoski, looking toward the excavation he had just climbed out of. He continued to stare, distracted by something in the distance.

Colbrook turned to see what was attracting Lowell's attention.

A laborer was standing at the top of the recently vacated pit, waving his hands and shouting to be heard over the noise of the workers clustered around the table.

Lowell started running towards him. Daud soon followed. With a startled expression, Rashad stumped after them. The laborer came forward as Lowell closed the distance, shouting, "Another find! Another find!"

Following after Lowell, Colbrook reached the pit not long after Daud. A small stream of workers began moving back to the hole. Cavoski returned with his camera, now perspiring heavily, probably wishing only one item had been purchased. Coslovich trudged along at a snail's pace, his enthusiasm depleted beyond his reserves.

As Colbrook took up a position at the top of the pit, he noticed Graf making his way across the sandy landscape towards the assembling workers. Lowell was already down in the hole, directing the excavation. A minute later Coslovich arrived and positioned himself next to Cavoski, somehow finding the energy to say, "Let's try for more reaction shots. Might be a good idea to pick up an establishing shot while you're at it."

Graf was soon shouldering through the crowd, pushing his way closer. Watching Graf's approach, Colbrook slowly backed away from the excavation. His view of the pit, the ladder, and the Serbians was soon blocked by a mass of laborers. When he was sure he could not be seen by anyone near the pit, he walked directly to Lowell's tent.

He found the Egyptologist's quarters empty. Having made his way to the center of the tent and alongside Lowell's camp bed, he dropped to one knee and reached under the canvas-covered frame, finding the corner of a gray shoebox and sliding it out from under the cot. Lifting the lid, he removed a compact 9mm pistol from the box. The magazine was filled to capacity. The cartridges were of no better quality than the firearm itself. He replaced the magazine and checked the chamber. It was empty. Everything seemed to be in working order. He stood up and forced the gun into his pocket, pulling his shirt down over it. Pushing the empty box back under the cot with his foot, he headed for the door.

Outside the excitement continued.

Working his way into and then through the crowd, Colbrook reached the side of the pit opposite Graf and Coslovich. Cavoski was leaning over the pit with the video camera. A laborer had hold of his sweat-soaked shirt to prevent him from toppling in.

Lowell was on his knees at the bottom of the pit, brushing sand away from a buried object. A face was gradually revealed in black stone, a depiction of a wig carved on the top of the head. Soon the upper torso and arms came to light, bare of any garment. The statue was that of a man, maybe slightly less than two feet in length.

Looking up from the bottom of the pit, Lowell shouted for all to hear, "Get a box ready!"

The laborers repeated their preparations as before. A plywood box was rapidly lowered down to receive the statue. A few turbans were tossed below for use as padding, and then ropes were lowered and secured for lifting.

Graf and Coslovich stood watching the activities below. Rashad, in imitation of Cavoski, leaned dangerously forward over the pit, two laborers holding his belt to steady his precarious balance.

The wood box was hauled up, carried a few feet from the hole, and then placed on the ground for all to see. Lowell stepped from the top of the ladder, his expression one of profound satisfaction. Colbrook made his way to his side.

"A priest of Amen," declared Lowell. He was squatting by the statue, staring closely at the figure. "It's black diorite. By the design, I'd say Thirtieth Dynasty. It's made to look like an older piece, resembling something from the Old Kingdom, but look at the face—see the faint hint of a smile? And the torso—much too realistic. Definitely not older than the Late Period. It was a time of revival. They were copying old objects but rendering them with greater plasticity."

"So it's the same age as the temple," said Colbrook.

"Certainly seems about right," replied Lowell. He had taken a small brush from his shirt pocket and was now sweeping off the top of the head. "It's a shame we've lost the lower legs and plinth block. I've told the excavators to clear a larger hole. Maybe we can find the fragments. All the same, it's a fine example of Late Period workmanship."

It would be very surprising, thought Colbrook, if they found any fragments of the statue in that pit.

"I recall you saying the temple was dedicated to Osiris," interjected Graf, who was now standing opposite Lowell.

"Amen was still revered and worshipped in most of the oases— the temple of Hibis being a perfect example," said Lowell. "And worship of one cult figure does not preclude another."

The smiling faces of content workers surrounded the Egyptologist on all sides. Colbrook suspected they were due for a bonus payment as a result of the morning's success.

Coslovich, on the other hand, stared blankly at the statue. He was probably thinking about the nuisance of having transported it around in the back of the minivan, running the very real risk that their vehicle might have been randomly searched by the Egyptian police.

Cavoski moved back and framed the beaming faces of the laborers, sweeping the shouldered camera in a wide pan. Lowell stepped in front of the lens and said a few words about the find, kneeling to point out the salient features of the statue. The Serbians were not taking their sound work very seriously, simply relying on the microphone mounted on the camera. Colbrook stepped away, not wishing to end up in the shot. Graf soon joined him.

Both men drifted through and then away from the assembled laborers. When they had moved some distance from the crowd, Colbrook asked Graf if he was going somewhere.

Graf stepped around a shovel lying in the sand and replied, "I'm leaving in the afternoon. I'm going with a convoy into Sudan."

"How long does that usually take?"

"A few days."

They had both stopped walking. Graf turned, watching Coslovich pacing around the statue. "The aqueduct maps are in Lowell's tent. In the bookshelf. A black binder. They're pretty rudimentary."

Colbrook nodded in reply.

"Most of the shafts you're probably planning on using to gain access to the fort are heavily silted up," Graf informed him. "It will take considerable effort to clear them. Don't waste any time. This dig will be closing down in two weeks. Everything has to be finished by then."

A group of Egyptian workers had assembled around the original granite statue. Lifting the plywood box, they carefully carried it to Lowell's tent and disappeared inside. Reappearing, they wandered over to the crated diorite figure, waiting for the Egyptologist to give them the signal to move it. The other laborers had resumed their previous positions in and around the many scattered pits. The dig site was slowly returning to normal.

With a sweep of his hand Lowell indicated that the second statue should be carried to his tent. He walked away from the Serbians, who were now preparing to bring their equipment back to their quarters. Lowell approached Graf and Colbrook. His face seemed even ruddier than normal.

"Remarkable finds," said Colbrook as the Egyptologist walked closer. "I guess I'll have to keep quiet about them until the SCA clears the artifacts for public release, though with the long delays involved in publishing it probably won't matter."

"I've spoken with Rashad already," said Lowell. "He'll clear them. There's nothing controversial about the artifacts. It's pretty obvious what we have."

"That's convenient," said Graf.

"About the only benefit of being forced to have an SCA inspector on site," replied Lowell. "But don't tell Rashad I said that."

"I'd give you a hand with the cleaning," began Graf, "but I need to continue preparations for the upcoming convoy."

"Shouldn't take long anyway," responded Lowell. "Well, I better get to work." He nodded to Colbrook, and began strolling towards his tent.

When the Egyptologist had disappeared into the tent, Graf suddenly declared, "I always thought there was something a little odd about this dig."

Colbrook was only vaguely paying attention to Graf. He was watching a distant stream of dust billowing across the desert to the west. It was an approaching vehicle.

"Looks like Lowell has another visitor," Colbrook said.

The vehicle gleamed in the sunlight.

Graf slowly turned in the direction of Colbrook's gaze.

"Looks new," said Graf absentmindedly.

Colbrook did not reply. He continued watching the vehicle draw steadily closer. As it approached he realized he had seen it before—parked outside the Karnak Club. It was painted a distinctive metallic blue.

"Toyota full-sized pickup," declared Colbrook.

He awaited Graf's reaction.

"Someone's in the back," said Graf.

The pickup was slowing to make the final turn toward the dig site. Chrome and glass flickered in the sunlight, the large alloy wheels flashing like solar beacons. Two men rode in the open back, their clothing unmistakably Egyptian. Both wore turbans and the ubiquitous *galabiya*, but what Colbrook found most disturbing were the automatic rifles slung from their shoulders. The truck did not slow, but barreled straight towards them.

It slid to a stop in the sand, not more than thirty feet away.

The two men in the pickup's bed jumped to the ground, their rifles pulled tight on their backs. Colbrook waited for the driver to exit, watching the armed men carefully.

The driver's door swung open and Nedic stepped out.

Colbrook looked around for the guards that were supposed to protect the archeological team from looters and bandits. They were nowhere to be found. He had not seen them at all that day.

Nedic looked much the same as Colbrook remembered him, although he had exchanged his dark and nondescript clothing for lighter and more casual wear. He did not appear to be armed, but that was not surprising considering the firepower he had in tow.

"Any luck?" Graf asked Nedic as the oversized Serbian approached on foot.

Nedic ignored the question. He was eyeing Colbrook's begrimed clothes.

Graf turned to Colbrook. "Mr. Nedic is part of the documentary crew."

The two armed Egyptians stood motionless.

"Expecting trouble?" asked Colbrook.

Nedic only glared at him.

"I see you've hired some new men," said Graf.

"Let's get out of the sun," declared Nedic. His English was serviceable but thickly accented. "Where's Coslovich and Cavoski?"

Colbrook glanced over at Graf, waiting for him to react. After some hesitation, Graf began walking in the direction of the Serbians' tent. Colbrook followed Nedic. The two armed Egyptians took up the rear.

They soon reached the tent, and Nedic ushered Graf inside. The two Egyptians waited for Colbrook to follow. He pushed through the loose canvas flaps and stepped onto the wooden floor inside. The gunmen remained outside.

Graf stood on the right side of the tent, resting one arm on a stack of equipment cases. Standing next to him was Coslovich, wiping his dusty face with a damp cloth and muttering something about the infernal desert. Cavoski was seated in a plastic lounge chair facing the entrance, drinking from a large clear plastic jug of water. He put it down on his lap with a slosh. His face was pink from exhaustion, his mesh baseball cap tilted back on his head. On his right stood Nedic. He appeared even larger in the confines of the tent, his bullet-shaped head quite menacing at close quarters. His face was fixed in a scowl.

Looking at Colbrook with a decidedly unfriendly gaze, Nedic began talking very rapidly in Serbian. Cavoski and Coslovich listened, occasionally glancing over at Colbrook during the one-sided conversation. Nedic suddenly stopped talking, waiting for a response. Coslovich said a few words while Cavoski nodded. Graf was staring at the floor. Colbrook had no idea what they were saying, and assumed the same went for Graf. The conversation went on for quite some time, clearly shifting from topic to topic.

Finally Cavoski looked up from his chair and said to Colbrook, "Why were you at the Karnak Club on Friday night?"

"To meet Lowell. To find out if I could visit the dig site," replied Colbrook. "Ask Graf. He was there."

Graf nodded in agreement.

Cavoski turned to Nedic and spoke quickly in their native tongue.

Nedic tilted his head back, and staring down the bridge of his nose asked, "Who are you working for?"

"I only work for myself," stated Colbrook, looking directly at Nedic.

Splashing water on his face, Cavoski said, "He wants a share of the deal."

"We told him about the Roman gold," explained Coslovich, tossing the cloth into a plastic trash can.

"I'm still taking my full share," insisted Colbrook. "You'll have to cut him in on your percentage."

Nedic glared at him.

Cavoski shrugged. "Nedic is still very suspicious of you. I tried to explain. He followed you in Luxor. He says you tricked him."

"What do you expect—look at him," answered Colbrook. "For all I knew he might have been a competitor. Tell him he needs to buy some shoes with softer soles. He's about as inconspicuous as an elephant wearing wooden clogs."

Nedic flexed his hands and simultaneously managed a crocodilian smile. "Don't let my accent deceive you. I'm not stupid. I know what you're talking about."

Cavoski said a few words to Nedic in Serbian. Nedic was scowl-
ing again when he directed his attention to Coslovich. The director
was brushing sand from the knees of his pants, muttering something
about the tripod being covered in grease and staining his clothes.

Talking exclusively in Serbian again, Nedic spoke for several
minutes without even the slightest glance in Colbrook's direction.
Interspersed throughout his diatribe the name *Vukasinov* was liber-
ally sprinkled. Both Coslovich and Cavoski interrupted him from
time to time. A heated argument was soon taking place between
the three Serbians.

"What does he want?" inquired Graf.

Coslovich turned to look at Graf, his face grim. "Do I have to
translate?"

"We've already agreed on this," replied Graf. "He can't just barge
in here and make new demands."

"He's not taking orders from us anymore," declared Coslovich.

Graf had a worried expression on his face. Colbrook moved his
hand closer to his pocket, his fingertips resting on the edge of the
pistol's handgrip.

"I make the decisions now," said Nedic with a snarl. He advanced
on Graf, his face twisted into a fury. "I think it's time you cooperate. No more games."

"I will not," said Graf. His voice was steady, but his face showed
fear.

"You have no choice," declared Nedic. He was within an arm's
reach of Graf.

"Get this lunatic away from me!" exclaimed Graf. He looked to
Coslovich for assistance. The Serbian director stepped in front of
Nedic, holding up his hand.

"Get out of my way," growled Nedic.

Coslovich moved aside.

"You don't have a choice anymore!" shouted Nedic. He was
smacking his fist into his open palm.

Graf backed up into a stack of equipment cases. He was reaching
into his pocket, fumbling to pull something out. A small revolver
appeared in his hand. He pointed it at Nedic.

The burly Serbian struck Graf's outstretched arm with the back of
his fist. The revolver fired, the bullet deflecting with a sharp *slap!* off

the reinforced corner of a steel case before striking the large plastic jug of water resting on Cavoski's lap. The cinematographer stared at the mark on the corner of the case, but soon turned his gaze closer to himself, watching in shocked disbelief as water slowly emptied through the bullet hole located halfway up the clear jug onto his leg. Nedic's second blow sent the revolver flying from Graf's hand. It struck the floor and discharged into the ceiling of the tent, a bright spot of sky showing through the solid canvas.

Graf dove for the revolver as Nedic kicked at it, sending it spinning under a shelf. With Graf now off balance, Nedic drove his fist into his stomach. Grunting in pain, Graf sat down abruptly on a large fiberglass equipment case, doubled over in agony.

Colbrook had his hand poised over his pistol. Out of the corner of his eye he saw the two Egyptian gunmen peering into the tent. When they could see Nedic was still on his feet and Graf was not, they backed out.

Coslovich had ducked when the gun had first gone off, and was now looking at Nedic with his mouth open. It was obvious he had not anticipated the sudden violent outburst. Cavoski lifted the plastic jug from his lap, placing it gingerly on the floor as if potentially explosive. The bullet had sunk to the bottom.

"What kind of game are you playing?" Nedic demanded, looming over Graf.

Graf looked up with a pained expression, still holding his stomach.

Reaching behind his back, Nedic pulled out a pistol that had been concealed in his waistband. It looked like a toy in his large hand. He pointed it at Graf. "Tell me—or I will kill you."

"You can't," groaned Graf. "You can't kill me."

Nedic stared at Graf.

"He says he's found a very good hiding place," explained Coslovich. "He's the only one who knows where it is."

Nedic lowered the gun. He was breathing hard, still staring at Graf.

Colbrook started to relax, his hand moving away from his pocket. Nedic appeared to be coming to his senses. Then the big Serbian turned his head slightly and winced. Blood was seeping through the left side of his shirt, just above the hip. Nedic touched it with his hand. The first bullet had actually grazed him.

"You're a liar," declared Nedic hoarsely. He lifted his handgun and fired a single shot into the center of Graf's chest.

Colbrook watched in disbelief as Graf pitched backwards off the equipment case, his arms flailing outward as he hit the floor. He lay still, his feet propped up on the container. A crimson stain began to spread across his shirt.

Nedic returned his gun to his waistband and stepped sideways, moving around the large case. He rolled Graf's body over and began searching it. Scraps of paper fluttered from his hand as he rifled through the open shirt pockets. He looked at them for a few seconds each, flinging them aside. When he checked Graf's pants pockets he found a set of keys. He threw them across the floor in disgust. They slid almost to Colbrook's feet.

While the mad Serbian continued his futile search, Colbrook slowly bent down and retrieved the keys. No one seemed to be paying any attention to what he was doing. He stared at the key ring before closing his hand over it. On it were the keys to the Isuzu, along with several others.

He started backing quietly in the direction of the entrance.

"Where's Lowell?" grunted Nedic, continuing the search. He was not finding anything of interest. "He must know something."

He rose and stepped toward Colbrook.

Halting, Colbrook watched Nedic advancing. The burly Serbian had his gun out again, and was waving it around in a menacing fashion. Colbrook did not doubt he might use it again.

"What about you?" Nedic barked.

"We already told you he knows nothing about—" began Cavoski.

"I'm not asking you," growled Nedic. He walked closer to Colbrook. His hovering face was covered in a thin film of sweat. "Where is Lowell?"

An engine started outside.

Nedic charged through the tent flaps. Colbrook followed.

Lowell was pulling the driver's door of an old Land Cruiser closed, a cloud of bluish smoke already coming from the tailpipe. Maneuvering the vehicle rapidly in reverse, streams of sand shooting out from under all four tires, the Egyptologist gunned the engine and swerved away from the tents.

Nedic was already running across the sand towards the blue

pickup, the armed men trailing him practically tripping over their *galabiyas* in the sudden race to keep up.

Colbrook gripped the set of keys tightly and increased his own rate of travel. The workers had stopped digging and sifting, their faces turned in the direction of the tents. There was an eerie stillness in the air. Colbrook kept running, ignoring the inquisitive looks he was getting from afar.

Up ahead Nedic had reached the blue Toyota pickup, his thugs almost at his heels. The two Egyptians vaulted into the open bed. Nedic practically tore the door off the truck getting in. The engine roared to life seconds later, the tires churning sand as the truck made a tight turn, racing after Lowell's Land Cruiser.

Colbrook sprinted towards the Isuzu. As he reached the side of the vehicle he took one last look in the direction of the desert track. Nedic was driving away in a billowing cloud of dust, the two Egyptians holding on for dear life.

Climbing into the Isuzu and pulling the door closed, Colbrook reached for the ignition. As soon as the engine started he stamped on the gas pedal. The vehicle slewed over the soft sand. Violently spinning the wheel, he eased the gas pedal halfway off the floor and then steadily pressed it down again. The truck accelerated. He grabbed at the seatbelt, pulling it across himself and latching it.

The windshield Graf had so carefully cleaned was already coated with a film of sand. Through it Colbrook focused on the thick plume of dust trailing Lowell's Land Cruiser. At roughly half that distance Nedic's blue pickup was barreling along at a suicidal rate of speed, leaving an even larger dust trail in its wake.

Colbrook guided the Isuzu onto the packed sand road. It soon became very rough, with large ruts and loose rocks strewn about unpredictably. Swerving and accelerating around the more obvious obstacles, Colbrook held the wheel tightly. The truck bounced violently at times, the seatbelt keeping him from being tossed out of the seat. As the surface of the road deteriorated Colbrook knew the vehicles up ahead would be forced to slow down. That was already the case with Lowell's Land Cruiser, but not so with the pickup. The Serbian kept blasting along as if he were on a paved road. He did not slow until he reached some of the sharper curves. Lowell's vehicle was now only a hundred yards or so ahead of Nedic's.

Colbrook managed to approach the blue pickup without blowing a tire or destroying the Isuzu's suspension. The two Egyptians riding in the open back were so badly shaken by the bone-shattering ride that they did not react to his presence. They gripped the sides of the truck, their rifles swinging wildly on their backs. Their mouths were moving, but their eyes were shut. Colbrook suspected they were praying for deliverance.

It was soon apparent that Nedic knew he was being followed—the pickup started swerving from side to side. Lowell's truck was now only fifty yards ahead, rapidly approaching a section of the roadway consisting of a series of short turns crossing the face of a steep downward slope. At the bottom of the hill was the paved road leading to Baris. Lowell's brake lights flashed intermittently as he began to negotiate the alternating curves.

Colbrook swerved to pass the Toyota pickup on its right side, but was soon forced to drop back to avoid a certain collision. He accelerated again until his grill was practically touching the back bumper of the blue truck. Giving the gas pedal a quick jab with his foot, he smacked forcefully into the back of the pickup. The two Egyptians stared at him with astonishment as they were tossed about, bouncing off the rear window and the plastic liner covering the truck bed in rapid succession. The pickup suddenly surged forward, disappearing in a cloud of swirling dust.

A dull thud came from the passenger side of the Isuzu, accompanied by a loud whistling sound. There was a ragged hole in the windshield just above the dashboard, and another hole in the plastic of the dashboard itself. Fluid began dripping from the glove compartment. A second thump came an instant later, the right outside mirror disintegrating in a dispersing cloud of plastic and glass. Swerving violently to the left, Colbrook strained to see through the billowing dust.

The view cleared as he rounded a sharp corner, and he found himself staring directly into the back of the pickup truck. The two Egyptians were kneeling down, their rifles held low for maximum stability. Flashes came from both muzzles and at the same instant the hood of the Isuzu shook under the incoming rounds. A series of holes appeared as if by magic on the sloping metalwork. Turning the wheel sharply to the right, Colbrook eased off the accelerator.

He pulled the 9mm pistol from his pocket and placed it on the passenger seat.

Having allowed some distance to open up between his vehicle and Nedic's pickup, Colbrook was now free of the blinding cloud of dust. He could see Lowell's Land Cruiser almost at the bottom of the hill, accelerating and about to move off the sand and onto the narrow paved roadway that continued on towards Baris.

Nedic abruptly swerved off the track into a series of low descending dunes in an attempt to bypass the slow switchback turns Lowell had traveled down. It seemed the Serbian planned on aiming his vehicle straight down the sandy incline. Colbrook had little choice but to follow, though he had reservations about the viability of such a maneuver.

As the blue pickup gained speed on the slope, the two Egyptians stood up, bracing their arms against the roof of the cab while holding their automatic rifles.

The drop down the face of the first dune was not difficult, and Colbrook steered the Isuzu into position to ascend the next. Ahead the blue pickup reached the shallow depression between the dunes and then suddenly surged forward, rocketing up towards the ridge at the top of the next dune. In a spray of flying sand the pickup began descending again, its rear wheels briefly airborne as it cleared the slender peak. Where Nedic had learned to drive with such skill and daring was anyone's guess, but he was making considerable gains on Lowell.

Colbrook followed the pickup's tracks through the sand, mimicking Nedic's techniques as best he could. He was halfway down the second dune when the Isuzu suddenly twisted sideways on the loose face of the dune, both right wheels leaving the ground. Reacting quickly to avoid the imminent rollover, Colbrook swerved hard in the opposite direction. The right wheels struck the ground and dug in, sending sand spraying against the windows. After a measured use of the accelerator, the Isuzu's path straightened. Colbrook continued on his downward journey, his eyes locked on the pickup's tailgate.

Lowell's Land Cruiser was now on the pavement and gaining momentum. Nedic was clearing the last dune, the blue pickup fishtailing down the flowing sand on the other side. The Egyptian gunmen still faced forward, leaning on the cab.

Colbrook pressed hard on the accelerator to clear the last ridge, landing almost on the front bumper as he came down on the other side, his view momentarily blocked by a dense cloud of onrushing sand. When it cleared, the pickup had reached the paved road and was speeding after Lowell's disappearing Land Cruiser.

Slowing to turn towards the paved roadway, Colbrook braced himself as the Isuzu bounced violently onto the asphalt shoulder. He swerved into the middle of the road, pushing down on the gas pedal. The engine howled.

The pickup definitely had the edge in horsepower—aerodynamics were another story. With their *galabiyas* flapping in the wind and their guns pointing forward over the cab of the truck, the two gunmen waited for their opportunity. Lowell was clearly not able to fathom the speed at which Nedic intended to drive his truck, and it was not long before the distance between the Land Cruiser and the pickup diminished significantly.

Colbrook struggled to match the pickup's speed—he could not match its acceleration. Glancing over at the pistol lying on the seat, he knew its effectiveness from this range was questionable at best.

It soon became clear that Lowell was aware of the approaching danger, but the narrowness of the road left him little in the way of options unless he felt inclined to go off-road. The armed Egyptians struggled to steady their weapons on the roof of the pickup's cab, their heads low, looking down the sights of their rifles. Colbrook heard the chatter of their fire.

The rounds all struck very low on the Land Cruiser, carrying off parts of the license plate and bumper. A few seconds later the taillights were blown off, one of these remaining remarkably intact as it sailed up and over the pickup. The underside-mounted spare tire bore the brunt of the next sustained burst, the rubber exploding off the rim, propelled by the sudden release of air pressure. The whole wheel detached, sparking as it skidded across the road.

Colbrook swerved to miss it, fighting to keep the Isuzu on the road. It was rocking wildly from side to side. The speedometer was hovering around eighty. He saw parts of the back bumper of Lowell's Land Cruiser bouncing down the roadway, along with strips of chrome and rubber spinning and scattering away into the desert.

Lowell was slowing down. The Toyota pickup was still gaining speed. Colbrook had his foot to the floor. The Egyptian gunmen were kneeling again, their rifles aimed out the side of the pickup as Nedic closed on the Land Cruiser. Lowell was still losing speed, and it did not take long for Nedic to draw alongside him. The Egyptians were very proficient in the time they had available to accurately discharge their automatic weapons. They appeared to be trying to destroy as much of the vehicle as possible without actually killing Lowell in the process.

The rear windows of the Land Cruiser vanished in an instant. The back door handles and lower plastic body trim came off next. Riddled with countless holes, the side panels were beginning to peel away from the underlying frame. The roadway was coated with gleaming bits of wreckage, with more being added every second. Colbrook approached within a car length of the pickup.

Suddenly one of the Land Cruiser's rear tires blew off in a cloud of gray smoke. Seconds later the disintegrating vehicle swerved off the pavement and began to slow in the deep sand bordering the road.

The pickup shot past the wrecked Land Cruiser. The Egyptians turned to examine their handiwork. Not fancying a repeat of the last encounter, Colbrook already had the pistol out and the window down. He fired two quick shots, one aimed at the wide back window of the pickup, the other at the rear tire. He missed the tire, but hit the window. Ignoring the possibility of braking, Colbrook struck the pickup square on the tailgate.

The impact forced one of the gunmen to let go of his rifle and grab for the side of the truck. The rifle flew from his hands, ricocheting off the grill of the Isuzu and disappearing from view. The second gunmen managed to hang onto his rifle, but fell violently to the bed of the pickup when Nedic made an unexpected maneuver. When he sat back up he had a dazed expression on his face.

With the gunmen temporarily incapacitated, Colbrook dropped back from the crushed tailgate of the Toyota and accelerated forward until he was alongside the truck. He drove with his right hand on the wheel, his left still holding Lowell's pistol. The dazed gunman struggled to untangle his rifle strap from his shoulder. The unarmed Egyptian watched in disbelief as Colbrook calmly took aim and fired at the truck's rear tire. The bullet sparked off the rim.

Dropping behind the pickup, Colbrook took aim again, struggling to line up the sights with the missing back window. His new plan was to shoot Nedic or the windshield.

The dazed gunman had by now disentangled his rifle strap and brought the barrel of his rifle up. Colbrook fired the pistol again. The bullet went low, penetrating the center console of the pickup with an explosion of splintering plastic. Nedic swerved in reaction, but straightened the vehicle seconds later. Colbrook was not so lucky—the gunman still had half a magazine left.

A hail of bullets slammed into the front of the Isuzu. The grill exploded into tiny fragments, taking most of the radiator with it. Both headlights shattered and the front hood began to disintegrate under the closely spaced impacts. All of this, along with paint chips and bits of flattened steel, flew up over the windshield and into the slipstream like industrial confetti.

Colbrook swerved, trying to avoid the next series of incoming rounds. Lifting his foot from the gas pedal, he flung the pistol into the passenger footwell, gripping the almost uncontrollable steering wheel with both hands. Seconds later he heard a loud *pop!* and the steering wheel spun itself forcefully to the left. He began slowing the Isuzu, trying to regain control. A sudden jolt told him he had gone off the pavement, and then his view was blocked by a cloud of swirling sand. He felt like he was flying for several long seconds, and then the truck began to roll. When he opened his eyes he was hanging sideways in his seat by the seatbelt, the Isuzu resting on its right side. The engine died seconds later, a row of red lights flickering across the instrument panel. The sound of a long skid pierced the numbing stillness, followed by the whine of the pickup's transmission in reverse.

Fumbling with the seatbelt, Colbrook managed to unlatch it and maintain his position by holding onto the steering wheel with his left hand. Stretching and reaching down with his right arm, he was able to retrieve the handgun. It was lying against the inside of the passenger door below him. Gripping the pistol tightly in his right hand, he pulled himself back with his left arm. Poised in this position he waited, listening. The sound of the pickup's engine grew louder and then passed with a roar. It was moving in the direction of Lowell's destroyed Land Cruiser.

Transferring the gun into his belt, Colbrook pulled the keys from the ignition and pushed them into his pocket. He grabbed the edge of the doorframe above the open driver's window, pulling himself up and onto the side of the wrecked truck. He paused for a moment, his feet dangling inside the vehicle. Lifting his feet out, he slid across to the bottom of the door. With a quick twist of his legs he dropped onto the soft sand below. The underside of the Isuzu was facing the road, the roof facing the desert.

Walking to the blacktop, Colbrook looked in the direction he had just driven from.

In the distance the Land Cruiser was parked at the edge of the pavement, the blue pickup idling at its side. The driver's door was open on the Land Cruiser, and Lowell was being forced at gunpoint into the passenger seat of the pickup truck. He appeared to have sustained no serious injuries. At half that distance one of the Egyptians was retrieving his battered rifle from the middle of the road. The pickup started rolling forward, headed in Colbrook's direction. It slowed just enough to allow the gunman carrying the recovered rifle to swing himself over the crushed tailgate.

Running back to the Isuzu, Colbrook dove to the ground behind it, the roof inches from his shoulder. The blue truck went blasting by, heading towards Baris. The two Egyptians were crouched low in the cargo bed, their heads down. Colbrook could see Lowell inside the cab, looking back at the wrecked Isuzu through the missing back window of the once gleaming pickup.

11

Colbrook stood in the narrow band of shade afforded by the toppled Isuzu and watched for approaching vehicles. Half an hour had
elapsed, and still no one had driven past. He was now forced to
imagine the possibility that he might be stranded for hours in the
hot desert. It was already past eleven o'clock in the morning, and
the sun was growing stronger every minute. Baris was at least four
miles away to the north, a distance not negotiable on foot without
an ample water supply.

Just when all hope was evaporating into the dry air, an old dump
truck lumbered up from the south. Colbrook dashed into the road
and started waving his arms. The driver slowed the truck to a
crawl, stopping several yards short of him after much squealing of
brakes.

Colbrook lost no time in making his way to the passenger door.
The chrome handle was almost too hot to touch.

With rheumy eyes and a leathery countenance, the old Egyptian
man hunched over the large steering wheel gave Colbrook a friendly
nod, greeting him wholeheartedly with *sabáah al-khayr*. He wore
a spotless brown *galabiya* and a small white skullcap. As soon as
Colbrook pulled the door shut the brakes were released, the driver's
bare feet working the clutch and the gas pedal simultaneously. A
pair of sandals sat on the dashboard.

After explaining the wrecked Isuzu as the result of his inexperi-
ence in dune driving, Colbrook soon realized the driver had little
understanding of English. He simply nodded at any statement. It
certainly made it easier for Colbrook during the short drive to

Baris—the man asked no questions, and therefore he was not ob-ligated to provide any answers.

Not a single vehicle passed them as they approached the town, and Colbrook now realized how fortunate he had been that the dump truck had turned up. On the outskirts of Baris the driver pointed at a dirt road leading to a substantial date-palm plantation. Downshifting, he guided the heavy vehicle onto the rudimentary road and stopped. Colbrook thanked the man in the best Arabic he could assemble, and jumped down from the cab, pushing the door closed. With a quick wave to the smiling driver, he strode towards the many low mud-brick structures that made up the outer fringes of the remote desert town. The truck rumbled away into the grove of date palms.

Stopping at a gas station to buy a bottle of soda to quench his raging thirst, Colbrook stumbled upon a small desert tour operator in the adjacent garage. Though the owner greeted him with much interest, at first he refused to drive him to Luxor, declaring that he only provided local tours around the Kharga Oasis. He finally gave in when the price Colbrook was willing to pay reached double what anyone could reasonably expect for the trip. When the man backed his vehicle from the building's interior, Colbrook realized why he had not been enthusiastic about the long drive—it was a Land Rover that looked to be several decades old.

Unfortunately there was no better option at the moment. As a precaution Colbrook purchased several large jugs of water—four gallons each—and stocked the empty ice chests in the back of the truck with non-perishable food.

After fueling the vehicle and filling several additional fuel cans that hung from a sturdy frame on the back door, they departed. It was now the hottest part of the day, and the Land Rover was not air-conditioned. Their only relief from the heat was the breeze blast-ing through the windows as they drove. While this worked well enough at high speeds, when the truck slowed to climb inclines and negotiate turns, the sweltering heat soon returned.

Adding insult to his already grubby appearance, Colbrook was slowly being coated from head to toe in a fine powdery dust kicked up by tires that were too wide for the fenders.

With plenty of liquid refreshment and assorted snacks remaining, they arrived in Armant a little after four o'clock. They crossed over the Nile on the bridge south of Luxor, and twenty minutes later were in Luxor, parked in front of the huge temple complex along the river. Tourists crowded the sidewalks, streaming towards the imposing ruins, their heads covered in hats of all shapes and sizes, their cameras gripped in keen anticipation. Colbrook paid the driver the rest of his fee and then gave him a little extra, telling him to have a reputable mechanic thoroughly check his vehicle before making an attempt to return to Baris. The driver happily agreed, but Colbrook suspected he had no intention of doing so—being baked to death was a worthwhile risk if there was a chance to pocket a few extra Egyptian pounds.

The Rover rumbled off.

Standing on the sidewalk in his rumpled and dusty clothes, Colbrook pulled Graf's keys from his pocket. One which had caught his eye earlier had a green plastic tag affixed to the top with the words *George Hotel* printed on it. He asked a nearby street vendor if he knew where such an establishment was located. The man gave him directions, and Colbrook purchased an ice-cream sandwich from his cart as a token of good will.

It did not take long to find the hotel—a small building away from the bustle of the tourist-infested areas, and almost adjacent to the train station. The outside was covered in narrow wooden balconies and small windows with metal bars. It retained a certain charm despite its aging facade. A brass placard above the main entrance indicated the hotel's name in large block letters, the date following—1924—apparently specifying the year of its construction.

Colbrook pushed through the glass doors, stepping into the lobby. It did not have a reception desk, and he soon realized why. A row of mailboxes on the inside wall suggested it was more akin to an apartment building, with most of the residents apparently staying for longer than just a few days or weeks. Pulling the keychain from his pocket again, he examined the key with the green tag. A small engraved letter C and the numeral 2 were barely visible on the neck of the brass key, almost worn away with age. Glancing at the doorways on the ground floor, he could see they all started with the letter A. He started up the narrow staircase, heading for the third floor.

Except for the quiet hum of air conditioning and the patter of his shoes on the tiled stairs, the building was silent. He reached the third floor and turned into a short hallway. Only four doors were visible, two on the right side of the hall and two on the left. All of the doors were closed except the last one on the right, which was open just a crack. Slipping Lowell's handgun from his pocket, he approached the open door, his shoes noiseless on the carpet.

It came as no surprise that painted on the door was C2. Even less remarkable were the obvious signs of a forced entry. The jamb and a considerable portion of the door edge were squashed and twisted from the use of a pry bar in the hands of someone who was clearly capable of exerting considerable force. It was also clear why the door was not properly closed—the deadbolt and doorknob latch were both damaged beyond repair. He had more than a suspicion who had been wielding the pry bar.

Listening for any sounds from inside the apartment, Colbrook pushed the door open with his foot

It looked as if a tornado had swirled through the room, flinging the contents in every direction. Furniture was overturned, drawers pulled out, lamps flung into the corners, and couch and chair cushions torn apart with methodical disintegration. The small kitchen was emptied of its contents—glasses, cookware, silverware, and crockery, all lying in a heap on the floor. The refrigerator and dishwasher were pulled from their positions, their doors swung open.

Stepping gingerly over the threshold, Colbrook entered the apartment. The carpeting was cut in several places and rolled back. Paintings had been pulled from the walls and tossed to the floor. A cabinet which had apparently once held a television was dashed practically to pieces, the television itself lying broken on the floor. Moving carefully through the ransacked room, Colbrook walked towards what he assumed was the bedroom.

It was much the same—everything torn apart and thrown about. The mattress was propped up against the wall, a long cut down its center, white foam bulging from its sides. The nightstand was flipped over, the ceramic lamp smashed to bits. More clothing littered the floor, most of it visibly trampled. The bathroom yielded similar results. The shower curtains were pulled down, the toilet tank cover was removed, all the personal grooming items were scattered on the floor, and the sink cabinet plundered to near destruction. The search had been thorough and complete.

Slipping the handgun into his pocket, Colbrook stepped from the bathroom back into the bedroom. He took one last lingering look around, and then returned to the living room. Weaving through the littered wreckage, he swung the battered entrance door aside and walked back out into the carpeted hallway, pulling the door into the same position it had been earlier.

Descending the stairs two steps at a time, Colbrook reached the lobby without incident. He had been lucky so far—apparently no one had come either in or out of the building during the time he had been inside. Walking briskly to the glass doors, he pushed through them to the street outside.

His senses were immediately assaulted by the heat and noise of Luxor in late afternoon. Pausing to look at the nearest street sign, he made a line for the Sharia Cleopatra, the less crowded thoroughfare on his right.

Crossing at the intersection, he started to make his way northwest. The sidewalk was primarily lined with residential buildings, with a few shops interspersed along the way.

He had already made up his mind to return to his own apartment. There was little he could do to help Lowell under the circumstances, and though he entertained the idea that Nedic might still be residing in the high-rise hotel nearby, he suspected that the trigger-happy Serbian had gone somewhere else—somewhere more secluded.

Pushing on toward the river and the ferry, Colbrook assumed it was likely he was being followed. The sidewalk was becoming quite crowded, and after he had glanced over his shoulder several times without locating anyone suspicious, he stopped beside a street vendor sitting on the crumbling curb. His wares consisted of several boxes full of old softcover books. Bending forward to examine the titles, Colbrook worked his way around the cartons so that he was facing in the direction he had just come from. The crowd continued to surge past. Only one man stopped walking, choosing instead to examine a cell phone that he had removed from his pocket.

He was a thin Egyptian wearing a tan *galabiya*. He had a large bushy mustache, the rest of his face covered in dark unshaven stubble. His head was covered with a white turban, small and tightly wrapped, looking much like a large onion perched atop his skull. His face was gaunt and drawn. A long horizontal scar bisected his forehead, curving down into his left eyebrow. He fiddled with the buttons on the cell phone, staring at the small screen. Several times he placed the phone to his ear as if listening.

Colbrook was not fooled by this behavior. He would need to either lose or incapacitate the man before returning to the Amenti House—preferably before crossing the Nile. He was not surprised Nedic had someone waiting at Graf's building. The Egyptian man had probably been instructed to follow anyone who took an interest in Graf's plundered residence. Nedic was clearly an old hand at this game.

Still examining the selection of books, Colbrook watched the man with the mustache continue to loiter on the sidewalk. He was now turned in the opposite direction, staring at the tips of his polished black shoes while holding the phone to his ear. A few seconds later the man swiveled his head, looking back at the sidewalk bookseller. Colbrook stepped away from the cartons of books and began walking again, still heading for the Nile.

A few hundred feet down the sidewalk Colbrook stopped in front of a cobbler's shop and watched the proprietor mending a pair of shoes. His tools were spread across a leather apron on a wooden box, while an antique sewing machine stood ready on a nearby table. He worked with a small hammer around the sole of a shoe, tapping at short nails. His client, an older man who was smoking, sat patiently on a metal stool in his socks.

Out of the corner of his eye Colbrook could see the man with the bushy mustache looking through the window of a nearby bakery. He was only fifty feet away, his onion-shaped turban quite distinct. With his right hand tucked inside the long center placket of his *galabiya* and his other hand hanging limply at his side, he waited for Colbrook to resume walking.

Moving away from the cobbler's shop, Colbrook increased his pace. He began searching for an alley that connected with another street, preferably one less crowded. After a few minutes he located a narrow gap running between two buildings. In a patch of sunlight at its far end a chestnut-colored horse was drinking water from a large concrete basin. Without even a backward glance, Colbrook

abruptly stepped into the shaded alleyway. He moved down it rapidly, approaching the thirsty beast. When he reached the other end
he found that the horse was standing in front of a large stable. It
appeared to be a depot of sorts for the many horse-drawn carriages
that plied the streets of Luxor, a place where drivers could bring
their horses for feed and water. There was room to house at least
a dozen animals comfortably.

The adjacent street seemed to end at the stables, branching into
two narrow cobblestone paths. Several empty carriages were parked
alongside the stable.

Colbrook brushed past the concrete trough. The horse continued
drinking. Once clear of the large animal, on his immediate right he
could see a row of empty stalls. Only one appeared to have a horse
inside. A quick glance over his shoulder told him all he needed to
know—the Egyptian man with the bushy mustache was approaching, jogging down the alleyway.

Dodging the plentiful horse droppings, Colbrook made a line for
the occupied stall. He ducked under the wooden door just as the
Egyptian man burst from the alley. Scrambling quickly to the rear
of the stall, he was careful not to spook the horse. Apparently quite
used to people, the animal largely ignored him, continuing to hang
its head out of the open upper door. Colbrook pulled the handgun
from his pocket, pressing himself against the boards that made up
the divider between the stalls.

Outside, the Egyptian skulked along, stopping and looking into
each stall. As the man drew closer, Colbrook jammed the gun
into his pocket. Snatching a heavy pitchfork from the back of the
stall, he waited for him to appear outside the door. A tense minute
passed. He wondered if bushy mustache had given up and turned
back. The horse swished its tail and then started to act restless.
Colbrook edged closer to the front of the stall, trying to determine
the cause of the horse's uneasiness. He was only slightly surprised
by what he saw.

The mustached man was crawling on all fours through the space
beneath the door of the stall. The top of his turban looked like a
giant mushroom cap. He was moving slowly, his head down, his
knees bearing the brunt of his shuffling crawl. A dagger of dama-
scene steel was gripped purposefully in his right hand. He looked

up with a startled expression. At the same instant Colbrook stepped forward and brought the wide handle of the pitchfork down on the back of the man's head.

The turban may have provided some protection against the blow, but it was clearly insufficient. He dropped like a felled tree.

Dragging the unconscious Egyptian to the back of the stall, Colbrook began searching for the cell phone he had seen earlier. He found it in the front pocket of the man's shirt. Tossing the tiny phone to the floor, he began grinding it into pieces with the heel of his shoe. When he was satisfied with the results, he put the pitchfork to its intended use and methodically covered the senseless man with hay.

Walking back to the front of the stall, he picked up the fallen knife. He dropped it into a large drain in the concrete floor. It slipped between the metal grates, splashing into the pipe below. Pushing open the stall door, Colbrook slipped out. He turned for a moment to secure the door, and then began walking briskly in the direction of the alley.

Emerging onto the Sharia Cleopatra, he continued down the street in a northwesterly direction, heading for the Nile. Reaching the Sharia al-Karnak, he crossed over it and made his way to the Corniche an-Nil. Standing briefly by the iron rail, he watched ferries and small craft of assorted types and sizes crossing the river. Groups of tourists crowded the sidewalk, talking loudly about their day's adventures and where to find a cool place to take a meal. Colbrook weaved his way through the sightseers, moving towards a concrete staircase that provided access to the river below. He pulled a few water-stained Egyptian pounds from his pocket in preparation for boarding a public ferry, and began descending the steps.

Walking out onto the largest pier, he approached a group of tourists waiting to cross the river. Many of them were wearing knapsacks and waist packs, and most had bottles of water in their hands. Hats abounded. Strolling along, Colbrook soon realized he was getting many astonished stares. Had he been an Egyptian it was doubtful anyone would have thought much of his appearance, but he was obviously not an Egyptian, and his torn and dirty clothes, his matted hair, and his dust-caked visage caused him to become the object of immediate attention. He strolled by an ogling backpacker in long knee-covering shorts, who had probably previously fancied himself the most adventurous person in the crowd, and continued to walk to the end of the pier.

A large ferry was moored on the other side of the river, its passengers just beginning to disembark. It would be at least another fifteen minutes before the vessel would return for the next group. Colbrook was growing weary. His condition was in some ways amusing, but it was becoming a problem. He was too conspicuous.

Close to shore several feluccas were battling for air. A few large river cruisers motored by, passengers crowded along the deck rails with their cameras ready. A rusting motor launch churned through the river, bringing workers from west to east, a faded Egyptian flag flying from its upper deck. A number of smaller motorboats buzzed across the water in both directions, some ferrying passengers.

One of these motorboats swiftly passed the end of the pier, going north. Suddenly it made a sharp turn, narrowly missing a felucca, and roared by in the opposite direction. It was a plain white fiberglass outboard, the three passengers inside all looking toward the pier. The boat slowed a few hundred yards up the river, making a wider turn as it nosed to the north again. It soon approached the pier, the sound of its engine dropping in pitch. Another sharp turn brought it parallel to the dock, the man at the wheel skillfully bringing it in broadside.

The motorboat bumped up against the wooden edgings on the pier not twenty-five feet from Colbrook. The three passengers were unquestionably Egyptians, two of them relatively young, one considerably older. The oldest wore a turban and *galabiya*, while the two younger men had short-cropped hair and were without head coverings of any kind. Both sported western-style clothes—one was in jeans, the other in khakis. The captain of the boat wore a red baseball cap and was clothed in a blue *galabiya*. From the darkness of his skin he looked to be Sudanese or Ethiopian.

The two younger men clambered from the boat, stepping onto the pier. They stood nearby, talking loudly in Arabic over the idling engine. While the captain was securing the small vessel, the older man with the turban waved to Colbrook. He was shouting something in broken English. Colbrook walked closer, trying to understand him. Soon it became obvious he was asking if he needed a ride across the river. Colbrook waved back, realizing he had a chance to skip the ferry and reach the opposite shore without waiting. He hurried towards the motorboat.

As he stepped carefully from the side of the pier and into the boat, the captain greeted him in a friendly way. The older man motioned that he should take a seat on a padded shelf that circled the interior of the motorboat. Colbrook seated himself facing the pier. The two younger men were now climbing back into the boat. The one wearing khakis quickly undid the lines, dropping them into the bottom of the boat, while the one in jeans sat opposite Colbrook. The captain resumed his position at the controls.

The younger man wearing the jeans held out his hand from the other side of the boat. Colbrook shook it.

"I'm Nuri," he said with a wide smile. Pointing to the man in the khakis who was taking a seat at his side, he declared, "My brother Azim."

"Martin," said Colbrook.

Nuri motioned towards the older man in the turban. "My uncle has recently run into financial difficulties. He owns the boat."

"Well, I'm certainly glad you stopped," said Colbrook. "What's the charge?"

"Ten pounds."

Colbrook pulled some bills from his pocket, holding them out to Nuri as he leaned forward.

"Yusuf," said Nuri. He was looking at the older man. "Look, we've made some more money." The turbaned man nodded. He was not so talkative now. Nuri took the bills and handed them across the small boat to him. The older man pocketed the money, mumbling something unintelligible in Arabic.

Colbrook leaned back, watching the two brothers. They did not look very similar to him, but did appear to be roughly the same age.

"Harith. Let's go!" shouted Nuri. He was yelling at the captain.

The motorboat gradually turned away from the pier, picking up speed as it changed its course to the west. When they reached the middle of the river Harith slowed the boat as quickly as he had throttled it forward. The engine dropped to idle. They were now drifting slowly northward with the current. Colbrook could not find any reason why they had stopped.

Nuri rose from his seat, lifting the cushion he had been sitting on. Azim was gazing fixedly at the bottom of the boat. Colbrook stared in disbelief at Nuri. The friendly Egyptian was retrieving a very large diving knife from under the seat. The blade was at least ten inches long, featuring a square tip and a serrated edge on one side. With deliberate slowness, Nuri slipped the lanyard hanging from the bottom of the handle over his wrist, twisting the knife tightly in his hand.

Azim finally looked up, his face devoid of emotion. He was waiting for Nuri to make his move.

Colbrook glanced over at Yusuf. He was as still as a pharaonic statue.

Nuri dropped the seat cushion with a thump. The boat was rocking gently now.

Colbrook stood up and reached for his gun, slamming his left arm into Yusuf's chest. The older man howled in pain, pitching backwards. Nuri lashed out viciously in the same instant, the polished blade flashing by. The square but razor-sharp tip missed Colbrook's face by only an inch. He did not think the end of such a knife was intended to be sharpened, but someone had spent a lot of time working on this one.

Colbrook felt something pulling at the back of his belt. It was Yusuf, trying to keep himself from falling overboard. Colbrook slammed his elbow into what he assumed was Yusuf's head. He heard a scream followed by a splash.

Azim now had a length of rope in his hand. He was yelling something at Nuri.

Colbrook yanked the gun from his pocket, his thumb tripping the safety. He stood with his feet apart for maximum balance. The boat was rocking more violently now, a result of the abrupt departure of Yusuf.

Both Azim and Nuri froze when they saw the gun.

Harith was looking back from the controls, an expression of disbelief spreading across his face.

Splashing and spluttering noises came from the side of the boat. Yusuf was struggling in the water, his *galabiya* floating like a giant jellyfish under his arms. He was not a very good swimmer, but he seemed to be able to stay afloat.

Backing slowly towards the stern, Colbrook covered the three men with the pistol. "Give him a hand. Pull him back into the boat." He waved the gun at Harith, who was closest to the floundering Yusuf.

Harith did not move.

"Nuri. Pull him in," demanded Colbrook.

Nuri did not move.

Harith finally did. He slammed the throttle forward.

Colbrook lost his balance in the sudden acceleration, his feet slipping on the smooth fiberglass. He fell backwards, his lower back connecting solidly with the engine cover. Briefly stunned by the impact, he looked up to see Nuri and Azim charging.

Azim was hurtling towards him, the length of rope clearly intended for his neck.

Colbrook brought the pistol up. The boat rolled violently just as he pulled the trigger, the bullet missing its intended target, blowing out the windscreen in front of Harith, who shouted something unintelligible and abruptly cut the engine. Azim splashed into the water on the side opposite Yusuf, having inadvertently thrown himself overboard. Nuri collided with Colbrook, slashing with the knife and connecting only with fiberglass. They both tumbled across the bottom of the boat.

Colbrook was now on his back.

Harith had abandoned the controls, his face rigid with fear.

Colbrook tried to raise the pistol, but Nuri had his arm pinned down with one knee and his shoulder immobilized with the other. The glint of the knife flashed before his eyes, the blade sweeping down again. He jerked his head to the side, kicking at Nuri's stomach with his feet. The knife tip sank into the fiberglass hull only inches from his ear.

Nuri dexterously avoided Colbrook's feet, retaliating by kicking at his gun hand. The knife swung wildly by from the opposite direction, scraping across the engine cover. Nuri's shoe rose, and when it came down Colbrook felt a stinging pain as the fingers of his gun hand were mashed under the hard plastic sole. He squeezed the trigger again. The report was muffled this time.

He had blown a hole through the bottom of the boat.

It was not a small clean bullet hole, but a crack.

The Nile began trickling in.

Nuri's looming face was contorted with rage.

Colbrook involuntarily released the gun after a second blow from Nuri's foot rendered his fingers useless and numb. The pistol slid away and disappeared into the sloshing water collecting in the stern. Nuri suddenly let go of Colbrook's shoulder, propelling himself backwards and to his feet. He was grasping the knife tightly again, his hand resting on the hot engine cover as he balanced himself. He did not seem to mind the fact that his hand had just been burned.

Colbrook sat up, staring at his own hand. All his fingers were still attached, though at least three of them were turning a pale shade of purple. He scrambled away from the stern of the boat, turning to face Nuri, who was now advancing with the knife held low and to the side. Harith had regained his senses and was trying to restart the engine. It sputtered and died, a cloud of blue smoke rising behind Nuri's arched back. A river cruiser was drawing near, its bows already too close for comfort.

Azim was doggy-paddling towards the stern of the boat. He was not very far away—a few more paddles and he would be within an arm's reach of the boat. Yusuf, on the other hand, was a speck in the distance, bobbing helplessly in the water and drifting slowly towards the eastern shoreline.

The back of the motorboat was considerably lower in the water than it had been, flooding faster than Colbrook had thought possible. The river cruiser was now practically on top of them, bearing down on the foundering boat. It seemed a collision was imminent from where Colbrook stood.

Nuri was oblivious to the oncoming danger.

A horn blasted a sudden ear-piercing warning. Nuri turned in surprise.

Harith was yelling now, twisting the ignition key violently.

The ship began to clear them—barely.

As it glided by Colbrook could see the faces of passengers on the top deck staring down at the motorboat. Typical of its design, the ship was sitting very low in the water. The wood railing on the lower deck was not more than six feet away. Colbrook could smell the diesel exhaust and feel the low vibration of the engines.

Harith suddenly got the motorboat's engine started. It sounded insignificant and puny compared to the rumbling diesels beside them.

Stepping up onto the edge of the motorboat's hull, Colbrook launched himself towards the side of the larger vessel. He heard Nuri yelling something to Harith, but he was already toppling sideways, his arms stretched to their fullest.

His hands found purchase on the ship's lower wooden rail located only inches above the deck, and he was suddenly yanked from the motorboat by the forward momentum of the river cruiser. The pain in his arms was excruciating, but he held on. As he spun free of the motorboat his legs dropped into the river with a splash. His arms felt like they would shortly be pulled from their sockets. He heard shouting from the upper deck of the cruiser. He turned to look back, his arms wrapped around the wooden rail. Nuri and Harith were rushing to the side of the motorboat, struggling to stay on their feet as the small vessel rolled over the bow waves of the large ship.

A shout came from much closer and Colbrook turned his head to look up. From the other side of the rail a man was reaching down to grab his arms. He was yelling the word *lunatic* over and over. Colbrook sensed another man had joined him—he wasn't paying strict attention to what was going on overhead—and both his arms were now being pulled at with considerable force. Flailing his feet out of the water, he tried to gain purchase on the smooth hull of the vessel with his soles, but his shoes continued to slip. The strength in his arms was fading quickly.

His legs splashed back into the water, twisting him around painfully. He tried to pull himself forward, but the flow of water was too strong. Exhausted, he leaned his head back, looking upwards. He could see passengers crowded along the rail on the top deck, staring down at him, mouths open, eyes wide, fingers pointing. It was all very impolite. The least they could do was toss him a line.

The sound of the high-pitched outboard motor soon mixed with the splashing and rumbling sounds of the larger vessel. Colbrook swiveled his head, sensing by the disturbing reaction of the onlookers that something was terribly wrong.

Harith was maneuvering the motorboat alongside, pushing ever closer to his dangling legs. The two men on the rail above Colbrook had been joined by several others. They were all shouting at the two

Egyptians in the motorboat, telling them it was too dangerous to attempt a rescue that way, but the motorboat kept coming, seemingly intent on crushing him between the two vessels—exactly the point of Harith's maneuvers.

Harith was proficient at the controls, and would probably soon succeed. Colbrook kicked upwards while the group of men pulled at his arms. His feet found the ledge the rail was fastened to just as the motorboat smacked into the side of the vessel, almost exactly where he had been hanging a second before. The men aboard the river cruiser were shouting at Nuri and Harith to back off. Resting in this awkward position, Colbrook could see that his rescuers now totaled more than a dozen men. Some of them were kneeling, trying to grab his feet. It was a gallant effort on their part, but his feet slipped all the same, plunging his legs into the water again.

Several men at the rail tried to grab him under his arms. One of them pulled at his injured hand. Colbrook stifled a howl of pain. Exhaustion was setting in. When he was almost on the verge of letting go and taking his chances in the water, he felt himself being lifted even higher. Some of the rescuers had leaned over the rail and were now holding his shirt. Fabric began to rip, seams failed, buttons flew. He swung wildly back out over the water, hands grabbing at him.

The sound of the whining outboard grew louder, and Colbrook struggled once again to find a foothold on the river cruiser's hull. He managed to get his feet back onto the margin of the deck, his upper body swaying out over the water.

Harith pounded into the larger vessel. Colbrook could see Nuri standing knee-deep in water alongside the engine, trying to bail the motorboat with a small bucket. A few seconds later the motorboat's outboard died, flooded with water. Nuri dropped the bucket. The Nile began pouring over the transom. The sudden weight of the inrushing water sent the bow shooting almost upright for an instant, throwing Harith from the controls. Nuri looked around in a panic, water now up to his waist.

With much effort, the men on the cruise ship finally managed to pull Colbrook over the rail, shouting invectives at the sinking motorboat. Colbrook dropped in exhaustion onto the teakwood deck.

"You better get help," said one of the men.

Colbrook could see another man hovering over him. He was wearing a bright yellow shirt and gray pants. Rolling onto his side, Colbrook gradually sat up. The man in the yellow shirt grabbed his shoulder, keeping him from falling over.

"I'll be fine," grunted Colbrook. He leaned his back against the exterior cabin wall, breathing heavily. A dozen tourists stared at him in disbelief.

The walkway was narrow, just wide enough for two people to pass one another. Large windows lined its entire length, identical blue curtains hanging inside of each. The man in the yellow shirt had joined the rest of the group. They were all now watching Colbrook more with curiosity than concern. Some of his rescuers were rushing away to get assistance.

"That was a crazy stunt," declared the man in the yellow shirt. "You must be nuts."

Colbrook was too tired to explain or argue the matter. He was slumped forward in his filthy and now mostly wet clothes, resting on his right elbow.

Near the midsection of the ship, where a break in the superstructure was visible, Colbrook saw two men emerge from a side door, hurrying towards him. One was undoubtedly another passenger—he wore checkered shorts and running shoes—while the other was an Egyptian man in a spotless white uniform. From the gold insignia visible on his epaulettes, he appeared to be the captain.

He was shouting at Colbrook. "Crazy man. You very nearly got yourself killed! Mad, absolutely mad!" He continued to rant in this fashion for several minutes until the man in the checkered shorts finally interrupted him by asking if the ship had a doctor.

"Does he need medical attention?" inquired the captain. He peered down at Colbrook.

"No—I'm fine," declared Colbrook. This was not entirely accurate—his fingers were quite numb. However, they seemed to work, and that was all that mattered for now.

Another man was making his way down the narrow deck. On his belt was a holstered revolver, the weight of it noticeably sagging his brown trousers. He was the ship's security guard. Walking with a purposeful stride, he approached with a frown. He stared at Colbrook, taking in the ridiculous site of his dust and dirt covered upper body and his wet and dripping pants, socks, and shoes.

"Slight mishap," said Colbrook, rising shakily to his feet. "I don't think that boat had its proper certification."

The captain was turning to look at the sudden commotion behind him.

The men on the deck were rushing to the rail. The motorboat was almost completely submerged, Nuri and Harith floundering in the water.

"I'd better radio for some help," said the captain. "Although why I should assist anyone who repeatedly collides with my ship is beyond me."

He started to walk away in an angry mood.

"Don't bother," said the security man. He was pointing off the starboard side.

Colbrook watched as a felucca glided up next to the sinking vessel, its crew tossing out lines to Nuri and Harith. Further downriver Azim and Yusuf were being taken aboard a much smaller boat.

The captain turned his attention back to Colbrook. "You come with me. I'm detaining you for further questioning."

"I'll check his papers," declared the security guard.

"You can stay in a vacant room until we reach Edfu. Under lock and key, of course," added the captain.

"Edfu?" questioned Colbrook.

"That's where we're heading," stated the captain. "I'll personally escort you to the police station myself when we get there. I'd drag you into the Luxor station, but I'm not going to delay the trip. This is an expensive cruise."

The passengers murmured their approval.

"Do you know the chief of police in Luxor?" asked Colbrook, staring at the captain.

"No—should I?" he replied.

The security guard interrupted. "I've met him. Why?"

"I think it's best if you contact him," declared Colbrook.

The passengers were staring at Colbrook again, and the captain waved for them to disperse.

"It's imperative that the police chief be notified of the latest developments," explained Colbrook.

The security guard had a smile on his face. "There's a phone at the back of the ship. Should I call from there?" His voice was filled with sarcasm.

"A wise choice," replied Colbrook. "Lead the way."

He shuffled after the guard, his shoes leaving muddy footprints on the teakwood boards. The captain brought up the rear.

Stepping around the corner of a wide vertical beam which marked the aft wall of the last cabin, Colbrook stood looking out from the stern at the foaming wake trailing for some distance behind the vessel. The motorboat had vanished beneath the surface of the Nile.

A companionway filled most of the rear deck, rising to the open deck above. The steps were covered in wide rubber strips for safety.

Against the windowless back wall of the last cabin were several metal boxes with hinged access covers. Most were marked with red or green crosses, indicating the nature of the contents inside, but some were labeled with enigmatic pictographs. One which Colbrook recognized immediately had the outline of a telephone handset painted on it. The security man reached for this box, snapping open a metal handle in the center of the panel. The cover swung loose on its hinges.

With a vague look of amusement the guard lifted the telephone receiver and pushed a button. He waited, the handset held to his ear. A minute passed in silence. Finally the guard mumbled something in Arabic into the phone. Another minute of silence passed.

The captain stood at the corner of the deck, blocking Colbrook's access to any other part of the ship.

Colbrook leaned against the taffrail, staring down into the churning water below. The Luxor temple was already fading in the distance, the ship at least a mile or two upriver already. A simple river crossing had turned into a major inconvenience. Edfu was seventy miles away.

The security man was motioning him over. Colbrook walked to his side.

"What is your name?" asked the man, covering the lower portion of the phone's handset.

"Colbrook."

The man lifted the handset to his ear, speaking rapidly in Arabic. Colbrook detected his name being said with some frequency. A few tense seconds elapsed, during which the man only listened. His previously amused face was now serious. He was talking in short sentences, stopping frequently. He was studying Colbrook out of the corner of his eye. A particularly loud burst came from the other end of the phone, the man snatching the receiver away from his ear with a pained expression. Not long after, the guard replaced the handset, closing the panel with some difficulty.

"Well," said Colbrook. "Did you reach him?"

The man turned with a look of embarrassment. "Yes. I was able to contact him."

"And?"

"He told me we should do everything possible to assist you."

Colbrook looked at the captain. "I'm going to need transport down the river."

"You want me to turn the ship around?"

"No. Nothing that drastic," replied Colbrook. "There must be a small boat on board."

The captain pointed at a large metal chest bolted to the deck near the rail. A davit with two lengths of chain hanging beneath it was not far from the steel box.

Colbrook crossed the deck, examining the instructions on the top of the box. The captain quickly motioned him aside, and reaching down released the catches. Colbrook watched as he skillfully removed the side panels. Inside was a large inflatable boat with a plywood floor. A small outboard motor was mounted on its transom, tilted to the inside. The boat was already inflated. The security guard walked over and assisted in maneuvering the boat from its container. Soon it was sitting on the deck alongside the aft companionway.

"Let me get a crewman," said the captain. "Someone who is properly trained for this sort of work. Someone who will come back with the boat." He walked briskly away, returning a few minutes later with another man in naval uniform. His was a simpler outfit, without insignia or epaulettes. He told Colbrook his name was Mohammed.

It took some time to attach the boat to the davit, but once it was secured it was lowered very quickly into the river. Mohammed rapidly descended a metal ladder near the davit, stepping expertly into the swaying and splashing inflatable. The ship was cruising at its usual speed, and it was clear the small boat was meant to be launched from a stationary vessel. Colbrook swung himself onto the ladder, dropping into the inflatable a few seconds later. Mohammed appeared to be enjoying the impromptu adventure.

A few quick pulls on the starter cord and the little engine roared to life. Colbrook undid the lock chains under Mohammed's direction, and the crewman gradually rotated the engine down into the water. A plume of spray erupted as he engaged the propeller and throttled the engine to a higher speed. The inflatable boat cleared the stern of the ship, making a wide arc out into the middle of the river before heading north. Colbrook sat in the bow, watching the surface of the Nile up ahead.

The sky was tinted with purple hues, the sun a pale orange orb through the thick haze to the west. Ferries crossed in the distance, their decks crammed with passengers returning from the west bank. Feluccas of all sizes prowled the river in both directions.

Colbrook pointed to the western shoreline as they continued north. "Move closer to that side!" he shouted.

Mohammed steered for the river's west bank. As they approached shallower water, reeds and thick vegetation blocked their view of what lay beyond the muddy shore.

"Take it north a bit further!" yelled Colbrook over the noise of the engine.

The boat slowed and began moving parallel to the river's edge. Colbrook watched the landscape with close attention, searching for familiar landmarks. The dirt road he had traveled on by donkey was now visible through occasional gaps in the rushes. Soon he spotted the top of the Amenti House, the cluster of densely planted palm trees around the structure providing a distinct visual clue as to its location.

"Take us in!" Colbrook pointed to a break in the vegetation.

The boat turned sharply and surged towards the shore. As they moved into the shallows, Mohammed turned off the engine and let the inflatable glide towards the muddy bank. With a slight bump the front of the boat grounded on the dark muck. Colbrook stood up, staring at the fifteen-foot stretch of oozing mud. He stepped out of the boat.

His leg disappeared up to the shin, a fetid odor strong in his nostrils. When he was sure he would sink in no further, he swung the other leg out. With some difficulty he managed to lift his first foot from the muck and plant it a stride ahead of the other. Slogging forward in this fashion, at times almost knee-deep in the reeking mud, he managed to reach the dirt road.

He turned to wave to Mohammed. The crewman held up his arm in response, recognizing that Colbrook was—by the standards recently established—okay, and pulled a paddle from the bottom of the boat. Using this to free the inflatable from the mud, he paddled some distance away from the shore and into deeper water before starting the engine.

Colbrook turned from the river and began walking down the dirt road. He recognized many of the houses and narrow side streets he had passed on his earlier journey by donkey. Trudging along in his torn and dirty clothes, he wished he had a donkey at his disposal now.

The air was warm and still. Dark shadows were already forming at the base of the Theban hills, the sun sinking lower in the western sky. The noises of the day's journey faded behind him, and in the enveloping silence he heard only the steady sound of his own footsteps. As he neared the street the house was on, a brown and white dog ran out of a nearby residence and watched him passing by. Soon he reached the high stone wall of the Amenti House. The front gate was closed. He paused, looking up at the three-story structure for a moment.

Entering the grounds through the gate, Colbrook walked along the gravel pathway, heading for the stairs that would take him up to his apartment. He was halfway across the recently watered lawn when he heard a cry of astonishment from above. He stopped and looked upwards. Beckwith was standing on his balcony, a book gripped in his hand as he leaned over the rail.

"Hold up a minute!" he cried out. "Where have you been?"

Colbrook stood on the path, his clothes plastered to his weary frame. He did not offer an answer to the Egyptologist, but just stared up at him.

"I'm coming down," announced Beckwith.

Colbrook was about to reply, but when he saw Beckwith disappear into his apartment through the sliding glass doors, he began

walking slowly towards the gated staircase on the side of the building, searching his pocket with his swollen fingers. He felt Graf's
keychain before locating the key to the apartment. He was surprised
he still had anything in his pocket.

He was unlocking the gate when Beckwith jogged up to him carrying a small cardboard box. Apparently the taxi driver had made
good on his word.

"What in God's name happened to you?" demanded Beckwith,
staring at Colbrook's mud-encrusted garments.

"I'll explain later, but first I need to change my clothes and take
a hot shower."

"Of course—of course," murmured Beckwith.

Pocketing the key, Colbrook swung the gate open. He motioned
for Beckwith to precede him up the stairs. The Egyptologist appeared hesitant at first, but after Colbrook assured him he was
actually doing him a favor, he slowly mounted the steps.

"I need someone to watch from the roof," said Colbrook, locking the gate and following Beckwith up the stairs.

"Are you expecting visitors?" asked Beckwith.

"Not welcome ones."

When they reached the roof, Colbrook sat down on one of the
wicker chairs under the trellis. He kicked off his muddy shoes and
then stood up, emptying his pockets. Coins and bills rained down
onto the wooden table, followed by the tightly folded shipping paper, the wrinkled filming permit, assorted tickets, and a crumpled
hotel receipt. Graf's keychain landed with a final resounding thud.

Beckwith put the cardboard box down on the wooden table.

"The shabti is genuine," he said.

Colbrook, struggling to pull off his muck-covered socks, replied,
"That doesn't come as a surprise."

12

When Colbrook returned to the rooftop it was bathed in the golden glow of the setting sun. He was wearing clean clothes and carrying a folded towel under his left arm. Despite the fact that he was rid of the visible filth he had acquired over the past twenty-four hours, he knew some things could not be so easily washed off. His unexpected dip in the Nile caused him real concern, and it was with foreboding thoughts of bilharzia that he had searched his small collection of medicines for an appropriate treatment. He had been elated to find Biltricide among his pills, and in sufficient quantity that he would be able to avoid dealing with the medical establishment altogether, though self-quacking was not something he was always eager to undertake.

Seating himself in a wicker chair under the trellis, he waited for Beckwith to join him. The Egyptologist drifted away from the wall and walked to the table, lowering himself into the other wicker chair. Colbrook leaned back, his badly bruised hand now resting on the folded towel. He thanked Beckwith for keeping watch while he had attended to his deplorable condition. For a minute neither said anything.

Finally Beckwith spoke.

"I've been keeping watch on the road. I haven't seen anyone suspicious," he said.

Colbrook nodded. "I'm not too worried. The only way up here is the stairs."

Beckwith was staring at the cardboard box containing the shabti. He reached for it, brushing aside the papers, coins, and keys, sliding the box closer to himself. Lifting the lid and removing the small figure, he held it up.

"A souvenir," declared Colbrook.

Beckwith examined it, turning it slowly in his hands. "Where did you get it? A street vendor? A bazaar around here? I doubt you found it just lying around somewhere."

Colbrook was silent until Beckwith looked up from the shabti.

"I bought it," he replied.

Beckwith resumed his scrutiny of the ancient object, peering at the faded hieroglyphs on the back.

"How well do you know Gus Lowell?" asked Colbrook. "Have you known him for a long time?"

Beckwith studied the bottom of the little statue. "I've known him for at least twenty years. Just as a colleague really. Egyptology is an unusual field. There aren't too many working Egyptologists. Most of us cross paths at symposiums, lectures, and fund-raisers. Those are the largest gatherings. Why—does this have something to do with Lowell?" He held up the shabti, as if it might answer the question.

Colbrook was silent again.

"How much did you pay for it?" Beckwith asked.

"Three thousand Egyptian."

"A fair price," muttered Beckwith. "What did the dealer tell you about it?"

"He said it was Twenty-sixth Dynasty," replied Colbrook.

Beckwith nodded. "Seems about right. I'd agree with that."

"The owner's name is missing, but it does have spell six of the Book of the Dead on the back," stated Colbrook. "At least that's what the dealer said."

"Your man knows his artifacts. Dare I ask where his stall is located?"

"He doesn't deal publicly."

Beckwith put the shabti back into the box, carefully closed the lid, and placed it on the table. He turned to Colbrook with a grave expression. "I don't know what you're involved in, or how Lowell fits into all this, but purchasing illegal antiquities is a major offense in Egypt. You could receive jail time and be forced to pay a considerable fine if someone could prove you knowingly purchased this item as a legitimate artifact and not as a replica souvenir. I wouldn't try to take it out of the country if I were you."

With a wave of his undamaged hand, Colbrook dismissed the comment. "I plan on leaving it here."

"I'm beginning to think you haven't been entirely honest with me," said Beckwith.

"About what?" asked Colbrook.

"Are you really a travel writer?"

Colbrook flexed his sore fingers, wincing in pain. "No. I'm not."

"What else haven't you told me?"

Colbrook managed a half-hearted smile. "You have a lot of questions."

"You're not providing many answers."

"I usually don't," said Colbrook.

Beckwith was about to reply when a metallic clang sounded from the garden below.

Colbrook reacted instantly. He flipped open the folded towel on the arm of his chair, revealing the Glock pistol. Gripping the gun in his still partially numb hand, he rose from the chair and quickly walked to the front wall. He searched for the source of the noise, staring down into the garden below.

The gardener was walking lazily down the gravel path, collecting his tools. He carried them over to a large storage bin.

Beckwith arrived at Colbrook's side and looked down. "He always does that at the end of the day. He's here for a few hours twice a week."

Colbrook made his way back to the wicker chairs, the Glock held loosely at his side. Settling down into his chair, he placed the pistol on the wooden table.

Beckwith stared at the firearm as he lowered himself into his own chair. He looked across the table at Colbrook with a worried expression, but said nothing.

"An occupational requirement," explained Colbrook, nodding towards the compact firearm. Leaning forward with a creaking of wicker, he added, "I think it's best if I explain my situation so you don't get the wrong impression."

Beckwith waited.

"I'm involved in an investigation," began Colbrook. "It indirectly involves Gus Lowell, but primarily deals with a man named Carl Graf. Do you know Mr. Graf?"

"I've met him a few times," said Beckwith. He looked at Colbrook with a slight frown. "He's active in diplomatic circles. Has an aid agency, if I remember correctly. Many friends in the Supreme Council of Antiquities. Well connected, one might say."

"That's him," said Colbrook with a nod.

"Lowell told me Graf is very good at obtaining funding for non-profit operations," Beckwith declared. "He seems to think Graf is indispensable when dealing with international and local agencies. The man to have on your side—or so he said."

"All very true," replied Colbrook.

"What is Graf under investigation for?" inquired Beckwith.

"I'm not at liberty to discuss the details, but let's just say he acquired something very valuable in his travels beyond the Egyptian frontier. Something he planned on selling for a considerable profit to the highest bidder."

"Antiquities?" asked Beckwith.

"I can't say," replied Colbrook brusquely.

Beckwith looked thoughtful. "As I said before, Lowell is the man to speak to if you want to know more about Graf. I really don't know much about him beyond what others have told me."

"Lowell isn't exactly available for questioning."

"Has he shut his dig down already?"

"I just came from his dig," said Colbrook. "Lowell has already left, but not voluntarily."

"Has the SCA shut him down?" asked the Egyptologist.

"Not yet," replied Colbrook. He was staring at his hand again. His thumb was turning a shade of purple he had not seen before. "He has more serious problems than the SCA. Graf appears to be the cause."

Beckwith seemed to be thinking again. "I know Graf has a residence in Luxor, but I can't remember the—"

Colbrook picked up Graf's keychain from the table. He separated out the key with the green tab. "George Hotel. I just came from there. It's been ransacked quite thoroughly."

"Ransacked?"

"Yes."

"And who did the ransacking?"

"Not me."

"Where did you get the keys?" inquired Beckwith.

"They're Graf's. I picked them up out at Lowell's dig."

Beckwith looked confused. "Isn't Graf usually in Sudan?"

Colbrook shook his head. "Not anymore."

"Where is he?"

"Dead," stated Colbrook.

Beckwith sat in stunned silence.

"He was shot." Colbrook paused. "You're probably wondering why I have his keys. It's not because I killed him. I borrowed his truck. It was an emergency."

"You drove his truck all the way from Kharga?"

"No," answered Colbrook, tossing the keys back onto the table. "Though that was briefly my plan. And I hoped to bring Lowell with me."

Beckwith was staring at the keys. He seemed intrigued by something. He reached for them.

"They're not much use anymore," said Colbrook. "The truck's been wrecked."

Beckwith was not listening to him any longer. He was examining one of the keys. He held it apart from the others. "You said these were Graf's?"

Colbrook nodded.

"What was he doing with this?" asked Beckwith, holding the key up in the low, raking sunlight.

Colbrook stared at the tarnished key. It looked much older than the others. It was also an unusual shape, but he did not see the significance of Beckwith's question.

"This is no ordinary key," declared Beckwith solemnly. "Do you see that number engraved on the top? The one that starts with the letters *TT*?" He handed the keychain to Colbrook so he could inspect it closer himself.

Colbrook peered down at the dull brown key. "You mean this number?"

Beckwith nodded. "Do you know what that is?"

"No."

"It's a tomb number," said Beckwith.

Colbrook looked up from the key.

"*TT* stands for *Theban Tomb*," explained Beckwith. "It's a key for a tomb in the Theban necropolis."

Colbrook placed the keychain back down on the wooden table. "Do you know where this particular tomb is located?"

"No," replied Beckwith. "The scale of the necropolis is considerable. Almost four square miles in all. There are more than four hundred numbered tombs. It would be impossible to remember the locations of them all."

"I assume there's a map," remarked Colbrook. "Some means of correlating the number to a physical location."

"Of course. I have several myself," replied Beckwith. "If I had to guess I'd say it's somewhere around the Qurna area."

"Qurna?" questioned Colbrook.

"Arabic names are used to define the various sections of the necropolis. Drawing an imaginary line from north to south behind the funerary temples, starting with Seti I, we have el-Tarif, Dra Abu el-Naga, el-Assasif, el-Khokha, Abd el-Qurna, Qurnet Murai, and finally Deir el-Medina—more commonly known as the workmen's village."

Colbrook nodded. "What about the Valley of the Kings?"

"The tombs in the Valley of the Kings all start with the letters *KV*," replied Beckwith. "It's a whole separate numbering system, exclusive to that area. The same goes for the Valley of the Queens, which naturally uses *QV*. This tomb is in an area typically referred to as the tombs of the nobles."

"So it's much smaller than any king or queen's tomb," observed Colbrook.

"More than likely," replied Beckwith. "A good-sized non-royal tomb might be between one thousand and two thousand square feet. Many of the tombs in the Valley of the Kings are four to eight times that size. It's true there are also very small ones, like Tutankhamen's, but those are exceptions."

"What are the chances the tomb is open to the public?" inquired Colbrook.

"Very little," said Beckwith. "There are fewer than fifteen in that area accessible to the public. I've been in all of them many times over the years. I don't recognize the number on the key. It must be a more obscure one. Most of the smaller tombs are in poor condition, and a considerable number are just plain unsafe. They're closed off to prevent further damage or looting.

"When tombs were first secured it was done primarily to keep the local inhabitants from living in them. Many were used as dwellings. They're quite cool in summer, relatively speaking, and comfortable in the winter. The inhabited tombs were eventually purchased by the government, most more than a century ago. The systematic numbering system came later. Of course, even when iron gates and steel doors had been installed, bolted to frames and fixed into concrete, the tombs were not considered completely protected. A force of tomb guards was formed as a further deterrent.

"There's a long history of illegal antiquities digging in the Theban necropolis. The tourist industry has probably mitigated it somewhat in modern times, but no one doubts that it still goes on to this very day. And there's plenty of corruption."

Colbrook stretched his tired legs.

"The guards are on duty for twenty-four hours every other day," continued Beckwith. "They take turns throughout the week. Not every tomb in the necropolis is individually guarded, of course. Usually three or four men will guard a group of tombs. The exceptions are the tombs that are open to visitors during the day. Those are always individually guarded." He paused, looking at Colbrook. "Bribery goes a long way. Usually twenty pounds will open any tomb. Most guards think of it as an honest supplement to their meager salaries."

Colbrook looked at the outlined hills to the west, their peaks still glowing with the last rays of the setting sun.

Beckwith's wicker chair creaked. He turned to Colbrook, his face impassive. "What I would like to know is how Graf acquired the key in the first place."

Both men sat for a few more minutes in silence, watching the sky change colors. The hush of twilight washed over the rooftop patio, and the promise of a cool night could be felt in the gentle breeze. Sheep were bleating somewhere on the road below.

"I think we'd better look at those maps of yours," said Colbrook suddenly. He rose from his chair, looking down at the Egyptologist.

Beckwith was frowning, but not entirely in a disapproving way.

"Why do I get the feeling you intend to enter this tomb?"

Colbrook reached down and scooped up the keys, dropping them into his pocket. "Because that's what I intend to do," he replied.

Beckwith's apartment looked like a small library. A large wooden bookcase covered the only windowless wall, filled with hundreds of volumes. Near the sliding glass doors a large desk was positioned with an outside view, looking out over the garden below. Two laser printers, an inkjet printer, and a large laptop computer filled the desk. Printed pages lay scattered about. Many were amended with hand-scribbled notes. Where desk space had proved insufficient, the floor had become a substitute for both additional computer equipment and books. The only area clear of research materials was the small kitchenette and the table adjacent to its entrance.

Beckwith was already rummaging around when Colbrook pushed the door closed.

"It should be in these," muttered the Egyptologist. He carried several large rolled-up maps to the kitchen table. Flattening one out, he stared at it for a few seconds before letting it roll up on itself. Pushing it aside, he started to unroll another one.

Colbrook moved to the table.

"Ah, here it is," Beckwith announced. He was staring at the open map on the table. Holding it down with his forearm, he moved the salt and pepper shakers from the center of the table, placing them on the top corners of the sheet. Securing the bottom edge with his elbow, he leaned forward and began tracing across the paper with his index finger.

Colbrook looked down at the map. It was a detailed line drawing showing both modern roads and towns and the ancient tombs and structures of Thebes. Hundreds of small squares were scattered across the landscape, each with its own number. Dotted and dashed lines surrounded, followed, and crossed certain features, indicating, Beckwith informed him, new discoveries, or in some cases, just negotiable paths. In a few places handwritten coordinates were scribbled as a locating aid. Other labels revealed the period of construction of the tombs in certain shaded areas, with such designations as *Second Intermediate*, *Ramesside*, *Old Kingdom*, and *Seventeenth Dynasty*.

Beckwith put on his reading glasses, his head hovering closer to the map. He suddenly straightened. "I found it. It's right here," he said, pointing to a spot near the center of the map. "It is in the Abd el-Qurna area."

Colbrook peered at the small square. It looked to be somewhat separate from the other tombs clustered in the region.

"I know the area reasonably well," continued Beckwith. "The government recently demolished a great many homes that had been built over the tombs on the lower part of the hillside. Primarily Eighteenth Dynasty burials." He tapped his finger on the map. "This tomb is near the top of the hill."

Colbrook was examining the roads and paths marked on the map. He reached into his pocket and removed the keys, setting them down on the bottom edge of the sheet.

"You know," Beckwith said, "I think I may have an explanation for how that key ended up in Graf's hands."

Colbrook stopped studying the map and glanced at Beckwith.

"A few years back Lowell did some clearing work on a Theban tomb," explained the Egyptologist. "It was a very short project. Just a few weeks, I think. I don't remember the tomb number, but it was definitely in this area." Beckwith stepped closer to the table and drew an imaginary circle on the map with his finger. "It's possible Lowell acquired this key during his brief work there. Certainly not standard practice by any means, but nonetheless he might have done so. Apparently he forgot to return it. He must have given it to Graf at some point. Why, I can't imagine."

Colbrook could, and if Lowell had been even remotely aware of Graf's intentions regarding the sealed tomb, it would only be a matter of time before Nedic found out about it. Lowell's main interest would be saving his own hide, not protecting a dead man's secret. Lowell might be an experienced Egyptologist, but he was unfamiliar with the methods of coercion practiced by those who engaged in the criminal arts.

"I may have a dig report for this tomb," declared Beckwith. He moved to an overflowing shelf of books, running his fingers along the spines of what appeared to be thin booklets. Pulling one out, he gazed down at the cover. "If there is one," he muttered to himself, "it should be in here."

Walking to the kitchen table, he began flipping through the pages. Colbrook continued to study the map.

"Here we are," Beckwith noted with some satisfaction. He put the booklet down on the table, pushing it towards Colbrook. "It's a typical Eighteenth Dynasty rock-cut tomb." He turned the page. "There's even a diagram."

Colbrook peered closely at it.

"That's the entrance." Beckwith reached down to indicate the location. "This short corridor leads into the transverse hall. After that is the second corridor, a fairly long passage that leads into the burial room. Some call it the chapel."

"What's this?" questioned Colbrook. He was pointing at a small outlined box on the diagram.

"That's the niche. The statue of the owner was placed in there," replied Beckwith. He then tapped his finger over a series of large, roughly square shapes drawn inside the chapel with dotted lines. "These are the burial shafts. The tomb has four of them."

"Are the shafts open?" Colbrook asked.

"Probably. Normally you'll find just loose boards covering them," answered Beckwith.

"How far down do they go?" questioned Colbrook.

"It depends. I'd say on average at least ten to fifteen feet. Some are deeper. That's just the shaft itself, mind you." Beckwith pointed at the diagram again. "See these gray squiggly lines here? That's the side chamber at the bottom of the pit. The burial chamber. They run laterally for about fifteen feet, and they're just a bit narrower in width than the shafts. That's where the coffins containing the mummies were placed. The lower chamber was then sealed with stones, and the shaft was filled up with rubble and sand, though some dispute that theory and believe the shafts were originally sealed with large stone slabs."

"I take it the burial chambers are accessible."

"Most of them have been opened and investigated at some point. This tomb appears to be no exception," replied Beckwith. He turned to the next page in the dig report. A series of black and white photos showed the wall decorations of the tomb. He turned the booklet so Colbrook could see them better.

"The limestone from which the tombs were tunneled is of poor quality. In order to provide a smooth surface for painting, plaster was used as a final finish. The artists then decorated the tomb walls. The current theory about the location of these scenes is that they relate to the room's association. For example, the transverse hall is connected with the world of the living, so it's here where we find scenes of everyday daily life. The long corridor that connects to the chapel typically shows the burial procession, as if one were entering into the realm of the dead, and the chapel itself is painted with scenes of offerings for the dead. Fitting, since this is where the burial shafts are located and the cult statue was set up."

"What's this line here? The double dotted line."

Beckwith leaned closer to the diagram. "Looks like an incursion." He turned his head to look up at Colbrook. "Incursions are tomb builders' mistakes. They happened when a new tomb was being tunneled out and there was an accidental breakthrough into an older one. It was more common than you would think. There was no master plan."

"So two tombs can be connected."

"These were at the time of the incursion, but this newer tomb was abandoned. You can see in the plan that there's no exterior access door. The whole thing was filled in shortly after it was started," explained Beckwith.

"Part of this looks like it might still be open," said Colbrook. "In this area." He pointed at the plan.

"It might be," admitted Beckwith. "Hard to say by just looking at the diagram. Egyptologists frequently block off an incursion after they've determined it isn't worth exploring further, usually because it's too unstable to dig in."

"If you were going to hide something in a tomb like this one," asked Colbrook, "where would you hide it?"

"Maybe the burial chambers, if you could get down into them," replied Beckwith after a few seconds of thought. "Or, in this particular case, maybe the incursion, if it's at all clear. It depends on the size of what you were hiding."

Colbrook studied the diagram.

"I can probably make arrangements to enter it," said Beckwith.

"I'm going there now," announced Colbrook, picking up the keys and putting them back into his pocket.

"Everything is closed," Beckwith told him. "You'll be stopped by the tourist police. You can't get near these tombs in a car. You'll have to use donkey paths. And then there are the spotlights on the hillside, lighting up some of the tomb entrances. You'll have to avoid those. Even then—" He looked at Colbrook. "I'd better go with you. I know the way."

Colbrook held up his badly bruised hand. "Are you sure?"

Slipping his reading glasses from his nose, Beckwith folded them and lowered them into his shirt pocket. He had a determined expression on his face. "I may look like an armchair scholar, but I assure you I have considerable experience in dealing with troublemakers. When I was actively digging I dealt with my fair share of disgruntled workers and lurking tomb robbers."

Colbrook was somewhat amused by Beckwith's sudden change of demeanor.

"Threats go a long way in these parts," Beckwith added. "They always have." The Egyptologist strode over to his desk. He yanked open a drawer, rummaging through its contents.

Colbrook walked closer to the desk out of curiosity, not sure what to expect.

When Beckwith turned—quite suddenly—he was holding a large revolver in his hand.

Briefly startled, Colbrook did not say anything for several seconds. Beckwith looked at him with a faint smile, obviously satisfied at the reaction he had elicited by the display of the vintage firearm.

"My God," said Colbrook, "it's an antique."

"Webley Mark Six. Manufactured in 1926—the last year they made them apparently. Never had the occasion to use it, but it's certainly a highly effectual prop. It's a top-break revolver." Beckwith opened the firearm, the barrel and cylinder rotating downward together on a hinge forward of the trigger guard. "Opening it also works the extractors. Similar to a double rifle. It's ingenious, don't you think?"

"It would be more effective if it were loaded," replied Colbrook, wondering when the Egyptologist last had occasion to handle a double rifle.

"The bullets are in here somewhere," said Beckwith. He put the revolver on the desk and started searching through another drawer.

A few seconds later he held a mustard-colored cardboard box in his hand. It was creased and faded.

"How old are those?" questioned Colbrook.

"Not as old as the gun," answered Beckwith. He carefully opened the carton, revealing the cartridges. Pulling one out and holding it up in the light, he said, "That's a .455-caliber bullet."

"Since I'm as unfamiliar with the Theban necropolis as I am with top-break revolvers," responded Colbrook, "and it will be dark soon, it would be a great help if you came along. But we have to go now. I suspect we're not the only ones looking for the tomb."

Beckwith began loading the cylinder, slipping the cartridges in one by one. When he was finished he snapped the revolver shut. Taking a handful of extra cartridges, he dropped them into his pocket. He turned to Colbrook.

"How many rounds have you got?"

Colbrook reached into his pocket and pulled out a spare magazine. He slid the magazine back into his pocket.

"I guess you're not going to tell me what Graf hid in the tomb," said Beckwith.

"You'll know when I find it." Colbrook removed his own firearm from his belt. He pressed the catch on the handgrip with his thumb, releasing the loaded magazine into his hand. Checking the chamber to be sure it was empty, he gently used his right index finger to pull the trigger, finding that he could apply sufficient pressure to complete the double-action pull. He took the pain as a good sign—at least his fingers were no longer numb. He replaced the magazine. "We'll need transportation."

"No worry," replied Beckwith. He put the revolver down on the table. "I don't have a car—it's too much of a hassle to own one as a foreigner—but I've got a friend who lives nearby. His name's Rafiq. He runs a taxi service. I'll give him a call."

Colbrook nodded in reply, looking at his watch.

Walking to the bedroom door, Beckwith disappeared for a moment. When he returned he was wearing a windbreaker. He picked up the heavy revolver and placed it into an inside pocket where it was not all that conspicuous. He then reached for the telephone on his desk. Dialing, he held the receiver to his ear. As he waited he opened a desk drawer and removed a four-cell flashlight.

"No one is answering," Beckwith said after a minute. "He must not be home."

"Just call another taxi," suggested Colbrook, growing impatient.

Beckwith hung up the phone. "I have a better idea. We'll just borrow his car. I've done it before."

"He's probably using his car. Like you said, he's not at home."

"He bought a new one last year. His old one is always parked by his house. I walk by there all the time. In fact, I just saw it this afternoon," replied Beckwith. He slipped the flashlight into the front pocket of his jacket, moving towards the door.

The sky was already filled with the pinpoints of many stars. A sliver of the moon was rising in the east. Crickets chirped in the garden, and the outside lights attracted a myriad of flying insects. The gravel crunched under their shoes as they walked towards the front gate.

Beckwith led the way. He turned right when they reached the road, moving quickly to the southwest. Colbrook was now wearing his own windbreaker. Beneath it he wore the shoulder holster, the Glock secure under his left arm. A small but powerful LED flashlight was in the jacket's right pocket, along with the cell phone Mercer had given him. He kept pace alongside the Egyptologist. The road was difficult to see in the dim light, and more than once he narrowly avoided stepping into a pothole which Beckwith's familiarity with the roadway allowed him to easily avoid.

A cool breeze was blowing off the Nile, mixing with the warm air still rising from the road. When they reached the first intersection, Beckwith turned right. They followed this road for a short distance, and a few minutes later stood outside a small brick house. A single electric lamp illuminated the porch, but the windows were all dark. A tan Mercedes station wagon, circa 1983 or so—a diesel, from the smell of it—sat parked in a weed-filled gravel patch forming the front lawn. Beckwith made for the car without the slightest hesitation in his step.

Opening the creaking front door, the Egyptologist dropped into the driver's seat. He leaned forward, his hands fumbling for something on the dashboard.

Colbrook opened the passenger door, looking inside the vehicle.

"Rafiq showed me how to do it," explained Beckwith. "The car was once stolen."

He pointed at the hole in the dashboard where the ignition switch would normally have been located. Several wires covered in black tape protruded from the opening.

Colbrook slid across the plastic seat, swinging his feet inside. He did not pull the door closed.

Beckwith was now holding two of the wires. He touched them together. The engine coughed and started. He turned to Colbrook with a smile. "I'm sure you're glad you brought me along now."

Colbrook pulled the passenger door closed. Beckwith settled in behind the wheel, swinging the driver's door shut.

The engine promptly stalled.

Coaxing it back to life several times, Beckwith finally managed to get the old Mercedes into gear without incident. He switched on the headlights and pulled out onto the road, turning sharply around. Making a left at the intersection, they soon passed the Amenti House, heading more or less northeast along the riverfront on the unpaved road. A few minutes later Colbrook could see the taxi depot up ahead. It was deserted. The sightseers had long ago crossed the river to their hotels on the east bank.

Beckwith slowed at the depot, making a left onto the paved road that provided access to the numerous sights on the west bank. They passed a few restaurants and a gas station in Gezira, a small town located directly across the Nile from Luxor. A minute later they were near the Arabian horse stables, approaching the primary police checkpoint.

Beckwith turned to Colbrook, his face lit by the glow of the dashboard lights. "I'll tell them there's a meeting at the Gordon House. There isn't, but it's a good place to park. The police will probably recognize me, but they won't know who you are. Don't say anything—I'll make up the story."

Colbrook nodded. He could see the large hut on the side of the road marking the location where the police checked vehicles. The hut itself was poorly illuminated, but the uniformed man who stood by the side of the road soon turned on a giant flashlight slung by a padded strap from his shoulder. He stepped out into the road, flashing the light, motioning for Beckwith to stop.

The Mercedes rumbled and shook as it rolled up to the checkpoint. Beckwith cranked down the window, waiting for the officer to make his way around the front of the station wagon. The odor of diesel exhaust was strong. Beckwith said, "Hello. Egyptology meeting at the Gordon House. My friend Dr. Colbrook." He pointed at Colbrook with his elbow, his hands still on the wheel.

The officer leaned closer, peering inside the station wagon. His face showed little concern. He grunted in reply, holding the heavy flashlight back from the side of the car with his arm. Soon he turned to wave down a vehicle approaching from the opposite direction. Beckwith struggled to crank the window back up, driving slowly forward while he did so.

Beyond the checkpoint the road was newly paved and followed a very straight course toward the Theban hills. Colbrook watched out the window as they slipped past the Papyrus Institute and then the shadowy forms of the Colossi of Memnon. They passed several donkey carts—farmers bringing their vegetables back from the market, Beckwith explained. Sugarcane fields stretched away on both sides of the road, the stalks shifting perceptibly in the nighttime breeze.

No one was at the ticket office or the tourist police building. Beckwith made a right turn onto the road that passed between the long row of funerary temples to the east and the tomb-covered hills rising to the west. Colbrook knew the paved road continued for several more miles before reaching the access road that led to the Valley of the Kings, but Beckwith turned off before they even reached the Ramesseum—the funerary temple of Rameses II—which lay mostly in ruins to their right.

The Gordon House turned out to be nothing more than a one-story brick building with a low, dome-shaped roof. It was painted white, or had been at one time. Most of the paint was peeling from the stucco finish. The windows were small and poorly fitted. More than a few appeared to have been broken and crudely repaired. The building was deserted.

Through the thick belt of palm trees bordering the roadway Colbrook could just make out the rising hillside where many of the tombs were located. It stretched away to the northeast, glowing in the illumination provided by a series of large ground-based spotlights. At the bottom of the hill a motley collection of houses dotted the landscape, the dim light inside of them revealing unmatched, odd-sized windows and doorways.

Beckwith maneuvered into the empty parking lot, swerving to a stop near the back of the building where they could not be observed from the road. Pulling the wires apart, he shut off the engine. Colbrook pushed open the passenger door, stepping out onto rough asphalt. Beckwith joined him after quietly closing the driver's door.

They both stood surveying the landscape.

A lone car swept by on the road, its yellow headlights reflecting off the gleaming asphalt. A few children chased each other across the shallow ridge to the north, their laughter breaking the silence and then fading with them as they moved behind the outline of a house.

"We're lucky. It's quiet." Beckwith turned and started to walk towards the northern edge of the parking lot, away from the road and trees. He gestured up at the artificially illuminated hillside and said, "We'll have to avoid walking near the lights if we want to reach the tomb without being noticed. The guards can be bought off during the day, but at night it's a different story."

Colbrook stared at the steeply rising ground that lay before them. The spotlights were not evenly distributed, and the very top of the hill faded away into inky blackness. In the distance beyond it an unearthly yellowish glow filled the night sky.

"Those dark spots are the tomb entrances," Beckwith explained. "The ones that look like rows of open doorways are actually short rows of square columns carved into the bedrock—the pillared porticos of the few remaining Middle Kingdom *saff*-tombs. Those narrow, lighter strips of ground are the footpaths used by the visitors, the indefatigable tomb guards, and anyone else who cares to venture into the Theban hills."

Beckwith pointed to a narrow *wadi* up ahead. "If we walk down this way first, away from these houses, we can start climbing the hill when we're some distance from them. I'd rather avoid the usual pathways, especially the easier ones, because more than likely we'll be accosted by some local asking for *baksheesh*, or worse, we'll be stopped by a tomb guard who lives around here. It's also a way of avoiding the lights."

Colbrook nodded in agreement, and began walking towards the

wadi. They made their way down the gravelly path, descending into the narrow valley.

Beckwith stopped frequently to check his bearings with some lit landmark nearby. They were moving along the base of the hill, slowly making their way across the rocky bottom of the *wadi* on what appeared to be an infrequently used footpath. The crushed stone that littered the ground was for the most part light in color, and Colbrook found that it was relatively easy to see where he was stepping. When they had gone several hundred feet into the *wadi*, Beckwith looked upwards, indicating they would have to start climbing.

They ascended the hill, weaving from side to side to avoid a straight climb. The hillside was not particularly steep, but the loose stones made it difficult to get a solid foothold. The Egyptologist seemed to have the agility of a mountain goat.

Stopping to look back down into the valley, Colbrook could see the roadway and the funerary temples below. The spotlights were already blocked from direct view, and the ridge they were ascending was in deep shadow.

Above him, Beckwith continued up the hillside. Colbrook began climbing again.

A few minutes later Beckwith stopped, apparently now aware of the distance that had opened up between them. Marching upward, Colbrook closed on the Egyptologist.

"Just a few hundred feet and we'll be at the top," Beckwith informed him. "There's a stone wall running the length of the ridge. We'll follow that almost to its end, staying on the shadow side of the wall. That way we'll be out of view from below. Even if a tomb guard sees us now, they won't be suspicious of me. I've been climbing around these hills for years." The Egyptologist adjusted his footing. "Of course when it's dark I'm usually going in the opposite direction." He turned abruptly and began the last leg of the climb.

Crossing the ridgeline, they stepped onto a well-worn path. A low stone wall weaved across the shard-covered ground. Without a word the Egyptologist began working his way along the top of the hill on the narrow path that followed the wall.

Halfway down the steep slope on their right was a row of tomb entrances partially hidden in the shadows created by a spotlight several hundred feet below them. Short pathways connected these entrances to another track which closely paralleled the one they were walking on, though it was at a much lower elevation. Along the sides and top of each tomb entrance the hillside was cut back and shored up with stone walls. Some of them had stacks of rocks covering the lower half of their doorways.

Beckwith only gave these tombs a passing glance. There did not appear to be any way of reaching them from where they were walking—the drop along the whole right side of the ridge was precipitous. The narrow path continued to twist along the hilltop, dipping and rising with the uneven ground, but always closely following the rock wall. Colbrook tried to see the road below, but the glare of the spotlights aimed up the hill made this impossible. Beyond the lights nothing could be seen at all. The view down the left slope of the ridge was blanketed in darkness, that side of the hill rapidly descending into a ravine below.

Beckwith suddenly slowed his pace.

Colbrook could see a man walking towards them, the glow of a cigarette very distinct against his face. He was wearing what appeared in the darkness to be a blue or black *galabiya* and a small white turban. His leather sandals were almost noiseless on the sandy path. In his right hand he gripped a large walking stick.

Beckwith said something to him in Arabic in a low voice. The man replied with a few words, and continued smoking, leaning lazily on his staff. Beckwith stood beside him in conversation for several minutes. Colbrook waited patiently for the outcome. Finally the man sat down on a large rock at the edge of the path, removing a pebble from his sandal. He nodded to Colbrook, and Beckwith bid him good evening in the usual Egyptian fashion. They continued on.

"Tomb guard?" whispered Colbrook.

"No. Just a local," muttered Beckwith in a low voice. "Out for some cool air."

The path was wider now, and Colbrook walked at Beckwith's side as they climbed yet another gradual slope. More tomb entrances were visible below in the flood of artificial light, some noticeably larger in scale than others, but all of them basically of the same design. Most appeared to be marked with painted signs, both over the door lintels and at the beginning of the access paths. None had stones piled in front of their doors. Beckwith confirmed that these tombs were open to the public during the day.

Reaching what seemed to be the highest point of the hill, Beckwith halted. The source of the unearthly glow coming from the north was Hatshepsut's temple, illuminated by a variety of lights located both within and without the edifice, providing a vast theatrical effect. From the ragged ridge that circled the mortuary temple, several spotlights flooded the valley below.

They continued on, and soon Colbrook could see into the shallow depression they had been moving towards for the last five minutes. Beckwith clambered over the stone wall and began descending a narrow gravel-strewn path.

When they reached the bottom of the depression, Beckwith stopped for a moment to look up the opposite slope. A row of small tomb entrances dotted the hillside. He stepped closer to Colbrook and in a low voice said, "It's over there. The one all the way on the left." His arm was outstretched, his hand pointing towards a rocky cleft.

Colbrook stared in the direction the Egyptologist was indicating. A dark rectangle too even to be a natural rock formation was vaguely visible. He turned to Beckwith. "Where are the guards?"

"If there are any nearby, they're down below us," Beckwith replied, still looking towards the crevice. He held out his flashlight. "Here, take this in case yours goes dead. I'm going to have a look around the other side of this hill. I want to see if there's a tomb guard walking on the Deir el-Bahri side. If there is, I'll try to draw his attention away from this area if he comes toward it. In the meantime, climb up to the tomb and get inside as quickly as possible. If the door is made up of bars, you can put the padlock back on from inside and lock it again. That way if someone happens along, a tomb guard or somebody out for a nighttime stroll, they won't realize anyone's inside. Just don't turn the light on until you're in the entrance corridor."

Colbrook nodded in understanding, taking the flashlight. He moved quickly along the steep path, turning to look back when he was halfway up. Beckwith was crossing the slope below him, heading northeast. Resuming his climb, Colbrook negotiated the loose stones on the incline. Reaching the ledge on which the path to the tomb was located, he made his way rapidly along the precipitous trail, soon arriving at the shadowy crevice.

As he passed into the darkened cleft, the outline of a square opening gradually appeared. He moved closer to it. A crudely lettered sign was affixed over the doorway. The number was badly faded, but it matched the one engraved on the key in his pocket. The entrance was free of rocks, though a few large ones were on the ground nearby. The door itself was made up of a series of iron bars welded into a heavy frame, with evenly spaced gaps between them. The top and bottom edges of the door were reinforced with solid metal panels. A transom of sorts, made of narrower bars, filled the space above it. All of the ironwork was rusted. A battered padlock hung from a ring below the U-shaped door handle.

Colbrook removed the keychain from his pocket. Pulling the large padlock upward and locating the keyhole, he carefully inserted the key. When it was fully seated he twisted it, giving the lock a quick downward tug. It did not open. He worked the key slowly out of the bottom of the padlock, fearing it would get jammed. He inserted the key again, this time pulling down with more force as he turned it.

The lock popped open.

He lifted the padlock from the metal ring and pushed against the door. It creaked in protest, opening only a little more than a foot when he put his full weight against it. He stepped sideways through the narrow gap.

Pushing the door slowly shut, he reached between the iron bars and looped the padlock shackle back through the retaining ring, snapping it gently closed. Slipping the keys into his pocket, he turned away from the door.

The flashlight in his hand came to life, its beam stabbing narrowly into the hollow darkness.

13

The walls of the passage were rough, gouged rather then chipped, blackened by the countless fires of centuries of inhabitations. A faint odor of stale air mixed with the lingering smell of burnt wood. The floor was packed dirt, bits of ancient and modern debris embedded in its uneven surface. Unadorned, the short corridor behind the iron-barred door opened into the first chamber—the transverse hall. Everything faded into blackness beyond that point, out of the reach of Colbrook's flashlight.

A few short steps brought him into the transverse hall. Roughly eight feet deep and thirty feet wide, the chamber revealed no obvious secrets. Instead of vivid wall paintings there were only blackened and scarred surfaces, most of the smooth finishing plaster having long ago disintegrated and taken the artwork with it, leaving behind little more than the fragmentary remains of paintings and the fractured bedrock they had once covered.

After making one circuit around the transverse hall, checking the walls for any obvious signs of recent activity, he began examining the packed dirt floor. Nothing appeared to have been disturbed here either, and the only object of note was an iron bar lying on the ground against the front wall. It appeared to match the gauge of those used in the door. He turned his flashlight upwards.

Like the walls, almost all of the plaster once covering the ceiling had long ago fallen down. There was nothing of interest overhead, only a moldering wooden brace that some archeologist in the remote past had installed for safety's sake.

Moving in the direction of the deeper corridor, Colbrook briefly stopped to examine the only section of substantially intact wall paintings within the transverse hall. He recognized them from the photos in the dig report. Shifting the flashlight from side to side in the dead silence of the tomb, he could not help but marvel at the fine detail painted into a marsh hunting scene. It was a remnant of what must have been a remarkable series of panoramas. He turned his attention to the long passageway.

Anyone hoping for a more intact collection of wall paintings in this part of the tomb would have been in for a disappointment—the beginning of the downward sloping and narrow passageway was in even worse condition than the transverse hall. The floor was littered with stone and plaster fragments and appeared to contain more than the odd reminder of mummified remains—tattered wrappings, the occasional tooth, and shards of broken bones. Colbrook knew many of these tombs had been used for mass burials in the later periods of pharaonic Egypt, and he distinctly remembered reading about one Egyptologist who had uncovered more than fifty mummies in a single tomb, stacked like cordwood.

Moving down the slender passage, playing the flashlight across the walls and floor, he continued his search. Halfway down the corridor the walls were smoother, the layer of finishing plaster largely intact. Some of the paintings in this section were still bright and colorful. One of them stood out from the rest: it was the tomb owner's mummy being carried on a bier, a procession of mourners following in its wake. Colbrook walked by the line of grief-stricken friends and relatives with the eerie feeling that he was not an entirely unwelcome intruder.

A doorway gradually emerged from the darkness at the end of the passage, only slightly narrower than the corridor itself. A band of boldly executed hieroglyphs in a well-preserved ochre pigment marched around its outer edge. He stepped through the opening into what he knew was the largest of the chambers—the chapel.

It was at least fifteen feet in depth and close to forty feet in width. Two giant pillars of stone carved from the bedrock were near its center, their surfaces crumbling and cracked in many places. The ceiling was vaulted and painted in a geometric pattern that resembled a woven carpet. A classic *kheker* frieze—at least it had been noted as such in the dig report—encircled the top of the walls.

Between the pillars, against the western wall, a large niche was visible. Colbrook crossed the chamber. Much to his disappointment the recess was empty. There was only dust and fragments.

Turning from the niche, he aimed his flashlight at the ground and began walking towards the corner of the chamber. The wall to his left was marked with uneven patches of plaster and the remnants of colorful tomb paintings, but the majority of it was only rough rock, entirely devoid of the plaster finish. The floor was packed dirt, untouched as in the other chambers.

Making his way cautiously forward, Colbrook located one of the burial shafts. It was covered by wooden boards loosely fitted together. They were black with age and warped at the edges. Kneeling down and resting the flashlight on the floor, he lifted one of the planks, sliding it to the side. With a large gap now showing between the pieces of wood, he picked up the flashlight and edged closer to the hole.

Roughly square, it descended at least fifteen feet straight down. There did not appear to be an accessible burial chamber at the bottom. The walls were smooth, the floor choked with broken stones. He arranged the board as it had been, blocking the shaft.

Moving along the short side of the chamber—the northern wall—he began searching for signs of an opening. It was here that the dig report indicated an incursion had taken place during the construction of a nearby tomb.

A stack of medium-sized stones rested against the middle of the wall. Behind the stones were a few old boards standing upright, similar to those he had observed stretched over the burial pit. After further examination of the blockade, he decided to forego the removal of the stones and boards until after he had walked the perimeter of the chapel. There were still three more burial pits to check.

The second pit he found in the corner opposite the first. It was completely uncovered except for a single wooden beam positioned across its center. A frayed piece of rope only a few feet long hung from the middle of the beam. Walking up to its edge, Colbrook aimed his light down the shaft. At the bottom he could see the opening to a lateral burial chamber. Though it seemed unlikely Graf would have risked descending into such a deep pit, he could not entirely discount the possibility.

Both the rope and the wood beam were old and showed no signs of recent activity, but Beckwith had mentioned a few other interesting details about burial pits. Colbrook moved to the opposite edge of the hole, looking for another mode of descent. In the corner of the shaft, rectangular notches were cut into the opposing smooth walls, vertically spaced every foot and a half. There was little doubt they were of ancient construction. He turned away from the pit.

Passing the opening he had entered the chamber through, he walked cautiously to the opposite corner, the beam of light rippling over the floor ahead of him. If the tomb diagram was correct—and so far it had proved to be—two more burial shafts should be located at this end of the room.

He found them at almost the same time. They were in close proximity to each other—only six feet separated the openings. Both were uncovered and in very poor condition, the walls being roughly hewn and crumbling. Of similar depth, one contained mostly rubble while the other was more or less clear at the bottom. Neither appeared to have been touched in ages, and they did not have wall notches. Colbrook guessed these shafts were later additions, probably dug for descendants of the original tomb owner.

Making his way back across the chapel lengthwise, he stopped to briefly examine the two carved pillars. Their limestone surfaces were mottled and chipped, but otherwise solid. He found nothing that resembled a cavity or niche, and moved back towards the breached wall, his intent to remove the obstruction and gain access to the adjacent unfinished tomb.

The stones covering the boards were not heavy, but they had been stacked with skill; the joints between them were tight. With the flashlight placed safely aside, he began pulling the stones off one by one, carefully rolling them into a small pile. He favored his right hand, using his left for the heavy lifting.

The air slowly filled with a thin haze of dust as each rock was removed. A few minutes later only the boards remained. Working these loose, he pulled them free and stacked them against the wall. The opening was quite narrow.

Taking the flashlight in hand, Colbrook began to creep his way into the opening on his hands and knees. The slight upward incline of the tunnel floor made his progress even more difficult, and the awkwardness of having to hold the light while simultaneously scrambling forward hindered him further. After six or seven feet the floor leveled out somewhat and the passage widened considerably, though the ceiling height changed very little.

Gradually the space over his head increased, and he was finally able to move at a half-crouch, shuffling along on bent knees instead of crawling. The passage ended at an open chamber roughly fifteen feet square and tall enough to stand in. The walls were only partially chiseled, and in many places uncut rock projected from their surfaces. The ceiling was smooth and level, but the floor was covered with a considerable layer of rubble.

Rising slowly from his stooped position, Colbrook studied the small room, sweeping his flashlight across the floor and walls. On the opposite side was another opening, a wall of broken rocks inside it. The only way into the unfinished chamber was the way he had come.

Working his way across the rubble-choked floor, he began to examine the room in detail. Nothing gave the impression of having been moved or rearranged in any way. His gaze met with only countless chips of stone. He reached the blocked opening, shining his light at the wedged rocks, searching for any gap or crevice. It was packed solid. He began to walk around the perimeter of the room.

Something glinted in the beam of his flashlight, half-buried under a stone. He stepped closer to it, using the side of his shoe to carefully push the rock out of the way.

It was a battery—a D-cell.

He picked it up and examined it. The expiration date was not for another five years.

Digging through bits of rock where the battery had been with the tip of his shoe, he found nothing else. He moved towards the opposite corner, crunching his way across the uneven stone debris. Soon he was near the opening he had entered the chamber through. He aimed the flashlight into the remaining unexplored corner. A large flat stone caught his eye, leaning sideways across the angle formed by the junction of the unfinished floor and wall. Picking his way over some sharp rocks, he stared down at the slab.

He pulled at it with one hand to see if he could move it aside, but found it was heavier than it looked. Kneeling on the floor, jagged rocks digging painfully into his shins and knees, he put the flashlight down and grasped the stone with both hands. Tilting it towards himself until it reached a vertical position, he gave it a sharp tug, shuffling back as it toppled over.

A small, neat mound of flat stone shards was revealed. Removing these with both hands, he began digging through a layer of loose sand. A few inches down he struck metal.

It was a tea tin.

He pulled it from the shallow hole, staring at the dusty cover. It was a brand he did not recognize, but looked to be of Turkish origin. He carefully worked the lid off.

Inside the tin was a small, hinged plastic case.

He slowly removed it, placing the empty metal container on a nearby stone. Snapping open the latch on the plastic case, he directed the flashlight at its interior.

The contents appeared to be a pair of standard ballistic eye protectors—combat-rated safety glasses.

Placing the flashlight down and holding the plastic case in front of it, he studied the protective eyewear more closely. While they certainly resembled a variety commonly used by members of the U.S. armed forces, further examination revealed some marked differences.

The frames were constructed of a very unusual dull black metal, tapering to an almost flat temple at the sides, and covered with a shiny rubbery substance along the length of the two curving ear pieces. An elastic strap was permanently connected to the ends of these. The metal band above the lenses—the part that crossed the brow—was slightly wider than usual, as if adding reinforcement. It was here that Colbrook found the almost microscopic engraved lettering—X01-NV.

Lifting the eyewear from the case—a case that did not appear to be up to the manufacturing standards of its present contents—he turned the protective glasses in the light. They were much heavier than they looked, and completely stiff to the touch. The lenses displayed an oddly luminescent quality when direct light struck them, despite their colorless glass. When held at an angle, the glass—or very dense plastic of some sort—looked as if it contained a clear liquid. A wire, hair-thin, ran around the perimeter of the lenses, disappearing into the metal band above them. Each lens was almost flat in the middle, curving only near its edge.

Still kneeling in the direct illumination of the flashlight, Colbrook gradually unfolded the glasses. Pulling the strap behind his head, he slipped them on.

Night turned to day.

There was something otherworldly about the view.

The room appeared to be fully illuminated. It was not quite the same as daylight, but it was very close. The colors seemed accurate, though in his current surroundings he could not be sure how accurate. Engineers sometimes exaggerated.

A very faint glow was coming from the peripheral edges of his field of view. He imagined it was how the chamber might look with diffuse overhead lights. It was a scene without discernible shadows.

Holding his hand in front of his face, he tested his depth perception. It had not been affected in the least. Looking down, he could see the glowing bulb in the flashlight, but could not perceive the light beam itself. He lifted the glasses, gazing down at the flashlight. The beam of light was now quite visible. He repositioned the eyewear. Clearly what he could see through the lenses was not formed by visible light.

He picked up the tea tin and placed the empty case back inside it. After snapping on the lid, he arranged the tin roughly where he had found it, but did not bury it. He lifted the flat rock back into the corner again, concealing the tin from immediate view. Opening his jacket pocket he put Beckwith's flashlight alongside his own. Neither would be necessary anymore.

Making his way to the access shaft, he crouched down, scrambling through the passage. When he reached the limit of upright travel he knelt down and began crawling forward. It was much easier now that both hands were free and he could see without even the hint of darkness.

Emerging into the chapel, Colbrook dusted himself off and stood surveying the quiet chamber for a moment. It was remarkable how little he had noticed before. He had not been able to take in the room in its entirety, his view restricted to the flashlight's narrow beam.

Entering the confines of the long connecting passageway, he walked steadily toward the transverse hall. At the end of the passage he stopped, looking across the chamber and into the entrance corridor. The iron door was closed and locked, but something was lying outside on the ground. It appeared to be a bag or knapsack.

Colbrook edged back into the passageway, his eyes fixed on the tomb door.

Outside a man stepped close to the iron bars.

It was Nuri, the illustrious knife-wielder from the motorboat. Having evidently made a full recovery from his unintended swim in the Nile, he was apparently not satisfied to spend a quiet evening at home nursing his scorched hand. Instead he was outside a tomb in the Theban necropolis, brandishing a pair of bolt cutters. The murmur of several low voices now filtered down into the passage. It did not sound like Arabic being spoken—it sounded like English. A very loud snapping noise echoed through the tomb, followed by the scraping of metal on metal. Very abruptly the iron door creaked inward on its rusty hinges.

Colbrook darted back down the long passage, moving with increasing speed towards the chapel. A clang of metal echoed through the tomb just as he stepped into the chapel. He made a direct line for the burial shaft spanned by the wooden beam, kneeling down when he reached its edge. It was the deepest of the four shafts, easily twenty feet straight down.

Poised there, his head turned so that he could listen for any sounds coming from the front of the tomb, he heard distant voices and footsteps.

They were growing louder with every passing second.

Scrambling to gain a footing on the wall notches, his shoes sliding down the chiseled stone surface, he found purchase on one with his left foot. Shifting his weight and gauging the distance to the next notch with his right foot, he managed to set both his feet securely. With his hands now placed in the topmost recesses, he began dropping notch by notch into the shaft. Without the benefit of the remarkable night-vision system he would have broken his neck many times over.

When he reached the bottom he looked into the burial chamber. It was roughly ten feet by ten feet. The ceiling was less than six feet high. Except for scraps of old wood and scattered pieces of broken pottery, it was empty. He crawled into it.

Lying sideways on the limestone floor he strained to hear something that would tell him who was with Nuri. Still breathing heavily from his quick descent, he tried to imagine what was going on in the chambers above him. Minutes slowly passed in silence. Finally he heard a dull tapping noise, as if the walls were being tested with a hammer. Not long after he saw dirt trickling down the corner of the burial shaft, as if someone had stepped near its edge.

The noises grew louder with every passing minute. A distinct voice echoed from above. It was Nedic, demanding a rope.

Colbrook quietly removed the Glock from its shoulder holster. Rolling onto his stomach and resting the bottom of the handgrip on the ground, he waited, staring at the smooth floor of the burial shaft. It would not be long before he was found.

A minute or two passed in relative silence, broken only by the sound of more footfalls. Then someone started talking nearby. For a second Colbrook was almost convinced it was Beckwith, but the voice soon grew louder and more defined. It was not an English accent—it was an Australian accent. It was Lowell talking to Nedic. He was in an argument with the Serbian.

"I don't even know what you're looking for," said Lowell. "Why do you keep asking me?"

"What about these holes?" asked Nedic gruffly.

"Burial shafts," replied Lowell. "Trust me—they're all empty. Graf wouldn't have gone down into one of those alone."

"Who said he was alone?" questioned Nedic meaningfully.

The end of a coiled rope landed with a dull *thwack* at the bottom of the burial shaft, the rest of it snaking back up to the surface.

"Check it," demanded Nedic.

Rocks and pebbles soon fell from overhead, some even rolling into the burial chamber. A smoky haze of dried dirt drifted down from above. Nedic was shining a large light down into the shaft, shifting it from corner to corner. Colbrook heard the sound of Lowell beginning his descent with the assistance of the rope, the tips of his work boots scuffing the soft limestone. It would not be long before he reached the bottom.

Colbrook gripped the compact pistol tighter, awaiting Lowell's appearance. The work boots were the first thing he saw, and then Lowell's knees as he crept closer, leaning forward to peer into the lateral burial chamber. The Egyptologist thrust his head and upper body into the chamber itself, a small but powerful flashlight gripped in his hand. Colbrook scowled, aiming the Glock at the Egyptologist's face.

Lowell froze, his expression one of shock. He looked terrible. His eyes were sunken and black. The normally messy mop of reddish hair was even more disheveled than usual, filled with an assortment of pebbles and dust. Buttons were missing from the front of his shirt and a large bruise showed on his collar bone. He had clearly not expected to find anything in the burial chamber, least of all Colbrook aiming a gun at his head and wearing a pair of what appeared to be protective glasses.

Nedic yelled down impatiently from above. "What did you find?"

Lowell's mouth opened as if he were about to speak, but nothing came out. He exhaled a ragged breath, his lips twitching as he did so.

Colbrook lifted the pistol ever so slightly, holding his breath.

Lowell slowly turned his head upwards, his eyes gleaming with exhaustion. He rose from his crouched position, his voice echoing upward with a barely detectable stammer from the bottom of the shaft. "Nothing—I found nothing. It's empty like I said."

Colbrook breathed normally again.

The burly Serbian was apparently talking to Nuri now, his voice fading. Lowell began climbing the wall notches, the rope looped around his arm as a safety measure. Several minutes of relative silence followed the Egyptologist's exit from the shaft, during which Colbrook could faintly hear someone winding up the rope.

Rocks rumbled somewhere. The sound of wood boards being violently thrown aside filtered down into the burial chamber. They were examining the stones and planks he had removed to expose the unfinished passage. Nedic's voice grew louder. He seemed to be arguing with Lowell again.

Nedic was inquiring about the small side tunnel—the incursion. Lowell was replying, but his voice was too low to understand.

"Give me the big flashlight," said Nedic forcefully, interrupting the Egyptologist. "You go in first. I'll follow."

"You'll have to crawl to make it through," said Lowell. "It's even smaller than it looks. It doesn't go anywhere. I was in here a few years ago."

"Move!" exclaimed Nedic.

"What if a tomb guard shows up?" protested Lowell, now speaking much louder. "We'll never hear anyone once we're inside the other chamber."

"Nuri will keep an eye out for anyone at the entrance," said Nedic. "Anyway, the tomb guards aren't armed."

"True—but the tourist police are," declared Lowell. "And they're not known for being too particular about who they shoot."

Nuri mumbled something unintelligible. Shortly afterwards the sound of footsteps passed very near the top of the shaft. Apparently Nuri was making his way back to the tomb entrance.

The tomb was soon eerily silent.

Colbrook slid the Glock back into its holster and crawled from the burial chamber. He looked up, listening intently.

If there was anyone still in the chapel, they were not making any noise. Using the wall notches, he climbed the side of the shaft as quickly as he could manage. When he reached the top he gradually raised his head above the floor.

The chapel was empty.

Nimbly stepping from the topmost notch, Colbrook swiftly made his way to the long connecting passage. He peered down its length, listening for a moment. Moving quietly down the passage, his footfalls noiseless on the packed dirt floor, he slowed as he reached the transverse chamber. Nuri was standing in the short entrance corridor. He was staring through the iron bars of the tomb door at the level courtyard outside, an AK-47 slung from his shoulder.

Colbrook backed slowly against the wall so that he could easily look in both directions. The night-vision glasses created a remarkably disconcerting sense that he would be spotted if Nuri were to suddenly turn from the tomb door, even though he knew that the rifle-toting Egyptian could not possibly see him without the aid of a flashlight.

He soundlessly pulled the gun from the holster again. Softly tapping the handgrip against the limestone wall, he awaited Nuri's reaction. As the Egyptian was turning and reaching for his flashlight

Colbrook darted forward into the transverse hall, moving rapidly towards the front right corner. Staying close to the wall, he began making his way silently in the direction of the short entrance corridor, on an intercept course with Nuri. He stopped to retrieve the iron bar that he had found earlier.

The Egyptian stepped into the transverse hall, his flashlight aimed at the long passageway. He was searching for the source of the noise, moving deeper into the tomb. Colbrook swiftly knelt down and picked up a small chunk of loose plaster from the floor. He tossed it toward the opposite end of the hall. It broke apart when it struck the floor, pieces scattering in all directions.

Nuri spun to his right, away from Colbrook. While his flashlight remained shining on the spot where the plaster had landed, he reached behind his back with his free hand, tugging the rifle from his shoulder. The weight of the heavy weapon shifted and the strap got caught on his bent elbow. He grabbed at the swinging rifle with his other hand, losing his grip on the flashlight. It dropped to the ground with a clatter, and the tomb—at least from Nuri's point of view—was plunged into darkness.

Nuri's movements were uncertain now that he was unable to see, but he managed to get a solid grip on the rifle, lifting it back onto his shoulder. He could not find the flashlight. Kneeling, he began sweeping his hand from side to side, searching for it. Several times he came very close to finding it, but all hope was finally lost when he accidentally kicked it with his foot.

The flashlight rolled far from his reach, the lamp now shattered.

Nuri fumbled in his pocket and came up with a book of matches. He tore one off and scratched it across the starter strip. The flame flared up for an instant and then burned weakly. Holding the match in his wavering hand, he advanced toward the far wall of the transverse hall, searching for the cause of the noise. He shuffled forward a few more paces, as if expecting to see a tottering mummy. With a sudden curse he dropped the spent match on the ground, rubbing his burnt finger. He began tugging at another match.

Colbrook returned the pistol to its holster. He walked rapidly forward with the iron bar held high. Nuri seemed to sense that someone was nearby and dropped the matches, bringing his rifle to a waist-high shooting position. Stepping around the unseeing

Egyptian who was now frozen in terror, Colbrook brought the iron bar down with all the velocity he could impart to it, striking Nuri in the back of the head. The Egyptian went down like a stone, his rifle slipping from his lifeless hands as he collapsed.

Grabbing him by the shirt collar, Colbrook dragged him to the far corner of the transverse hall. The back of his skull was clearly fractured. Colbrook retraced his steps and retrieved the AK-47.

Walking to the tomb entrance, he propped the rifle against the wall, pulled the door inwards, and stepped outside.

It did not take long to locate Beckwith. He was kneeling behind a boulder near the opening of the narrow defile which led to the precipitous footpath. Under normal circumstances it would have been a very good hiding place.

Colbrook began walking towards Beckwith. The Egyptologist was crouching lower, trying to conceal himself behind the large boulder. Not particularly interested in being shot by a Webley at close range, Colbrook called out several times in a subdued voice, declaring his identity.

Beckwith finally stepped from behind the boulder. He was staring at Colbrook with a perplexed expression on his face.

"I've taken care of the homicidal watchman at the door," began Colbrook in a low voice, "but Lowell is still inside with a mad Serbian named Nedic."

Beckwith said softly, "I saw them go in. There was nothing I could do. I knew they weren't tomb guards."

"I'm going back in to get Lowell," said Colbrook. "Stay where you are, and don't use your gun unless you absolutely have to. If you do decide to use it, be damn sure it isn't me you're shooting at. The big Serbian, of course, is expendable."

Beckwith nodded with an anxious look. The gun was still in his jacket pocket. He was peering at Colbrook's eyewear.

"Did you see anyone else?" asked Colbrook quietly. He looked around the courtyard, examining the steep hillsides and rocky outcroppings above it.

"No one," whispered Beckwith. "Not even a tomb guard."

Colbrook waited until the Egyptologist had resumed his position behind the boulder before walking quickly back to the tomb entrance. He stepped through the opening and picked up the AK-47.

Turning, he swung the heavy iron door closed. The hinges were not squeaking as loudly as before.

Navigating the long passageway and entering the chapel, he walked over to the more rudimentary burial shafts on the left side of the room. He stood and listened for a moment at the edge of the first shaft. Releasing the magazine from the rifle, he dropped it down into the deep pit. The clatter of metal on stone was muffled but audible. He walked a few paces to the next shaft and dropped the whole rifle into it, barrel first. The initial impact sounded like a hammer hitting a rock, and then the rifle tumbled sideways onto the rubble bottom. The echo lasted for several seconds.

Colbrook took up a position behind one of the thick pillars—the least likely place for Nedic to shine his light. From here he had an unobstructed view of the incursion opening. Kneeling down, he pulled the Glock from its holster.

Several minutes elapsed, and then, barely detectable at first, the sound of someone struggling through the small passage gradually filtered into the chapel. Either the search was over or the recent noises had alarmed Nedic. Lowell's head emerged from the cramped opening in the wall. The Egyptologist crept all the way out of the passage, slowly rising to a standing position, his flashlight pointed at the floor. The knees of his pants were coated with stone dust. He was waiting for Nedic to appear.

Loud cursing soon identified the arrival of the Serbian.

Practically tumbling from the hole, Nedic quickly regained his feet. He was carrying a giant flashlight, which, as Colbrook expected, he promptly swept across the underground room. Staying low, Colbrook only rose to his earlier crouched position after the Serbian had directed the light in the opposite direction, towards Lowell.

"Turn off your light," demanded Nedic.

Squinting into the glare, Lowell snapped off his flashlight.

Nedic wore a rumpled black linen shirt with the sleeves rolled up almost to the elbows and a pair of dust-caked black jeans. Dull black boots completed his garb. He was clearly prepared for a nocturnal outing. Slung from his shoulder by a thin nylon strap was a Heckler & Koch MP5 submachine gun, providing the means by which he intended to dispatch his enemies or—as it was beginning to look to Colbrook—his intimidated associate.

"I'm not finished with you," spat Nedic. His left hand continued to grip the flashlight while his right leveled the MP5. He steadied the gun, aiming it at Lowell's chest.

In a quavering voice Lowell replied, "I've told you everything I know. I don't even know what you're looking for. Graf never told me anything."

"You're going to end up like Graf," barked Nedic. His temper was as predictable as his choice of firearms—small, expensive, and deadly.

Lowell was panic-stricken.

"I'm going to give you one last chance to tell me where—"

The large flashlight exploded into a thousand flying pieces as an ear-splitting pistol shot echoed through the stone chamber. Calmly stepping from behind the pillar, Colbrook covered the Serbian with his gun.

Nedic remained absolutely still for several seconds, the remnants of the plastic flashlight handle still gripped in his hand. He was as good as blind without the light, and Lowell was in no hurry to turn on his own. The Egyptologist had fallen to a sitting position, his arms raised protectively.

"Drop the gun," ordered Colbrook.

Nedic chose to drop the flashlight handle.

Colbrook fired a shot at the ground just in front of the Serbian. The impacting bullet sent up a spray of dirt and rock dust. Finally coming to his senses, Nedic tossed the MP5 aside. He stood staring in the general direction of Colbrook, into what to him was the black void of the tomb interior, uncertain of his predicament.

"Follow my directions and no one will be seriously injured," began Colbrook. He took a few steps forward, edging closer to Nedic, but staying well out of his reach.

Lowell now rose from the floor. His voice was filled with apprehension. "Colbrook, is that you?"

"Get the rope, Lowell," said Colbrook. A coiled length of high-tensile strength climbing rope was lying next to the shaft Lowell had descended earlier. "Don't turn on your flashlight."

"I can't see anything. How can I get it?" questioned Lowell.

"I'll tell you where it is," replied Colbrook.

After a minute of continuous instructions as to where to walk,

how to turn, and when to reach down, Lowell stood with the length
of rope clutched in his hands.

Nedic had not moved. He stood listening to the conversation, his
face expressionless. In a sarcastic voice he blurted out, "You never
had me fooled. I was on to you from the beginning. Travel writer,
treasure hunter—ha!"

Ignoring Nedic's remark, Colbrook directed Lowell to hand the
end of the rope to the Serbian.

"What now?" asked Nedic. "Am I supposed to hang myself?"

"Tie it around your waist," stated Colbrook without emotion.
"You're going into the burial shaft."

"You can't—" began Nedic.

"If you prefer, I can just shoot you in the leg right now," interrupted Colbrook.

Nedic started tying the rope around his waist.

"Lowell," said Colbrook, "throw the other end of the rope in
my direction." When the rope landed not far from where he stood,
Colbrook quickly retrieved it from the floor. He made his way to
the shaft that was spanned by the wooden beam, securing the rope
to the substantial timber while keeping an eye on Nedic.

The Serbian was growing restless in the dark.

Colbrook then directed Nedic to walk to his right, towards the
shaft with the wooden boards across the top. A few of the planks
had been shifted in the earlier search, but most of them were still intact. A resounding crash echoed through the tomb as Nedic walked
unwittingly over the dried boards. He let out with a bellow, falling
rapidly down the shaft, the excess rope unwinding swiftly from
where it rested on the floor. The rope pulled taut seconds later. The
beam creaked.

Walking slowly to the shaft, Colbrook looked down. Nedic was
hanging just a few feet above the rubble-strewn bottom, swaying
like a fish hooked on a line. The rope had worked its way under
his arms as a result of the sudden restraining force, and was pulled
tight across his upper chest. He was cursing and spitting out dust
at the same time.

Colbrook knelt at the edge of the burial pit. He hadn't thought
it would be quite that close, but then again the length of the rope
and the depth of the pit were variables he had only been able to

roughly estimate by eye. Peering down at Nedic, he declared, "Answer my questions and I'll let you climb out. If you don't cooperate I'll just cut the rope."

Nedic spat at the ground, pulling himself upwards with his arms in an attempt to relieve the pressure of the rope around his chest.

"Certainly pays to buy the best rope—don't you think?" asked Colbrook. "I'd like to know where I can find Vukasinov. And don't tell me he's not in Egypt."

Nedic replied with a string of curses.

"I'm going to cut the rope now," said Colbrook with conviction. "Some unsuspecting archeologist will no doubt find your remains one day."

"Wait!" shouted Nedic hoarsely.

"Well?" inquired Colbrook. "I don't have all night."

"He's renting a houseboat," grunted Nedic.

"Where is it?" demanded Colbrook, slipping the Glock back into its holster. "For your sake, I hope it's tied up somewhere."

"South of the Luxor temple. It's moored permanently," said Nedic in a raspy voice.

"What does it look like?" asked Colbrook.

"Like a floating house. It's bright yellow. You can't miss it!" shouted Nedic in a hollow voice. "Follow Sharia al-Walid down to the passport office!"

After describing in a more subdued tone how to find the houseboat from there, Nedic continued to slowly turn on the rope, his face tilted upwards.

"Now get me out of here!" he roared.

Colbrook removed a small pen knife from his pocket and began sawing at the rope. The cut fibers parted rapidly as he worked, the strain of Nedic's weight assisting in severing the rope. It pulled apart with a sudden snap, sending Nedic plummeting the last few feet to the bottom of the pit. The broken rope slithered away into the shaft.

"Are you crazy!" shouted Nedic. "We had a deal!"

Rising to his feet, Colbrook said loudly, "I need you out of the way for a while." He turned, ignoring the muffled shouting coming from the bottom of the shaft.

Lowell had not moved from where he had been left standing.

"Turn on your flashlight," instructed Colbrook.

Several minutes later, with Nedic's shouts now almost inaudible behind them, they reached the tomb's entrance. Lowell pulled the iron door closed as they stepped outside into the still night, and Colbrook put the cut padlock back in place. As an extra measure he jammed a flat stone between the hasp and the loop. One direct hit would probably knock it out, but performing such a feat from inside the tomb would be difficult, especially from the bottom of a burial shaft.

As they turned and walked away from the gate, Beckwith stepped from behind the boulder, zipping his jacket closed.

Colbrook removed the night-vision glasses, holding them out to the approaching Egyptologist. Beckwith mumbled something that sounded apologetic, but tried them on anyway. After a few seconds he returned them without a word.

"Well?" asked Colbrook, putting them back on. "Was it worth the trouble?"

"Remarkable," said Beckwith. "Absolutely remarkable."

Colbrook glanced at Lowell.

"Don't look at me," said Lowell defensively. "I never knew about them."

Walking swiftly towards the entrance of the defile with both Egyptologists following him, Colbrook led them down the steep footpath to the shallow depression. He did not require Beckwith's assistance to find the way back to the car.

The Mercedes station wagon did not appear to have been tampered with or searched, but Colbrook made a quick circuit around the vehicle anyway. He peered underneath it and then checked the tires.

"No one followed us," declared Beckwith.

"You can never be too careful," replied Colbrook.

Opening the driver's door and dropping into the front seat, he quickly located and touched together the two exposed wires sticking through the dashboard. The engine rumbled to life. Beckwith got into the passenger seat, Lowell into the back seat.

Colbrook accelerated out of the parking lot, leaving the headlights off. As the station wagon picked up speed on the blacktop road, Beckwith suggested a shortcut. Colbrook called out the approaching landmarks and turns so that Beckwith could properly direct him. Lowell never said a word as he swayed from side to side in the back seat.

Using dirt side streets of limited serviceability, Colbrook managed to work his way to the ferry landing area without passing the main checkpoint and tourist police headquarters, but more than a few stalks of sugarcane dragged under the front bumper when he stopped the car by the moldering concrete dock.

Leaving the engine running, Colbrook pushed open the driver's door and stepped out. Beckwith slid over into the vacated seat. Lowell remained in the back seat.

"Go back to the house," instructed Colbrook, tossing some sugarcane stalks away. "Keep an eye out for anyone suspicious. Make sure you aren't followed. If you are, go someplace else." He took the night-vision glasses off and placed them into the pocket of his windbreaker.

Beckwith nodded, pulling the door closed. The headlights came on and the Mercedes slowly pulled away, maneuvering around several large potholes.

After the taillights disappeared around a corner, Colbrook walked down to the Nile.

On the other side of the parking area a rotund man hovered over a smoking, glowing metal drum, feeding sticks and scraps of wood into its open top, flames flaring up with every new addition. His *galabiya* hung limply from his shoulders, his mostly bald head gleaming eerily in the flickering yellow light.

Behind him on the edge of the river a small boat was tied up. The hunched figure of a man sat in the bow, his face only visible in the brief gouts of flame. Slipping from the vessel as Colbrook approached, he held up his hand in greeting. He appeared to be as old and withered as some of the mummies in the Cairo Museum. His craft proved to be a wooden rowboat fitted with a barely serviceable outboard motor.

The crossing to Luxor was uneventful.

Colbrook marched along the Corniche heading south. He passed many expensive hotels illuminated like Christmas trees, and considerable numbers of docked river cruisers, at times more than three abreast in the water. As he continued south, streetlights diminished in number and the buildings became smaller and more dilapidated. He was no longer in a tourist-frequented area. Reaching into his pocket he removed the night-vision glasses and put them on.

Turning onto a sloping dirt road that followed along the Nile's marshy banks, Colbrook could smell the river before he saw it. A thick wall of vegetation blocked his immediate view of the smaller docks that dotted the water's edge. As he walked past the ends of the narrow wooden piers, he slowed to look down the length of each. Most had small feluccas tied up alongside them, their bows rubbing against the old tires used as bumpers. After passing an empty stretch of shoreline he reached a pier that turned out not to be a pier at all, but a railed gangplank that led to the door of a bright yellow houseboat.

It sat low in the water, parallel with the river. Calling it a boat was not entirely accurate—it had neither bow nor stern. It was a moderately large house sitting atop a series of shallow pontoons, the barge-like structure at the waterline supporting the house-like superstructure that would have looked more at home on solid ground. Further observation revealed metal pipes at both near corners of the floating house, connected to metal pins on the shoreline which in turn were thoroughly embedded into concrete pillars. Ropes and chains provided additional anchoring should the metal pipes ever come loose from their fittings. A thickly insulated electrical cable ran the length of one of these permanent hawsers.

The house itself was vaguely French Provincial in style, rising two stories above the river. False stonework and stucco provided the exterior trim and finish, and tall sliding glass doors substituted for windows. Matching balconies in ornate iron finished out the Old World ambiance. The roof was practically flat, with only a slight pitch detectable from the center beam to the roof's edge. A narrow walkway ran the length of the first floor, a few folding chairs scattered about on its faded wooden surface.

Colbrook followed the electric cable to a metal box affixed to a wooden pole near the road. Ignoring the warning labels glued to the outside, he opened the cover and peered inside. As he suspected, a single breaker lever provided the means by which power could be cut in an emergency. He closed the box.

Concealing himself behind a large flowering shrub only a few paces away from the electric box, Colbrook waited. A man like Vukasinov would not be without guards of some sort. The railed walkway was empty, and except for the incessant buzzing of large airborne beetles and the occasional hoarse croak of a frog, there were no sounds coming from the direction of the houseboat. Several minutes passed, and then he heard voices. The door opened.

It was Harith, the expert motorboat captain.

He was looking down the gangplank. After a few seconds of observation, he stepped back inside and disappeared. The door remained open.

Suddenly a shorter man stepped into view, his hands grasping a thick rope attached to something heavy. He was slowly backing towards the doorway. It was Azim.

Harith soon reappeared. He was carrying the opposite end of a large burlap sack. Azim continued shuffling backwards, struggling to pull the rope over his shoulder as he turned to face out the open door. Something swayed heavily inside the burlap sack. It looked like a body.

As they cleared the doorframe Harith hooked his foot on the edge of the door and pulled it closed.

Soon they were out on the gangplank, moving at a quicker pace but still hampered by their awkward and weighty load.

Colbrook pushed aside some leaf-covered branches. Harith's end was now slipping in his hands, and he was forced to halt, gathering up more burlap as he did so. Azim rested against the railing chain, his face registering profound annoyance at the delay.

Finally clearing the gangplank, the two men moved towards a rusted Fiat sedan. It was parked near a giant clump of rushes almost at the river's edge. Once alongside the vehicle they abruptly dropped their burden. Colbrook heard a muffled shout. There was movement inside the burlap bag.

Azim savagely kicked the sack. The movement suddenly stopped.

With much cursing and grunting, the two men began maneuvering the cargo into the back seat of the small car. Pushing and pulling, they managed to get the burlap sack inside.

Slamming the rear doors shut, both men moved to the front of the car. Harith dropped into the passenger seat. Azim got in behind the wheel. The engine started with a growl, and amidst a cloud of exhaust the Fiat turned sharply away from the river. The car disap-peared moments later, the sound of its engine fading.

For several minutes Colbrook remained still. Then he unzipped the front pocket of his windbreaker, removing the cell phone. Keep-ing an eye on the houseboat, he quickly dialed a number from memory. Still kneeling in the weeds behind the shrub, he waited. Soon he was talking in a low voice, never pausing to allow an inter-ruption from the other end. When he finished he turned the phone off and placed it back in his pocket.

It was time to determine if Vukasinov was alone.

Rising from his concealed position, Colbrook strode to the elec-tric box. Swinging the cover out of the way, he reached in and pulled the breaker lever down. The lights in the houseboat went off. He closed the cover, resuming his position behind the shrub.

A buzzing noise began, followed by a distant but loud *pop!*

About a quarter of a mile upriver a transformer box on a utility pole had blown. The lights were now out for at least half a mile along the river in both directions. A strong electrical odor filled the air.

The houseboat remained dark.

Quietly crossing the gangplank, Colbrook crouched behind a folding chair on the front deck, looking for any sign of movement inside.

Lowering the night-vision glasses for a few seconds, he saw a flicker of candlelight coming from one of the upstairs sliding doors. Raising the glasses back in place, Colbrook once again drew the Glock, making his way to the front door. It was closed but not locked.

Pushing through the heavy door, he found himself standing in a long, narrow hall. Several other doors connected with it. They were all closed. A metal staircase went up to a landing which connected the two sides of the upper floor otherwise divided by the cathedral-style entrance hall. There was something lying near the bottom of the stairs.

It was a man, flat on his back on the tile floor. He was wear-ing polished black shoes and a tan *galabiya*, his head covered in a tightly wound white turban.

Colbrook drifted forward.

It was the mustached man who had followed him after his visit to Graf's apartment.

His face was covered in spattered, drying blood, his sightless eyes staring up at the ceiling. Two bullet holes, closely spaced together, were visible below his left shoulder.

Colbrook stepped around the dead man and quickly ascended the stairs, thankful for the sturdy metal treads which allowed him to move almost soundlessly.

A door on the upstairs landing to his right was open. He removed the very unusual variant of protective eyewear and placed them in his pocket. A faint, flickering light was coming from the doorway. He continued moving towards it until he could see inside. Heavy curtains and a densely woven oriental rug made for a luxurious environment, emphasized by a giant bed constructed of ornately carved wood. Several lit candles stood on a nightstand large enough to substitute for a breakfast table.

A man sat on the edge of the bed, facing away from Colbrook. He wore a maroon-colored robe, the collar turned up. The back of his head was covered in thinning gray hair. He seemed to sense that someone was watching him, because he slowly turned towards the door, rising to his slippered feet.

Colbrook raised his gun, stepping into the room.

The man's heavily lined face registered little emotion. Somewhat on the short side, he made up for his lack of height by his sheer bulk. He had the upper body of a bullfrog, standing on legs that seemed insufficient for his size. Wrinkling his gray mustache in apparent distaste, his blue eyes peering out of their prematurely sunken orbits with a bold gaze, he raised a shaggy eyebrow while reaching down with an exaggerated flourish to cinch his rumpled robe. Before he closed it, Colbrook caught a glimpse of blue and white vertically striped pajamas. If the robed man was scared, he certainly did not show it.

Colbrook pushed the door silently closed with his foot. "It appears the Serbians have taken to Egypt. Is it the abundant sunshine or the ancient history that draws them, I wonder?"

Expecting a bullfrog to have a bullfrog's voice, Colbrook was surprised at the remarkably polite and cultured voice with which the gray-haired man soon spoke.

"Sarcasm. The sign of a man who is sure of himself."

"Very true," replied Colbrook. He waved his pistol in the direction of the divan at the foot of the bed. "Why don't you take a seat, Mr. Vukasinov."

Showing no surprise at the mention of his name, Vukasinov turned to seat himself on the low, backless couch. Easing down onto it, he looked up, his eyes narrowing. Colbrook kept his distance, the gun never wavering from its target.

"You seem intent on living up to the reputation ill-informed reporters and politicians once attributed to many of your countrymen," said Colbrook.

"Mr. Graf," said Vukasinov, "should have stayed within his range of experience—sanctioned corruption."

"As opposed to the unsanctioned variety," said Colbrook.

Vukasinov looked thoughtful. "Graf came to me, not the other way around."

"And you supplied him with whatever he wanted," declared Colbrook.

Vukasinov almost smiled. "Of course. I'm a business man."

"Besides selling, you also broker deals between those who want to buy and those who have something to sell."

"A rare opportunity," remarked Vukasinov. "And one which I would rather soon forget."

"Trouble?" questioned Colbrook.

"It's to be expected," said Vukasinov solemnly.

Colbrook studied the stocky Serbian very carefully, paying particular attention to his hands and the pockets of his robe. "What do you know of Graf's partner?"

Vukasinov looked up, his eyes shifting to the gun.

There was a long silence before Colbrook spoke again.

"Because we both know that helicopter crash was no accident."

14

Vukasinov answered the one question Colbrook was most interested in with only minimal attempts at evasion. There was little doubt that he was a veritable fount of information—far more useful alive than dead—but when the aging Serbian reached for a snub-nosed revolver concealed in the deep pocket of his robe, as a man in his predicament is liable to do, Colbrook permanently ended the career of the arms dealer with a single well-placed round.

Leaving the houseboat behind, Colbrook proceeded south along the river, where he soon found an Egyptian who offered to take him across the Nile in his motor-fitted felucca. The man had been skulking about his vessel in the dark, his head wrapped in a woolen scarf. He proved to be almost as deaf as he was blind, and it was with much difficulty that Colbrook managed to direct him to the proper dock.

The ferry landing on the western shore was mostly deserted at this time of night, but a few stragglers still pestered him for *baksheesh*, some even boldly following him as he began to walk in the direction of Ramla. When he was finally alone on the road, he slowed his pace. The night-vision glasses were safely zipped into his coat pocket, and he now removed them guardedly. He was growing accustomed to wearing them.

Making his way down the grassy edge of the damp road, Colbrook caught a glimpse of the Amenti House through the thick vegetation. Though it was still some distance away, he could see the pinpoints of light coming from the small accent fixtures in the garden and the large lamps affixed to the building itself. An orchestra of frogs and insects hummed away in the underbrush as he walked. A strong odor of dank vegetation came from the swampy ground bordering the Nile.

The roadway was empty, and with the exception of a few startled cats, nothing else crossed his path. He continued to make his way cautiously towards the Amenti House, a layer of slippery mud gradually building up on the soles of his shoes.

Approaching the high wall outside the three-story building, he saw nothing suspicious or unusual as he stepped through the gate and into the garden. Walking on the wet grass to avoid making any noise on the gravel walkways, he began systematically examining the grounds. When he was convinced there was no one lurking in the bushes he returned the night-vision glasses to his jacket pocket. Cutting across the lawn, he made his way to the front door. On his approach to the covered entryway he heard the distinctive rumbling sound of a sliding door opening.

Beckwith appeared on the balcony above. He was carrying the Webley revolver, his face worried and drawn as he leaned over the railing. The lights were out in his apartment. Colbrook suspected he had been watching the road from inside.

"Any trouble?" asked Colbrook, looking up.

"No trouble at all," said Beckwith. "Lowell's having a lie-down. His ordeal has left him badly shaken."

"Did anyone come by?" inquired Colbrook.

"Nary a soul," said Beckwith.

Colbrook nodded, moving onto the gravel side path. He quickly unlocked the staircase gate, and after securing it, walked up to his own apartment.

Entering the kitchen, he sat down at the table. He removed the cell phone from his pocket and carefully dialed a number. Several seconds later he began talking, slowly and clearly, as if giving instructions. When he was finished he closed the phone and started towards the refrigerator. It was going to be a late dinner.

The next morning Colbrook visited the police station in Luxor. It was just after nine o'clock when he sat down in Hassan's office. The police chief was already at work, stacks of scribbled papers and forms spread across his desk. His head was covered with a plain brown baseball cap, concealing his short-cropped graying hair. He was wearing a red polo shirt and faded jeans.

The police chief gazed at Colbrook with a saturnine face.

"You won't believe how busy I've been lately," said Hassan. "It's like the floodgates of mayhem have opened up in Egypt."

Colbrook remained expressionless.

Hassan suddenly became cheerful. "I'm glad you stopped by, though. There are a few things I'm hoping you can clear up." He pushed some papers aside and leaned forward. "So what did you come here to tell me?"

"A tomb was broken into last night."

"Where is this tomb?" asked Hassan.

"Abd el-Qurna."

"Why didn't you contact me earlier? I must ring the tourist police and antiquities security force immediately," insisted Hassan. "Which tomb is it?"

Colbrook told him, adding, "They're not antiquities thieves. They planned on using the tomb for storing drugs."

Hassan expressed his disbelief at such a scheme.

"They're more than likely still inside," said Colbrook. "One of them is a very dangerous man. Precautions should be taken." He paused, looking directly at Hassan. "The one with the fractured skull shouldn't give you too much trouble."

Hassan had an odd look on his face when he reached for the telephone on his desk. He dialed and waited. His eyes briefly met Colbrook's as he began speaking rapidly in Arabic. His last words sounded like direct orders. He put the handset down, pushing himself back from the desk in his rolling chair.

"Should I assume this has some connection with the boat incident yesterday?" he asked.

"Not directly," Colbrook answered in a self-deprecating tone. "That was simply poor judgment on my part."

Hassan seemed to be pondering something for a moment before he spoke. "Apparently there's been another incident on the river. A foreigner was found stumbling along it about fifteen miles north of here. He was incoherent and using part of a deflated life raft as a head covering." Hassan shook his head sadly. "He has a very, very bad sunburn."

"Can you give me a description of him?" questioned Colbrook.

"Long straggly hair and a beard," replied Hassan. "He was wearing a faded yellow and green T-shirt and shorts."

"I followed a man who fit that description," admitted Colbrook. "I lost him several days ago when he boarded a river cruise. His shirt wasn't faded then."

"We assume he came from the river somewhere," said Hassan, "but we've had no reports of any large vessels sinking in the Nile, so I'm not sure what to make of the life raft."

"Hasn't he told you anything?" asked Colbrook.

"No. He's suffering from sunstroke. He's under observation in a local hospital."

"My guess is that he was taking river cruises to determine which vessels were most suitable for transporting narcotics," said Colbrook. "He must have encountered some kind of trouble."

Hassan reached into his pocket and removed a small maroon-colored booklet with gold Cyrillic lettering and a double-headed eagle on the cover. It was in a clear plastic bag. He held it up in front of Colbrook. "He was carrying this. It's a Serbian passport."

"I'm well aware of his nationality," stated Colbrook. "He's one of many criminals I've been tracking."

"I would be very interested to hear who the others are," said Hassan.

"When I have one of them cornered with a shipment of drugs, I'll contact you immediately," Colbrook declared.

Hassan put the passport back into his pocket. He reclined in his chair with a sigh.

Colbrook could tell he wasn't finished.

"There's been some interesting news from the Kharga Oasis recently. You wouldn't happen to know anything about that, would you?"

Colbrook shook his head. "I haven't heard anything."

Hassan leaned forward. "A prominent aid worker was found shot dead in his truck outside of Baris. That's a small town at the southern end of the oasis. Practically the middle of nowhere actually."

"Bandits?" questioned Colbrook.

Apparently Coslovich and Cavoski were more clever than he had given them credit for. Somehow they had managed to transport

Graf's body to the overturned truck, making it look as if he had been killed in it. It was a shame, their filmmaking talents going to such waste. They would have been better served in the fictional genre.

Hassan nodded. "Probably bandits. The truck was pretty badly shot up from what I've been told." His hands were now resting on the arms of his chair. "And on the same day, not far from the earlier incident, two foreigners were arrested by the tourist police. They were digging in a Roman fort out in the desert," said Hassan. "Looking for gold apparently."

"Treasure hunters," muttered Colbrook. "I didn't think they existed anymore."

"We get all sorts of crackpots in Egypt," replied Hassan. "The pyramids seem to be a magnet for them." He paused, looking directly at Colbrook. "But that's not the strangest part of the story."

"What's that?" asked Colbrook.

"They were Serbian nationals," declared Hassan.

"Remarkable," said Colbrook.

"My thoughts exactly," said Hassan.

Neither spoke for a moment.

Fixing his gaze on Colbrook, Hassan asked, "Are you working alone?"

"As far as I know," replied Colbrook.

"We rescued a man from some kidnappers last night," explained Hassan. "He's an American."

There was a long silence.

"The station received an anonymous call. We were tipped off to look for a red Fiat sedan heading south from Luxor along the river. The caller even gave us the car's plate number."

"Did you trace the call?" asked Colbrook.

Hassan shook his head. "The call has proved untraceable. There's no information about the number, the phone used to make the call, or even what tower the call was relayed from."

"Very suspicious," said Colbrook.

"A security team patrolling the Luxor bridge was contacted immediately. They headed north along the river. When they spotted a red Fiat sedan that matched the caller's description, they stopped it and surrounded it," said Hassan.

"Who was in the car?" asked Colbrook.

"Two Egyptians and the American."

"What have the Egyptians told you?"

"Nothing," answered Hassan. "They were both armed. They resisted. Both were shot dead. The American was lying in the back seat, heavily restrained. He claims to have no idea why he was kidnapped."

"Who is he?"

"His name is McKinnon," replied Hassan. "He says he's a tourist. I've advised him to leave Egypt." Hassan reached for a folder on his desk, and pulling it closer to himself, opened it. Inside was a glossy photograph. "This was taken just after his rescue."

Colbrook took the photo from Hassan and studied it.

The man in the picture was wearing brown knee-length shorts and a floral-print shirt. His head was crowned with a bright blue baseball cap.

It was the man from the *Papyrus*.

"Do you know him?" asked Hassan.

"I met him at a tourist site," answered Colbrook. "And I think I know what must have happened." Colbrook handed the photograph back to Hassan. "Apparently someone saw me talking to him. They must have assumed he was working with me."

Hassan placed the photograph back into the folder.

"In that case," he said, "I'll keep him under guard until we can get him out of the country. His position is even more precarious than I thought."

"A diplomatic flight is arriving later today," said Colbrook. "I can arrange to have him put on that. Where is he now?"

"At his hotel," replied Hassan. "I have two of my best men assigned to him."

"Send him over to where I'm staying in about an hour," said Colbrook. "I'll be waiting for him there."

"Nothing must happen to him," warned Hassan. "We prefer tourists to leave with a good impression of our country."

"Don't worry," Colbrook assured Hassan. "I'll make sure he leaves safely."

Half an hour later Colbrook was back on the rooftop patio of the Amenti House. The sky overhead was cloudless, and the day was already uncomfortably warm. Beckwith and Lowell had joined him at the table only minutes before. Lowell sat to Colbrook's right in a wooden folding chair. Beckwith was seated in the other wicker chair, wearing a photographer's vest. His camera was on the table.

There was a long delay before Beckwith finally said, "How do they work? I mean the night-vision glasses."

"If I really knew I couldn't tell you, but since I don't, I can't give away any secrets," stated Colbrook. "As far as I know it's a purely optical device, without the considerable drawbacks of a conventional system. Those limitations are lack of accurate color, and, more importantly, lack of depth perception. Current night-vision technology relies on an image created by electronic light amplification, so it's similar to looking through a video camera. These aren't like that at all. They operate based on a different form of energy emitted by all objects—invisible to the eye, only changing it to visible light through the optical conversion system."

He leaned forward.

"There are only three people who really know how they work," summed up Colbrook. "And I'm not one of them."

"Now what?" asked Beckwith. He seemed genuinely disappointed that the adventure was over.

Colbrook settled back into his chair. "Haven't you ever heard of a diplomatic bag?"

"In spy novels," said Lowell.

Colbrook gave him a disapproving glance. "They're real. Not the bags, of course, but the concept behind them." When no one interrupted him he continued. "Any parcel marked as a diplomatic bag has immunity from search or seizure. Article 27 of the 1961 Vienna Convention stipulates this status."

"And you have such a bag?" questioned Beckwith.

"No. If I carried one out of the country I would immediately have to go into retirement. By definition, anyone carrying a diplomatic bag with proper documentation stating they're a diplomatic courier is granted temporary diplomatic immunity, while those who are official diplomatic couriers have permanent immunity," said Colbrook. "Don't you see the problem that would create? I would be forever connected with the American embassy in Cairo. Anyone who arrives as a travel writer and leaves carrying a diplomatic bag will never be treated by the Egyptian government—or any other government which obtains knowledge of this status—as a normal visitor again."

"I see your point," stated Beckwith.

"The solution," said Colbrook, "is to assign someone else to carry the bag out of the country, as if it's normal diplomatic material. Preferably this person should be an individual who already has obvious connections with the U.S. government, such as an embassy employee."

"And you've found such a person?" speculated Lowell.

"He's headed this way aboard a diplomatic flight as we speak." Colbrook looked down at his watch and then rose from his chair, declaring, "If you will excuse me for a moment, I have a package to prepare." He disappeared down the stairs to the apartment.

When he reappeared he was carrying a shoebox-sized parcel, wrapped heavily in packing tape—close to half a roll, in fact. He placed it down on a low table located a short distance behind his chair, concealing it behind a potted plant. He returned to his chair and sat down.

"Who built them?" asked Beckwith.

"A small privately owned company you've never heard of," replied Colbrook. "When the government intelligence apparatus failed to take appropriate action, I was retained by them."

A car door slammed in the road below. Colbrook stood.

"Is that the courier already?" asked Beckwith.

"No," said Colbrook. "Just someone I've agreed to look after. An American tourist who ran into some trouble. Indirectly, it was probably my fault. He'll be leaving on the courier flight."

Colbrook excused himself and descended the stairs. He walked to the gate by the road. Two Egyptian police officers and the American in the bright blue baseball cap were standing outside. A suitcase was resting on the ground near the police car. Colbrook swung the gate open.

"Hello, Mr. McKinnon," he said, holding out his hand. "Sorry to have caused you so much trouble. Believe me, these things happen very infrequently."

McKinnon looked mildly surprised. Then he laughed and shook Colbrook's outstretched hand.

"The travel writer from the cruise," he said. "I thought you seemed a little suspicious."

One of the police officers carried McKinnon's suitcase over, and Colbrook took it from him.

"Have a good trip home, Mr. McKinnon," said the other officer with a friendly nod.

The two neatly uniformed men climbed back into the police car. The doors slammed and the engine started. Colbrook led McKinnon through the gate as the police car drove away.

"A diplomatic flight will be leaving from Luxor airport in a few hours," explained Colbrook. "You have a seat on it." He pushed the gate closed and they walked along the gravel path.

"Free of charge?" inquired McKinnon.

Colbrook nodded. They neared the stairway leading up to the roof. "It's the least the U.S. government can do."

Colbrook led McKinnon up the stairs. The suitcase was fairly light for its size. When they reached the top of the stairway, he guided McKinnon across the patio towards the table. Beckwith and Lowell rose in greeting. McKinnon introduced himself.

"These men are both Egyptologists," explained Colbrook. "That's Dr. Beckwith, and this is Dr. Lowell. They're helping me with my investigation."

"What sort of investigation is it?" asked McKinnon. "Chief Hassan wouldn't tell me anything. He just said there was some sort of mix-up and that it was imperative I leave Egypt immediately."

"Antiquities smuggling," explained Colbrook.

"Big money involved?" guessed McKinnon.

"That's the only reason to smuggle things," replied Colbrook. He placed the suitcase in the shade under the trellis, about ten feet from the table. "I'll see what I can find in the way of refreshments. I also have to make a phone call, so I might be a while. Beckwith can show you around the garden and point out the very rare species of birds that he's identified."

"I could use a stroll," admitted Beckwith, reaching for his camera.

McKinnon took his cue from Beckwith and Lowell, and the three men headed for the stairs leading down to the garden.

When they returned about fifteen minutes later, Colbrook was sitting at the table with four large beverages. He was keeping flies away from the glasses, not an easy task considering the persistence of the notorious Egyptian variety. Beckwith, Lowell, and McKinnon joined him at the table.

"Nice place," said McKinnon. "Do you always stay in lodgings like this?"

"Not usually," admitted Colbrook with a smile.

He picked up a large glass of cold lemonade and handed it to McKinnon.

"A diplomatic courier is due within the hour," explained Colbrook. "I've told him you'll be returning with him."

"Where exactly does this diplomatic flight go?" asked McKinnon.

"Djibouti," replied Colbrook.

McKinnon considered this, and finally shook his head. "I don't even know where that is."

"The southern end of the Red Sea," replied Colbrook. "A couple of hours away by air. You'll be transferring there to a flight heading back to the U.S. Probably a military transport of some kind."

"I don't mind," said McKinnon. "I'm looking forward to it. Sounds like it should be interesting." He drank some of his lemonade, and then put the glass back on the table. "I think I'm going to need my sunglasses up here."

He rose and walked further under the trellis to where Colbrook had placed the suitcase. Facing away from the table and kneeling in front of the piece of luggage, he unlatched it. Opening a zipper, he began rummaging around. Several seconds passed before he closed the suitcase, the latches snapping solidly shut. The next sound that came from his direction was metal sliding on metal.

McKinnon turned, moving towards the table, his loose-fitting rayon shirt fluttering in the warm morning breeze.

He was holding a large pistol.

It was a Model 1911—a .45-caliber Colt—and it was carefully aligned with Colbrook's chest. McKinnon's thumb drew the hammer back.

Colbrook sat unmoving.

Beckwith was as still as an Egyptian tomb painting.

Lowell stared at McKinnon in disbelief.

"Please leave your hands on the table, Mr. Colbrook. We wouldn't want anyone to get hurt, would we?" McKinnon's face was like a mask, devoid of all expression. His eyes glittered like a snake's. "Now that I have your full attention, I'd like you to do something for me."

"Something tells me you're not a tourist," said Colbrook.

"No. I'm not," admitted McKinnon with an unpleasant chuckle. The gun remained steady in his hand, never wavering for an instant from its target. "I'd like the night-vision glasses. I won't ask for them twice."

Colbrook pondered the request for several long seconds.

"You shouldn't have gotten off that cruise," he finally said.

"Oh?" McKinnon's eyes narrowed.

"That's what got me thinking," explained Colbrook. "Only two people didn't make the return trip."

McKinnon waited, the pistol motionless in his hand.

"It took me two phone calls and a houseboat search to figure out who you were," stated Colbrook. He paused. "You're the buyer's agent."

"You think you're really clever, don't you?" responded McKinnon.

"I know that you're a retired intelligence officer, and that you accept retainer fees from foreign governments. Apparently your pension wasn't sufficient, and you weren't interested in the usual standbys—research foundations, private security, or writing your memoirs," said Colbrook.

"Everyone's a writer these days," declared McKinnon with a snarling laugh.

"You told me you were working on a novel," said Colbrook mockingly.

"I was just making conversation," replied McKinnon with an alarming grin. "I was trying to act like everyone else. Not many lone travelers on that ship."

"I'll admit you had me fooled at first," said Colbrook. "And even after I suspected you were not who you appeared to be, there was one thing I couldn't figure out."

"What's that?"

"How you knew who I was."

McKinnon was still grinning. "Well, how did I know?"

"You didn't," said Colbrook.

McKinnon's knuckles were growing white on the pistol's grip.

"And you didn't realize your mistake until you arrived here," added Colbrook. "It would be interesting to know who you're working for, though I can probably guess. The amount of money involved and the nature of the technology certainly limits the possibilities. Whoever it is, it's a government unwilling to deal directly with a man like Vukasinov. You should have been more careful with him yourself. You should be at the bottom of the Nile right now."

"I'm still waiting for those night-vision glasses," stated McKinnon. His smile had long since faded.

"You planned on eliminating the Serbians and Graf from the transaction and keeping the payment yourself. Am I right?"

"Go on," said McKinnon. "It doesn't matter now does it?" His finger was firmly on the trigger of the Colt.

"But like everyone else, you had no idea where Graf had hidden the night-vision glasses," continued Colbrook. "You had little choice but to rely on the Serbians, which of course is what you were supposed to be doing. But they weren't going to give them to you without the money they were promised, and the buyer wasn't going to provide you with the funds without a demonstration. You needed someone inside of Vukasinov's operation. Someone you could promise a few million to carry out your treacherous plans. Gvero was your choice. His disappearance caused you some trouble."

"It's a shame your investigative powers will be lost forever," said McKinnon.

He raised the Colt slightly, adjusting his aim. Colbrook watched as his finger started to squeeze the trigger.

An eardrum-shattering explosion rocked the patio.

It was Beckwith's Webley.

McKinnon lowered his eyes in disbelief, a crimson stain spreading from shoulder to shoulder across his shirt. He stumbled against the table and slumped forward onto it, the Colt dropping to the wood surface. A cloud of dense smoke drifted across the rooftop.

Colbrook turned to Beckwith. "What did you do that for?"

"He was about to kill you," replied Beckwith indignantly. "I saw the trigger moving."

Colbrook pushed his chair back from the table and rose to his feet, picking up the Colt.

"Why are you carrying the Webley?"

"After what happened last night, I was taking precautions," explained Beckwith. "It fits perfectly into the lower pocket of my photography vest. Why else would I be wearing this thing? It must be ninety out here."

Lowell was staring at McKinnon's slumped form, his face ashen gray. A rivulet of blood was running across the table towards him, and when it neared the edge he got up and staggered backward.

Colbrook stepped towards Beckwith, pointing the Colt at the tiled floor. He squeezed the trigger. The hammer dropped with a loud *click* but the pistol did not fire.

Reaching into his pocket and pulling out a two-inch long tapered metal pin and a slightly shorter spring, Colbrook held them out in his hand for Beckwith to see.

"The firing pin and firing pin spring," declared Colbrook. "They're relatively easy to remove from a Colt Model 1911. Most modern handguns would require complete disassembly. With this vintage Colt I didn't even need any special tools."

Beckwith was speechless.

"I probably should be thanking you," admitted Colbrook, "but you have no idea how many people wanted to interrogate this man."

Half an hour later, all signs of McKinnon's demise had been removed. The tiles, chair, and table were cleaner than they had been before. The patches of dampness and small puddles on the tiles were evaporating quickly, but for good measure Colbrook directed Lowell to water all of the potted plants and leave the hose in a conspicuous spot.

When this work was completed, Beckwith and Lowell dropped down into their chairs.

Colbrook's cell phone buzzed in his pocket. He turned it off without even looking at it. Staying under the trellis, he walked to the wall by the exterior stairs and began to watch the road below.

A silver Peugeot station wagon was approaching. The condition of the car was considerably better than most vehicles in the area, and Colbrook was not surprised when it pulled to the side of the road near the wall's gated entryway. Three men clambered out into the dusty street.

The driver wore a large turban and a *galabiya*, and was clearly recognizable even from afar as Abdullah from the City of the Dead. The front-seat passenger was undoubtedly Harry Mercer, wearing an ordinary short-sleeved shirt and jeans. The back-seat occupant was a man Colbrook did not recognize. All three rapidly passed through the front gate and crunched their way along the gravel path, heading for the side staircase.

"The courier has arrived," declared Colbrook dramatically.

Lowell and Beckwith both started to rise from their chairs.

"This shouldn't take long," said Colbrook, waving them both back into their seats.

Mercer was the first to arrive on the roof. He was soon followed by Abdullah, who bowed his turbaned head in greeting and took up a position near the top of the stairs. He was still wearing the dilapidated sandals. The man Colbrook did not recognize introduced himself as Thomas Hastings. He was short and slightly heavy around the middle, with thinning brown hair. A pair of small eyeglasses were perched on his beak-like nose. His clothing was nondescript: a pair of wrinkled gray trousers and a white button-down shirt. He carried a black hard-sided case in his right hand, roughly the size of a briefcase, but about twice the usual depth.

Both Egyptologists stood and introduced themselves. They offered their chairs, but everyone preferred to stand. Beckwith and Lowell sat down again.

Mercer started the conversation.

"Everything is set. The plane is waiting at Luxor airport," he said.

Colbrook nodded. He turned to Hastings. "This must be a welcome change from your usual desk job."

Hastings managed a smile despite his visibly nervous disposition. "A perk of working for the State Department. At least that's what Mercer said. I don't really care for the responsibility of handling state secrets."

Colbrook grinned. "Oh, I don't think we're dealing with state secrets." He looked at Mercer with exaggerated uncertainty. "Are we?"

"Just routine nonsense," chuckled Mercer.

Colbrook lifted the heavily taped cardboard box from the table. He had moved it from the smaller table when Lowell had started watering the plants. "The all-important package," he said solemnly.

Hastings brushed past Beckwith's chair, placing the black case on the table. He unsnapped the locking fasteners. Opening the lid and never taking his eyes off the box, he allowed Colbrook to position the parcel inside. Locking the case, Hastings lifted it from the table and stepped back alongside Mercer. The whole procedure did not take more than a few seconds to complete.

There was an awkward silence.

Beckwith looked up at Hastings and said, "What is your usual job?"

"I'm a State Department translator in Djibouti. I specialize in Arabic," answered Hastings. He managed a more cheerful expression. "Not too many people have even heard of Djibouti."

Beckwith nodded, smiling to show that he was just making conversation. "I've never been there, but I know where it is. Along the Ethiopian coast. Where the Red Sea meets the Gulf of Aden."

"Isn't there some sort of American base there?" asked Lowell.

"That's where I've been working for the past year," said Hastings.

Abdullah was fidgeting with a pack of cigarettes in his breast pocket.

Colbrook cast a sideways glance over the wall. Down below in the road a boy and a gray donkey were wandering along at a snail's pace. The boy was casting furtive glances in both directions as he went. He took up a position not far from the silver Peugeot. Apparently Mercer had no age limit for his operatives.

"Well, we must be getting to the airport," said Mercer. "The pilot declared engine trouble over the Red Sea in order to divert to Luxor. Someone might start poking around the plane."

"That's quite a diversion," noted Colbrook. "And, I'm assuming, an even more miraculous repair."

"It's a Lear 45 with less than a hundred hours on the engines," admitted Mercer with a wry smile. "We should be in Djibouti before lunchtime."

Abdullah removed the car keys from his pocket with a loud jingle, moving towards the stairs.

Mercer tapped his watch. "We don't want to keep the pilots

waiting." He glanced around the patio and then turned to Colbrook. "Wasn't there supposed to be another passenger?"

"Not a passenger," said Colbrook. "Just a rug. It has to go to the cleaners."

He pointed to a large rolled Oriental carpet resting on a low bench behind some planters in the shade of the trellis. It was folded over once and tightly secured with heavy twine.

Colbrook led Abdullah and Mercer across the patio, and they positioned themselves to lift the rug. Soon Lowell and Beckwith joined the effort. Hoisting the rug up, the five men moved towards the staircase. Hastings stepped aside to let them pass.

As Colbrook neared the stairs he looked down over the wall. The gray donkey was now cropping grass on the opposite side of the road, the boy standing at its side.

By the time they reached the bottom of the stairs Mercer had broken out in a sweat, and when they reached the Peugeot he remarked that he suspected the rug was woven on a lead backing. Hastings stood by the side of the car holding the black case with both hands as they struggled to fit the rug into the cargo area. When flies began to circle his head, he climbed into the back seat and pulled the door closed. With a final shove from Mercer, the rug cleared the opening. Abdullah immediately swung the hatch closed.

"What kind of rug is that?" questioned Mercer. "An Isfahan?"

"No," replied Colbrook. "I believe it's called a McKinnon."

After the silver Peugeot disappeared from view, Colbrook led Beckwith and Lowell back up to the rooftop patio. All three sat down at the table.

Beckwith turned to Colbrook. "Do you mind if I ask you a question?"

"Go ahead," replied Colbrook.

"How did Graf acquire the night-vision glasses?"

"A helicopter crash," said Colbrook. "But it all started with a security issue involving his aid operation in Sudan. The Displaced Fund."

Lowell wiped beads of perspiration from his forehead.

"I've heard of it," admitted Beckwith.

"That's not surprising," replied Colbrook. "Graf's agency has been working out of Egypt for some time. It makes sense as a base of operations when your work is primarily being directed at Sudan, at least from a logistical point of view."

"What sort of security issue are we talking about?" questioned Beckwith.

"Graf's convoys were vulnerable to attack. Both men and vehicles were sometimes lost in the violent hijackings," said Colbrook.

"That's certainly a problem," stated Beckwith. "What's the point of providing aid if the supplies never make it through."

"Graf had similar thoughts," replied Colbrook, "which is why he purchased weapons on the black market to arm a small security force to protect his convoys. I don't doubt it worked. But by attempting to solve one problem he created another. After the aid was successfully delivered by armed convoys, the relatively hapless populace was targeted with even greater violence. So Graf took the operation a step further. He armed the aid recipients, not just his convoy security forces."

"I'll be damned," declared Beckwith.

Colbrook nodded. "It gets worse. Once he had a deal with a major arms supplier, he began selling weapons. He became a gunrunner, plain and simple, using the protection of his aid organization to regularly smuggle weapons across the border between Egypt and Sudan, and then distributing them throughout sub-Saharan Africa. His supplier was a Serbian arms dealer who was more than happy to provide the weapons as long as Graf paid for them—which he clearly did. The numbers were small at first, probably only a few hundred firearms in total, but when Graf realized that his gunrunning enterprise was generating substantial financial returns, he continued to increase the arms shipments. In doing so he created a logistical dilemma."

Lowell stared at the ground. Colbrook continued.

"Graf needed a place to stockpile all the weapons flowing in. He couldn't get them out of Egypt fast enough to avoid having to store them at least on a temporary basis. Most of the legitimate aid materials came through the port at Alexandria, and were then trucked directly to staging depots. But these locations were unsuitable for weapons storage because they were frequently inspected by the Egyptian authorities. Much too risky. He needed someplace to conceal them along the established convoy route, someplace with an existing infrastructure. That's how the dig near Baris came into the picture."

Colbrook gave Lowell a deliberate glance.

"Graf contacted me," explained Lowell after considerable hesitation. "I already knew him from many previous social engagements related to Egyptology. He claimed he could provide some private funding for the dig site. No doubt some wealthy friends of his, I assumed. I never asked. Graf knew I was embroiled in a dispute with the SCA over the construction of a magazine to hold any artifacts I uncovered. I didn't have sufficient resources to construct one. He guaranteed that a considerable portion of the funds could be used to build such a structure."

"And that was what Graf was most interested in," said Colbrook. "With the funding secured, construction began on the magazine. It's easy to imagine what happened after it was finished."

Colbrook directed his gaze toward Lowell again.

"Graf told me he wanted to store valuable medical items inside," said Lowell. "I wasn't suspicious at first. Anyway, I hadn't found much at the site and wasn't in a position to argue the matter." He paused. "The magazine was filled almost within the first week. He also rented a small lot of land in Baris and had a fence put up around it. He kept his trucks there, hiring independent drivers who were paid well for their work."

"But surely you must have known what Graf was really up to," protested Beckwith.

Lowell shifted uneasily in his chair. "I eventually realized what he was doing, but by then it was too late."

"And the SCA inspector?" asked Colbrook.

"He found out what was going on. Even threatened to contact his superiors," replied Lowell. "Graf offered Rashad ten times his normal salary. Obviously the authorities were never contacted."

"Graf was running a terrible risk either way," continued Colbrook, "but one day a remarkable find changed everything. Lowell stumbled across an aqueduct in the desert, not far from the dig site. It turned out to be of vast size and depth, with many tunnels branching off in all directions, some of them running for miles underground. Graf realized he had the answer to his storage problems.

If he could find a means of getting his crates into the aqueduct he would no longer have to risk storing everything in the magazine and at his truck lot. I located one of the weapons caches myself, but I never did find the entrance used for getting the supplies into the aqueduct. I suspect they either opened a shaft from above, winching everything down on cables, or found a lateral access passage large enough to just roll the crates inside."

"They were winched down from above," Lowell said. "The hole was covered over with sheets of plywood and a thin layer of sand when not in use. It's about two kilometers from the dig site."

Colbrook nodded. Now he knew where Graf and the Serbians had gone the night he had searched their tent.

"With the weapons safely stored in the aqueduct," Colbrook went on, "Graf really did only have medical supplies in the magazine. Not exactly in accordance with SCA regulations, but not something that was going to get him thrown into an Egyptian prison for the rest of his life."

"How did they get the weapons into Egypt in the first place?" questioned Beckwith.

"I assume the arms came from the Black Sea into the Mediterranean," said Colbrook. "A large commercial vessel—a freighter—probably stayed offshore near Alexandria. Smaller local boats retrieved the cargo during the busy port hours and transported it up the Nile. When they reached the limit of the navigable portion of the river, the crates must have been transferred to trucks and driven south. In some cases—one of which I can personally verify—the weapons were then loaded onto passenger ships for the next leg of the journey. The final stage was by truck."

Beckwith shook his head in disbelief.

"It was all very clever," said Colbrook. "The legitimate aid came through the port at Alexandria as expected, while the weapons came up the Nile disguised as supplies for the dig near Baris. But what other choice did Graf and his arms supplier have? The Red Sea and the Horn of Africa are heavily patrolled."

"None of this explains the night-vision glasses," protested Beckwith. "And what about the helicopter crash?"

"That's the most interesting part of the story," replied Colbrook. "From Graf's point of view it was nothing more than a very dangerous sideshow, so to speak, but in the end directly caused his undoing—that and his partner's impatience in receiving his share."

"Partner?" questioned Beckwith.

"Graf did not act alone. He had an accomplice. An associate from his UN days."

Beckwith waited expectantly.

"Like almost everyone involved in international aid," continued Colbrook, "Graf had an insatiable appetite for control over people, and he wanted that power to wield as he wished. There's nothing quite like watching a whole village empty out onto an airfield in keen anticipation of your arrival, and Graf was sure he had the popularity of a rock star in the regions he operated within. No doubt he told himself many times how much more he could accomplish with additional funds at his disposal."

"Why is it that men are never satisfied with the power they already have?" asked Beckwith. "They always seem to want more."

"History invariably proves that to be the case," responded Colbrook. "And the results are usually disastrous. Graf's situation was no different."

Beckwith's silence was a cue for Colbrook to continue.

"Graf's willingness to take extraordinary risks to fund his aid operation culminated in a daring and dangerous plan," explained Colbrook. "His partner's access to classified information revealed the existence of the night-vision system and the rigorous testing schedule, making it possible to set an elaborate trap. They knew it was not simply an improvement of existing technology but a significant breakthrough in a scientific sense. On the open market there was almost no limit to where the bidding might reach on such an item.

"Armed to the teeth, and with a small posse at his heels that he had personally equipped, Graf crossed over the border into Sudan one fateful day. He drove to a carefully selected village, one he had been to many times before while pursuing his so-called humanitarian work, and during the night staged a mock raid. With the village cleared out, he proceeded to set fire to many of the buildings. For an added effect old truck tires were also burned to create thick smoke. With a considerable blaze going, he sent an anonymous distress call indicating that an actual raid was taking place. This worked its way through official channels to Camp Lemonnier, home to a Joint Special Operations Task Force in Djibouti.

"His partner's intelligence turned out to be accurate. A helicopter was flying not far from the village, conducting a not so routine long-range aerial refueling mission. It diverted from its intended course for a simple reconnaissance run. Graf and his minions were waiting. When the helicopter passed overhead its tail rotor was shot out with carefully directed automatic-weapons fire. The aircraft spun out of control and crashed moments later. Within minutes the helicopter was surrounded by armed men. The pilots and the flight engineer succumbed to their wounds and were quickly buried in a sand pit nearby. The helicopter was subsequently looted for its parts."

"How do you know all this?" questioned Beckwith.

"I was at the crash site not long before I arrived in Egypt," replied Colbrook. "I also observed the delivery of circuit boards taken from that very same helicopter to a man in Qena only four days ago. The helicopter parts are relatively worthless compared to what Graf was really after."

"The night-vision glasses," declared Beckwith.

"There are only two operational sets of those in existence," said Colbrook. "Only the pilot was wearing them. The co-pilot was using a conventional system. With the critical item secured, Graf went back to Egypt. He contacted the Serbian arms dealer, ready to make a deal if a suitable buyer could be found. I should point out that Graf stood to make hundreds of millions of dollars from this transaction. There was a catch, though. The Serbians wanted a demonstration. They had to be convinced the technology existed and actually worked before they would initiate talks with potential buyers."

"Well?" asked Beckwith. "Did Graf give one?"

"Yes. He did," replied Colbrook. "But only to the Serbians he had been dealing with already—the documentary crew, to be exact. And not without reservations."

"And the arms dealer agreed to sell them after that?"

Colbrook nodded. "Of course. But Graf was now in a vulnerable position. He knew he had to hide the night-vision system until the deal went through. He knew the Serbians would gladly make the sale without him if they could gain possession of the glasses themselves. He stashed them where he was sure no one could ever find them—in the Theban tomb."

"It was a good hiding place," said Beckwith.

Lowell shifted uneasily in his chair again.

"Despite all of Graf's preparations, a simple problem threatened to derail his plans," continued Colbrook. "Lowell's dig was nearing the end of the season, and the funding was almost exhausted. Although the concession was his for the foreseeable future, he had to close the site on the agreed date. The magazine would be locked until he returned for the next season. Graf recognized the problem that would create. He had to do something to prevent this from happening. His trucks would become suspicious traveling to a closed dig site. My assumption is that he asked Lowell if he could obtain a digging extension from the Egyptian authorities." Colbrook turned to Lowell. "Am I right?"

"Under very unusual circumstances," said Lowell, "such as finding a tomb or a spectacular set of artifacts, extensions will be allowed for a few more weeks. This is necessary to secure the site and catalog the items before storage."

Colbrook forged ahead. "Well, nothing of the sort appeared likely to turn up at the dig," he remarked, "but Graf soon changed all that with the help of his Serbian associates. They set up shop at the dig site as a documentary team. They also provided the additional funding necessary to keep the dig going. The Egyptian authorities did not find any of this to be unusual or suspicious, as it's quite common. While the Serbians proceeded with their documentary shoot, arrangements were made to buy genuine antiquities from unauthorized dealers." Colbrook stared at Lowell, who was now frozen in his chair. "The documentary crew purchased the artifacts during their many production-related travels, and hauled them back to the dig site."

Beckwith studied Lowell for a reaction. The red-haired Egyptologist did not even blink.

"Lowell then proceeded to bury them," announced Colbrook deliberately. "I saw it with my own eyes."

Beckwith's face clouded over as he considered the implications of such an Egyptological outrage.

"I also followed the Serbians when they picked up the artifacts," said Colbrook. "A man named Hamed residing near the Seti temple has quite a collection of antiquities in his basement." He turned to Beckwith. "Incidentally, that's where I acquired the shabti."

Beckwith was still struggling to come to grips with the previous statement.

"The Serbians soon notified Graf that they had found a potential buyer. Unfortunately for Graf, the buyer also wanted a demonstration. Graf insisted that the buyer accept the Serbians' guarantee, without an actual physical inspection. He was not willing to part with the glasses until he had the money. For very good reasons he did not trust the Serbians, or anyone else for that matter."

"Who would," grunted Lowell, obviously relieved that Graf had become the topic of conversation again.

"Graf continued to stall for time, knowing that if he acted too hastily and handed over the night-vision glasses, he ran the risk of being cheated or killed," said Colbrook. "He ignored request after request for a demonstration. What Graf didn't understand was that the Serbian arms dealer—Mr. Vukasinov—had already been contacted by Graf's partner in crime, now growing impatient for his share of the sale. Acting on the assumption that Graf's partner would be able to locate the glasses, Nedic was given a free hand to bring Graf into line by any method of coercion short of killing him. Things didn't quite work out that way, and ultimately Graf was killed by Nedic. Then Vukasinov had his trouble with McKinnon, who was supposed to be working for the buyer but was really working for himself. The rest you know."

"You seem to have missed something of great importance," said Beckwith. "What about this partner of Graf's? The one who had access to classified information. Where is he?"

"Identifying him did present a problem," admitted Colbrook, "but after I talked to Vukasinov last night, the situation was clarified immensely."

"How so?" Beckwith asked.

"I know for certain who he is," answered Colbrook.

"Who is he?" asked Beckwith.

"You've already met him," replied Colbrook.

"I have?" Beckwith seemed skeptical.

"The State Department translator," said Colbrook.

"But you gave him the glasses," objected Beckwith.

"No I didn't. The box contains only a few pieces of silverware from the kitchen drawer."

Beckwith was at a loss for words.

"He's been very thorough about covering his tracks. He can be better dealt with outside of the usual channels." Colbrook paused meaningfully. "We had to resort to different tactics in order to provide an appropriate punishment."

"You mean the United States government?" inquired Beckwith.

"I mean the two other men you just met," explained Colbrook, "and myself. We don't trust the government to handle these sort of things anymore."

Lowell was watching Colbrook very carefully.

"There are no coincidences in this line of work," said Colbrook. "Hastings was chosen for the position of temporary diplomatic courier with a very specific purpose in mind. Mercer and Abdullah are taking him to a parking lot in Luxor. They'll transfer him to another vehicle. He will be instructed to drive this car down the road leading to the airport while Mercer and Abdullah follow. This automobile contains a considerable quantity of narcotics in the trunk—about thirty kilos of cocaine to be exact. Before our friend from Djibouti reaches the airport he will be stopped by the police. Naturally this will involve a search of the vehicle. Under the circumstances, Hastings will have a hard time explaining himself."

"What about his diplomatic immunity?" asked Lowell.

"He has none. The papers are forgeries. He never had any immunity," answered Colbrook. "Do either of you know the penalties for drug trafficking in Egypt?"

He looked at both Egyptologists. Apparently they did.

Colbrook's cell phone buzzed. He opened it and listened. The call ended only seconds later.

Beckwith looked at him with growing curiosity.

Colbrook closed the phone. "That was Mercer. The plan went without a hitch. Hastings has been taken into custody."

Lowell almost seemed to be enjoying himself now.

"There is still one thing I don't quite understand," said Colbrook, turning to Lowell. "It's about your dig."

"What about it?"

"You went along with a lot of questionable activities to keep the site operating," observed Colbrook. "You took some big risks, mostly for Graf's benefit."

"A very hazardous course to follow," agreed Beckwith. "If you had been caught not only would your concession have been permanently revoked, but you would never have been allowed to set foot in Egypt again."

Colbrook studied Lowell. "I'm surprised you didn't eventually go to the authorities."

"You know the kind of people I was dealing with," replied Lowell. "They would have killed me."

"Maybe," declared Colbrook. "But I think you could have figured out some way of managing it."

Lowell did not respond.

"That total station is very sophisticated," said Colbrook.

"It makes surveying a lot faster," reasoned Lowell.

"I guess you had to be careful around those aqueducts," remarked Colbrook.

"We didn't want to accidentally dig into one."

Lowell did not seem to be enjoying himself so much anymore.

"There is one question that remains," said Colbrook, looking directly at Lowell. "What is it you're really digging for?"

Colbrook sat and listened—not to Lowell's answer, because for the moment there was none—but to the distant sounds drifting off the river in the warm morning air. His visit to Egypt had gone better than he had expected.

"And don't tell me it's Roman gold."

www.ingramcontent.com/pod-product-compliance
Lightning Source LLC
Chambersburg PA
CBHW020816260626
47169CB00003B/696